THE
BULLET
GARDEN

Also by Stephen Hunter

Bob Lee Swagger Series

Point of Impact

Black Light

Time to Hunt

The 47th Samurai

Night of Thunder

I, Sniper

Dead Zero

The Third Bullet

Sniper's Honor

G-Man

Game of Snipers

Targeted

Earl Swagger Series

Black Light

Hot Springs

Pale Horse Coming

Havana

THE BULLET GARDEN

An Earl Swagger Novel

STEPHEN HUNTER

EMILY BESTLER BOOKS

ATRIA

NEW YORK LONDON TORONTO SYDNEY NEW DELHI

**EMILY
BESTLER
BOOKS**

ATRIA

An Imprint of Simon & Schuster, Inc.
1230 Avenue of the Americas
New York, NY 10020

First Emily Bestler Books/Atria Books hardcover edition January 2023

EMILY BESTLER BOOKS/ATRIA BOOKS and colophon are trademarks of Simon & Schuster, Inc.

For information about special discounts for bulk purchases, please contact Simon & Schuster Special Sales at 1-866-506-1949 or business@simonandschuster.com.

The Simon & Schuster Speakers Bureau can bring authors to your live event. For more information or to book an event, contact the Simon & Schuster Speakers Bureau at 1-866-248-3049 or visit our website at www.simonspeakers.com.

Manufactured in China

1 3 5 7 9 10 8 6 4 2

Library of Congress Cataloging-in-Publication Data has been applied for.

ISBN 978-1-9821-6976-3
ISBN 978-1-9821-6978-7 (ebook)

To the novelists of The War, some great,
some not so great, whose work illuminated my youth . . .

Anton Myrer, *The Big War*
Nicholas Monsarrat, *The Cruel Sea*
Edward L. Beach, *Run Silent, Run Deep*
Irwin Shaw, *The Young Lions*
James E. Bassett, *Harm's Way*
John Clagett, *The Slot*
Norman Mailer, *The Naked and the Dead*
John Hersey, *The War Lover*
Joseph Heller, *Catch-22*
Leon Uris, *Battle Cry*
Herman Wouk, *The Caine Mutiny*
James Jones, *The Thin Red Line*
George Mandel, *The Wax Boom*
John Ashmead, *The Mountain and the Feather*
Richard Matheson, *The Beardless Warriors*
Robert Gaffney, *A World of Good*
Harry Brown, *A Walk in the Sun*
James E. Ross, *The Dead Are Mine*
Thomas Heggen, *Mister Roberts*
Denys Raynor, *The Enemy Below*

My! People come and go so quickly here!

Dorothy Gale (Judy Garland),
The Wizard of Oz,
1939

PRELUDE: CASEY

6–8 June 1944

Roger

"No, no," said Basil St. Florian. "*Bren* guns. We need the Bren guns. It is simply not feasible without Bren guns. Surely you understand?"

Yes, Roger understood but he was nevertheless unwilling.

"Our wealth is in our Bren guns. Without Bren guns, we are nothing. Pah, we are dust, we are cat shit, do you see? Nothing. NOTHING!"

Of course he said "*Rien,*" for the language was French, as was the setting, the cellar of a farmhouse outside the rural burg of Tulle, Department of Corrèze, in the region of Limousin, 250 miles south and east of Paris. Basil had just dropped in the night before, with an American chum.

"Do you not see," Basil explained, "that the point in giving you Brens was to wage war upon the Germans, not to make you powerful politically in the postwar, after we have pushed Jerry out. FTP Communists, FFL Gaullists, we do not care, it does not matter, or matter *now*. What matters now is that you have to help us push Jerry out. That was the point of the Bren guns. We gave them to you for that reason, explicitly, and no other. You have had them eighteen months and you have never used them once."

3

"I will not give you Bren guns," said Roger, "and that is final. Long live the Comintern! Long live the *Internationale*! Long live the great Stalin, the bear, the man of steel! If you were in Spain, you would understand this principle. If you—"

"Dear Roger, listen to the American lieutenant here. Do you think the Americans would have sent a fellow so far as they've sent this one just to tell you lies? This fellow is an actual son of the earth. His pater was a farmer. He raises wheat and cows and fights red Indians, as in the movies. He is tall, silent, noble. He is a walking myth. Listen to him."

He turned to the American and then realized he had, once again, forgotten the name. It was nothing personal; he just was so busy being magnificent and British that he couldn't be troubled by small details, such as American names.

"I say, Lieutenant, what was the moniker again?" He thought it was remarkable that the name kept slipping away on him. They had trained together at Milton Hall outside London for this little picnic for six or so weeks, but it kept slipping away, and whenever it did, it took Basil wholly out of where he was and turned his attention to the mystery of its disappearance.

"My name is Leets," said Leets, in English, accented in the tones of the middle plains of his vast homeland, the Minnesota part.

"It's so strange," said Basil. "It just goes away. Poof, it's gone, so bizarre. Anyhow, tell him."

Leets also spoke French with a Parisian accent, which was why Roger, of Group Roger, didn't care for him, or for Basil. Roger thought all Parisians were traitors or bourgeoisie, equally culpable in any case, and that seemed to go twice for British or American Parisians. He didn't know that Leets spoke with a Parisian accent because he'd lived there between the ages of seven and fourteen while his father managed 3M's European accounts. No, Leets's father was not a farmer, not hardly, and had certainly never fought red Indians; he was a rather wealthy business executive now retired, living in Sarasota, Florida, with one son, this one, in occupied France playing cowboys with the insane, another a naval aviator on a jeep carrier that had yet to reach the Pacific, and still a third 4-F and in medical school in Chicago.

Roger, namesake and kingpin of Group Roger, turned his fetid little eyes upon Leets.

"I can blow the bridge," said Leets. "It's not a problem. The bridge will go down; it's only a matter of rigging the 808 in the right place and leaving a couple of time pencils stuck in the stuff."

But Basil interrupted, on the thrust of an epiphany.

"It's because you're all so similar," he said, as if he'd given the matter a great deal of right proper Oxonian thought. "It has to do with gene pools. In our country, or in Europe on the whole, the gene pool is much more diverse. You see that in the fantastic European faces. Really, go to any city in Europe and the variety in such features as eye spacing, jawline, height of forehead, width of cheekbones, is extraordinary. I could watch it for days. But you Yanks seem to have about three faces between you, and you pass them back and forth. Yours is the farm boy face. Rather broad, no visible bone structure, pleasant, but not sharp enough to be particularly attractive. I fear you'll lose your hair prematurely. Your people do have good, healthy dentition, I must give you that. But all the plumpness on the face. You must eat nothing but cake. It goes to your face and turns you rather *ballonishish*, and it's bloody hard keeping you apart. You remind me of at least six other Americans I know, and I can't remember their names either. Wait, one of them is a chap called Carruthers. Do you know him?"

Leets thought this question rhetorical and in any event it seemed to tucker Basil out for a bit. Leets turned back to the fat French Communist.

"We can kill the sentries; I can rig the 808 and plant the package, and it doesn't even have to be fancy. It's simple engineering; anyone could look at it and see the stress points. So: pop the tab on the time pencil and run like hell. The problem is that the garrison at Tulle is only a mile away, and the minimum time I can get the bridge rigged is about three minutes, because we have to go in hard. When we shoot the sentries, it'll make a noise, because we don't have silencers. The noise will travel and the garrison will be alerted. Meanwhile, I have to get down and lash the package just so on the trusses. They'll get there before I'm done. So my team will get fried like eggs if we're still rigging when they show. That's why we need the Brens. We've only got rifles and Stens and my Thompson. I need two Brens on the road from Tulle with a lot of ammo to shoot up the trucks as they come along. You can't disable a truck with a Sten. Simple physics."

He went on to explain the ballistic arcana of the circumstance, citing bullet weight, composition, inherent accuracy, muzzle energy and velocity, down to numbers as per cartridge. It was very impressive—if you were twelve. Here it was met with eyes pickled in distraction by all involved.

"Right," said Basil. "Well presented, Lieutenant Bates. Quite fascinating. Now see here, Monsieur Roger—"

"*Non!*" said Roger, spraying them with garlic. He was a butcher, immense and powerful but also garrulous and intractable. He'd fought in Spain, where he was wounded twice. He was almost grotesquely valiant and fearless, but he understood the primitive calculus of the politics: the Brens were power, and without power Group Roger would be at the mercy of all other groups, and that was more important than the prospect of 2nd SS Panzer Das Reich using the bridge to rush Tiger tanks to the Normandy beachhead, as intelligence predicted they would surely do.

"My dear brother-in-arms Roger," said Basil, "the bridge will be blown, that I assure you. The only thing in doubt is whether Lieutenant Bates—"

"Leets."

"Leets, yes, of course . . . whether Lieutenant Leets and his team of maquisards from Group Phillippe will make it out alive. Without the Brens, they haven't a chance, do you see?"

"Phillippe is a pig as are all his men," said Roger. "It is better for them to die at the bridge and spare us the effort of hunting them down to hang after the war. That is my only concern."

"Can you say to this brave young American, 'Lieutenant Bates, you must die, that is all there is to it'?"

"Yes, it's nothing," said Roger, looking like he had a train to catch as he turned to Leets. "'Lieutenant Bates, you must die; that is all there is to it.' All right, I said it. Fine. Good-bye, sorry and all that, but policy is policy."

He signaled his two bodyguards, who, after rattling their Schmeissers dramatically cinema-style, rose and began to escort him up the cellar steps.

"Well, there you have it," said Basil to Leets. "Sorry, but it looks like your number is up, Lieutenant. You get pranged. Sad, unjust, but inescapable. Fate, I gather. Ours not to reason why, et cetera, et cetera. Do you know your Tennyson?"

"I know that one," said Leets glumly.

"I suppose one could simply not go. I think that's what I'd do in your shoes, but then, I'm not the demo man; you are. I'm the head potato, so I'll supervise quite nicely from the tree line. As for you, if you decide not to go, it would be embarrassing, of course, but in the long run it probably doesn't make much difference whether the bridge goes or not, and it seems silly to waste a future doctor of all the fabled Minnesotas on such a local Frenchy balls-up between de Gaulle's smarmy peons and that giant, stinking, garlic-sucking red butcher."

"If I catch it," said Leets, "I catch it. That's the game I signed up for. I just hate to catch it because of some little snit between Group Roger and Group Phillippe. Stopping Das Reich is worth it; helping Roger prevail over Phillippe is not, and I don't give a shit about red or white guerillas."

"Yet they can't really be separated, can they? It's always so complicated, haven't you noticed? Politics, politics, politics, it mucks up everything. Anyhow, if you like, I'll write your people a very nice letter about what a hero you were. Would you like that?"

As with much of what Basil said, the words were pitched in a key of meaning so exquisite, Leets couldn't exactly tell if St. Florian was serious or not. You could never be sure with Basil; he frequently said the exact opposite of what he meant. He seemed to live in a zone of near comedy where nearly every damned thing was "amusing" and he took great pleasure in saying the "shocking" thing. The first thing he said to Leets all those weeks ago at Milton Hall was "It's all a racket, you know. Our nobs are trying to wipe out their nobs so they can get all the wog gold; that's what it's *really* all about. Our job is to make the world safe for Anglo-American nobs."

Now Basil said, "I can, however, in my tiny British pea brain, concoct one other possibility."

"What's that?"

"Well, it has to do with a radio."

"We don't have a radio."

The radio was lashed to André Breton's body—which, unfortunately, had hit the earth at about eight hundred miles an hour when André's parachute ripped in half on the tail spar of the Liberator that had dropped them the night before. Neither the radio nor André were salvageable, which was why Team Casey was down 33 percent strength before its other two-thirds landed under their chutes a minute or so after André had his accident.

"The Germans have radios."

"We're not Germans. We're the Allies, remember? Captain, sometimes I think you don't take this all that seriously."

"I speak German. What else is necessary?"

"This is crazy. You'll never—"

"Anyway, here's my idea. I cop a German uniform tomorrow and walk into the Tulle garrison headquarters at eleven a.m. With my command presence, I will send Jerry away. Then I will commandeer his radio and put in a call. A fellow owes me a favor. If his groundwork is solid, it just might work out."

"Jerry will put you up against a wall at eleven oh three and shoot you."

"Hmm, good point. Possibly, if Jerry is distracted . . ."

"Go ahead, I'm all ears."

"You blow something up. I don't know—anything. Improvise—that's what you chaps are so good at. Jerry runs to see. While Jerry's got his knickers up his bum, I enter the garrison headquarters, all Savoyed up, Jerry-style. It's easy for me to commandeer the radio, make my call. Five minutes and I'm out."

"Who are you trying to reach on radio?"

"A certain fellow."

"A fellow where?"

"In England."

"You're going to radio England? From a German command post in occupied France?"

"I am. I'm going to dial up Jack Cairncross of the Code and Cypher School at some grotesque country monstrosity. He's some kind of higher pooh-bah there and there are sure to be lots of radios about."

"What can he do?"

"You didn't hear this from me, chum, but it's said he's one of the reds. Same team, just different players, for now. Joe for king, that sort of thing. Anyhow, he's sure to know somebody who knows somebody who knows somebody in the big town."

"London?" asked Bates—er, Leets—but Basil just smiled, and Leets realized he meant Moscow.

Basil

So Basil turned himself into a passable German officer with little enough trouble. The uniform came from an actual officer who had been killed in an ambush in 1943 and his uniform kept in storage by the Maquis against the possibility of just such a gambit. It smelled of sweat, farts, and blood. It was also a year out of date in terms of accouterments, badges, and dinky geegaws, but Basil knew or at least believed that with enough charisma he could get through anything.

And thus, at 11 a.m., as Leets and three maquisards from Group Phillippe prepared to blow up a deserted farmhouse a half mile out of town the other way from the bridge, Basil walked masterfully to the gate of the garrison HQ of the 113th Field Flak Battalion, the lucky air boys who controlled security here in Tulle. The explosion had the predictable effect on the air boys, who panicked, grabbed weapons and other dangerous, frightening (to them) equipment, and began running toward the rising column of smoke. They were terrified of a screwup because it meant they might be transferred somewhere actual fighting was possible.

Basil watched them go, and when the last of several ragtag groups had disappeared, he strode toward the big communications van next to the château, with its thirty-foot radio mast adorned with all kinds of Jerry stylistics; this one had a triangle up top. These people!

It helped that the officer whose uniform he wore had been a hero, as the vivid clutter on his chest indicated. One medal in particular was an emblem of a tank, and underneath it hung three little plates of some sort. The other stuff was the usual porridge, and it all signified martial valor, very impressive to the distinctly non-militaristic Luftwaffers who didn't know tuppence about such stuff but recognized what they took to be the genuine item when it appeared.

Basil got to the radio van easily enough, chased the duty sergeant away by proclaiming himself Major Strasser—he'd seen *Casablanca*, of course, and knew no German had—of Section III-B Abwehr Paris, working for the legendary *Herr Major* Dieter Macht, whom Basil actually knew.

He faced a bank of gear, all of it rather scienced-up in an array of dials, switches, knobs, and gauges set in shiny Bakelite.

The transceiver turned out to be a 15 W.S. E.b., a small, complete station with an output power of 15 watts, just jolly super and what the doctor ordered. The frequency range embraced those used by the British and the mechanics for synchronization between transmitter and receiver were very advanced. Two dials up top, a midpoint dial displaying frequency, the tuner below, and below that buttons and switches and all the foofah of radioland. Had he a course on it somewhere in time? Seems he had, but there was so much, it was best to let the old subconscious take over and run the show.

Die Maschine was very Teutonic. It had labels and sub-labels everywhere, switches, dials, wires, the German gestalt in one instrument, insanely well-ordered yet somewhat over-engineered in a vulgar way. Instead of "On/Off," the switch read literally "Makingtobroadcast/Stoppingtobroadcast Facilitation." A British radio would have been less imposing, less a manifesto of purpose, but also less reliable. You could bomb this thing and it would keep working.

The machine crackled and spat and began to radiate heat. Evidently it was quite powerful.

He put on some radio earphones—the noise of static was quite annoying—found what had to be a channel or frequency knob, and spun it to the British range.

He knew both sides worked with jamming equipment, but it wasn't useful to jam large numbers of frequencies, so more usually they played little games, trying to infiltrate each other's communications and cause mischief. He also knew he should flip a switch and go to Morse, but he had never been a good operator. He reasoned that the airwaves today were totally filled with chatter of various sorts and whoever was listening would have to weigh the English heavily, get interpretation from analysts, and alert command; the whole process had to take days. He decided just to talk, as if from a club in Soho.

"Hullo, hullo," he said each time the crackly static stopped.

A couple of times he got Germans screaming, "You must use radio procedure! You are directed to halt! This is against regulations!" and turned quickly away, but later rather than sooner someone said, "Hullo, who's this?"

"Basil St. Florian," Basil said.

"Chum, use radio protocol, please. Identify by call sign. Wait for verification."

"Sorry, don't know the protocol. It's a borrowed radio, do you see?"

"Chum, I can't—Basil St. Florian? Were you at Eton, '28 through '32? Big fellow, batsman, ginger. I was on the Harrow eleven. June 23, '33. You got a century that day, out for 126 wasn't it?"

"Actually, it was 127, edged it to third slip."

"Ah, right. The wicket was deteriorating a bit, funny bounce. Good showing, though. You had a smashing classic cover drive. Beautiful to watch."

"The god of batsmen smiled upon me that day."

"I was at fine leg, damned good if I say so myself. I dismissed you, finally. You smiled at me. Lord, I never saw such a striker."

"I remember. Who knew we'd meet again like this? Now, look here, I'm trying to reach the code mucky-mucks at that ghastly Toad Hall. Chap named Jack Cairncross. Can you help?"

"I shouldn't give out information."

"Old man, it's not like I'm just anybody. I remember you. Reddish hair, freckled, looked like you wanted to cosh me. Remember how fierce you were; that's why I winked. I have it right, don't I?"

"In fact, you do. All these years, now this. Know which hut he's in?"

"No idea. Can you help?"

"I can get you Bletchley Central. Let me see, yes, via the day code they'd be King-Six-Orange, then. Let's make you Freddie-Seven-Pip. I'm going to have Evers do a patch."

"Thanks ever so much."

Basil waited, examining his fingernails, looking about for something to drink. A nice bottle, say, of something red from '34, anything would do, '34 was such a fine year. He yawned. Tick-tock, tick-tock, tick-tock. *When* would this Evers fellow—

"Identify, please."

"Is this King-Six-Orange?"

"Identify, please."

"Freddie-Seven-Pip. Looking to speak with your man Jack Cairncross. Put him on, do you mind?"

"Do you think this is a telephone exchange?"

"No, no, but nevertheless I need to talk to him. Old school chum. Need a favor."

"Identify, please."

"I can't remember. Something like Freddie-Pip. Listen carefully: I am in a bother and I need to talk to Jack. It's war business, not gossip."

"Where are you?"

"In Tulle. Tulle, France."

"Didn't realize the boys had got that far inland."

"They haven't. That's why it's rather urgent, old man."

"This is very against regulations."

"Dear man, I'm SOE. You know, the dagger boys. I'm actually at a Jerry radio and at any moment Jerry will return. Now, I have to talk to Jack. Please, play up for the game."

"SOE, public school, weekends in the country, all that then. I hate you all. You deserve to burn."

"We do, I know. Such officious little pricks, the lot of us. I'll help you light the timbers after the war and then climb into them smiling. But first let's win it. I implore you."

"Bah," said the fellow, "you'd best not put me on report."

"I shan't."

"He is, in fact, no longer here. The Scot beggar has left us for the nobs at Six."

"Can you patch me through, then? It's rather urgent." Basil could hear hubbub in the yard. Had the air boys returned?

"I suppose I must, Seven-Pip," said his inquisitor with a tragic sigh.

More clicking and buzzing and whatever magic lurked in the wires and antennae of His Majesty's secret apparatus was again put to the test, until somehow Basil's voice had been repurposed to the rotting old buildings on Broadway.

"Station K. Identify."

"Ah, I think it's something Seven-Pip. Does that help?"

"Observe security protocols, if you please."

"Look here, it's one of your old boys, Basil St. Florian. Everyone at Broadway knows Basil St. Florian."

"I need the code word before—"

"FREDDIE! That's it. Freddie-Seven-Pip!"

Authenticated, Basil waited again until he was shunted at last to some office or other, one hoped close enough to the target.

"Philby."

"Yes, see here, I need to speak with—Kim? Kim Philby, can that be you?"

"It is indeed, Basil. Why, I'd know that voice anywhere! Lord, how I've missed those nights we tried to empty all the gin bottles in Soho."

"What gay lads we were!"

"You're off blowing up Jerry's kitchens, are you?"

"Actually, Kim, I am. And that's why I need a chat with your chap Cairncross."

"That one? The Scot? Dour as haggis in vinegar."

"Can you get him on the blower for me?"

"Of course. But Basil, do call back, anytime. I'd love to hear your adventures. You've much to tell, I'm sure."

In a minute or so, another voice came over the earphones.

"Yes, hullo."

"Jack, it's Basil. Basil St. Florian."

"Who?"

"We met at the Citadel briefing with all the other senior code breakers. I'm with one of the hugger-mugger outfits. Was all banged up. Last year in the war rooms."

"Oh, that. Rather fuzzy, but if you say so."

"Right, Jack. Now, see, here's the thing. I need a favor, do you mind?"

"Well, depending, of course."

"I'm to go with some rough chaps tonight to set off a firecracker under a bridge. Nasty work, but they say it has to be done."

"Sounds fascinating."

"Not really. Hardly any wit to it at all. You know, just destroying things; it seems so infantile in the long run. Anyhow, our cause would be helped if a gang in the area called Group Roger—have you got that?— would pitch in with its Brens. But it's some red/white thing and they won't help. I thought you had Uncle Joe's ear—"

"Who did you say you were? Good heavens, man. People may be listening."

"No inference or judgment meant. I tell no tales, and let each man enjoy his own politics and loyalties as I do mine. That's what the war's all about, eh? Let's put it this way: if *one* had Uncle Joe's ear, *one* might ask that Group Roger in Tulle vicinity pitch in with Brens to help Group Phillippe. That's all. Have you got that?"

"Roger, Brens, Phillippe, Tulle."

"Thanks, old man."

"It's not like you can just ring them up, you know. But I'll give it a whirl."

"There's the lad."

Basil put the microphone down, unhooked the earphones from around his head, and looked up into the eyes of an *Oberleutnant* and two sergeants with machine pistols.

Leets looked at his Bulova. It had been an hour, no, an hour and a half.

"I think they got him," said his No. 1, a young fellow called Leon.

"Shit," said Leets, in English. He was at a window in the upper floor of a residence fifty yards across from the gated château that served as the 113th Luftwaffe Field Flak Battalion's headquarters and garrison. He held an M1 Thompson submachine gun low, out of sight, and wore a French rain slicker, rubbery, and a plowman's shabby hat.

"We can't hit it," said Leon. "Not four of us. And if we got him out, on the surprise aspect of it, where'd we go? We have no automobile to escape."

Leon was right, but still Leets hated the idea of Captain Basil St. Florian of the Horse Guard perishing on something so utterly trivial as a bridge in the interests of one Team Casey that existed out of a misbegotten SOE-OSS cooperative plan, silly, cracked, and doomed as hell. Strictly a show, thought up by big headquarters brainiacs with too much spare time, of no true import. He knew it—they all knew it—and had known it in all the hours in Areas A and F and whatever, disguised golf clubs, mostly, where they'd trained before deployment to the god-awful food at Milton Hall. As the Brit had said, it probably didn't make any difference anyhow. He cursed himself; he should have just planted the charges without the Brens and taken his chances on the run to the woods. Maybe the Krauts wouldn't have been quick enough out of the gates to get there and lay down fire before he rigged his surprises. Maybe it would have been a piece of cake. But you couldn't tell Basil St. Florian a thing, and when the man got an idea in his head, it crowded out all other concerns.

"Look!" said Leon.

It was Basil. He was not alone. He was surrounded by adoring young men of the 113th Luftwaffe Field Flak Battalion and their commanding officer who were escorting Basil to the gate. Basil made a brief, theatrical bow, shook the commander's hand, and turned and smartly strode off.

It took a while for him to reach the outskirts of town, but when he hit the rendezvous, Leets and the maquisards, by back streets and fence jumping, were already there.

"What the hell?"

"Well, I reached Jack. Somehow. He's to make certain arrangements."

"What took you so long?"

"Ah, it seems the previous owner of this uniform had an illustrious career. This little trinket"—he touched the metallic emblem of a tank with its three tiny plates affixed serially beneath—"signifies a champion tank destroyer on the Eastern Front. The Luftwaffers wanted to hear war stories. So I ended up giving a little performance on the best ways to destroy a T-34. Good god, I hope none of the fellows—they seemed like good lads—try that sort of thing on their own against a Cromwell. I just made it up. Something about the third wheel of the left tread being the drive wheel, and if you could hit that with a *Panzerfaust*, the machine stopped in its tracks. Could there be a third wheel? And I don't believe I specified left from which perspective. All in all, it was a rather feeble performance, but the *London Times* critics weren't around, just some dim Hanoverian farm boys drafted into the German air force."

"You made the call? You got through?"

"Why, it worked better than our trunk lines. No operator, no interference. It was as if Jack had been in the same room. Amazing, these technical things these days. Now, what's for dinner?"

Leets

Leets applied the last of the burnt cork to his face. Burning corks had turned out to be no picnic, but finally he managed to do a reasonable job of masquerading his broad, uninteresting, and very white American balloon face against the darkness. He looked like a potato that had fallen off a truck.

He was now ready, though he felt more like the football player he'd been than the soldier he was, so packed with gear very like the shoulder and thigh pads that had protected him in Big Ten wars. He had a Thompson gun, seven mags with twenty-eight .45s in each, the mags in a pouch strapped to his web belt, as were six Gammon grenades, Allways fuzes packed with half a stick of the green plasticky Explosive 808. They were all ready to have their caps unscrewed, their linen lines secured and tossed to explode on impact. They smelled of almonds, reminding him of a candy bar he had once loved in a far-off paradise called Minnesota. He had a wicked, phosphate-bladed M3 fighting knife strapped to his right outside lace-up Corcoran jump boot, which was bloused neatly into his reinforced jump pants, an OD cotton slash-pocketed jump jacket, model of 1942, almost like Hemingway's safari coat over his wool OD shirt with his silver first lieutenant's bars and the crossed rifles of infantry, as

19

he'd been a member of the 501st of the 101st before his French got him recruitment by OSS. Then, too, a Colt .45 automatic on the web belt, seven fat cartridges in the mag, two more mags on a pouch on the web, a black watch cap pulled low over his ears so that he looked like one of the lesser Our Gang members. He also carried a satchel full of Explosive 808, and time pencils—that is, Delay Switch No. 10—a tin of five of them in the satchel with the 808 for quick deployment. He weighed about a thousand pounds.

It wouldn't be a sneak-and-plant-and-run job. It would be more like a 1934 bank job: go in shooting, take (in this case, plant) the loot, and run. It should work but if reinforcements from Tulle got there before they made it to the woods, they'd be dead ducks, as the Germans—even incompetent Luftwaffers—could hose them down with MG-42 fire from the guns mounted on the trucks.

That's where the Brens came in. The Brens could drive the trucks back, even destroy them, scatter the easily frightened Luftwaffers. The whole thing turned on the Brens.

"Great news, chum," said Basil. "You have Brens!"

"What?"

"Hmm, it seems that Roger had a change of mind, or perhaps an order from higher HQ. In any event, even as we speak, Roger and his two Bren gun teams are setting up on the slope overlooking the road from Tulle, three hundred yards beyond the bridge."

"Do we know that for a fact?"

"Chum, if Roger says they're there, then they're there."

"I wish I could actually see the guns." But he looked at the Bulova he wore upside down on his wrist and saw that it was 0238 British war time, so it was time to go.

"Okay," he said, "then let's get it done."

"Well said, Bates. I'll be with the other boys in the wood line. We'll lay down fire from our end."

"You can't see well enough to do any good, and that goddamn little peashooter won't frighten anyone." Leets indicated the Sten machine carbine that hung around Basil by sling and looked as though it had been assembled from random tubes out of the discard bin by a committee of dull plumbers—a 9mm sub gun that fired too fast when it fired at all and then its bullets did little good when they got there, if they got there at all.

"Bates, it can't be helped that their stuff is so much better than our stuff. We make do with what is. We do our bit, that's all. You know the tune: Guns and drums and drums and guns, hurroo, hurroo."

"Sorry, Captain. I'm a blowhard, I know. Just venting because I'm scared shitless. Anyhow, thanks, what you did was swell; it was, I don't know—"

"Stop it, Bates. Just go blow up your damned bridge and it's back to tea and jam."

The Bridge

Leets was having some trouble breathing. His stomach was edgy, his fingers felt like greasy sausages from someone else's body, and he wanted only to sleep. He'd felt this way before games sometimes. He'd been a tight end—usually, because of his size, a blocker—but there were a few plays in the book that designated him as receiver and he both loved and hated that opportunity. You could become a hero. You could become a goat. It all happened in a split second in front of fifty thousand yelling maniacs cram-packed into Dyche Stadium or some other Big Ten coliseum. Once, memorably (to him at any rate), he caught a touchdown ball on a freakish lucky thing-of-beauty pass from Otto Graham that he'd ticked with a finger, popped into the air, and snatched while himself falling. He was a hero who knew he'd been lucky and secretly felt he didn't deserve the Monday of acclaim he'd gotten. It was his favorite memory, it was his worst memory. It came to him now in both formats.

The car rolled onward; no wonder they called them coffee-grinders: a little tin pot of a thing powered seemingly by rubber bands. Chut-chut-chut, it went. Leon drove. Leets was in the front passenger's side with the Thompson. In the backseat, in fetal positions, were Jerome and Franc, good guys, kids really, all with Stens. They'd have trouble getting out, so it was up to Leets, really. He'd deliver the first blows for freedom in this part of France. He felt sick about it, but it was increasingly obvious that it didn't matter how he felt, since what would happen would happen and if the Brens were there, thank God and Basil St. Florian, and if they weren't, Dad would be so upset.

A bottle was produced. It came to Leets with a small glass. He poured some bitter fluid: man, it kicked like a mule, JESUS CHRIST! He grasped for breath, poured another tot, and held it over for Leon to gulp down.

"*Vive la France!*" said Leon, completing the transaction.

"*Vive la France!*" came the salute from the rear.

Vive my ass! thought Leets.

They entered the cone of Luftwaffe arc light, and immediately the two sentries at the gate raised hands, began to scream, "HALT! HALT! HALT!" They were kids also, a little panicked because no cars ever emerged from the darkness out of nowhere and they themselves didn't know what to do, open fire or run and get a sergeant. Their helmets and weapons looked too big.

It was murder. It was war but it was still murder.

Leets rolled from the Citroën and put three into each boy from the hip at a range of about ten yards. The Thompson seemed to point itself, so hungry to kill, and under his delicate trigger control convulsed spastically three times in a tenth of a second, then three times more in another tenth of a second, leaking incandescence and noise, and the boys were gone. He pivoted, brought the gun to his shoulder, zeroed in on the guardhouse through the aperture sight to the wedge at the muzzle, and feathered off the rest of the magazine, holding the butt tight into his shoulder, watching the wood and dust splinter and leap as the rounds struck, glass shattered, a door broke, punctured, and fell.

The gun empty, he reached into his pouch pocket and pulled an already primed Gammon. With a thumb he pinned the little floppy lead weight at the end of the Gammon linen against the side of the bag, feeling the slight squishiness of the clump of 808 inside, cranked slightly to the right to the classic QB pose so he could come off his right foot, and launched a tight spiral toward the guardhouse fifty feet away, following through Graham–style. As the bomb sailed through the air, its weighted linen wrap unfurled, and when it separated it popped a restraining pin inside the Allways fuze, arming that gizmo to detonate on impact. That was the genius of the Gammon: when armed, it was volatile as hell, but it always went off.

Great throw: the guardhouse went in a blade of light and percussion, making Leets blink, stagger, have a momentary loss of reality. So fucking loud! His men were next to him, emptying Stens into the wreckage and at fleeing figures.

"*Un autre,*" said Leon. Another.

Leets got another grenade out, pinned the weight, and this time put more arm into it. It sailed into the darkness where presumably Germans still cowered, perhaps unlimbering weapons, but the explosion was larger than the last: the Gammon power depended wholly upon how much 808 was packed about the Allways, and evidently Leets had been a little overexcited on this one.

Dust rose, half the lights went out, burning pieces of stuff flew through the air; it was all the chaos and irrationality of an explosion. Hearing was gone for the night. Leets paused for a second to get another magazine into his Thompson, made sure the bolt was back, and raced forward into the madness.

He reached the center of the span, when a volley of rifle shots kicked dust and splinters up. He flinched, realized he wasn't hit, recovered. The fire surely came from the other end of the bridge, where a small security force had been cowering, uncertain what to do. Fortunately, the Luftwaffers were as poor at marksmanship as they were at aggression, and so all the shots missed flesh. Leets answered with another long burst from the reloaded Thompson while his comrades chipped in with Stens.

"Throw some bombs," he ordered, while he himself went to the railing of the span, looked over it.

It was not an impressive bridge. It was, in fact, a rather pathetic bridge. But it would do well enough to support the weight of a fifty-six-ton Tiger II tank, a column of which under the auspices of SS Das Reich now headed toward it on the road to Normandy. Leets had seen the structure at daylight: two buttresses, heavy logs, no apparent stone construction except at the base. He simply had to detonate enough 808 where the truss met the span to disconnect the support; the span would collapse of its own, or at least cave in enough to prevent passage of the heavy German vehicles; it needn't be pretty or dramatically satisfying. A little tiny bang would be fine, just enough to get a little bit of a job done.

He knelt, slipped the Thompson off its sling and the satchel of 808 to the ground. He reached into it, pulled out the tin of the time pencils, and beheld the five six-inch-long brass tubes, each with a tin-wrapped nodule at the end. The problem with them, god dammit, was that as clever as they were, they were somewhat retarded in their firing rate. Supposedly they were set to fire a primer in ten minutes, but just as often they went in eight or nine or eleven or twelve. It was a matter of how quickly the acid in a crushed ampule ate through a restraining wire that, when it yielded, allowed the spring-driven needle to plunge into the primer, which went bang, causing the larger, encasing 808 to go bang as well.

So Leets took them out now, all five of them, discarded the tin, and stomped hard on the proper ends of the pencils. Immediately a new odor arrived at his nose, that of the just-released cupric chloride as it sloshed forward from the shattered vials in five pencils and began to eat at the metal. He wanted them cooking now, eating up the minutes so that when he and the boys fled, the Germans didn't have time to pull the pencils free. He put them in the bellows pocket of his jump pants, buttoning it tightly.

He squirmed over the railing, eased himself down, flailed with a foot for mooring on the truss, found it, and carefully lowered himself until he was beneath the bridge span.

Suddenly he heard a racket far off. Oh, Christ, he almost let go and plummeted twenty-five feet to the sluggish stream bed below. Were they shooting at him? But then he recognized the glorious workman's hammer-like bashing of the Bren guns, knowable because of their wonderfully slow rate of fire, which enabled gunners to stay longer on target than our poor Joes with their faster-shooting BARs.

Goddamn, good old Basil! Basil, you snotty, arrogant, cold-blooded aristo, goddamn you, you got me my Brens and maybe I will get out of this one alive.

Vive le Basil!

Brimming now with excitement and enthusiasm, he called up to Franc.

"Eight oh eight, comrade!"

Franc leaned over, holding the satchel. It was a stretch—Franc dangling the satchel by its strap off the edge of the bridge, Leets clinging to the truss, grasping at the thing, which seemed somehow just out of reach—but in what seemed a mere seven hours, he finally snared it securely and pulled it in.

He was monkey-clinging to the truss now, his feet secure on a horizontal spar, crouched under the span, where it was damp and pungent, where no man had been in fifty years or so. He tried to find a way to attach the satchel itself, but in wedging it against junctures, he could never feel it was secure enough to consider it planted. Ach. It was so awkward.

Christ, his muscles ached everywhere and he could feel gravity sucking at his limbs, urging him downward into the muck below.

Finally, he managed to moor the satchel between his knees. Then, holding on with one hand, he unsheathed his M3 knife from his boot sheath and cut the canvas strap on the satchel. Now, what to do with the knife? He couldn't quite find the angle to get it back into the sheath, so he tried to slide it into his belt, and of course at a certain point it disappeared and hit the water below.

Goddamn! He hated to lose a good knife that way. It was odd how annoyed he was at the loss.

Anyway, he liberated the satchel from between his knees, wedged it into the truss, and used the long strap to bind it securely. He pawed at the gathered crunched material to find a passage to the explosive, and at last his fingers touched the sticky, gummy green stuff. He smelled almonds again.

He reached into his bellows pocket carefully, since it was at a radical angle and the pencils could easily slip out. Then, one by one, he removed the pencils and jammed them into the wad of 808 stuffed in the satchel nested in the bridge.

They always said: use two to make sure. He used all five and made certain in his orthodox midwestern way that each one was secure and driven in deep enough so that gravity wouldn't pull it out.

God, I did it, he thought.

It seemed to take an hour to clamber back up to the bridge span itself, and Franc and Leon pulled him while the third maquisard hammered away with the Sten periodically.

On the span he was elated, yet also exhausted.

"Whoa," he said in English, "wouldn't want to do that job over." Then, reverting to French, he said, "Friends, let's get the hell out of here!"

He grabbed his Thompson, ran back down the bridge, past the blown-out guardhouse, deserted, sandbagged gun pits with their silent

88s pressing skyward, the wreckage and small fires from the Gammons; now it was only a question of the long run up the hill to the tree line in the darkness, waiting for the boom from the—

That's when he noticed the Brens were no longer firing.

That's when he saw a German truck scuttle over the crest of the road, stop, and begin to disgorge troops—many of them—while on top a soldier unlimbered an MG-42.

Leets did a quick tumble through the facts as he thought them to be and concluded that, yes, Team Casey had a chance.

Luftwaffe troops, basically antiaircraft gunners; their rifle marksmanship and combat aggression had to be somewhat deficient. It was dark; untrained, unbloodied troops didn't care for the dark. They weren't sure where they were going, and at best they'd put in a half effort, each fellow thinking, I don't want to be the one guy who dies tonight.

"Okay," he said to his three musketeers, "we'll go ahead by leapfrogging. As each guy runs, the other three pour fire on les Boches. When you hold on them, aim a man high, or your rounds won't reach the target. Three rounds, no more. Shoot, move, don't stop no matter what. We spread out, try and go about fifty yards per spurt. Up top they'll be covering us. We don't need the damn Brens; we're fine."

"Fuck that fat Roger," said Leon. "He is pig filth, swine, a screwer of mothers and babies."

"That communist shit. The reds should be rounded up after the war and—"

"We will visit Roger, I promise you," said Leets. "Now, come on, guys, let's get a move on."

Franc went first, then was passed by Leon and finally Jerome. Leets crouched behind a sandbag revetment and had a wild, insane, heroic impulse. Maybe I should stay here, cover them, and keep the Krauts off until the bridge blows.

Then he thought, Fuck that.

He was moving, was past Franc, past Leon, almost to Jerome, moving through fire that was sporadic at best, now and then licking up a spit of dust in the general area, and he'd heard nothing blazing by his ears, which would show that Jerry had zeroed in on them.

The flare popped, freezing him.

Flares? These clowns have flares?

He looked back to the bridge and beheld with horror the reality that two more trucks had arrived, in the dappled camouflage coloring of 2nd SS Das Reich, and watched as from each truck spilled *Panzergrenadiers* in their camouflage tunics, hardened by years on the Eastern Front, a unit noted and feared far and wide as the finest of the SS divisions. These characters carried the new StG 44, something the Germans called an "attack rifle," with a high rate of fire. Oh, fuck, they could really lay fire with that sonofabitch.

How did they get here so fast?

Another flare popped, and then another, and the whole scene lit up, this puny French river valley, he and his three maquisards racing uphill through a landscape of flickering shadow as the descending parachute flares caught on the stumps of the so recently cut pines and threw blades of darkness this way and that, like scythes, the Germans still two hundred yards away but coming strong, the camouflaged *Panzergrenadiers* racing through and past the confused young Luftwaffers, and now, suddenly, from the ridgeline, a long arc of tracer as the MG-42s tried to range the target.

We are screwed, he thought. This is it.

The bridge went.

It wasn't the blossoming, booming movie explosion so familiar from the Warner Bros. backlot agitprop films but more of a disappointingly insubstantial percussion, lifting a large volcano of smoke and dust from the structure in the aftermath of a flash too brief for anyone to remember. Leets stole a moment in the fading parachute flare to examine his legacy: the bridge, as the dust cleared, was not downed, leaving a gap as if a mouth had been punched front-teethless, but the roadway span hung at a grotesque 45-degree angle, torquing downward, meaning the truss Leets had 808ed had gone but the other one held. It would take days to repair, or to detour around, and those would be days with no 2nd SS Das Reich at Normandy.

He stood, dumped a mag a man high at the nearest parade of SS *Panzergrenadiers*, and shouted to his guys, "Go, go, go, go!"

Franc took the first hit. He just slumped, tried to get up, then sat, then lay down, then curled up.

"Go, go, go!" screamed Leets, dumping another mag. He had three left.

Of the two maquisards, Leon, the youngster, made it closest to the tree line, and then a new flare popped and the German fire found him and put him in a beaten zone, and no man survives the beaten zone.

Jerome didn't make it nearly as far, and Leets had not gotten clear either, for he ran himself through a sleet of light and splinter as the Germans tried to bring him down, but in the second before he was hit he saw Jerome jack vertically from his runner's crouch and go down hard as gravity took hold of his remains and decreed it unto the earth.

The bullet struck Leets in the left hip. Man, did he go down, full of spangles and fire flashes and lightning bugs and flies' wings. His mind emptied; all visible movement ceased in the universe, and it went silent—I am dead, he thought—but he blinked himself alive again and saw SS coming up hard in the light of a new flare, holding their fire, for they wanted someone alive for the info before the execution, and he cursed himself for throwing out the cyanide tablet he'd been issued.

The pain was immense, and he tried to make it go away by rushing a mag change, lifting the ever-loyal, faultless best friend of the Thompson gun and running another mag, seeming to drive them back or down or whatever.

He was twenty-four.

He didn't want to die.

He tried to get through another mag change but dropped the heavy weapon. He got a Gammon bomb out but couldn't get the cap unscrewed. He pulled out his .45, jacked the slide, held it up stupidly without aiming, blinked in the bright light of another flare just overhead, and squeezed off a few pointless rounds.

The gun locked back. He saw two *Panzergrenadiers* quite close with their fancy new rifles.

Then the two Germans sat down as if embarrassed.

A wave of explosions wiped out the reality that was but a few yards ahead of him.

"There, there, Bates, chum," said Basil. "The fellows are here with a stretcher. I don't see any splintered bone, just huge purple smear from bum to cod. You might even live."

"Basil . . . I . . . what . . . get out of here . . . oh, for—"

But Basil had turned and was busy running mags through his Sten, as around him, the other maquisards fired whatever weapons they had.

Somehow Leets was on a stretcher, and being humped at speed the remaining few yards to the tree line.

"Basil, I—"

"There's the good chap, Bates, these fellows will take good care of you. Get Lieutenant Bates somewhere to medical aid. Get him out of here."

"Basil, you come too. Come on, Basil, we got the bridge. We can—"

"Oh, someone has to stay to discourage these fellows. They seem so stubborn. But I'll be along in a bit. We'll have that chat. Good luck, Bates, and Godspeed."

Basil turned and disappeared back into the forest. For Leets, it became an ordeal of not passing out as the maquisards heaved his sorry ass along a dark path until he seemed to be being slid into some kind of vehicle and then he did in fact pass out. But Basil was gone. He had disappeared into the great maw of the war, swallowed whole, for what? Well, not much of anything—a twisted bridge span.

And then he put it together. Someone ordered the Brens to withdraw, leaving us uncovered. Whoever, however, whenever, it was inescapable: *We were betrayed.*

Part One

SCEPTERED ISLE

CHAPTER 1

Parris in the Summer

God was late.

For six weeks he had been everywhere on the firing line. He was a deity with far-seeing eyes and an eerie professional calmness that separated him from every man any of them had known. He lectured, he taught, he named the parts and took them through the ceremonial intricacies of disassembly and assembly, and when the young recruits found themselves behind their spanking-new M1 Garand rifles, it seemed like he found time to kneel next to every boy—there were three hundred of them—issue gentle sight corrections, adjust a grip, test for a dominant eye, tighten a sling, slap a recalcitrant bolt handle forward, jiggle an en bloc clip of Government .30 into a breech, or press on the trigger-guard safety to which young fingers—the average recruit was 19.7 years old—were unaccustomed.

He never seemed to sweat, as if that human attribute was itself too intimidated to perform. He never cursed or humiliated or threatened, as did endlessly their daily custodians, the drill instructors; his way was soothing, as if he knew enough real bad shit lay ahead for them and had determined not to add to it. This disposition was part of a legend that was growing toward the ecclesiastical, while in fact he wore no ribbons on his tunics and never spoke of the islands he'd been on.

Though it was barely halfway through the year of our war 1944, it was said he'd already been on three. Most could name them: Guadalcanal, Bougainville, and Tarawa. The former was famous for its triple-canopy tropical rain forest, just the neighborhood for hiding the wily Japanese; the latter for its thousand-yard walk through the chest-high surf from amtracs hung up on unseen reefs while blue tracers flicked murderously through the air, killing randomly. He got through that. On the third day he'd been badly wounded, it was said, spending six months in the hospital. The Corps believed he'd seen enough combat and had assigned him here on Parris Island, the smudge of marshy land just south of Beaufort, South Carolina, and north of Georgia where young men were brutalized into Marines. He was the senior NCO in charge of Rifle Marksmanship, that central faith of the Marine Corps.

But where was he?

Did something dare impede the great Gunnery Sergeant Earl Swagger, or was this part of Marine stagecraft, designed to increase the aura around the man? They would never know. They swatted flies and sand fleas, glad of the island's singular mercy, which was a ramshackle roof built over the amphitheater that somewhat distilled the near-lethal sun, and talked among themselves, waiting, waiting, waiting. They were full of piss and venom. Culled hard over the weeks, those that remained yearned themselves to get to the islands and kill a bucketful of Japs. All considered themselves invulnerable, whether they were Harvard graduates—there were fourteen of those—or had flunked out of Frog Snot High School in Swampbilge, Mississippi. They thought they were crack shots on the nine pounds of Garand rifle death they lived with; they thought they could toss a grenade through a gun slot in a pillbox forty yards hence or go all Errol Flynn with their bayonets, outdueling the yellow enemy and their cruel samurai swords. All knew they would be heroes or die trying; none knew they might just die by whimsy, accident, or tropic fever. That was too much heaviness to the spirit to bear.

"Here he comes," came a call that became a ripple and then a wave as it coursed through the group. Indeed, a jeep came down Range Road through a meadowland of rifle acreage from a squad of administrative Quonsets a mile off, pulling up dust from the unpaved track. A PFC drove. Next to him had to be the gunnery sergeant his own self, big as life, maybe bigger, certainly the most interesting man any of them had ever met.

The sergeant bailed briskly from the vehicle, to be instantly attended by the DIs who supervised each platoon of the 3rd Recruit Training Battalion, and each gave a smart report to the effect that all were present and accounted for, meaning that the recruits were seated and rapt. This would be Swagger's last time to address the battalion as a whole and he had words for them.

Swagger was a solid six feet, immaculate in class A khaki shirt and, for the occasion, blue dress trousers with Marine red stripes, ending cufflessly in black oxfords so bright with shine you could signal a plane with them. His visored cap was white. He wore no tie but the shirt was starched hard, its array of pockets and plackets arranged to form a metaphor for perfect USMC-style order on the chest, and a perfect pie of T-shirt showed in the valley of the collar. No ribbons, just the dark three up and two down over the diamond on the sleeve that signified rank.

No one would call him handsome; no one would call him ugly. He was simply a Marine. His face had been baked in Pacific sun, so that it now resembled a Spartan shield picked up after the big fight on the Greek coast. It was a long, hard, lean face, unadorned by flesh. He had cheekbones like howitzer shells. His nose was a blade, its precision testimony to the fact that even while winning Pacific fleet light heavyweight champion in '39, he had been quick enough to keep it pristine. The jaw appeared to have been smelted from steel and the eyes were intense. They were also legendary. Every time he took a physical, naval aviation boys came calling to beg him to take a commission and an appointment to Pensacola and fly with them, because they knew he'd see the Zeros before they saw him. He, however, was a man of the gun, the land, the forest, and the hunt, and his skills and inclinations pointed him irrevocably in that way. Besides, generations of Swaggers had found the earth good enough to die on.

He went swiftly to the podium, not requiring the seated youngsters to rise, as he knew that would unsettle them for no point at all. He faced them.

"Good morning, marines," he said in a tone of voice familiar to military formations for a good five thousand years, and linking him to a long line of the foremen of battle who got them up the hill or across the river or through no-man's-land, whether the setting was Guadalcanal or Borodino. His variation on the NCO's voice had the softness of the mid-South to it, as he hailed from Polk County, Arkansas, but the tone could have been Zulu, Greek, Roman, Hun, even yeoman's as spoken in the mud of Agincourt.

"GOOD MORNING, SERGEANT," they replied, and he passed on any follow-up Corps-standard theatrical bullshit as in "Sound off like you got a pair" or "I can't hear you" to get them even more ginned up. Swagger thought such rhetorical excesses unnecessary and of no use to the combat-bound.

"I call you marines and not recruits because, though a week shy of graduation and assignment to your next units, you have all passed rifle marksmanship. You are therefore riflemen and are therefore entitled to the respect of men, for all of you fellows are now men, even that squeaky little redhead over there"—he pointed to Richie Murphy, a kind of battalion mascot who was officially seventeen but widely believed to be even younger—"and in short order will be facing Japanese infantrymen in places you never heard of, you can't pronounce, you couldn't find on no map because they aren't big enough. That's man's work. Only men can do it, and you have proven yourself. No matter how it turns out, know today you are a man and a marine."

They cheered themselves. They had earned it: by mastering the hard craft of the march, the compass, the push-up, the grenade, and most of all the rifle. In that discipline they showed the skill to lie flat and put rounds on targets to six hundred yards. It would be harder under fire, but if their luck held—nobody said it would—the fundamentals Swagger had pounded into them would get them through it.

"Now, you may have noticed, ain't no officers here today," he said.

Some had, some hadn't. But, yes, it was strange, as platoon commanders and battalion staff had been ever present over the rigorous nine weeks that had preceded.

"That's because I want to speak freely, with no reports being filed and investigators from the Navy Department showing up. So what I tell you ain't official Marine doctrine as vetted by the old men with stars on their collars. I'm just giving you straight shit, and I hope you listen on it and take it to heart. I believe it may save your life someday. But before I begin, let me ask: Is there a man here from Harvard University?"

In time a few hands raised. Swagger pointed to the nearest, and said, "All right, son, you come on up here."

The boy climbed onto the stage in his much-sweated-in herringbone twill dungarees. Though tall and slim, he wore the olive drab cotton poorly, so that it hung on him like pajamas, obscuring the crew athlete he'd once been and the war athlete he'd become. His cover was the pith helmet, a Jungle Jim thing that actually did its job against the sun no matter how goofy it looked. He was shod in boondockers, rough side out, giving him the aspect, however unlikely, of a man who made his living pushing a plow behind a mule. He came to attention.

"Stand at ease."

The boy's posture relaxed but still showed strength through core muscles.

"What's your name, son?"

"Sergeant, my name is Wallace F. McCoy, Sergeant," he said smartly.

"Now, McCoy," said Swagger, "I know on account of your fine university that you're a smart fellow. I'm guessing you have a good memory. Would I be right?"

"Well . . ." The boy paused. "Sergeant, I can name all the presidents and all the states. I know the table of elements, the Declaration of Independence, the names and stories of all the constellations. I've read every British novel ever written and all the poets and playwrights. I know the Pledge of Allegiance, Shakespeare's sonnets, the words to the Marine's Hymn, and I speak Spanish."

"That would seem to be what I had in mind," said Swagger. "Now I believe in that brain of yours there might have been room enough for something the Marine Corps taught you called 'The Rifleman's Creed.' Tell me I'm not wrong."

"Sergeant, you're not wrong, Sergeant."

"Excellent. Now I want you to recite it for me and all your chums in 3rd Recruit Battalion sitting out there. Speak it loud, so they can hear in the balcony"—there of course being no balcony.

"Sergeant, yes, Sergeant."

He turned, cleared his throat.

"Wait," said Swagger. "It works better with this." He leaned behind the podium and removed an M1 Garand rifle, the potbellied, eight-round .30-caliber semiautomatic weapon that made the American marine or soldier the best armed in the war. He handed it to the young man, who received it with accustomed hands, immediately cleared it to check that it was unloaded, again by regulation, then turned to face his cohort.

" 'This is my rifle,' " he said from rote memory. " 'There are many like it, but this one is mine. My rifle is my best friend. It is my life. I must master it as I must master my life. My—' "

"Skip to the brother part," said Swagger.

"Yes, Sergeant. 'My rifle is human, even as I, because it is my life. Thus, I will learn it as a brother. I—' "

"That's enough, McCoy. Stand easy."

McCoy went to parade rest, the rifle held precisely parallel to his right leg, secured by the grip of his right hand.

Swagger turned to the group.

"You all know that. The DIs have drilled it into your ears for eleven weeks. You have nightmares about it. You probably will remember it for the rest of your life.

"It was written in 1942 by a general named William H. Rupertus, commandant of the big base in San Diego. I had the privilege of serving with the general when he was a colonel in Honduras in the thirties banana wars. He was a fine man. I'd serve with him anytime and follow him anywhere."

He paused.

"And yet, marines, I'm telling you this one, not straight from the heart, but straight from the mud in which most battles are fought. It's bullshit."

The brigadier, a small gray thistle of a man who confronted reality under an iron-gray flat-top, hollow cheeks blackened perpetually by whisker that could not be shaved away, and eyes that looked like peep sights, was in conference with his senior staff in the big room just down from his office. All present wore perfectly starched class A khakis, open at the neck, short-sleeved, as much fruit salad as possible on chests, rank pins on collars and over their khaki slacks, highly shined brown oxfords. They looked like mushrooms with medals and suntans. They sat rigidly, they talked rigidly, they smoked rigidly.

The meeting had to do with construction shortfalls for the barracks to house incoming recruits for the newly designated 5th, 6th, and 7th Recruit Battalions. The new boys would be arriving by October and it didn't appear the barracks would be habitable until November.

The issue, therefore, was where to put the boys until the building could take them.

"I don't want them squawking about sleeping outdoors," said the brigadier in an iron voice under iron eyes. He smiled in the presence of grandchildren only, except he had no grandchildren and his only son had died on Guadalcanal. "They should be concentrating on their training. Besides, the DI magic doesn't work outside an intimate setting like a barrack. That's where he builds the marine into them."

"Sir," a colonel said, "maybe there's unused hangar space at Page. We could requisition cots, we could run lines with tarps to cut the room into more intimate space—"

But before the commanding officer of Parris Island's Page Field could object, the brigadier's aide entered, went swiftly to him, and bent over.

"Sir, call from Navy Annex," he whispered.

Whoa!

The brigadier was taken aback. Such direct communications were rare. Orders and policies generally drifted down the table of organization, each level getting its turn. And Navy Annex, where the commandant and his headquarters staff were now located while something called Henderson Hall was expanded for them, meant interest from the highest level. In fact, such things almost never happened. Something large must be on somebody's plate. He had to jump.

"Gentlemen, forgive the interruption. I have to take a call."

He turned, left, involuntarily making certain his gig line was straight, his fruit salad as precise as a Technicolor chessboard, his shirt bloused tightly, his shoes as bright brown as a cow's eyes, his one star freshly Brasso'd and gleaming on each collar wing. No one at Navy Annex could see him, of course, but he felt better prepared if he was as squared away as any headquarters officer.

In his office, he found another orderly holding the phone. He took it and a deep breath and said his name into it.

"How are you, Brad?" asked the commandant of the Marine Corps, a soft beginning that seemed to indicate the call wasn't to be remonstrative.

"Sir, I'm fine. We're working hard here to keep our programs on schedule and of high standard. I can send you a report if—"

"No, no, this is another thing."

"Yes, sir, how may I be of help?"

"You have Gunnery Sergeant Swagger down there, is that correct?"

"Yes, sir. Swagger's practically an institution. He turns out the best riflemen in the world. I hope you're not telling me his requests have been approved and he's off to the Pacific again. I'd hate to lose him."

"I wish I could help you on that one," said the commandant, "but I answer to higher parties. In about an hour, a B-17 from the Eighth Air Force"—those were the boys who were bombing the Reich from England!—"will put down at Page."

Was Page big enough? Well, if the pilots were good enough and the brigadier instantly understood that a far more normal procedure would be to land them at Naval Air Station Beaufort, twenty miles to the north. So this had to be highest priority.

"Yes, sir," he said.

"It will be carrying two men. One is actually a psychologist, the other a field officer, but both will be in civilian clothes, for reasons nobody cares to explain to me. Still, both should be treated with formal military courtesy. They are attached to an outfit that even I didn't know existed until a few minutes ago."

"I will arrange to have them picked up and—"

"No, I want you there to greet them."

"Yes, sir."

"I want you to have Swagger with you."

"Yes, sir."

"They may make him an unusual offer. I myself don't even know what it will be. It is of course entirely voluntary."

"I hear you, sir."

"However, and I can't emphasize this enough, I wish that he accepts it. I hope that you will make this clear to him and that you will add that you wish that he accepts it."

By long tradition of Marine culture, a senior officer's "wish" had the impact of a howitzer shell. It meant instant compliance, as in NOW.

"Yes, sir."

"They require a meeting with him to make their pitch. I am told that it is acceptable for you to sit in on it, both to communicate to Swagger that the Marine Corps is in approval here, and that you personally endorse Mr. Morgan and Mr. Leets."

"Yes, sir."

"You'd best get cracking," said the commandant.

"It was a Canadian fellow designed this," said Swagger to his three hundred zealots, now hanging on his every word and buzzed by his willingness to buck the hokum of "The Rifleman's Creed." He held McCoy's Garand high in one hand, at the perfectly engineered point of balance, so that his audience could appreciate the lethal architecture, the high engineering art, the functionality that was the best part of the beauty that the nine pounds represented.

"Now, let me tell you, Mr. John Cantius Garand wasn't in the Miss Lonelyhearts business. He didn't want to hold your hand, he didn't want to make you all happy-happy like the Easter Bunny does, he didn't want you to fall in love with what he was designing. It ain't your best friend. It ain't a girlfriend, your baby, your brother, your grandma on Thanksgiving who knows how to roast up them birds, your old uncle. It's not, no matter what General Rupertus, sitting in his office with a bottle of bourbon and all het up over Pearl Harbor, says. It's not *you*. In fact, it's your enemy."

He let that one sink in as the boys, most of them, even the fourteen from Harvard, gasped at the apostasy.

"It wants you dead. It will always be looking for mud to choke on, for rocks to bang, for grease to slip it out of your hands and fall hard, for rain to turn its steel rusty and erode out the grooves in the barrel. Its gas plug wants to vibrate loose so it don't get the right measure of recoil energy to operate reliably. Its rear sight wants to go out of zero, its front sight wants to bend, its sling wants to slip off your shoulder in the prone, its extractor wants to break so it don't eject and it ties up. I'm telling you, young marines, it ain't your girlfriend, and if you think it is, you will be sorry.

"Suppose you have to use someone else's weapon when Miss Marianne is blown up? Suppose you have to use Jap weapons? Suppose you get picked to replace the assistant machine gunner and now you got his dinky little carbine? Suppose you're on night patrol with a .45 and a knife? Are you going to get all Section 8 because your precious Miss Marianne ain't there? You cannot plan what's going to happen to you; you can only prepare for the most likely contingencies. The best way is to face the truth: it's a tool. Nothing more, nothing less. Its real good at what it does, if you do your part. We had Springfields on the 'Canal, and I'll tell you in every way this one is far better, the best in the world. If you do your part.

"And what is your part? Real simple. You maintain it every single goddamned second you are on the line. You do not get sack time unless you ram the barrel clear, oil the bolt channel, check the clicks on your sight, run a rag over the insides, look hard into it, test that the trigger guard is still locked into the action and that the action is still rigid in the stock. All of that, every night, before every patrol, every invasion, every assault, every opportunity the Marine Corps gives you to kill Japs.

"You will grow to hate the goddamned thing because it demands so much of you. But it don't care what you think. It only cares about itself and the springs and recoil energy and the parts and the levers that all work in perfect timing to make it operate. It ain't going to congratulate you when you hit a Jap at 240, or gun down a fleeing Nambu crew fast as you can trigger it, or pot a sniper in a high green tree who's been making life hell for you. You only impress it by working it hard every day.

"Maybe at the end of the war, your last day as you muster out and you go to the armory and sign it over to the battalion arms room for some other young green thing to use, maybe then, and only then, when you see Miss Marianne racked with all her girlfriends as you head out and back to your life, can you let yourself imagine that the goddamned thing is a gal that has a soul and is giving you a tiny bit of smile. At that moment, you will have earned it. So it's okay to smile back."

They rode in silence. It was beyond any service etiquette that an enlisted man, even a gunnery sergeant of vast experience, should ride in the backseat of a staff car with a general, even a brigadier. Thus, neither knew what to say as the car, which had showed unexpectedly at the rifle range amphitheater to acquire Swagger, rolled through the ranges, then into marshy land where Parris Island seemed as much liquid as solid and supported stands of vegetation that had once sustained the stegosaurus. Eventually, the road yielded to the dried-out southern tip of the island, where Page Field had been built to accommodate biplanes, then Wildcats, then Hellcats but never a bird as big as a 17.

"Gunnery Sergeant Swagger," the brigadier finally said, "you should know up front that some very important folks are involved in this party, and all of them, including me, hope that you'll enthusiastically embrace what is coming on."

"Sir, you know I am 150 percent Marine Corps, and if that's what the Marine Corps wants, I will provide it, same as any hill it told me to climb up under fire."

"I knew that to be the case, Sergeant. I did want to get it out in the open so there'd be no confusion. I think that—"

But at that moment a great roar engulfed them, followed by enough shadow to kill the sun for a second or two, and then it swept over them, just one hundred feet up, a B-17 on landing vector, its twin tires cranked down to embrace the ground shortly.

It was a huge plane by any standard of its time, wingspan one hundred feet, four Wright R-1820-97 Cyclone engines whose whirling props chewed the atmosphere like hungry tigers, its streamlined seventy-five-foot tube of fuselage broken only by double bubbles of shiny Perspex turrets, .50-caliber Messerschmitt-killers bristling from each, its proud tail itself a two-story blade for cutting the air. It was beautiful like the Garand was beautiful, out of the perfection of its design for the hard task it had been assigned.

"That's a B-17G, sir," said Swagger. "The latest model. Chin turret, double fifties in the tail."

"If they think coming to get you is worth pulling a ship off the missions to Germany, then that should give you some idea of how important this thing is."

By the time they arrived at the airfield, a rude collection of Quonsets and wooden shacks as well as new corrugated steel hangars on a spit of land which yielded at its tip to Port Royal Sound and a gateway to the Atlantic, the plane had come to rest, its nose up on tires half as big as a man, its tail down. Fuel trucks attended it, mechanics swarmed over it, some Marine pilots had gathered just to admire it. Army Air Forces officers, in waxy-brown A2 jackets and squashed forty-mission hats and huge teardrop sunglasses, supervised. No Air Forces enlisted men were visible in the ceremony of refueling, which even more suggested the plane was stripped for weight for its longer-distance job today.

The brigadier and Swagger got out of the car and were greeted by the exceedingly nervous captain who was now in command of Page, since the authentic CO was back at Base HQ, presumably still arguing overusing the extra hangars for the new recruit battalions.

"Sir, they're in here, sir," he said.

"Were they annoyed we couldn't be here to greet them off the plane, Mason?"

"Not at all, sir. Very friendly fellows, casual and joking. I have them in the pilot's ready room enjoying good Marine Corps coffee and I've promised them and their crew real eggs and bacon as soon as Cookie gets it together. They seemed to like that."

"Okay, fine, Mason."

Mason led them in, through a briefing room loaded with photos on the wall of famous air machines and their flyers, all in jaunty leather coats with diagonal rows of buttons or slanted zippers, all "Smilin' Jack" for the tremendous adventure of roaring through the air. The ready room was smaller, a comfy warren and fewer pictures with an alcove of lockers, a chalkboard with names and missions scrawled on it, and a sign that read: ". . . IN THE AIR, on land, and sea," from the "The Marines' Hymn."

One older, one younger. In suits, gray and brown. The ties were red, the white shirts had little buttons on the collars, the shoes, heavy for both, had patterns of perforations about them. They were like star maps in Florsheim leather.

One looked like the sort who'd be comfortable anywhere. His relaxed position on the central sofa suggested ease of being, quick study, confidence in charm and wit, and nimble mind.

The other, younger, had football written all over him. Pleasant, open face; blond crew cut; maybe, despite linebacker size and shoulders, a little less sure. One smoked, one enjoyed a mug of black joe, and they seemed to be chortling over something.

They rose, smiling.

"Gentlemen!" the older one said heartily, as if all were old pals meeting at a golf course watering hole, "thanks so much for accommodating us so quickly. Brigadier and, I presume, Gunnery Sergeant Earl Swagger, Marine Corps star and already a three-island vet."

This annoyed the shit out of Swagger; it was as if they were welcoming outsiders to their little club, not the other way around. It was also clear that they had no real interest in the brigadier, who took all this with dignity, but again it pissed Swagger off, because it upset the order of the world. All rule breakers start with the little ones, like these two, while working up to the big one that fucks everything up.

The brigadier nodded, let himself be ushered to a leather chair, while Swagger felt himself maneuvered toward another, better, closer one.

"We're not much on ranks in our outfit. I'm Bill Morgan," said the older. "This is Jim Leets. I'm the psychologist. He's the hero."

"Mr. Morgan, then, Mr. Leets, welcome to Parris Island, and please tell us how to help you," said the brigadier.

"Here it is: we have a bad jam-up in Europe," Bill Morgan said. "Our organization—it's supposed to be secret, but I don't think I'm betraying anything when I tell you we're called the Office of Strategic Services—"

"OSS," said the other, Leets. "We do spy stuff. We blow stuff up and kill field marshals and connect with the underground all over Europe. At least, that's the idea."

"Jim, tell them why we're here."

Leets, the younger, continued. "On highest priority we were assigned to find the best combat rifleman in American service. Didn't matter if he was a marine or a Boy Scout or an Army jeep driver. The deal is, we find him, we get him to Europe by the fastest route possible, and he starts working on our little problem."

"You wouldn't go wrong with Swagger," said the iron brigadier, unbidden. "He may be the best NCO in the Corps. He should be a colonel by now. Why he won't take a commission is something even the commandant has lost sleep over."

"So we hear."

"Can you tell me the problem?" asked Swagger.

"In one word," said the one called Leets, "snipers."

CHAPTER 2

Night Patrol

"Brooklyn!"

"What?"

"I said *Brooklyn*, god dammit."

"Jack, is that you?"

"I say 'Brooklyn,' you're supposed to say 'Dodgers.' Sign, counter-sign."

"I forgot."

"I'm coming across. Don't shoot me."

"Don't worry, I can't find my rifle."

"Hold it down, god dammit," commanded Sergeant Malfo in either a loud whisper or a soft yell.

Private Archer, of 2nd Squad, 1st Platoon, Dog Company, 2nd Battalion, 9th Infantry, Lightnin' Joe Collins's VII Corps, Omar Bradley's First Army, Ike Eisenhower's SHAEF, plunged into the cold water of a stream that ran randomly across this part of France that happened to be about twenty-seven kilometers west of Saint-Lô on the Saint-Lô–Périers line, where seven American divisions faced six German divisions.

The Germans seemed to be winning. Their position was solid, their gun pits well hidden, their machine-gun lanes laid out and staked, their artillery ranged, their elite SS Panzer units stationed to fly to attack points and torch the outgunned American Shermans. They were shrewd, tough, full of zeal and energy, and so pleased not to be in fucking Russia anymore they'd fight like lions.

The Americans, meanwhile, kept botching the skills of war, beginning with an intelligence failure that totally missed the primary difficulty facing the five thousand G.I.s ashore since D-Day: that before them lay a deathtrap of hills, forests, twisty roads and worst of all a maze-like array of eight-foot-tall, impenetrable headgrows. Other mistakes followed quickly: attacks in which preliminary shelling hadn't hit; getting lost on the complex of roads, out of coordination and communication, with all the commanders at each others' throats; and the Shermans reluctant to risk running into Tigers on the country roads, so they were always behind or had gone to the wrong place. The line had been static for three weeks—D-Day was four back, though neither of the soldiers had been there for it—and nothing seemed to suggest fortunes would change.

Archer, wet to the thighs, his Garand rifle held high over his head, scrambled up the bank, slipped in the mud, got some leverage, and rolled heavily into his squad's position, a gully hidden by foliage overlooking the stream and the meadow through the trees that he had just low-crawled across. By daylight it looked like a land of lush, romantic fantasy where Cinderella might have lived, but at night it revealed its true nature: a nightmare region full of vegetable walls, ditches, tricky, treacherous, unknowable, unmappable. And full of men who wanted to kill you. He breathed in heavily, glad to be alive, if wet and back from tonight's adventure in The War.

"Cigarette," he said to his friend on sentry duty, Private Gary Goldberg.

"Jack, I'm low."

"Mine got all wet when I fell in that fucking stream. Come on, Gary, give me a cigarette."

Neither of the boys—one twenty-one, the other twenty-two—were heavy smokers or had quite mastered the inhale action of the cigarette, but they were of an age and a disposition that mandated conformity, and the American army ran on tobacco. Some of the men claimed tobacco was the sixth food group, others that it belonged in with the vegetables.

Goldberg got a Victory pack of Camels out of the pocket of his M1941 jacket and flicked it out, a very Bogart/*Casablanca* move, and Archer took it, cupped it in the same Bogart style, pulled a Zippo, and fired up. He sucked in deeply, accidentally inhaled, had a brief spasm of coughing, but then got with it, settling back, enjoying the buzz.

Both were new, not only to the squad, the company, the battalion, the division, the corps, but also to The War. They were high-IQ draftees (over 115) who'd been sent to college for a year in the strange Army Specialized Training Program with the ultimate objective of turning them into officers. Then someone had noticed: What the fuck are we sending these guys to college for while the other guys are getting killed all over the world? Thus the program was suddenly ended and the formerly lucky boys were simply distributed into line units. This meant two things: that everyone hated them for being designated geniuses and for spending the last year safe and warm (and missing the rather hectic time the 9th had experienced in North Africa, in Sicily, and assaulting Cherbourg) and that they became friends for life, however long that might be.

Their little cigarette tête-à-tête was shortly interrupted by a rather intimidating noncommissioned officer.

"You okay, Archer? Goldberg, I almost tripped over your rifle. Pick it up."

"Is *that* where it is? Yes, Sergeant," said Goldberg.

"Goldberg, nix on the wisecracks. Save 'em for Broadway. Archer, talk to me."

"Well, I got pretty close to them."

"How close?"

"I could have used their latrine but the line was too long. Is that close enough?"

Sergeant Malfo wittily responded with a dead eyeball look that would have crushed ball bearings. He had that part of the sergeant business down pat.

"Spill. This isn't kindergarten. We gotta get out of here before the sun's up."

"Yeah, yeah. Okay, no engine sounds. No tanks moving in. Nothing at all to suggest they're going to attack anytime soon. Just soldier bullshit. A lot of pipe smoking—God, the shit they use for tobacco—and a lot of laughing. The Krauts seem to find the war very funny."

"I thought they were supposed to turn and run when they saw the mighty American war machine," said Goldberg.

"These guys just seemed . . . I don't know, really *happy*. They like this stuff. It's in their blood," said Archer.

"Bear down, Archer. Save the psychology for the chaplain. Any sign of artillery? You know, clearings in the woods, haulage trucks, piles of shells?"

"Nah. Now, I'm not saying not there. I didn't see so much in the dark. I didn't exactly get *into* the trench. It was more a radio experience. I listened hard and I didn't hear a thing that sounded like . . . like . . . I don't know. What I heard was mostly just stuff. Guys on the line. I don't think they'd be so comfortable if they were going to come at us soon. I saw the usual German solid work, what little I could make out. Barbed wire, machine-gun emplacements behind sandbags, a line of trench, rifle pits in front, to pick at us coming across the field, then fall back to the trench when we get close. If any of us are left to get close."

"Okay, good work. I'm going to radio it on."

He stood and the bullet hit him in the head. Back portion, left side skull, just below helmet, straight through, exiting in a blur of mess.

Neither boy had seen a headshot at close range before. The sergeant's skull seemed to evaporate into smear, a sudden spray of warm drops that neither wanted to examine pelted them, and the older man—Malfo had been all of twenty-five—seemed to melt. Goldberg had an incongruous memory of the Wicked Witch dissolving in *The Wizard of Oz*, while Archer, an engineering student at Purdue, thought of modern art, somehow, as if Malfo had become some crazed painting.

The dead sergeant flopped without grace onto the ground, making a sound that seemed like meat falling off a truck. Some more liquid splashed them.

Both young soldiers went hard to the earth.

"Oh, fuck," said Archer. "The Krauts can see in the dark."

Goldberg began to sneeze.

CHAPTER 3

Trees

"**S**ergeant," said Leets, "what brought us to you were rumors of an extremely successful anti-sniper program you ran on Guadalcanal in fall '42. We've heard the story from a variety of sources, each of them different. Now we'd like to hear from you."

Earl disliked nothing so much as talking about himself—unless he was on a drunk with seven or eight other sergeants, preferably in a whorehouse filled with jiggly Filipino dishes; then, of course, he wouldn't shut up. That would be how the story got around.

He turned to the brigadier.

"Sir, may I smoke?"

"Sure, go ahead, Sergeant," said the older visitor, Morgan. "We want you to be comfortable."

But Earl waited until the brigadier nodded. It was part of his war on men in suits, these two, yes, but generally men in suits everywhere.

He shook a Lucky loose from the pack in the pocket of his class A, lipped it, produced a burnished Zippo with "USMC" engraved on it, lit, inhaled deeply, then sent two lungfuls of smoke on patrol into the room.

The smoke lingered, separated into layers hanging heavily, forming its own weather system. More would soon join it.

"October, the rainy season. Everything had bogged down; we were low on supplies and energy, but not mud, plenty of mud. Our battalion was stretched thin but we had enough Browning .30s to hold them off when they came frontally. My company had high ground over a kind of meadow or gap or something, two hundred yards from a wall of rain forest. Believe me, nobody wanted to go in there, much less attack it. Thick, dark, wet, everything the Japanese love, everything the Americans hate."

He took another puff, savoring it. Exhaling, he sent another front advancing north to south, enveloping the suits, who had to bear up. But he miscalculated. The two men looked at him, gone in Earl rapture: it was like hearing about war from Achilles on a hill outside Troy just after the fight with poor Hector.

"They didn't have much artillery but they sure had snipers. Made our lives miserable. Couldn't move hardly till dark. It was a surprise and we paid for it dearly. I lost seven boys killed or bad wounded the first two days. We never suspected they'd be that good. They were hitting dead zero from at least two hundred out, maybe further. Where'd they get glass that good? Where'd they get ammo that good? Where'd they get men that good? How were they hiding that good?

"Tried everything. Artillery, air strikes—no air to speak of, no napalm, not then—counter-sniper teams, machine-gun sweeps, the works. Every day they hit someone, and we just got fewer and fewer, since no replacements were coming in. There were nights when, if they'd hit us hard, they'd have busted on through to the sea.

"Morale stunk, the boys were extra-jumpy, the officers sullen and scared. Yep, happens to marines too. That's what sniper war does.

"So I'm thinking: What don't we know about this shit? What questions ain't we asked? What do the Japs know we don't? I come up with one answer: trees.

"They had to be in trees. Sure, but which trees? Thinking harder, I reasoned out that they'd have to be stout, tall trees to get the elevation so they wasn't shooting uphill, which is always tricky. But what trees in a rain forest are like that? Nobody knew. So I went to the skipper and told him I wanted to do a one-man tree recon. I'd infiltrate down low in the dark and move into the rain forest. By day, I'd be trying to figure which trees, where were they, how could we ID them in the triple canopy, which was so dense, it obliterated everything.

"That's what I done. I learned that most rain forest trees are shallow of root and weak of limb and trunk. Banyans was one I recognized from the Philippines. Mangroves was another; it was the one that grew in water. Some palms, and shit on the ground like barbed wire, all tangled, thorny, tough. That jungle could take a man down hard and fast. The smell of rot. Everything wet and crumbly. Mud everywhere, some flowers. Lizards, birds, maybe monsters. But there was one tree that was strong and tall. It had kind of fins deployed from the trunk to make it sturdier, it looked kind of like something from another planet or another age. Not so many of them; I guess it could only grow in certain spots where it could get deep roots in. I later found out it was called a koa. But the name didn't matter; I just figured, if snipers were there, that would be the tree they were in. I managed to climb one: hard going for a light heavyweight, not easy, but happily there was no Jap in that one, though when I got up there I realized that one had been there. Obviously, they perch in one of them trees for weeks at a time, then move on before we get them zeroed. The thickness of the trunk was protection against random fire and artillery. Pretty good setup, and the Nip who'd been there had cut one limb for a rifle rest, just above a juncture where he'd sat.

"So the question was: How do we ID that tree so we can concentrate fire on it? From the ground looking up or from our line looking downhill, the jungle was so thick, you couldn't see nothing."

He took a puff. Even he had to acknowledge that what came next was smart. It saved lives. Boys got off that island that might otherwise not have. Made him happy. He'd done his duty that day.

"So I wiggled out a ways on a limb and cut off a branch. Looking at it carefully, I could tell that the leaves was significantly lighter than all the other jungle haberdashery. Couldn't see it from the ground, but . . . maybe from the air.

"I got back that night and the next night got a jeep to Henderson Field, which we just barely controlled. I found an Army Piper Cub pilot—I think they call it an L-4 in the Army—and told him my plan. So he and I flew over our positions that afternoon and he got me a big Army camera for aerial recon. Hardly been used, as all it showed was trees.

"A day later, the pictures come to battalion. We look at them, and sure as shit—"

Another deep draft of Lucky, toasty, smooth, and pure, bringing buzz and happy, producing another front of heavy weather on the same north-south axis, smothering his admirers. Suits. Outsiders. Know-it-alls. Fuck 'em.

"—from five hundred feet up, you could pick out the taller, stronger trees because of the color difference. They looked near white in the black-and-white photography. So we oriented the photo to the compass and from a certain arbitrary point downslope shot azimuths to each of the trees—fourteen of 'em, within Jap 7.7 range—to the battalion front. Next night I took a volunteer gun crew down the slope, we dug in at the selected point, oriented the tripod to the photos, and were able to set the gun by tripod clicks on each azimuth. I figured there was no point in waiting for daylight, because by that time the Japs would be in their shooting positions with the trunk between them and us. Plus, they could bring fire on us.

"So at 0430 we fired fourteen two-fifty-round belts of .30 ball along the azimuths that led to each tree. Figured the first hundred would cut a way through the foliage and the next hundred and fifty would spray the spine of the tree. Fire for effect, it's called in our talk. We got the water to boiling in the water jacket halfway through, we were firing so much, so fast. It boiled off and we had to refill from our canteens.

"Then we broke the gun down and crawled back up the slope, had a cup of joe, and caught some sack. The test was next morning. Would we catch same old sniper hell or what? And the truth is, we didn't. And we never did again, even when we moved into them trees and across the island. And no other battalions did neither."

"The Japanese aren't said to value life," said Bill Morgan. "Why do you think they didn't just reload the trees and take the losses for the damage inflicted?"

"I figure it was because their snipers were their best men: smart, great shots, dedicated, willing to die. They're the ones who make the outfit operate, probably NCOs with a lot of time on the trigger, been through China and Malaysia and the Philippines. It's one thing to sacrifice conscripts, but if you get your best killed, you're destroying yourself. Even the Japs ain't that stupid.

"I later heard from an intelligence officer that they'd intercepted some radio chatter, and the Japs thought we had some new weapon that could see in the dark and through the heavy canopy. Nah. It was just Swagger and Corporal Tommy Malloy, two PFCs and a John Browning .30 water-jacketed. Malloy was a terrific gunner. He earned his pay that night. Too bad he didn't make it off the island."

"Here's to Tommy Malloy," said this Leets guy. "God rest his soul. And may we find more like him."

Earl took a puff of Lucky in tribute to Tommy. Was that a moment of silence? Maybe this Leets got it, after all. Maybe he wasn't so bad as Swagger thought.

The two looked at each other, saying nothing.

Finally, Bill Morgan said, "I hope you'll excuse me a second, gentlemen. I have to make a phone call. Jim can keep you amused with magic tricks. He's good at that."

"I have calls to make as well, gentlemen," said the brigadier. "Back shortly."

The brigadier stood, Swagger rose, but the brigadier put out a hand, meaning: belay that.

He hastened out.

Swagger and Jim Leets were left alone.

"Do you blow stuff up, Mr. Leets?" Earl asked.

"Got a bridge after D-Day," said Leets.

"Sounds like fun."

"Seeing it blow was the highlight. But then we were jumped by Waffen-SS from God knows where. Lost some extremely good people. The SS executed a hundred French civilians in the town the next day. That's the bad part. No big deal, but I also caught a piece of German junk in the hip. Thought it had shattered my joint, but it must have been a ricochet and there was no penetration, only massive bruising, slow to heal, and you'll see that I walk with a limp. Just got out of the hospital in London a few days ago."

Earl said nothing, not his way. But he thought, Okay, bud. You're in the club.

Both the brigadier and Bill Morgan returned in nearly the same second. They reseated themselves without fuss.

"Okay," Morgan said. "I called DC, talked to General Donovan; he's our boss, Wild Bill, from the Great War."

"I met him, as a matter of fact," said the brigadier. "Great man. Medal of Honor in the Great War. Sergeant Swagger, if General Donovan is in on this, you're in good company."

"Yes, sir," said Earl.

"Go ahead, Lieutenant Leets," said Morgan.

"Here it is," said Leets. "We will leave in an hour or so, enough time for you to change to civvies and get your shaving kit. The Fort is refueling now. Straight shot to London. Ten, maybe twelve hours, depending on prevailing winds. Best to sleep, because you'll need it. Over there you will be assigned by Office of Strategic Services to investigate a sudden spurt in night sniper deaths inflicted in theater on our troops, holding up our entire offensive initiative. Colonel Bruce will detail-brief you. You will get all support and logistics via OSS as provided by the Army. You'll have carte blanche to travel, investigate, interview, and, we hope, develop an anti-sniper campaign similar to the one you deployed on Guadalcanal. Much wider front, of course. You will oversee its implementation—"

"Meaning I get to shoot too? Not just sit in a tent, waiting for results?"

"If that's what you want. You're calling the shots."

"When I'm done, I can come back to the Marine Corps? You'll use whatever influence you might have through the War Department into the Navy Department to get me back to the Pacific?"

"Again, if that's what you want."

Earl looked at the brigadier, caught a nod so imperceptible, any civilian would have missed it.

"Sure," he said, "let's do it."

"Excellent," said Morgan. "If nothing else, you'll be the first and certainly only man in the war to board a plane a marine gunnery sergeant and get off it a major in the United States Army."

CHAPTER 4

70 Grosvenor

As usual, the nightmares: the blue tracers floating in from the smudge of rock called Tarawa on the horizon that was a mile away through chest-high ocean. Wherever they flicked, they tore up the surface of the water, and if a boy was in the center of that disturbance, he'd next be seen floating facedown in a liquid cloud of his drifting blood. Then there was the up-close stuff on the 'Canal when the Japs thought they could overcome the positions on pure manpower and sent wave after wave, men dying for nothing in the hundreds as they came through the night, and the .30s just kept harvesting them, like wheat or Arkansas corn, in some places breaking through when the guns jammed on their own heat, which meant it became a knife-and-shovel fight in the dark. You did things to them you didn't want to remember but would never forget. That's what the knife was for, but even Earl knew it was bullshit and so tragically wasteful, thought up by men far away. On the ground, it's hard to hate a guy you've just sliced open from nipple to hip, but there wasn't time to process it, as another one was on you in a second.

And the big wound. It was like being in the center of an explosion.

You were blown out of your body, and when you came back to it you were wrecked. Legs, arms, all gone. A fog of fatigue that drew you into the sleep that was death. And when the shock lessened, the pain arrived, like someone corkscrewing into your chest on a lubrication of lava and gravel. You screamed, but no one heard you, there was so much noise, the sky filled with dust, smoke, blue streaks. And then a pair of eyes and then another. Two colored stretcher-bearers.

"Goin' be fine, boss," one said. "Me 'n' Marcus git you on back now."

And they did.

And when he woke in the aid station, the man next to him was Marcus, and Marcus was dead.

He awoke in the cold, vibrational dark of the B-17, chilled and yet thirsty. He'd awakened in many strange places; the Marines will do that for a man. It took him a second to get it organized, but then he had it, it was clear, and he knew that the fun was just beginning.

In an OD staff Ford, they drove through London, the newly uniformed major—after a stop at the Airborne logistics building at USAAF Station 486, previously RAF Greenham Common—and Leets in back. Silence. The city prowled by, its buildings, those that stood, old-time with ornamentation and fancifulness built into them. Far off, unnecessary barrage balloons floated at the ends of tethers, sandbags were built into walls everywhere to secure them against bombs that no longer fell, the traffic was sparse but the streets jammed. It seemed now a largely military city, as if the parade had ended and the men in uniforms, dozens of different ones, just milled about, looking for, as usual, liquor, women, and fights, in that order.

"Leets," said Earl finally, "brief me on Colonel Bruce."

"David K. E. Bruce. Two middle initials tell you something. Married to a Harriman. Wealthy. Connected. Charming, very social, which is his job. You will like him, as everybody does, but he'll seem more civilian than military. Yale or Princeton, I think, then into politics so 'getting along,' 'making allowances,' 'achieving compromises,' not tommy guns, are his preference. Wants to do diplomacy after the war, I've heard, and this is a great first step. But don't underestimate him. Smart as they come. Not a yeller or a martinet, not too comfortable with military etiquette. Has back-channel connections to the Roosevelt administration. Well-known in Washington. Knows wines, theater, literature. Reads both the *New York* and the *London Times*es each day. Well-thought-of by Brits."

"You know him well?"

"He visited me in the hospital after the bridge."

"Good man. I like an officer who understands who does the bleeding in this shit. Is he Sebastian's uncle? You related, Sebastian?"

Sebastian, the name of the driver, was a handsome kid who oozed privilege through every pore. A T/5 corporal, he had the kind of suave confidence that made Earl want to bust him in the mouth. He'd see if Sebastian could pass the Earl test. So far, not so good.

"Not by blood, sir. But his father and mine were at prep school—"

"That's all I need to know, Sebastian," said Swagger.

They pulled up to a building at last. It was dull, gray, nondescript, built sometime between Waterloo and the Somme, presumably by someone in a hurry, for it bore little ornamentation. No gargoyles, no inscriptions, no filigree, just your basic gray box, with a tiny bronze plaque by the double doors reading "70." It was evidently designed by someone whose only tool was a T square, as it was mostly a pileup of right angles through all four stories to a flat roof. Nothing marked it as significant or vital to the war effort, or a supersecret spy lair.

"This part of Mayfair," said Leets, "is kind of a little America. Down the street you'll see the American embassy. The Connaught Hotel is near Grosvenor Square too; it's bachelor officers' quarters for our people. You'll have a room there, as do I."

They entered to find a foyer with a civilian at a desk and four sharp-dressed Army MPs in white helmets and leggings, with .45s holstered and carbines at the ready. Their IDs got them into a hall that led to the elevators, which in turn took them to a fourth floor—the big guy was always up top!—and down a hall notable for its dowdiness, decorated in a style that might be called the Faces of Old Men. Pictures of Roosevelt, Marshall, Ike, Bradley, other weathered pork chops with stars on their collars, plus a few framed exhortations to security and patriotism, nothing to suggest the mayhem that this building was said to unleash. Entry into the last office yielded a view of a young woman sitting behind the desk in the uniform of a WAC lieutenant, next to a typewriter and two telephones.

"Lieutenant Fenwick," Leets said, "I'm here with Major Swagger to see the colonel."

"I'll notify him, Lieutenant," she said, smiling.

Maybe it was the smile, which showed a set of brilliant white teeth; maybe it was the quiet precision of the makeup, applied by someone who knew of such things; maybe it was the size of the eyes or the luster of their expressiveness; maybe it was the symmetry of the face, the tautness of the noble cheekbones, the aquiline perfection of the nose—but she was definitely a cover girl waiting for the flash to pop. Or maybe an actress, with a face that was still flawless when blown up three hundred times on-screen.

He thought too that he picked up a little something between her and Leets. They both did a good job at pretending to perfunctory engagement, but Earl sensed it to be performance, not authenticity.

"Gentlemen, please go in," she said.

Was this OSS or MGM? Another movie face. Bruce, mid-forties, looked like someone Earl had seen a few times twenty feet tall on a screen, but the name hadn't stuck. Maybe Walter, maybe Phillip or Kenneth? Probably Walter. Blade of nose, silver-gray hair brilliantined back, face too tan and lineless, eyes too bright and lively, mustache too trim, like a brush. He was in shirtsleeves, tie tight and cinched in a precise Windsor knot, the khaki shirt tailored perfectly, fitting as if poured over his still-lithe body. Not a wattle or jiggle anywhere; you'd think he rode to hounds every morning. Behind him, a cityscape of London seen only by generals and German Heinkel pilots stretched across two windows, divided only by a corner. Big Ben, the Houses of Parliament, Whitehall, Nelson on his column, the king in his castle, the view tourists used to pay Cunard hundreds for a gander at.

"Gentlemen, do come in," the colonel said.

Both men fronted the desk, came to smartly, saluted. Colonel Bruce threw a loose wag back, then stood.

"So glad to see you, Major. Welcome to our little tea party. Leets, how's the hip?"

"Sir, it's fine."

"I doubt that, but I admire your willingness to push on. Come, I don't want this too formal, it's too important for formality." He gracefully shepherded them to a sofa and leather chairs arranged at a fireplace. On the mantel, photos not of old men in uniforms but of the dogs he must have once raised at his estate, wherever that was.

"Please, sit down. Coffee? Millie, get us some coffee, will you?"

"Yes, Colonel," *Vogue*, July '39, called in.

"Major," the colonel asked, "thanks for pulling up stakes and getting here so quickly. How was the flight?"

Earl, face professionally stern, could not but yield to the colonel's warmth and modesty in its package of upper-class American perfection.

"Sir, it was cold and bumpy . . . and long. But I got enough sleep. Ready to go to work."

"Good man," said the colonel. "How do you like being a major?"

"Feels pretty much the same as gunnery sergeant. I guess it's legal."

"You may not have noticed, but one of the signatures on the paper you signed was General Eisenhower's. That makes it legal. That makes anything legal."

"Hope to be of service, sir."

"All right, let's get to it. You don't have time to waste and I don't either. You may wonder why you're here, in a building with the professors and code-breakers instead of at SHAEF HQ with soldiers. The reason, General Eisenhower decided and General Bradley concurred, is that SHAEF or Henderson Hall or the Ministry of Defense or the War Department— any military bureaucracy that considers itself important—is usually a nest of cliques, factions, plotters, coups, and countercoups. Politics. Everybody watches everybody and it's a wonder anything gets done with all the watching. We don't want you getting waylaid by any of that. You'll work from here, and your contact with regular army will be through liaison. We don't want you on the phone yelling at lieutenant colonels who won't return your call unless they hear from their boss."

"Yes, sir."

"Leets is a good man, knows the ropes. He'll get you anything you need. If he can't get it, my door is always open, as are several other doors in this building. Everyone behind those doors knows who to yell at. Every one of them gets his phone calls answered. Don't hesitate to pull rank. That is what rank is for."

"Thank you, sir."

"Now. Major Swagger, let me introduce you to an unfamiliar phrase: the bullet garden."

CHAPTER 5

The Bullet Garden

"Where are we?" asked Goldberg.

"In France, I think."

"Jack, I'm the comedy writer. Where in France?"

"Not inside our own lines. Not inside German lines. Somewhere in between."

"What do you see?"

Archer had taken his helmet off and kind of squished his head up through a tangle of vegetation so that he could view something other than the tangle of vegetation.

As much as they hated it, Privates Goldberg and Archer also loved this tangle of vegetation with its crest of dirt down the middle for a spine, its arboretum of interesting French flora twisted like barbed wire about everything, including their necks and faces, for it seemed to offer them some sort of camouflage from what they assumed were three thousand pairs of German binoculars searching for them.

"I see fences made out of this shit," said Archer, meaning the veg.

"I see meadows and clumps of trees. I see a line of trees that must be a road, though it would be sunken. I see what we've been seeing since this morning."

"Any Tiger tanks?"

"No Tiger tanks. No Germans. But . . . no Americans either. No Shermans."

It was about four in the afternoon. The sun had another three hours of work to do designating targets for snipers, and nothing could hurry it along.

"I say we wait for nightfall," said Goldberg.

"We'll get even more lost than we are now if we wait for nightfall. We'll walk straight into a prisoner-of-war camp."

"Maybe for you, Farmer Brown. For a Goldberg, it's a bullet in the head."

"I'm not a farmer; I'm an engineering student."

"So engineer us a way home."

The two had lain next to the fallen Sergeant Malfo for at least five minutes, frozen in terror and utterly incapable of movement. The only sounds they heard were the other patrol members as they hauled ass away from the site of the sergeant's sudden death. What had become of them, neither of the privates knew nor particularly cared.

After a bit, when they realized the German airborne wasn't about to parachute onto them, they got up and decided that it was time to vacate. Goldberg remembered his rifle, located the end that went up, and grasped it to his chest. He couldn't remember if the safety was on, but he also couldn't remember where the safety was. Meanwhile, Archer had been wise enough to snatch the dead sergeant's map case, hoping it might offer them some kind of guidance. But what good is a map when you don't know where you are?

They had wandered somewhere between abject fear and abject paranoia, with interesting flashes of panic, hysteria, and the urge for contrition, along hedges and across roads and through glades, keeping low, rifles at half-port, eyes opened like wide-screen lenses, encountering no signs of anything except cow life on earth, and when the sun reached its zenith they realized almost simultaneously that walking around in broad daylight in no-man's-land was a good way to get killed. The nearest sanctuary appeared to be a seven-foot wall of bush into which, oblivious to thorn and scratch, they had pressed themselves. If invisibility was the goal, they had not achieved it, as the faded khaki of the beat-to-hell American M41 jackets stood out against the lusher garden green of whatever sort of growing stuff had more or less absorbed them. But the artifice might serve against casual observation.

"Try the map again."

"I looked at the fucking thing a thousand times. It makes no sense to me. I see where we were, I see where we want to go, but I can't figure where we are."

"Orient it to something."

"There's nothing to orient it to. I don't see buildings, roads, a village, a hill, a stream. Nothing."

"What do you see?"

"This shit," he said. "Everywhere."

It was like a scene from a fairy tale, only set in hell. In its way, unlinked to the fact that it was full of men in *Feldgrau* who wanted to eat them for dinner, it could have been considered beautiful. That's why they called it the bullet garden. Green and rolling, it was crosshatched by more of these brush fences that turned it into a maze. Stands of trees knotted it, dips occasionally swallowed it, small humps of hill offered themselves up, stone walls that came and went made it more confusing. The dominant feature was this hedgerow thing, a wall of thatched hawthorn roots, raspberry bushes, lupine, violets, and greasy mud that had become more formidable through the centuries. From a little altitude it made more sense, but inside it you were in a puzzle, cut off from any longer view. It only followed to move in the lee of the hedgerow, rather than in the lush green meadow. But that was slow going, confusing, and seemed to lead to nowhere.

"We have to find something to orient on," said Goldberg, then added, "I can't believe I actually used the word 'orient' in a sentence. Twice, even."

"Why, it's like you're a *soldier* or something," said Archer.

"So orient, please. And hold the soy."

"That's *professional* comedy?"

"Bob Hope's people would have gobbled it up."

"Yeah, Bob Hope," said Archer, knowing his pal was no closer to Bob Hope than he himself was. But he squirmed, got the map out, wiggled, put on his glasses, took a few more peeks, and generally made like he knew what he was doing.

"Okay," he finally said. "Here's what I come up with. We do know that the sun moves from east to west. From that we can learn east, west, and, by elimination, north and south. We have to get west. Our lines are to the west, more or less. Theirs are to the east, more or less."

"Are you sure about that?"

"Actually, no. Because in war everything gets messed up and sometimes you end up attacking in the direction you came from."

"You're making my head hurt. Can't we just take the subway?"

At that point Archer unloaded a solution to their problem, which involved reading the east–west transit of the sun as a kind of central feature, figuring north and south from that, and therefore proceeding south until it was time to turn west.

There seemed to be something about a river in there somewhere, and he finished with a flourish.

"At the point of the bend in the river, we stop going that way. We head due west. The sun is setting sort of ahead of us. In a couple of miles, we should hit this road"—he pointed again to the map—"and our lines are just beyond. Remember yesterday evening, we crossed a road just after we started out?"

"Not really. But I guess it's okay."

"Don't forget your rifle."

"Jack, I have the rifle, but the safety. It's mysterious to me."

"Front of trigger guard. If it's pushed 'OUT' it's off safe. Gun go bang. If it's pushed in, no bang. Got it?"

"I really don't belong in the infantry," said Goldberg.

"Nobody does," said Archer.

They disentangled themselves from the hedgerow. It was like escaping a giant, ill-tempered octopus. All tendrils and crawlers and thorns scratching at them, puncturing them, drawing blood, tears, and sweat. Prickly annoyances severed, they assumed the scuttle position, bent forward, ready to move on, all equipment . . . well, most, present and accounted for.

"I think I lost a couple of grenades," said Goldberg, counting only the four of the six he'd been issued. They scared him, actually. He couldn't actually imagine setting a bomb to ticking in his hand, then throwing it. Or rather, yes, he could imagine it; he just couldn't imagine himself doing it.

"Don't worry about it," said Archer.

"Should I take my safety off?" he asked.

"No, because you're more likely to fall than run into a Kraut. If you accidentally fire, we could run into a whole lot of Krauts."

"Okay," said Goldberg, quavery in both heart and voice, but game to do his best. It was The War, after all.

They scuttled. It was not fun. Walking standing up would not have been fun either but it would have been easier. Instead, in the artificially constructed caution posture, bent double, nine pounds of rifle at diagonal across chest, six (or four) pounds of grenades on belt, plus bayonet and canteen, rucksacks full of candy bars, cigarette packs, socks, and even underwear changes and condoms (you never knew), they advanced in short stutter steps, pausing every fifty or so yards for a look-see. Each lower back signaled displeasure at the situation, but if they'd gone to a medic, he would have said, "Take two aspirin. If that doesn't work, tough shit," and gone back to his paperback copy of *No Orchids for Miss Blandish*.

They got to a juncture in hedgerows and, based on Archer's sense of the sun's direction toward the horizon, burrowed through. Also not fun. In the thorns, equipment snagged as they went over the crest, sliding down. But then, war isn't supposed to be fun. It's your job. It's what you do.

In this manner they proceeded, sweat eventually blossoming on all the danker body areas but including the undank forehead, where it slid down into eyes, bringing blur and salt, causing squinting, sniffing, general discomfort. Insects, attracted to the smell of greasy man meat, seemed to swarm even as birds made bird sounds, vegetation ignored them, and the sun moved, if warily.

Finally they came to a road. Blunder across it? No, sir. Not that dumb. Instead, they sort of lay up next to it. It seemed to be in a kind of trough, garlanded on each side by heavier rows of shrubbery and tree, the limbs interlocking overhead until they formed a kind of green tunnel in each direction. It reminded Archer of an Orrington Avenue, on which he'd grown up, a million years ago.

He kind of slid down the bank, got to the road—packed dust and gravel—looked each way hard for a minute or so, detected no sign of human activity, and then made clicking sounds, their version of "secret code," and Goldberg, much smaller and scrawnier, slid down the embankment. His helmet, not very tightly attached to his head, rolled around, threatened to pop off. He got it under control, gathered himself, adjusted his glasses.

"Let's—"

At that moment, the Tiger tank cranked around the bend.

CHAPTER 6

Bocage

"The French word—actually it's a Norman word," said Colonel Bruce, "is *bocage*. Ancient by any standard. Won't trouble you with etymology. Basically it describes a terrain featuring a checkerboard of pasture, woodland, brush, hill, hedgerow, farmer's fields plowed or unplowed, lots of cows and bumblebees, all set across a rolling landscape, heavily riverine, verdant beyond imagination. The G.I.s call it 'the bullet garden.'"

"It sounds like sniper territory," said Swagger. "Not a place to go walking."

"Not a place through which one advances an army. General Bradley's First Army has run hard against it and is now and has been and will be stuck for a long, long time. Why? Mainly, snipers. Thoughts, Major?"

"The Germans have been there for months. They know the ranges, the hides, the get-outs and fallbacks, the elevations and their own ballistics. They're all hard from Russia or Italy and won't make a beginner's mistake."

"It gets worse. Some of them, the most terrifying and morale-shattering, work at night. Maybe it's new technology, maybe it's closer range shots, maybe it's highly developed hearing capability which enables them to target our boys at night; we don't know."

"These night snipers. That's why I'm here?"

"Yes, Major. We need someone with the brains to approach the problem from a new perspective. We need him to come up with a counter program and fast. The war has stalled. The British are hung up too, but not as bad as we are. Ike is frustrated and losing bargaining power with Montgomery, the President is embarrassed, and the press is harping."

"Is there some kind of time limit, sir? What are the bigger parts in which this all fits?"

"We've got to break out. Something is planned, yes. We'd like a program in place and operating before then. No dates, no operation names, but I think the last week in July, a month off. So there's a lot of SHAEF pressure to produce. If you can shut down the night snipers, you will have made a major contribution. What are your needs?"

"First off, I want all technical ordnance intelligence on German sniper training, German sniper equipment, especially ballistics, German sniper tendencies in other theaters, particularly Russia, if possible."

"Millie, you're getting that?"

"Yes, Colonel," came an amplified voice.

"She's on intercom. She's taking dictation. Not too many Smith graduates do shorthand, but Millie's a whiz."

Swagger shot a look at the inert Leets, who was himself scrawling notes in a notebook. Nothing showed on his face, but his ears burned red, out of some significant emotional reaction. Swagger noted it.

"Go on, Major."

"Next I want our POW reports to see if we've taken any snipers alive. If so, I'll go to the camp and interrogate them. SS and regular army."

"I have to say, for whatever reason, you won't be finding too many sniper POWs."

"Most important, though, I want carefully culled casualty reports on entire First Army engagements since hitting this bullet garden. The culling should be along these lines: on all men killed by single rifle shots to upper body and head. Multiple wounds indicate firefight, meaning machine guns, grenades, artillery. The single-shot deaths may or may not prove sniper but it reduces the number considerably. I want time, date, and, if possible, circumstances. I want to calculate attrition rates by single rifle shot across the front. Not just at night. I have to figure out how that effort fits into the overall sniper campaign. We need to understand where are they most active, where the least. Does it shift? Do the night shooters move from sector to sector and, if so, how?"

Leets scrawled.

"That will take time and manpower," said Colonel Bruce. "But General Eisenhower's name on the order should prove helpful. Nice to have a four-star general backing you up."

"Sure is," said Swagger. "At a certain point, when we've broken the dope down far enough, Leets and I will head to the front and find survivors. We need to know exactly how the killing occurred and look for signs. Ejected shells, boot prints, shooting platforms improvised into trees and buildings. All of that is valuable. What do they shoot? Standard infantry rifle with a scope screwed on or a hand-built marksman's weapon tinkered over for maximum accuracy at long range and nothing else? What does such a weapon allow them to do? When do they shoot? What was the wind, the weather? Most importantly, is this new technology? Do they have some vision-enhancing technology we know nothing about?

"Then target selection. What is their preferred target? We have to know not only who they're hitting but who they're not hitting. Why A and not B? That'll tell us a lot."

"Excellent, Major. You're in Room 351. Large, used to be headquarters of an insurance company. Plenty of room for maps. Plenty of room for crates of documents. Leets will be your majordomo and can get you anything you need, top priority. He has all the phone numbers. Maybe every

Friday at 0900 you'll come up for a report? I may drop in once in a while, as will some of my staff or some cleared people from SHAEF. But you'll always be alerted before. In your office, it is to be understood, military etiquette is secondary to efficiency and results. You build the culture you want. Saluting or no saluting. First names, last names, rank, whatever. Nobody cares if you do or don't say 'sir' all the time. If you need me, call Millie and no matter where I am, she'll get in touch and I'll get back to you fast as humanly possible. Is that all square with you?"

"Completely, sir."

"Great, Major Swagger. Glad to have you aboard. One more thing, if I may."

"Yes, sir."

"Do you like parties?"

CHAPTER 7

Machine

In the industrial manufacture of death, no machine's design expressed its destiny more perfectly than PzKpfw VI Ausf. E. Thus, it haunted every GI's nightmares, it frightened every officer's deep reptile brain, it drove tactical planners bats, and it dominated the battle imagination of the western armies beyond comprehension.

Airplanes were more lethal, but they were specks in the sky. Artillery was more violent, tearing men from limb to limb, but it was far off and arrived silently, like a curse from God. Machine guns killed faster, especially when fields of fire were carefully interlocked, but good management of counter-fire and maneuver and mortar implementation could deter their impact. Barbed wire was not the dragon's teeth it had been in War One because the front was so mobile, changing, evolving or devolving, going liquid here and turning to stone there every day, sometimes every hour.

But the fucking Tiger! *PzKpfw VI Ausf. E, PzKpfw VI Ausf. E, burning bright, / In the forest of the night* . . . It laughed at the doctrine of streamline. It mocked irony, introspection, poetry, and whimsy. It scoffed at heroics, it crushed nobility, it shattered aesthetics, it shit on honor. It vanquished all that came before it, particularly any tanks that presumptively dared to stand against it. It whacked the Russian T-34s into atomic particles. Ask about Kursk. It turned Shermans and Cromwells into bonfires of the apocalypse, filling the atmosphere with the debris of burning metal and flesh.

Archer and Goldberg tried to melt into the ground as this rough beast approached. They were off the road, half shrouded in the weeds and flowers of France, sweating and pissing and issuing the gas of panic while their mouths filled with gray sand, their limbs went all spastic elastic, and their brains emptied of everything except regret for all the evil things they had done. Archer had once cheated on a math test because he was not going to let Jean Silverstein beat him out as valedictorian at Evanston High in 1942. As for Goldberg, he remembered a joke he'd stolen from Marty Greene and sold to Fred Allen for $5. Actually, he'd stolen two or three from Marty. Well, okay, it was four or five, maybe even six or seven. Marty was funny, but he was shy and his stuff would have died if Gary hadn't moved it along the chain. He had a brief image of apologizing to Marty, of the two of them going to Hollywood and becoming a comedy writing team, of Beverly Hills, the pink and black future of Cadillacs and dumb blondes with big melons and the company of other funny, sharp, clever Jewish boys like themselves. That is, if the Tiger didn't kill them.

Though of different faiths that were practiced in different languages, their prayers were identical, almost to the syllable.

PleaseGodpleaseGodpleaseGodpleaseGod!

It didn't match the formal elegance of either Old or New Testament, but it was all they could come up with at the moment as they lay fetid and craven in the vibrational zone of the thing, fifty-six tons on the hoof smashing remorselessly toward them, followed, they now saw, by a loose gaggle of *Panzergrenadiers*.

The machine—each caught a glimpse as they went hard to and into earth and tried to become one with the soil itself—was perhaps the single most masculine object in the world. It had no feminine curve, no whispers of softness, anywhere about its being. It was primarily that most male of constructs, the box, or rather several of them, all Krupp steel, arranged as if by a child on a carpet, held together by the blue purity of a welder's torch, then mounted on the biggest caterpillar treads in the world, about a yard wide, which in turn encompassed nine, count 'em, nine steel wheels staggered in precise density, giving traction at the insistence of the mighty engine capable of moving the whole construct virtually anywhere it wanted to go or through anything it wanted to go through. Here the word *through* meant penetration, violation, disruption: no house, no building, no wall—nothing erected by man—could resist its moods or whims.

It bristled with guns, most notably the famous 88mm cannon with a telescopic barrel, the most feared ground weapon of the war, which, so far, could outshoot any other tanks on either side. It quite routinely turned blots on the horizon into volcanos of melting steel and men. To see the length of the thing was to know that in far-off lands engineers toiled into the night, trying to figure out how to get something as big as an 88 on one of their own brazen chariots. Maybe it would happen—but it hadn't happened yet. A machine-gun snout protruded from the shelves of steel lower down, and up top, next to *Herr Kommandant*, another gun was at rest, ammunition belt dangling insouciantly from the breech.

Still, this particular panzer, as mighty a war dinosaur as it might be, sounded discordant notes. For one thing, the sloped castle keep of the turret was turned backwards as if in the reflective mode, not the predatory mode, contemplating where it had been (Russia?), not where it was headed (death?), and the cannon was itself depressed. *Herr Kommandant*, enthroned within the turret but seated so that his upper half was free to enjoy the health-giving benefits of German nudism, was a strange fellow, far from the black-coated, monocled Raymond Massey type of *Desperate*

Journey. Instead, he wore a beard and thick torrents of blond hair pushed back and had hung sunglasses on his broad, rather handsome face. He had a scarf wrapped around his neck. But he had no shirt on. He was smiling. He was happy. He was exactly what the Germans were not supposed to produce, an individual, freeborn and ecstatic to be so. He had no interest in the MG-42 on a steel pedestal next to him. Moreover, two other hatless German heads peeped out of the hatches forward, beneath the turret, and they too were pleased to be taking a day off.

Archer, who had come to rest with his head tilted to the right, saw all this as he saw the number 503 in heavy gothic script on the flank of the turret. Meanwhile the heavy infantry boys in support seemed themselves on some kind of lark. No marching here. Helmets off and strapped to belts, just *Feldgrau* cloth caps, those who wore them, nearly everyone smoking either pipe or cigarette, weapons slung haphazardly about the torso for comfort, not for fast action. If one of them was an officer or a sergeant, he didn't declare himself by uniform or disposition.

The noise of the heavy engine, the dust that even at cruising speed the tracks ripped from the fragile road, the buzz as the earth yielded to the mandates of the 700-horsepower grinder—it all reached such a crescendo that Archer could no longer take it. He put his face down, closed his eyes, and waited for a bullet to the head.

So too with Goldberg. His nerves almost gave out, but heroism didn't demand fine motor skills, only paralysis, at which he was a high master. He didn't see a thing.

CHAPTER 8

Are We Having Fun Yet?

"Parties?" said Swagger. He had to admit, he hadn't seen that one coming.

"Yes, Major, parties."

"No, sir. Not at all."

"That's the best news I've had so far. By the way, what would your definition of a great party be, just so I know for the future."

"Two guests, sir. Me and a bottle of Jack Daniel's No. 7."

"Now, that's a party I'd attend. Can you get me on the invitation list? I'd imagine it's pretty exclusive."

"So far, sir. But on V-E Day you're invited."

"Great. Major, I ask because . . . well, maybe you've heard the joke. If not, you will. OSS is sometimes nicknamed 'Oh So Social.' That's because the need for foreign-language skills and advanced analytical skills, plus a gift for conspiracy, deceit, and cold-blooded violence, seems to usually suggest the wellborn. They have too much time on their hands and love the thrill of the abyss."

"Yes, sir," said Swagger. It accorded with his sense of the world and he was not unimpressed by Colonel Bruce's acknowledgment of what was abundantly clear to anyone with a brain.

"These people are very bright, all of them. But when you put a lot of very bright people in one building, they almost always and almost instantly become involved in competition. And one of the things they squabble about endlessly is who gets invited to which party."

"I see, sir. Probably the same at Marine HQ in Washington."

"So I'm sent here to get along with the British and wage war on the Third Reich but I spend my days monitoring party invitation lists. Is this any way to fight a war? Well, you'd be surprised. A lot of business does get done. Some major initiatives only exist because two chaps shared a cocktail at Lady Diane's. So I suppose they are necessary. At the same time, human nature, alas, is eternally human nature, whether in wartime London, Berlin, Tokyo, or Washington. God, the wasted energy, the stupidity, the nonsense, the sheer folly. That's why I'd never write a book. Nobody would believe it."

"I understand, sir. I have no intention of going to any parties whatsoever and don't give a damn who does or doesn't. I intend to keep Leets over there so busy, he won't go to parties either. Right, Leets?"

"Yes, sir," said Leets.

"Very good news. I don't have to worry about getting you on the party list."

CHAPTER 9

Yes, They Have Some Bananas

The noise grew and grew and then it shrank and shrank. Finally, it was gone. Archer lifted his eyes and saw only a settling shroud of dust illuminated in late shafts of sun randomly sneaking through the canopy.

"Gary? Did you die?"

"Twice."

"Me too."

"I wet myself. Don't tell the guys."

"I won't if you won't."

"Deal. Man, did you see that thing? It was a dinosaur. It was a Tyrannosaurus rex. If it decides to eat you, it eats you. I feel like an hors d'oeuvre."

"I'd hate to be where it's going. When they buckle down for the game, they'd be hard to stop."

In his exhaustion and still febrile terror, Goldberg reverted to his native language: "Ets-lay et-gay the uck-fay out of ere-hay."

"Ammed-day ight-ray," said Archer.

Behind them, somebody said, "Ello-hay, oys-bay."

It was a German. With a big black gun.

CHAPTER 10

Paper Deaths

It took a while for the anonymous clerks of SHAEF to cull the necessary death reports from the casualty lists, and in the intervening time Swagger tried to make himself an authority on the German sniper.

What he learned was slightly surprising. The first was that, as a phenomenon, sniper war wasn't terribly interesting to Western intelligence. Therefore, no one had devoted intense scrutiny to it, and it was covered merely as an afterthought. As Earl sifted through the reports, he noted a curious lack of urgency, clearly reflecting a lower priority. Most reports were based on published secondary reports from German propaganda magazines, not secret-sourced documents as examined and translated cursorily by the British. Only the sudden and unanticipated success of the bocage catastrophe got their heads turned in the right direction at the expense of far too many G.I. lives, and Earl realized that his was the first direct, high-importance focus on the issue. But this indifference had its own parallel in the Germans themselves.

Though they, like all the major powers, had run a highly successful sniping program in the Great War, they had more or less abandoned it as they geared up for what became The War. This was because they had been so entranced with lightning warfare—blitzkrieg—and the development of armored and ground troop coordination, with Stukas thrown in for laughs, that they had bypassed the sniper, who was after all an exemplar of stationary warfare as fought in trenches.

For a long time, as they blitzed across Europe and halfway across Russia, that bias held. But the Russians, once they put a stop to German advances and hung them up in cities like Leningrad and Stalingrad, re-taught them the forgotten lessons: a man with a rifle and a scope could do severe damage to not only his targets but to all those standing near his targets and all those hearing from those who'd been standing near his targets.

Thus the Krauts got into The War sniper game late, which explained their lack of development. These fellows almost always fired the standard 8mm Mauser K98k but with a bewildering complexity of telescopic sights and mounts, most from the commercial sources, or so the authorities of army ordnance claimed. As they tried to come up with doctrine, they fumbled.

Their initial foray into an official weapon was coded Zf. 41 and it had a little long eye-relief 2x sight mounted halfway down the barrel where it seemed like a toy and had to be more appropriate for hitting squirrels than men, as the image would have been tiny to eyes twenty inches from the lenses. Moreover, its lens was so narrow—20mm—that its light transmission capabilities would be minimalized. It would be useless in stormy weather, dawn or twilight, deep forest, or even the shadows of ruined cities. What was the point?

Realizing this and dumping the program, they had commercial scopes from manufacturers like Ajack, Hensoldt, Zeiss, and J. W. Fecker, in a multiplicity of powers (2 to 10) and diameters, and a multiplicity of "graticules," as they called reticles, ranging from cross-hairs with different thicknesses to the hairs, post and line sometimes touching, sometimes not, and even target dots. Such a disparity of elements meant that it was up to each shooter to master his optics, as there could be no consistent doctrine.

What a mess!

Whoever was hunting the bocage was doing much better.

But who was that?

CHAPTER 11

Kurt

The German, who was in a T-shirt, seemed quite casual, except for the rifle with its curved stock and *Amazing Stories* ray gun look.

"The look on your faces when you saw this gun!" he said, delighted. "Man, that was something I'd like to have a photo of. Scared shitless? You were *beyond* shitless!"

Neither hero could think of a thing to say. Archer was silent. Goldberg gibbered like a fool.

"Okay," said the German, "let's go. Taking you to see Kurt. He'll figure out what to do."

"How do— What's with— I mean, why—" blurted Archer, his curiosity overwhelming the danger.

"The English? Man, I grew up in L.A. Five years. My dad was a cinematographer at RKO. Hope to get back there when this shit is over. Come on, let's go. We'll miss lunch."

The soldier led them down the middle of the road, hands up, to a bend, where they discovered the Tiger had halted and its crew and the soldiers had taken a break in the lee of a particularly high spurt of hedgerow under a cluster of shade trees, where they'd be spared the sun and the predation by Thunderbolt. The machine itself was still mighty and gigantic, bigger than any tank either G.I. had ever seen, dappled in the colors of the woods.

But the men attending *Die Maschine* hardly looked like avatars of blitzkrieg; instead, the get-together resembled a fraternity party: a lot of laughter and horseplay, maybe some girlfriend teasing or football chatter, some letter writing, some pipe smoking, some catching up on naptime. One played the harmonica, not "Lili Marleen" but jumpy licks from Benny Goodman.

The boss was the bare-chested, bearded sergeant sitting atop the fender of his vehicle as a fullback sits on the bench after his fifth touchdown that afternoon. Most of the pack was gathered around him, in fear, fealty, or admiration; who could tell?

He looked at them. He began with a critical strategic question.

"Have a banana?"

He was, indeed, himself having a banana. He did, indeed, have a bunch of bananas next to him, slightly greenish at either end. He handed it over, and both G.I.s took one. What were they supposed to do? Turn down a banana from a German?

He smiled at them. If they expected torture or at least a brutal grilling, it did not arrive. Instead, the German tanker said, "I'm Kurt." Then he spoke rapidly to the guy who'd captured them, who no longer held the rifle on them.

"Kurt wants to know if you're snipers."

"No, sir," said Archer.

"Good," said the first German. "Kurt hates snipers. Go ahead, eat your bananas."

Again, Archer and Goldberg flashed What-fresh-hell-is-this? looks, and then tore into the fruit. Actually, it was pretty good, if a little chewy. All that fiber. Good for the stool, good for the spirit.

"Good, yes?" asked Kurt.

"Yeah, I'll say," said Gary, a little overanxious to please.

Kurt spoke again to his translator. Was it German? Hmm, maybe yes, maybe no—after all, what did Archer or Goldberg know?—but it somehow didn't sound like Raymond Massey in *Desperate Journey*. The translator said, "He wants to know what you're doing out here so far beyond your own lines. You don't look like commandos or paratroopers or saboteurs."

Goldberg and Archer stumbled all over themselves. The message, though garbled, was something like "On patrol . . . sergeant killed . . . lost . . . wandering . . . no idea where our lines are."

Kurt listened to the explanation, then asked a question.

"Do you hunt tanks?"

"No, we *run* from tanks," said Goldberg.

"No, no," said Archer. "We were just on night patrol. We got lost."

"How many Germans have you killed?"

"Sir, none. I haven't even fired my rifle in combat. So far the war has been hiding and shitting in holes, usually the same one."

Kurt considered carefully.

"What should I do with you now? Do you want to join the German army?"

The two were dumbfounded, but the laughter suggested Kurt was joking.

Then he said, "I suppose I should turn you over to the SS . . ."

"*V latrine nehmoli najet havno,*" someone more or less said, or at least that's what it sounded like.

That set off a little explosion of bon mots, one liners and hoots about *nejdzniki*, whatever that was, all of it lost on the G.I.s.

"This guy is pretty funny," Archer muttered to Goldberg. "Maybe he could give you some material for Bob."

"I think we'd be a disappointment," said Goldberg to Kurt. "I'm a comedy writer for radio—"

"Hardly," said Archer.

"—and he's studying to be a farmer."

"Farming is good!" said Kurt. "Myself, I built automobiles. That too was good. Farming, autos, both for the people. And . . . what is 'comedy writer'?" The translator was now up to speed on the rhythms, and the words reached the guys almost simultaneously with the expression, though the syntax was sufficiently fractured to give it that Hollywood convention of foreignness.

"When people say funny things on the radio. It's not spontaneous," said Goldberg. "It's all written down. I'm the one who writes it. I'm the funny one."

"Theoretically," said Archer.

"Do you know Bob Hope?" asked the translator on his own.

"I know his people. You don't get to meet the star."

"No comedy on German radio," said Kurt. "They just yell at you."

"I hate that," said Goldberg.

"Okay, boys," said Kurt. "I guess not kill you. I no like killing people. Oh, so much killing I've seen! I could tell you but it make you cry. I don't mind blowing up tanks that are trying to blow up me and crew—machine against machine—but shooting actual people quite revolting. This is why Nazis hate me. They *like* killing people."

The two G.I.s nodded dumbly. Neither could think of a thing to say. Even professional quipster Goldberg came up dry.

"You promise me you won't kill Germans. Just hide in hole and shit and think up jokes. You, taller one, you think of corn."

"Yes," said Archer. "Definitely. Corn all the way."

"Go on, get out of here. Leave rifles and grenades—"

"They already left their rifles behind," said the translator.

"Well, take their grenades. Throw them in the pond. I don't want them near machine. And bayonets. Then send them on their way."

He turned back to them.

"Do you know way?"

"Uh, not really."

"Go west. Toward setting sun. Stay close to hedgerows. Hack through with those little shovels. Be careful of middle of the fields. Travel at night, but later, after sun has set, then quit when sun is about to rise."

That's when the translator quit, seeing his duty finished, but Kurt added, "*Davjte pozor na nejdzniki.*"

Nejdzniki again.

CHAPTER 12

Ammo

The ammo was the key, Earl realized.

The 8mm was not what he would have chosen as a sniper round, producing too much kick and, by reputation, too much muzzle flash and standard, but not notably effective, accuracy. Pretty much like the .30 of Garand and Springfield provenance. Could the 8mm be tamed by specialist ammunition? Possibly, but if they don't take the trouble to standardize the scope, it seemed unlikely that they'd go to the trouble to produce a specialized sniper round. And in fact their first sniper hero, an SS officer named Repp at an engagement called the Demyansk Encirclement in 1942, had used a Mannlicher sporting rifle, if the propaganda photos of him were to be believed.

Perhaps it was merely a reflection of intelligence analyst lack of interest in the topic, but if a special sniper-grade cartridge had been designed and issued since Repp's 122 kills in a single engagement, no reports of it had yet reached Allied intelligence.

At any rate, once the Germans rediscovered the power of organized sniping after Repp's feat, by late 1943 they went at the process headfirst.

They finally settled on a rifle and a scope, this one called Zf. 39, a K98f Mauser with a turret scope by Hensoldt. The schools, or so propaganda indicated, were numerous and rigorous, the biggest being at Vilnius in Lithuania. That establishment, by location, would provide shooters primarily against the ever-advancing Soviets; others were spread throughout the Reich, including the Motherland and its little brother, Austria. Perhaps those schools were sending their newly trained heroes to the bocage and maybe a couple of visits from the Eighth Air Force could shut them down and kill the future killers.

However, assuming the reports from the bocage were reliable and not overexaggerated (yet to be determined), the shooters in this part of France appeared, most of them, too salty to be recruits just graduated from a school. Maybe they were seasoned vets of Russia, with a batch of red kills to their credit. But it wasn't as if the snipers weren't desperately needed in Russia either, so Swagger doubted the Germans would pull their most productive soldiers out of the more urgent Russian battlefront and send them to Normandy. If that assumption held, the question would then still be: Where are they getting these guys? Who are they? Is it little Hans, the champion of the Frankfurt junior shooting club, all grown up? Or someone else from somewhere else?

CHAPTER 13

503

Hard to believe, but they were there.

Nobody had shot them. Nobody had thrown a potato masher grenade down their pants. It had been a long, stoop-shouldered, dash-and-squat progress across rural France, amid loveliness too beautiful to describe, but they were too anxious to have noticed.

Now they were collapsed in fatigue just a few yards from the actual beginning of American territory. They were a mess: drenched from stream crossings, bleeding from thorns, exhausted from the frequent long, long, low crawls across the pastures, and basically into hour 40 of sleeplessness.

Archer could make out sandbagged revetments and what he took to be the barrel of a .30 air-cooled in a gun notch. Shapes clustered behind, but butts, ever-present in all armies in the world, glowed in the dark. The odor of the tobacco was definitely American. After all, LS/MFT.

"We made it," he said to Goldberg.

"We just have to get through this part without getting shot to ribbons," said Goldberg.

"We'll take it real slow. No sudden moves, no shouts, nothing to get the boys riled."

"Got it."

"But, Gary—"

"What?"

"I've been thinking."

"Always a bad sign."

"No, listen. When we tell them about the last couple of days, maybe we ought to skip the Kurt-and-the-bananas part."

This had never occurred to Gary. When he hadn't been fantasizing about his own death, he'd been trying to imagine a radio skit built around a "funny" German who kept saying "Have a banana." He knew it was good stuff, but he just couldn't get the right angle on it. If Bob says, "Hands up, *Schweinehund*!" maybe Bing comes back with "Have a banana!" No, there was a beat missing. It needed another wrinkle, a complication. Maybe the response would be, "Hmm, pie or split?"

"Why?" he asked.

"You can't outguess these officers. You don't know how they'll take stuff. Maybe they'll say, 'Well, why didn't you grab your grenades and pull the pins and kill everybody, yourselves included?'"

"What, and ruin a perfectly good pair of pants!"

"I think that's our job out here. And we didn't do it. Instead, we had bananas with a batch of oddball Nazis, including a guy in a T-shirt from L.A. and a bearded nudist, and went our merry way."

"What I want to know is, where did they get the bananas?"

"I would say Germans are supermen, they can get anything they want. I mean, if you can build a Tiger tank, you can get a banana."

"So ix-nay on the bananas. And the whole Erman-Jay thing."

"Right. We saw the tank and the soldiers. Then we lay there another hour. Then we took off."

"The rifles?"

"We left 'em in panic when Malfo got his brains blown out."

"The grenades?"

"We never had grenades. They scare us."

"They do, but we're supposed to have grenades."

"So they can yell at us. They can put us on KP or send us to Graves Registration. But they won't put us in front of a firing squad."

"Americans coming in!" Archer called.

"Sign?"

Archer turned to Goldberg.

"Do you remember the sign?"

"Yeah, but it was a patrol sign. But that was yesterday. They've probably changed it anyway."

They were closer now. They crouched behind a tree and the sandbags were just a few yards away. The .30-caliber air-cooled barrel sticking out of it seemed to rotate toward them, or was that imagination? Now just this last little—

The machine-gun burst ripped up a hurricane of dust and twigs and other frags, the noise crashing, the flash blinding. It stitched its welcome into two feet of earth to their immediate right.

"JESUS CHRIST!" screamed Goldberg. "We're Americans!"

"Sign, god dammit!"

"Brooklyn," said Goldberg.

This time the machine-gun burst cut into trees, shredding them, spewing supersonic nuggets of bark everywhere.

"That was yesterday's sign!" the gunner called.

"We left yesterday," said Archer. "On patrol. Sergeant Malfo got hit by a sniper. I don't know where the rest of the guys are. We've been wandering around in the bullet garden all day."

"What unit?" came another voice.

"Ninth Division, 60th Regiment, 3rd Battalion, Dog Company, 2nd Platoon, 2nd Squad."

They could hear mumbling, maybe some arguing.

"Okay, come in slowly, rifles in both hands overhead. This gun is on you the whole way."

"We lost our rifles."

"Great," somebody who had to be a sergeant said.

They scrambled over the revetment to find themselves poked, prodded, examined by hobos who were actually other American infantrymen.

"You almost killed us," Goldberg said.

"I was *trying* to kill you," said the machine gunner. "That's my job."

"You're sure it said '503'?" Major Bingham asked Archer.

"I am, sir. Absolutely."

They were running on the fumes of the fumes, in waking hour 45 or so. This interrogation was occurring in the 3rd Battalion G-2 tent adjacent to battalion headquarters, about a mile back from the front, a dreary village of rotting, sagging canvas and unstuck pegs—too much wet in the earth to hold—in a debriefing that surprised both privates for its detail and intensity. Even Goldberg wasn't going for laughs anymore after his "I felt like an hors d'oeuvre" line got no smiles from the inquisitor.

"So let's go over this one more time," Bingham said, "because I want to be dead accurate before I forward to Nutmeg under a flag."

"Yes, sir," said Archer, who knew that Nutmeg was Regiment.

"Start with the map again."

What was with this guy? He looked like an English teacher and carried on like a homicide detective. His rimless glasses gave him the face of a Hawthorne expert. But it was no *Scarlet Letter*, it was the Scarlet Map!

Archer had told them over and over again he had no idea where they'd been, as they'd fled pretty much blindly through the night after the death of Sergeant Malfo. The map was at this time pointless.

"I can locate the site where we laid up near the German lines, sir. But after that, I have no idea where we went, which direction. Just away, you know? I mean, the guy had his head destroyed."

"He looked like a dead balloon," said Goldberg.

"And then Gary started to sneeze. I mean it was a ridicu—"

"How much time passed before you evacuated?"

"Seemed like an hour. Gary?"

"Seemed like ten hours. I got him all over me. Plus, I'm suddenly ka-chewing like an old man in a snowstorm. Maybe I'm allergic to death."

"So five minutes?"

"Yes, sir."

"Any sense of initial direction?"

"None, sir."

The intelligence officer sighed heavily, as if all of Job's woe had descended upon him. Or his show had closed in Boston. He took a pack of Camels out of his tanker jacket, lit one up, then offered smokes to the two privates.

"Go on," he said.

"Do you want me to skip to the tank part? It's just walking until then."

"Yes."

So Archer went through it again, the dive into the gully, the rumble in the earth as the giant war machine clanked by, the odd casualness of the Germans, especially the shirtless tank commander in the turret with the sunglasses. Nothing about bananas for lunch with the boys in gray.

"You're sure it was a Tiger?" for about the tenth time.

"Yes, sir."

"It wasn't a Panther? They have similar profiles."

"No, sir. I've seen a lot of dead Panthers outside Cherbourg. I've never seen a Tiger before. Big as a whale. This was a Tiger."

"It couldn't have been 508? '8' and '3' are easy to confuse, especially under pressure and if only seen for a second."

"It was 503," said Archer.

"Goldberg, you concur?"

"Sir, I was trying to insert myself into an ant hole at the time." No laugh. What an audience! The show *deserved* to close in Boston!

"Okay, I want you each to write a detailed narrative of the patrol. Not just the tank. *Everything.*"

"The sneezing?"

"The sneezing. Everything. Get busy now, get some coffee if you need it to keep going. But I want this getting to Division ASAP."

"Sir, may I ask? Why is '503' so significant?"

"It sounds like elements of 12th Panzer are infiltrating north. They've broken down into individual tanks so as not to attract air strikes. The '503' would indicate one of their most illustrious units, Abieltung 503, that is 503rd Heavy Tank Battalion. These guys are the best tankers in the world. They ate T-34s for breakfast in Russia. Twelve-to-one kill ratio. But it looks like they're trying to slip through the bocage without incident to get to the Brits and a landscape where their superiority can come into play. The Brits have to be alerted that the big bad wolf is at the door."

"Yes, sir," said Archer.

"You two boobs may have actually made a significant contribution to the war effort," said Major Bingham. "Good work."

"Thank you, sir," they said, each feeling maybe a little guilt in holding back on the banana affair. But still, it was the first compliment either had gotten in their own private war against Hitler.

CHAPTER 14

The Boy

Swagger had turned Leets into an errand boy by sending him off with Lieutenant Fenwick to round up office supplies: index cards, hundreds of pins, RAF Biro pens that applied ink via a tiny ball without smudge, in the dozens. Also, there had to be a maps office, so that was on the route too, as Swagger demanded maps in duplicate of the bocage areas of France, in all scales, from the whole VII Corps front down to individual village districts with their streams and gullies and winding cow paths diagramed. He saw what was coming as a map hunt before it became a sniper hunt.

That done, he went to Room 351, unlocked it to find a surprisingly large space with corner windows to admit the light, though no particularly impressive views of London. The ancient city, outside the T square of windows of 351, was just a grim stretch of low, indistinct buildings and trees, lacking anything of ceremonial or historical note. It could have been Fort Wayne. No one had even bothered to float barrage balloons in this sector. Nothing to protect.

Worktables had been provided and folding chairs. He noted a smallish office defined by a glass wall in the far corner that would become his own, he knew. He also found his driver and go-for T/5 Sebastian, sitting there, trying to look useful.

Sebastian snapped to but knew you didn't salute indoors, uncovered.

"As you were."

"Thank you, sir."

"Sebastian, is that the name?"

"Yes, sir," said the young man, who had one of those beautiful faces that belonged on a vase or a wall—and not a post office wall. His uniform, Earl noted, was superbly fitted, the Ike jacket lustrous and freshly pressed, the two T/5 stripes immaculately placed, as were the small collection of meaningless ribbons. No CIB, no wound stripes, no decorations for anything except attendance. His brown oxfords glowed, achieving a luster unobtainable on government leather.

"Okay, Corporal, we need a little talk here, alone, get some things ironed out."

"Yes, sir," said Sebastian.

"As I see it, you've got the best job in The War. No real responsibilities when kids your age are leading hundreds of bombers against German cities in broad daylight or taking patrols into triple-canopy jungle. No danger anywhere in your life except if you look the wrong way crossing the street and get hit by a cab. Three hots, a cot, probably an actual bed. I'm guessing there's a pretty jazzy social life in this city every night and you're a big part of it."

"I can't deny it, sir."

"I don't want to know the family details, but yours is fancy, and strings were pulled and that's why you're here instead of a shithole outside Saint-Lô. Harvard, right?"

"Yes, sir. Like my father and his father and—"

"In the islands, I buried plenty of Harvard boys. Guts shot out, heads blown off, chopped to ribbons by Jap bayonets. Just last week I was addressing a battalion of young riflemen about to head to the Pacific. I asked how many Harvard boys were there. There were fourteen. They thought it was everybody's war, despite family and brains that might keep them out of the explosion circus."

"Yes, sir."

"You seem to think the explosion circus is for other people. Your sort doesn't do dirty work."

"It's not that; it's only—"

The boy did look abashed. He swallowed dryly. This was probably his most uncomfortable exchange in the military. He had run out of words.

"Just on general principle," said Earl, "I'm about this far from shipping you out to the 1st Ranger Battalion. You can spend the rest of the war hanging off a cliff in subzero temperatures while being shot at by Krauts. How does that sound?"

"I'm afraid of heights."

"I'll bet you are. So you have one minute to explain to me why I should keep you around. What can you do? What can you bring me to keep you off that cliff? Make it quick."

"I can explain stuff."

"What stuff?"

"*This* stuff, sir. Everything, really. Professors would call it Realpolitik, meaning how it really operates and who's really powerful, not what the charts or newspaper stories say."

"Realpolitik? German word, huh?"

"They're not stupid. They know what they're doing. They were onto something with this concept. I'm talking about things Lieutenant Leets doesn't know. He's a hero; he sort of floats above it all. Very decent man, brave, loyal, earnest, hardworking. But he still thinks the Germans are the enemy. He's exactly the sort who will get destroyed in this place, not see it coming, not know why it came. He doesn't know the building is the enemy. Before you can defeat the Germans, you have to defeat 70

Grosvenor. I've been here since '42. I know everything, and that's intelligence you can use."

"Go on."

"I know who's red and who's FBI tracking red. I know who's secretly sleeping together. I know who's a homo. I know who's kind of weird. I know who's affronted by everything. I know who hates who and why. I know who's smarter than he seems and who's dumber than he seems. I know who works and who loafs."

"What's the first name?"

"Edwin. Edwin Gaines Sebastian. Ed."

"Suppose you give me some particulars, Edwin."

"You and Leets don't know that before you even start, you've got an enemy sworn to destroy you. I can name names. Major Frank Tyne in Operations. Why? Because of Operation Millie, his true objective in the war."

"Meaning?"

"He is in love with Lieutenant Fenwick."

"Who wouldn't be? She's a beautiful gal."

"But it's more than that. She's also wired into the New York–Boston hotshot class who really run things and regard the war as a minor interference in their business. That's why I'm here instead of that shithole outside Saint-Lô. I'm one of them. They like me. They like my father's money."

"Well, Edwin, at least you're up-front."

"Yes, sir. And that's why I know the value of Millie. If you marry her, not only do you get the number one swell dish in London, you're connected, your future after the war is settled, and it will be excellent. Brokerage or law practice partnership. Great houses on maple lawns overlooking the sound. Doesn't matter which sound, there'll be a sound. Access to the secret rooms in D.C. where the decisions are made. It's all foreordained."

"What does this have to do with Room 351?"

"Lieutenant Fenwick seems to have chosen Leets of all her suitors, and she had many. She went with the colonel to visit him in the hospital when he got back from France. I guess that's where it started. He was the hero, the only Jed who actually blew a German bridge on D-Day. She went back on her own a few more times. Now he's here permanently and they seem to be an item, and he's assigned to the building's hottest project, Room 351 with the mystery movie star from the Marine Corps, a true hero who shrinks the balls of all the would-be warriors around here."

"I thought I picked something up between them. It was the way they *didn't* look at each other."

"Yes, sir. Exactly. So, if Room 351 succeeds, Leets succeeds and looks bigger and Tyne looks smaller. So he doesn't want that success; the hell with the war. That means any dealings you have with him will be tricky, any requests will somehow get lost or derailed. Any rush orders will be unrushed. Any schedule will go off the tracks. There will be bureaucratic initiatives to take you over. That is, unless you know the way around the problems. And I do. That's what makes me a help. I can get you anything, fast and clean, through other Ts. The Ts hang out together. A Tech 5 at 70 Grosvenor can do you a lot more good than a Tech 5 clinging to a cliff at four thousand feet in the Italian Alps."

"Hmm," said Swagger. "I still like the idea of you on that cliff. But suppose you make a habit of giving me the intelligence every morning so I know what I'm facing that day. Who's going to come after me, when's it going to happen, what're my moves. Who can I punch, who can I beat down with Marine Corps profanity, who should I ambush up front, who should I avoid?"

"I can do that."

"Then get the coffee and don't wreck the car."

● ● ●

Enter Millie Fenwick. Millie, from Millicent, from the Fenwicks, you know, *the* Fenwicks of the North Shore. Millie was a lovely girl, clever as the devil. She graduated with high marks from Smith but never bragged or acted smart; got her first job working as a secretary at *Life* in Manhattan for the awful Luce and his hideous wife; spent some time on a Senate staff—her father arranged it—and then, when war came, she gravitated toward the Office of Strategic Services just as surely as it gravitated toward her. People knew where they belonged, and organizations knew what kind of people belonged in them, so General Donovan's assistants fell in instant love with the willowy blonde who looked smashing at any party, smoked brilliantly, had languid, see-through-anything luminosity in her eyes. Everyone loved the way her hair fell down to her shoulders; everyone loved the diaphanous cling of a gown or blouse to her long-limbed, definitely female torso; everyone loved her yards and yards of leg, her perfect ankles well displayed by the platforms of the heels all the girls wore. It was rumored that both Warner's and RKO had scouted her.

By '43 she'd transferred to London Station at 70 Grosvenor and become one of Colonel Bruce's assistants and wore the uniform of a second lieutenant in the WACs. She was in charge of the colonel's calendar, important for Oh So Social. She answered his phones or placed his calls, but it was more than that. She also knew the town and so was able to prioritize. The colonel was hopeless and said yes to every invitation in the days before she arrived on station. She had keen, perhaps even eerily prescient social instincts; she knew who counted, who didn't, which receptions it was important to be seen at, which could be safely ignored, which generals were on the ascension, which were on the decline, which Gaullist liaison officers could be trusted, which should be avoided, which journalists were helpful, which were not. She was indispensable, she was efficient, she was beautiful and brilliant at once.

Then what was she doing in a crummy office supply storage room with a dropout from medical school and a purple-pink continent of bruise still lighting up his hip? Actually, kissing.

Then some more kissing.

Finally, kissing.

"When will I see you again?" she said, when their lips came unglued. They were hidden behind shelves of paper supplies and beat-up English desk sets, plus more Biro pens, typewriter ribbons, sheets of carbon paper, unused mimeo machines, Dictaphones. A war runs on blood, gas, and paper, and they were in the paper part.

They were close. Body on body, breast on breast, loin on loin, thigh on thigh. If he let himself he could feel the garters holding her stockings up. He didn't let himself. It could lead to complications.

Breaths mingling, hearts beating in synchronicity, pulses racing, faces flushed. One more inch and it would have been sex; this was near sex, separated but by atoms against the possibility that someone would see and report to all what all already knew. It's what they had instead of sex in the forties.

"He's going to work us hard, I think," said Leets. "Twenty on, four off, for sleep. Maybe sleep here on cots. Lots of coffee. He just wants to get this over with and get back for his scheduled death on some island you and I and even he has never even heard of."

"Jim, I will miss you. If something breaks, let me know. Maybe you'll get a little time off and we can steal some privacy."

"Sweetie, I will miss you too. *So.* These last few weeks have been the greatest ever. Maybe getting hit was the best thing that could have happened to me."

"Don't say that."

"I guess I didn't mean it, really. Love you as I do, I'd give it all up to have Basil back."

"I'm not sure if it's your honesty or your loyalty that stole my heart.

Fortunately, you've got both. Plus courage and decency. And you make an excellent martini."

"The major's the hero type. I'm just an idiot who follows orders. He's like mad Basil, who saved my life at the expense of his own. Still can't figure that one."

"He saw in you what I see in you. The bright and hopeful future, earned, not presumed. He knew his kind would be obsolete with The War's end. He knew you could build a better world than he could dream of. God bless Basil, God bless the major, but let them enjoy their war in peace. Their big secret is how happy they are. They were born for it; nobody else was."

They kissed again. It was a standard movie thing, maybe in its way better for lack of backlighting and Hoagy Carmichael. Lots of fun, even if shot through with regret and doubt and sense of other issues calling. It was still the same old story.

"I've got to get back," he said.

"Me too. Ugh, and tonight I said I'd have drinks with Frank Tyne—"

"That guy? Good Lord, why?"

"Colonel Bruce asked me to. Frank has been writing memos about Room 351 and the colonel can't figure out what's going on."

"Nothing good, I'd say," said Leets.

CHAPTER 15

The Hunter

Tonight's beast was loud. Sometimes they were slow and careful, moving as silently as possible, gliding between trees, hopping on stones over water so as not to splash. They rested quietly, in the dark, and made good use of the land's natural features. Intelligence governed, not blind instinct.

But not tonight. This one was stupid. It made all kinds of noises, left enough sign to trail in a blizzard. You could track on shit and piss alone, for the rank odors of elimination trailed it and identified it on sheer miasma. Shoot into the smell of the shit and you killed. But even without that immense advantage, it presented him with others: it destroyed the foliage, looking like the path of a hurricane of shattered branches and torn limbs; it left huge, muddy tracks in the damp earth; and it made endless low sounds to accompany its clumsy efforts to navigate and remain directional. A fool could follow and track.

But he was no fool. Far from it. Slim, hard, tough, he was above all wise to the ways of wood and field. He had in his time faced and destroyed many beasts. Some came at the end of long stalks—days, even—the distance between hunter and hunted never opening, never closing, as they ranged over the land. Those were his favorite hunts, since he felt then he had earned his kill and the rifle shot was merely an afterthought. Others may have not offered much of a chase but fought valiantly at the end. Risking everything on one last, crazed charge to crush him, demanding of him the nerve to stand tall and calm as pounding destruction approached and shoot well at the last second, they required that he place the bullet precisely in the only spot it could find brain. That too was an earned shot, always worth the risk and always celebrated afterwards by a drink or twenty. He was so proud then, knowing he had the heart of a lion, the nerves of a hyena, the strength of the baboon. He never panicked. It was not in his mind to do so.

In fact, his mind was quite interesting. In it, things proceeded logically from causality, and he felt his excellence at his life's work came from that, not his physical attributes, however spectacular they might be. He had the knack for memorizing the landforms so that, even in dark or rain, he knew when his prey would be climbing or descending, which valley it would choose to follow on the principle that less climbing meant less energy expended and thus less time in the zone of maximum vulnerability. These animals were never clever. It was not in them to be clever. They didn't have a mind for strategy, for ruse, for disguised intent or counter-ambush. That was one disappointment.

The other was how easily they died. It was, he supposed with some melancholy, to be expected. The bullet was slim and fast, built to penetrate muscle and blood, to destroy the organs that were the motors of the body, to smash the brain that was the controller, to rip the heart that supplied the blood fuel to all parts. Some animals of the past had been difficult to kill; one had to love them for that. These, however, surrendered without a whimper, flattening to the earth almost instantly.

He had but one flaw. To his credit, he knew it. That was the memory of a woman. *Karen.* It came upon him suddenly, like an ambush. It took him out of his head. It rattled him, filled him with regret. It destroyed his certainty, his will, his ambition. He wallowed in a sludge of despond, a worthless soul praying for death to arrive sooner rather than later. She would win again, as she had already.

Karen!

But not tonight. That was, after all, the point. In mission was the only surcease from pain and memory. It alone—at least so far, in ways the liquor and sex had not—drove her image from the front of his brain, cramming it into a little faraway hole until the next time. *Karen!*

It was getting time to shoot.

He was well behind and had been still for a long time. Another hunter's gift: the gift of stillness. Most creatures had to shiver and twist and torque, reminding themselves they were still alive. Noises served the same purpose, as did, he supposed, the need to defecate or urinate. All announced and symbolized life, and if they were incapable of conceptualizing the self, their instincts nevertheless proclaimed it, loud and clear, to all in the neighborhood. I squirm, therefore I am!

The hunter is different. Stillness becomes him. It is as though he can reduce himself to inanimateness at the cellular level, will his systems to close down to the merest of oxygen sustenance level, to purge his brain of the need for constant visual stimulation. Pins and needles do not afflict the parts of him that touch ground, his neck never cranks in upon itself in pain; his need for water does not explode in his imagination; his lips, dryer than parchment, do not annoy him; his digestive system, in obedience to a will as achieved over long periods of self-discipline, has no desire to perform evacuation. He is close to animal death, unfazed by tremor or twitch or yip or gurgle. If hungry, his stomach walls do not vibrate; if uncomfortable, his muscles do not complain; if bored, his mind does not wander. He never gets horny. He finds nothing funny. He knows no awe. He never wants it to be over. This close to death, he is fully alive.

He checked his watch. Time approaching. He was low to earth here and could not get the shot he wanted, as the undergrowth was too dense. But he had already picked his spot, a stout tree that would sustain his weight for steadiness and at the same time give him shelter. He slithered to it, now a snake or a lizard, moving as if by rhythmic flexes from musculature beneath his skin. Noiseless, calm, unrushed, in his element.

He felt the beast's comfort ahead. They were like that, complacent anywhere, almost instantly. They lacked the predator's discipline to concentrate on alertness, which was why they died in such numbers. Odd bits of sound reached him, for the creature had no noise discipline either. It went with its confidence and sense of foolish invulnerability.

He reached the tree and in the darkness slid up to it, moving slowly on leg power, pressing his left biceps against it for steadiness. He could make this shot standing clear, but he knew himself never to be arrogant. If rest and solidity was possible, then it should be taken. It was a gift from whatever gods there were and one does not scoff at the gods out of arrogance. He whom the gods destroy first they make proud.

He rose, leaning into it, rifle sling spiraled about his arm for tightness when he went into the hold. His breathing was steady, his heart regular, his sense of time somewhat distended as he focused on the ceremony of the shot. The darkness was easing, bit by bit, in the east as, on schedule, that steady old bastard the sun drew close to the lip of the earth. The light seemed to ooze; it was a liquid looking for form to sustain it. It filled in details as it edged over the earth's rim, and the trees became structures of leaf and limb, the underbrush a riot of complexity, the flowers, a few of them, bursting into color as if explosions. The whole scene was active in its acquisition of singularity and identity.

He raised the rifle. It was the best in the world for this kind of thing. Superbly accurate by fate, it had been selected by the factory experts for this specialist's role, and made all the better. The surfaces of the trigger engagement mechanism had been stoned to smoothness, the action fitted precisely to the stock, the barrel floated for freedom of vibration, all of which supported the purpose. The scope, the world's best—boasting glass so flawless, it seemed to have been cut from sky itself—was harnessed to the rifle by a heavily engineered system of uncompromising reliability. A bridge builder's ingenuity had gone into its systems of lockdown, buttress, and engineering integrity. He himself, with the selected ammunition, had spent hours achieving dead zero at two hundred meters, at which most opportunities would present themselves and which would be out of the reach of his quarry's sight in the low just-predawn light.

As the scope came to his eye, the world increased in scale by a multiplier of four, which meant that the light increased in scale to that degree. He saw the head, he saw the shoulders, the back of the neck, and knew the perfect spot as the great Bell had discovered so many years ago. Imagine a lateral line from ear to ear intersected by a vertical line from the center of the target—not the anatomical center but the center as presented by the creature's posture—and place the point of the sight there. It was like a blade piercing the brain, isolated in space though flanked by two horizontal blades, the three of them designating the mathematic point of impact, which was, at this calculated range, identical to point of aim.

He thumbed off the safety, feeling a slight shudder as it snapped. His fingers reacquired the comb of the stock, knowing the wood intimately, knowing where to place themselves for maximum comfort and therefore security. The fore pad of his trigger finger came to rest on that lever, but just so, a feather's touch, no willed pressure, no sense of obligation or urgency.

He never fired. His subconscious administered that effort and it surprised him as much as it must have surprised his respondent two hundred meters away.

If there was noise, he didn't hear it; if there was recoil, he didn't feel it; if the powder released gases, he didn't smell them. He slid down the tree, knowing the excellence of the shot, and melted into the ground cover.

CHAPTER 16

The War of Pins

The boxes from SHAEF began to arrive by armed escort. Military policemen, white helmeted and white gaitered, delivered them and then, by arrangement, went to the canteen, where they had coffee and pastry until the day was done, though one at a time stood outside the door of 351, hand placed on the holster flap of his .45 automatic. You never knew when *Fallschirmjäger*s were going to drop by.

In the room, the three men worked. It was melancholy and ceaseless. The boxes mostly contained Form No. 1, "Report of Decedent," a banal one-page form from various theater cadaver collection points before shipment to the big cemetery at Blosville. Most of the documents came from platoons of the 603rd Quartermaster Graves Registration Company, which administered this part of the war for the various corps of Bradley's First Army. They had the worst job of the war. The dead were theirs.

Theoretically, as the Form No. 1s arrived, packed chronologically in the crates, they had been pre-culled and selected by Swagger's criterion of only fatalities by single bullet as designated in the "CAUSE OF DEATH" box. It was a crude distinction. Maybe the poor G.I. had only caught one of a fifty-round machine-gun burst. Suppose he'd been toppled by a Luger at close range when bumbling accidentally into a German position. Perhaps a single chunk of mortar shell, falling short, had replicated the wound profile of a bullet. All of those were possible, but all were outliers. The criterion, in its clumsy way, went a good bit of the way toward identifying the victims of the sniper campaign.

Leets tried not to think of what each Form No. 1 represented, or of the process by which the blank had been filled in. But he couldn't keep it out of his mind, seeing a private in a vast, tented mortuary, a democracy of the dead where white and colored, rich and poor, educated and ignorant, officer and enlisted, lay in rank on rank, in crude wood coffins on the ground. A man too sensitive to ontological meaning would go Section 8 in such a cathedral of the killed and have to be straitjacketed and led gibbering and drooling to the ambulance and then the bin. Thus the guys of the 603rd had to be of impoverished imagination who stooped, going from body to body and inspecting for wounds, identity, unit affiliation, and numbly doing the paperwork, recording time of death and condition of remains.

Even at one remove, it gave Leets the willies.

He supposed the poor kid of the 603rd doing the hard work grew inured to it. Perhaps he'd been sent punitively, because he was a screwup; perhaps he'd volunteered, hoping to go into the funeral industry postwar or having been in the funeral industry prewar. The boy, like a medic, was used to the impact of steel on flesh, and the necessary rearrangement of features that followed, anything from a single red hole dead center of chest to a sack of body parts that might or might not have been just one man. If that kid, whoever he was, could get through it, Leets determined that he could handle the paperwork at least, though over the long hours he could not put the sweetness and the softness and the nut-crunching beauty of Millie far from his troubled mind.

He worked hard. They all did. Shuffle, shuffle, note, record, and move on. Finish, so the material could go back to SHAEF and be reinserted into the industrial process of loss, The War–style, which would include notification of next of kin, alert to Payroll for pay cessation, invocation of insurance liabilities, entry in theater-wide casualty report to SHAEF and ultimately the War Department. It wasn't simple to die; it involved a lot of paperwork.

There were six possibilities of death. A red pin was officer/nighttime, black was NCO/nighttime, yellow was PFC or lower/nighttime, blue was officer/daylight, brown NCO/daylight, green was PFC and below/ daylight. Each went to a map designated by color.

It wasn't perfect, as the battalions of dead crawled across the big the- ater maps on the wall. Black and brown were hard to tell apart without intense scrutiny. *Nighttime* as well was too broad to be of much imme- diate use, as it included the minutes just before sundown and just before sunrise, along with those—not many—in the hours of true dark. The end product was six of the full-theater maps, each denoting a category of death via colored dot. They presented a selection of shapes: one linear, the others kidney shaped, tending to oval, some darker, some lighter in color. It was something that could at last be analyzed, and Swagger poured him- self into it. Nothing else existed. He told his two assistants to get lost. It was just him and the dots.

CHAPTER 17

The Poet

June 23, 1944
Somewhere in France

where i am, i'm ripe for slaughter
i am reduced to next day's fodder

there are mortars.
loud and smoky,
i cannot flee them.
those are orders

worse of course
are the snipers
they will sting you
they are vipers

And the Nazis are so nasty
their MGs go so fasty
makes no difference, heart or head
either one will make you dead

war i think is very thrilling
except for all that random killing

hope soon i'm homeward bound
if my luck has got turned round

a hundred-buck wound is all i ask
G-d should do that simple task
why so special do i think i be?
because of course—i'm me!

Your loving son Gary

"Don't send it," said Archer.

"Why not?" said Goldberg. "It's true."

It was another day in the bullet garden, Dog 2-2 style. Their foxhole faced a broad sweep of nothingness. They could see hedgerows and also hedgerows as well as hedgerows. Also: dead cows on their backs with bloated bellies, legs upward. Some fields seemed to grow them.

The land was empty but at any time could fill with Germans. The sky was clear but at any time it could begin to rain mortar shells. The atmosphere was calm but at any time swarms of bullets could rip across it. Plus, they had to shit in a hole. All of these things happened frequently.

"They don't want the truth," said Archer. "They want, 'Gosh, everything here is fine. The fellas are great. The new sarge reminds me of Uncle Ted.'"

"Uncle Jerry," said Gary.

"'Anyway, blah blah de blah blah. Love to all, even Uncle Jerry. See you soon. P.S.: Morale high, food great!' That's what they want to hear. That's what the censors will let you say."

"Well . . . ," began Gary, his mind flooding with clever ripostes.

But the new sergeant, a large, perpetually angry man named McKinney, who looked like the entire Notre Dame backfield, loomed over their foxhole.

"Okay, you two cracked eggs, vacation over. Archer, you find Bliko-wicz in the company area. You clean his BAR for him. He's been lugging it plus 340 rounds of ammo since I got here. He needs relief and sack time."

"I don't—"

"No such words in the United States Army. Only words are 'Yes' and 'Sergeant,' in that order. We need that gun maintained daily. It'll keep us alive. Goldberg, get on your bicycle and head back to Battalion G-2. They have some new maps in. Nice to know where we're going, wouldn't you say, Goldberg?"

"Yes, Sergeant."

"Now, that's my language. Learn from your buddy, Archer. Now, get—"

Mortars.

First the pop, hollow and stupid. Sounded like one of those Ping-Pong ball guns. Then the whistle. If it was soft, you'd probably live. If it was loud, you probably wouldn't. But it was hard to tell one from the other in a hormone rage of fear and dread.

"Hit the fucking dirt," yelled McKinney, piling in on top of them. Maybe there were actual atheists in foxholes somewhere, but not here, not today.

CHAPTER 18

The Restaurant

Major Tyne was nervous on the way over, which was not like him. He was a big guy, a former New York City cop. His ambitions were likewise big. He ran for and won the post of councilman on the city's raucous West Side, pushing hard on the I'll-control-the-Negro platform, which was called "I'll conk the niggers" by his staff. But as a councilman he met a better class of crook—the landed Irish gentry, high politics, law and brokerage partnerships, newspaper voices—and had a gift for doing and receiving favors, including cash and jobs. It was his true talent, although he'd been no slouch with the billy club either.

He was infected with toxic ambition. When war came, he looked hard at it and tried to figure what would earn him the most glory with the least risk. He came up with the OSS, where all the swells coagulated under the leadership of the highest of the high-table Irish of New York, William Donovan of Fighting 69th fame, and he pulled every string in the book to get in. He somehow succeeded, although no one particularly liked him, and he spent a year on Catoctin Mountain in Maryland teaching marksmanship and close-quarters combat to the French-speaking Ivy League poofs who would actually land behind enemy lines. He also lobbied incessantly, making calls, writing letters, sucking up like a whore at a rodeo, and finally got the coveted 70 Grosvenor assignment, ending up in Operations, where his "real-world experience" would supposedly come in handy.

The rumors persisted that he had done missions in France, killed Germans, liaised with the Maquis, was quite the party-poopin', paratroopin' tough guy. It was also stated or assumed that he was Wild Bill Donovan's best boy, with an open line to the big guy himself. He had started them all and they were patently untrue. He had conked quite a few Negroes in his time, and shot a pimp above 110th, but none of them wore *Feldgrau*. Additionally, he'd seen Donovan only a couple of times, on parade duty when the old man was driven down Broadway in a limo ahead of the Fighting 69th vets on Saint Pat's.

So now he was with Millie in a cab to the restaurant, trying desperately to think of something witty to say that didn't require the word *fuck* in one of its many variants.

"Sure hope a doodle doesn't land on us," he said, laughing heartily if fraudulently. "Those damn things sure put a damper on things, eh? And the ridiculous part is how randomly they fall. You're no safer in one place than another. And even if a Spit gets lucky and knocks one down, who's to say it'll crash in a worse place than it might have hit otherwise?"

Doodles were the topic du jour in London, early July 1944. Unmanned German jets, called V-1s, they were launched from France and pointed toward London. They weren't so much aimed as lobbed underhand, as with a beanbag. They simply fell from the sky when they ran out of fuel and fell, detonating four hundred pounds of high explosive. They went where wind and luck took them. You were lucky or you weren't, though some claimed if you heard one, and its engine suddenly cut off, you might have seconds' worth of time to take cover. But the fatalism was general all over London: if your name was written on *Herr Vergeltungswaffe-Eine* (Vengeanceweapon-1), that was it.

"They ought to let me take a squad of good men over there," he said. "Nothing like a dose of tommy gun medicine and TNT to close down a Nazi installation. I'm sure Wild Bill would approve."

"I'm sure the Germans would stop shooting them off if they knew they were upsetting Major Frank Tyne," Millie said, and Frank got that she was kind of sporting on him.

"Okay," he said, "I got a big mouth. Still, we ought to do something to those installations. I don't know, bomb or raid or something. I've sent several plans to the colonel with copies to General Donovan—well, you know that."

"And the colonel will read them. I'll put them in the top of tomorrow's pile," she said. Actually, she'd already placed them in the round file, so, swiftly incinerated, they were presumably part of the very vapors they now breathed.

The cab entered the darkened theater district, pulling up at a posh-looking spot, and the driver said, "'Ere we are, guvnor."

"Oh," said Millie, "Simpson's. How nice, Frank."

Tyne shoveled over a crunchy wad of bills and raced around to open Millie's door.

"Wasn't easy getting the ticket," he said. "This one's not for the commoners. I dropped General Donovan's name and here we are." Actually, he had a kid on staff whose dad was a two-star at SHAEF ("How else he'd get into our outfit, huh?") and he called Dad, who called this or that lord; Frank had no idea.

"It's the Waldorf Astoria of London," he said—wrong because the Waldorf was a *hotel* and it had a *dining room* while Simpson's was a *restaurant* and had *no connection* to a hotel.

Millie, he realized instantly, would see through the stab at swank and thus have no reaction, another dud move on his part. He cursed his own stupidity. If he'd still had a beat to walk, he would have done some conking tonight, just to let off steam.

He took her in, they walked past liveried chaps outside, and were greeted by the maître d' as if they were Lord Bosie's godparents. A lot of la-la was invested getting them into a room furnished in glowing oak with chandeliers and an opaque glass curvature as a ceiling. Old paintings adorned the walls, mostly horses and generals, so it was hard to tell them apart, and every square ounce oozed the highest of breeding, the most lavish of tastes. It looked like the place where the British Empire went to hide during the Blitz.

They were an odd couple: she looked like she'd stepped off the cover of *Vogue*, in a silky gown that merely suggested her lithe construction, easeful grace, and artful aplomb, while he trailed in dumpy American class As with his tiny issue of ribbons on his chest, bouncing along in the beat cop's lumbering cloppity-clop. Beauty and beast? Princess and knave? Slim and husband three, the rich one from Cincinnati? Something like that.

Once seated, he again reached for jokes not there. "That roof doesn't look like it'd be much good against doodles, does it?" he laughed, pointing at the frosted glass capping the room.

"I doubt the Germans would be so rude to interrupt us," she said. "At least a few of them still have manners."

Far off, a thunder-boom signaled touch down, from the direction possibly in Islington.

"See, he deliberately missed," she said with a smile.

Get to it, he thought.

"Millie, I'm so glad you agreed to come out with me tonight."

"Frank, the pleasure is all mine."

"I've had the impression you've sort of been ignoring me since—you know, the night the Jeds went in."

That one was of particular embarrassment. He'd been so proud of his part in it all and she'd been all of a sudden unusually open to him, so he'd taken her to the ops floor, and there they looked at the big map of France with all the Jed targets designated on it and a cast of dozens pushing pieces around it on guidance from live radio communiqués out of actual battle. She'd seemed fascinated by it.

He made up a little fib to make himself seem bigger.

"See this one." He pointed to a small town—Tulle, actually—on a small river that had a small bridge. Someone had written "CASEY" in crayon over it. "Maybe Das Reich comes that way. You know, Tigers and all, straight on into Normandy. So we had to blow it. Problem there was Casey had no Bren guns and thought they'd be visited by Krauts in trucks during the op. A Sten or a Thompson won't knock out a truck. So I found out what group in the area controlled the Brens—turned out it was red—and I went to communications, got them on the shortwave, and told them how important it was that our guys had the Brens. And that's how it happened. So if anything gets done tonight, it's because Team Casey has Brens for backup!"

"Oh, Frank," she'd said, "that's so wonderful," and touched his arm. It was the first time she'd touched him. The electricity was enough to fry Dillinger.

Then he'd invited her to his office for a nightcap "to celebrate," he said. Though the building was all abuzz with Jed frenzy, his little coop was dark and empty. Not that he hoped to uck-fay, not with a nice girl like Millie, but he wanted to know where he stood with her, maybe hold her close, smell her, nuzzle her neck, bank some encouragement. It was the forties, so a kiss, even sans tongue, would have been paradise. She was so goddamn beautiful and her father was so goddamned rich.

A glass of rye, neat, American stuff, bought for just this reason on the black market. A lot of eye contact—hers were as big as lamps, deep and brown and serene, unblinking and inviting—and just when it was getting interesting . . . he fainted.

"I just wanted to explain. I don't know what happened. Maybe it was all the pressure of supervising the Jed teams. Maybe it was the excitement that my teams were finally going in and that this was the night. Maybe my blood pressure got the best of me. I just hope it wasn't something for you to hold against me."

"Frank, whatever gave you that impression?" she asked.

"Well . . . I can't seem to get you on the phone. When I drop by to deliver something to the colonel, you're so all-business. It's just a feeling I had."

"Frank, it's a terrible time."

The drinks came. His a straight shot of Jameson, hers a martini, which, after a first sip, she would not touch.

"It's so busy since the invasion," she went on. "I even feel a little guilty about tonight. The colonel's got appointments, meetings, inspections. Scheduling, drivers, sometimes quarters—it all has to be arranged. And the parties. His job *is* to go to parties and talk up the outfit. And you know what an organizational mess he is. I have to keep it all running straight, I have to supervise the list for his own parties—"

"Somehow I'm never on the list."

"Frank, it's business. It's not pleasure, believe me."

"I suppose."

"Anyway, that has to come first. We all know that. That's what's going on."

"Well . . . I keep hearing about you and Leets. You know how people will talk. I mean, are you *seeing* him?"

"Oh, my goodness, Frank! Where did you ever get that idea? I went with the colonel to visit him after he came back. We got along. I visited him a couple of times. Frank, he's a hero who doesn't act the part. In fact, he was upset at the way CASEY turned out, not proud!"

"Well, he doesn't have much to be proud of. He SNAFUed in a bad way. He got his teammates killed and everybody said it was probably the British guy, Basil St. something, who did the real stuff. And none of it would have happened if I hadn't gotten them the Brens! The colonel needs him more for public relations than as anything else. We had to have a hero and Leets was the lucky guy who got on the hero bus. The people who really know what's what all say that."

"Frank, I wish you wouldn't talk poorly of Lieutenant Leets. He's a very fine young man, a football hero, in fact, and he just wants to do his duty. He's going to be a surgeon after the war. He went to a fine university and—"

"I just don't want you blinded by all the lights shining on him. I saw the photos on the damage CASEY did to that bridge. It wasn't much. It didn't cost the Germans a damned thing."

This was a lie. He hadn't seen the recon photos. Nobody had. They were still classified top secret while the Eighth Air Force damage assessment team got around to them, but it had put a much higher priority on strategic recon of damage to German industry, its true bread and butter. So the bridge photos would sit until someone got around to them, sometime in 1956. They were notoriously slow on this. By their way of thinking it was only a dinky bridge blown up by somebody else.

"Frank! Really, let's change the conversation."

"Millie, I have to ask where I stand with you. I just can't stand not knowing. It's making me crazy! I mean, do I have a chance? I know a dozen guys are in love with you and maybe I'm pretty far down the list, but just give me a chance. I will be someone big after the war; I will make you proud. I have ambitions. You—"

"Frank, really. There can't be an 'after the war' for any of us until there's an actual 'after the war' for all of us. Everything else has to be put aside."

"Okay, okay, I hear you. But I'll always be here for you. If there's anything you need, I can get it for you. Nylons, lingerie, perfume, anything. I can—"

"Oh, the hors d'oeuvres! They look so good. Oh, Frank, let's eat, I'm starved. And then I think you should take me back to the office, because I've still got work to do."

He smiled, thinking: I am going to fucking massacre that prick Leets.

CHAPTER 19

Meeting

The colonel was due at 11. He said he'd have some brass from SHAEF and First Army with him, but not to worry, they were just messenger boys with too much junk on their collars. But everybody was looking for progress and he hoped that the Room 351 operation had something to show for the two weeks of effort.

Earl had definite ideas about how to present. He wanted all the maps mounted on the wall but all shielded so that he could unveil them in chronological order. He was afraid if the various idiots tried to apprehend it all at once, they'd get all screwed up and the whole thing would fall apart. The art of the pitch was to keep it clear, quick, with a good sense of suspense toward a climax, leading to a single conclusion. It had to be a story, in other words.

"It's got to be simple enough for officers," he said.

But at a certain moment, late, he got some eye contact from Sebastian, meaning: I have eyes-only dope. Earl said to Leets, "Lieutenant, why don't you go upstairs and wait with Lieutenant Fenwick to bring the brass down here."

Leets didn't need a second prompting to kill time with Lieutenant Fenwick: he nodded and took off.

"Okay, Sebastian. You look like the cat that swallowed the chicken. Spit it out."

"Sir," he said, "I have it on authority that Major Tyne in Operations has sent a blistering memo to the colonel, with copies to SHAEF intelligence, and finally to E Street"—meaning General Donovan, at the E Street HQ in Washington, boss of all bosses, Mr. OSS himself—"raising a rumpus about Room 351. It was only summarized to me by the T who delivered it to both the colonel and to communications for transmission. I'll summarize. He says he thinks that Room 351 is wasting resources and manpower in that nearly two weeks in, it has produced no actionable material and nothing seems to be on the horizon. Meanwhile, its presence at 70 Grosvenor is so disruptive, it's interfering with the 'real' work of OSS. He thinks it should be sharply cut back and placed under jurisdiction of Operations, since it obviously is intended to reach an operations phase, and that it should report directly to him. No one should have the operational carte blanche Room 351 has. He also thinks that your position should be clarified and wonders if rumors suggesting you are actually a Marine NCO are true and, if so, you should be immediately reduced in rank to the equivalent E-7 of the Army, and required to address all officers via protocols of common military courtesy."

"Who is this fuck again?"

"Ah, some extraneous major in Operations. He's like a vice president without a real job. He just sort of wanders around, stirring things up, trying to get himself promoted. He claims to have been the mastermind behind the Jeds, but everybody knows that's bullshit. He claims he has Irish connections, being an ex–New York pol. He likes to pretend he has Donovan's ear."

"Why're his shorts up his crack over me?"

"It's not you, it's Lieutenant Leets. Tyne's one of the hopeless dopes who thinks he has a shot at Lieutenant Fenwick and is all browned off because he isn't getting anywhere with her, while she's widely known to be sweet on the lieutenant."

"Is this high school?"

"Pretty much, sir. Do you want me to draft a reply or counter for your signature, to counteract quickly?"

"No, that's how you get a crybaby reputation and they tune you out. What we have to do is shortcut our plans, move ahead to the next stage, maybe overstate the importance of our findings. Then find a way to crush this bug. I hate to play these fucking games, but if you're going to work in a building instead of a foxhole, that's what it takes."

"Yes, sir."

"Good work, Sebastian. It's always good to know who's trying to fuck you over. Plus, you get another two weeks in London before you report to 1st Ranger Battalion."

"Yes, sir, thank you, sir."

Leets and Colonel Bruce showed up with two geldings from SHAEF. Both appeared a few degrees below room temperature. Not your combat leadership types, these two were pale men in their late thirties, one bald, one balder. They wore rimless glasses—Earl had seen a famous painting of a farmer standing with his grim wife in front of a Gothic farmhouse once, and that memory, unattached to time, place, circumstance, flittered through his memory—and had faces unpatterned by emotion.

"Brigadier Stacy, SHAEF G-2," said the one.

"Colonel McBain, First Army G-2," said the other, not that there was much difference between them. Etiquette forbade handshakes or routine human courtesies, so Earl gestured them to seats placed in front of the west wall, which they took.

"Gentlemen, I hope you'll find this interesting and worth your time," he said.

"Please proceed, Major."

He began by explaining his sniper criterion, waited for objections, encountered none, and went on.

"Yes, sir. Now direct your attention to the six maps on the wall. I've had them covered because I want to show them chronologically. Less confusion that way."

No response.

"Corporal," Swagger said, and Sebastian removed the sheet from the first map.

"This map represents all casualties in theater killed by the single bullet standard," said Earl. "The time period here runs from June eighth, when First Army troops moved into the area to two days ago, as derived from Graves Registration Form 1s. It makes clear what a big sniper problem you've got."

The two—Colonel Bruce sat behind—looked intently at the carnage represented before them. It was the Cotentin Peninsula as currently contested by First Army. It was the purple dot nightmare, a documentation of swirling, chaotic aggression, as the German reaper took them all, long, short, and tall, good, bad, lazy, smart, by the violent whimsy of industrial war making.

"It tells us what we know. Snipers everywhere. You got 'em on the line, you got 'em on patrol, you got 'em day or night, you got 'em behind the lines. By our count, you've lost more that fifteen hundred men to snipers in the last few weeks."

"We've all seen the casualty reports, Major. We're interested in the night sniper problem, not the day casualties. Please move on," said one of the bald ones bloodlessly. But Earl liked that both he and the other were taking their own notes, not arriving with a staff of go-fers, door openers, and yes sayers. In other words: serious men.

"Yes, sir, that's our focus too. We're headed there. Corporal, go ahead."

The young man removed another sheet from the map.

"These green dots record theater-wide deaths in a category we call daylight non-leadership. That is, ranks E-3 and down, your basic G.I. Joes."

The map looked like an attack by killer eels. Sweeps of curvy green dots seemed to obscure the geographical information below as reptile forms formed a formation slowly advancing horizontally through the bocage.

"You'll note the way the kill pattern traces our own line pattern on a week-to-week basis. That means our fellows are getting hit in their own positions, and as the lines move slowly, so do the hits. Where it's dense is where we were stalled out. So this would be PFCs and privates.

"This represents sound infantry deployment of precision marksmanship at the battalion level. The German knows what he's doing, and he places his sharpshooters where they're most inclined to encounter targets in daylight."

Another map. Much less dense, but tracking more or less along the same lines as before.

"Leadership, meaning E-5 and above. Daylight. Not really a problem, because these guys are experienced and have other responsibilities than holding ground and looking over brush fences. Questions?"

None.

"All right, let's get to the night action."

He nodded and down came the fourth sheet. Map No. 4 was without eels; instead it seemed random dots splattered across the landscape, though not terribly dense and spotted by occasional outliers.

"Non-leadership after dark. Let me define 'dark.' We chose fifteen minutes before true sunset, as calculated by your meteorologists, to fifteen minutes after true dawn as our definition of 'dark.' So these are your infantry night patrol deaths. Sergeant or second lieutenant takes a squad out to check German dispositions. Occasionally, firefights will develop in the dark, and I'd read these as firefight deaths, not sniper related. The shooting is pretty indiscriminate. Some people get hit as they withdraw or on the approach. That's what happens if you patrol aggressively, and if you don't, you have no idea what's happening, and you get hit in company strength or larger and lose far more."

"Did it occur to you to separate the night casualties into zones according to hour of night, Major."

"It did, sir. That's also interesting. I'll get to it shortly."

"Excellent."

Sebastian exposed the fifth map. By now the spray of dots had solidified into deep and dark magenta, the color of spewing blood before it oxygenates, and they roughly followed tendrils out beyond the American lines. They represented a higher, more organized form of carnage.

"Bingo," said Earl. "This category is leadership, nighttime. They're hitting sergeants and junior officers, those that lead the patrol. All or almost all headshots, by the way, an interesting finding. Mostly to the back of the head, on a kind of three-quarters angle between the ear through-line and center-head through-line. That's the preferred shot, and it's too common to be anything except acquired by practice, discipline, and experience."

He let the graphic of so many dead young leaders sink in for a second.

"You know what this means. It gives the troops fear that the Krauts have some kind of night-vision technology. They can see in the dark. Doesn't matter if it's true or not, but it sure as hell flies through the platoons in a hurry, and its effect is that the patrolling will be less aggressive and too prone to panic even in the absence of the sniper. They won't go as far and as hard, and they'll turn back early. That's the strategy, the big picture."

"We're seeing that all through First Army," said Colonel McBain. "You can't make the men do more, because, to them, more is death. Go on, Major."

"The small picture is that, at the squad level, it all but destroys that patrol that night. The men see their leader hit in such a destructive way, and they panic and break up. Any firepower advantage with our BARs and Garands is immediately lost. Our guys wander, some into German lines, some into areas the Germans have flooded so they drown, some so beat up in the mind that when they do get back, they aren't much good for a while."

"It's everywhere," said McBain. "General Bradley calls it the 'sniper disease.'"

"So the questions would be: How do the Germans identify the patrol leader and kill him? Do they have that night-vision technology so refined, they can read rank in the dark? How do they find our men in the first place so unerringly? Do they know where they're going? Is it an intelligence leak to be plugged? Have they developed a pattern read on your people and can make predictions that solid? Then why do they always take that three-quarters-angle shot? Why do they like that shot? Then how do they get out of there? Then who? Is it one guy? Is it a squad or special unit whose existence might come up in radio intercepts, espionage results, aerial recon? Is there an HQ site to be bombed or raided? I'd happily take a team in. I know Lieutenant Leets would join me. But anyway, has it left a paper trail? Do we have sources that can get into their files? Maybe the Russians would."

"I doubt they'd share," said Colonel Bruce. "They're allies, but not *that* allied."

"Have you compared our 'leadership deaths' to the same in other theaters, Major?" asked McBain. "Is it possible this is, again, just war? Snipers, after all, are trained to hit leaders."

"I happen to have some acquaintanceship with the campaigns on Guadalcanal, Bougainville, and Tarawa, sir. The marines had a sniper problem, and while nobody broke the ranks of the killed down like this, that's because no such pattern existed. Moreover, there was no night sniper activity. In that war, the deaths pretty much reflected the dispersion of the ranks in the command. More privates than sergeants, more sergeants than lieutenants, more lieutenants than colonels, more colonels than generals, and no generals."

Neither senior officer said a thing about the reference to the marines on the three islands.

"Okay, last map. Some answers, I think."

Hmm, strange: it was identical to the one before.

Was this a joke?

No, wait. The pins were of different color, though intermixed, being mostly green and a little red, giving the display a kind of Macy's-at-Christmas splendor.

"I'm afraid you'll have to explain this one to us," said Colonel Bruce.

"It was Lieutenant Leets's idea. He saw it. Let him tell. Leets?"

"Yes, sir," said Leets, rising from the dark. It hadn't been his idea. It was Swagger all the way, all of it, but Swagger didn't want it turning into *The Swagger Show*, knowing that in certain kinds of wars that set you up for destruction.

"The idea was to identify the night patrol leadership deaths by hours, meaning first hour from sunset to first hour before sunrise with a different-colored pin for each hour. I thought we'd need a lot of pins. But it turned out we only needed two kinds of pins, green for the half-light of dawn and red the half-light of sunset. That's when the majority of the hits took place. In dead of night, the darkness remains just as mysterious to the Germans as to us."

"That suggests that, as of yet, there's no technical night vision at play here," said Swagger. "They're hitting in low light but it's enough for them to see from a good way out, making a specific shot on a small target, even waiting till it's turning into the right position. They could easily shoot mid-torso, which is doctrine to all the armies of the world, but they wait longer for that peculiar shot. We can only speculate on why."

He paused.

"So, Major," said the brigadier, "speculate. That's why you're here."

"I'm guessing a small mobile unit of men in a largely independent unit. They are deployed in an unsophisticated manner, never in coordination with other units, a tactical subtlety the Germans would normally be more than capable of. They just go here and there. We can tell when a group of them move north, because you get a bunch of night kills in a northern sector for a few days. Then they move south, and that's where the kills occur. They seem to report to no one. They're on their own, contrary to the Wehrmacht practice. I'm guessing the SS, with sponsorship high up that gives them their freedom."

"How big a unit?"

"We note that there's never more than twelve night hits, so I'd put the unit at twelve superb shots. They may have special training, special tactics, special capabilities. They target leadership on down to patrol leaders. They know if they do that they spread fear and paralysis. They're the ones who have First Army shitting in its pants and bottled up on the roads."

"Okay," said McBain. "But who are they?"

CHAPTER 20

Sleet

"You go," said Archer.

"No, you go," said Goldberg.

"You both go, clowns," said Sergeant McKinney.

Ulp. No choice. Direct order.

Archer shimmied through. It was a burrow in the hedgerow, chopped by G.I. shovels through the spine of dirt and root, the vegetation sheathing it hollowed out by severe application of bayonet over several hours.

Archer emerged from the mucky tunnel into bright sunlight infused with filaments and patches of green from the vegetable universe around them. He saw ten or twelve of his buddies just ahead, kneeling nervously in the sunlight, waiting on everyone else. They'd formed up into a loose skirmish line. No fire came at them yet, as the Germans a hundred yards away were either waiting for their shooting lanes to fill with targets or had withdrawn the night before. Every man went tight and concentrated into himself.

"Uggk. Agghhkk!" Goldberg was stuck.

Somehow his canteen had come half-loose and only one hook secured it to his combat suspenders, and the aluminum jar of water had managed to hook itself into a loop of root.

Archer poked it with his rifle butt, it came loose, and his buddy managed to squirm through.

Goldberg never quite made a convincing infantryman. He was so scrawny that no belt or strap could cinch tight enough. His combat suspenders in fact suspended his cartridge belt, but—being heavy with M1 clips in pouches, an entrenching tool, a first aid pack, and grenades—it slopped around his narrow waist, always reorienting itself. Sometimes the shovel was in front, sometimes in back, depending. The sloppy fit of the M41 field jacket, with its vast peak lapels, its flaps and buttons everywhere—it looked like half a slime-green zoot suit jacket—complicated the issue still more, as it gathered where it shouldn't, formed pleats everywhere, worked its way too far left or right, and offered sleeves that wouldn't stay rolled and fell below his fingertips, tangling up things to yet another degree of confusion. The canvas leggings, meant to seal his boots off from the world and thereby preclude the entry of rocks and pebbles to them, couldn't be gathered tightly enough to (a) do their job and (b) stay secure. Thus, they twisted and scrunched at will. He had to insert rolls of TP to fill up the space and moor them, but that was an imperfect improvisation, as the rolls compressed with usage and lost their effectiveness. Then, despite every effort made by various volunteers in the squad, the webbing in his helmet liner never really secured itself to his head. Consequently, the steel pot itself, capping the liner, owed no fealty to any particular directional mandate of the head and rotated randomly, sometimes correctly aligned with his face, sometimes fully backwards, but usually somewhere in between. The rifle seemed gigantic in his pale hands, and since he had never made friends with it, it compelled him to yet more awkwardness and, by comparison to his five feet six inches and 117 pounds, suggested he'd been issued one of those giant basic training cutaway models to illustrate the working of the operating rod. The pallor of his thin but freckly face and the magnification of his wire-framed G.I. glasses inflating his hyperintelligent, hypersensitive eyes all suggested a What-is-wrong-with-this-picture? puzzle. He was always out of breath—that is, when he arrived at all. Thus discovering him in a bocage meadow about to attack an element of 7. Armee, LXXXIV. Armeekorps, 353. Infanterie-Division, under Oberst Mueller seemed ludicrous. No matter, here he was.

"Get going, god dammit," the sergeant bellowed from behind. "This ain't no picnic."

"See?" said Goldberg to Archer. "I thought it *was* a picnic."

They got themselves motivated to join the half-assed line of kneelers as behind them a few more squad mates scrambled out, supervised by Tarzan McKinney, new to platoon and squad in replacing the late Malfo, but not new to The War.

Give it to him, he did his job. He ran to dead center of his line, then outward a few feet. He had a tommy gun and seemed to be dressed in grenades. He checked a watch, worn NCO-cool–style inward on his wrist.

And he had a plan. It wasn't just to witlessly race into implanted German machine-gun fire. Instead, he'd instructed the platoon's best rifle grenadier to infiltrate the hedgerow at 0300 and slither forward through the grass a good fifty yards and there go as flat as flat could be. The contraption he carried was most notably a festival of the Ms so beloved by official U.S. Army nomenclature: an M1 rifle with an M1909 blank .30 round chambered, an M1 grenade projector muzzle adapter (22mm), an M1 grenade appliance with four spring-metal prongs defining a grenade-sized hold space into which would be inserted, pin pulled, lever locked in a lever-restraint compartment a Mark 2 fragmentation grenade. If it worked, and it usually did, the power of the blank round would propel the grenade appliance from the barrel and it would separate from the grenade proper, thus freeing the safety lever and arming the nasty little bastard. A second or two after landing, the grenade fuse would inform the grenade charge that it was party time. Lots of stuff would get blown up, hopefully a German machine gun or two.

The plan held that the grenadier, five feet three inches of crazy-brave Pole named Blikowicz, of Pittsburgh, Pennsylvania, would remain flat prone until the attack launched at 0730 in position with just half an eye open. Theoretically, the hero Blikowicz's life depended on the deception: the Krauts would not pick him out within the wild grass and various styles of flower and plant that obscured it. When the platoon got in its position and began its move, no doubt the Germans would open up with their heaviest lawn mower, called an MG-42, which fired—or so Goldberg swore he saw in *Popular Mechanics*—five thousand rounds a minute. It was on Blikowicz to note the muzzle flash, rise fast, and, with his good instincts for geometry and loft, loose his grenade into the flash. That would be that. Having lost its main advantage and being spread thin, the Krauts would undoubtedly fall back.

"It's a good plan," Archer had said.

"Not as good as mine," said Goldberg, "which is we return to London, catch up on our sleep, take a good shower, and go out for a beer."

"You don't even drink beer," said Archer.

"For that," said Goldberg, "I would learn."

"Our mortars opening up," McKinney said. "Get ready."

And indeed, the weather turned to 100 percent chance of destruction. The sky seemed to fill with arcs of dark blur, since the shells didn't move fast enough to invisiblize themselves. They rose, lost interest in ascension, then fell, and a hundred yards beyond they detonated.

Loud. Scary. Also frightening, plus terrifying as well as deeply intimidating. Each bomb hit, ruptured, released a hot spew of energy, steel, and bad breath, and caused commotion to rule within its limited cone of destruction. Such a sound! Hurt the ears, made you cringe and wince, even as a rush of hot wind snorted twigs in your face. Smoke and debris exited the strike in good order, then lost shape and disorganized into a gray haze that drifted everywhere. It smelled like somebody was burning Hitler's socks. Pricks of something—dust, cinder, frag, pulverized branch, German femur, who knew?—blew hard against the crouching men. The far hedgerow seemed absorbed by this new front of very angry weather, and the sounds were so major they seemed to beat tattoos on eardrums. It was the Boom-Boom Room at the midtown Van Barth without the syncopation and the shimmy and the babes in nylons. Just the boom-boom part.

"Let's go," screamed the sergeant.

"Better never than late," said a smileless, bloodless, parchment-lipped Goldberg, afraid equally that he was going to die or piss in his pants.

"I missed Confession," he said to Archer.

"You're not Catholic," said Archer by way of explanation.

"Now you tell me," said Goldberg.

The two high-IQs rose and, hunched and forlorn, started the nightmare walk toward what was either enemy positions or just bushes.

It was an attack. Why was it happening? Who had ordered it? What was the point? Was this trip really necessary? No one knew. The best theory was that armies, being armies, are supposed to attack once in a while just to show they remembered what they were. But it wasn't a big attack with thousands of troops scurrying across a front the size of three counties in Texas. It was a sort of small attack, one company, four platoons, moving in synchronization across four bocage meadows that abutted each other, to the accompaniment of a mortar barrage, bazookas, light machine guns, and rifle grenades. This meant noise, noise meant smoke, smoke meant confusion, confusion meant danger, danger meant death. But who could say no? After all, as people kept reminding them, it was The War.

The line hardly charged but more or less kind of drifted forward, each individual looking ahead for inspiration to Sergeant McKinney, who stopped now and then to hoist Thompson to shoulder and release a burst. He was shooting at the smoke and hitting it too. Was he hitting anything made of flesh? Hard to tell. Maybe he was just showing off, a little combat theater for a somewhat tough-to-please audience. He sure looked the part.

"Should we be shooting?" said Goldberg.

"At what?"

"I don't know. Stuff."

"I just see smoke, but what the hell."

Archer wedged his M1 into his side, clamped it still with his elbow, shoved the safety off at the front of the trigger guard, and fired once. Except that the whizzers that suddenly came pouring out of the thing—hot spent brass casings—signified more than once, not that he had any sense of pulling the trigger eight times. He had felt no recoil, seen no smoke. As an experience, it left zero impression.

The empty clip popped up like toast at Sunday breakfast and the rifle stopped shooting.

That meant yes, he had fired eight times, but it was so unusual, the details didn't quite register. He just carried the thing and hadn't actually fired it in several months. It still worked, he was happy to note.

"Come on, Gary, let those bastards have it!"

But of course Gary couldn't remember how to get the safety off; then, when he did, he found it too mucked in gunk to fire.

"I'll just go *bang*! Maybe they won't notice," he said to Archer.

The Germans finally noted they were being assaulted. It seemed they too had mortars. In various locales around the field, fountains of turf and grass erupted, unleashing a devil's breath of wind. The air filled with hummingbirds. A man fell, another ran to him. Another fell.

"Come on, god dammit!" shouted McKinney up ahead, then he plunged forward. Heroism was his business. Less enthusiastically, our non-heroes, now animated by the war between fear (go back!) and shame (go forward!), scuttled along, somewhat passive-aggressively. At least

Archer was consumed in the drama of reloading, which meant pulling another en bloc clip of eight .30s from a pouch, inserting it into his breech, shoving it in so hard with his thumb it threw the little lever that let the bolt fly forward. Not easy to do while walking through a shower of mortar shells. Each of these new phenomena brought with it a contribution to the symphony of percussive tonalities, so loud a fellow couldn't hear himself think, even if he could think of something to think of. Goldberg, for his part, just felt like an imposter. He was a Jew in the middle of some WASP ceremony, mysterious and dangerous.

A machine gun opened up. This alarming development announced itself in the form of globs of green light floating up from the hedgerow and curving toward them. It looked like neon sleet. It was so pretty, it was hard to imagine each chunk of light was death its own self. Associated with the show came noise, which sounded like a chain saw versus a radiator, as the German gun emptied five thousand rounds in a single minute toward them—well, eight hundred. Someone burned another pile of Hitler's socks. The air was loud and occupied, filled with unclassifiable optical illusions, unknowable flying pieces of alternating shape and speed, sparks and gobbits of pure heat, flaming butterflies.

At this point—sequence ambiguous; no one could actually pinpoint it—Blikowicz got his grenade launched and it hit three-quarters down the hedgerow, where it detonated with a thunderclap and a bladelike flash of hostile intent.

Fuck, it was loud! Everybody went down, waited, and indeed the gunfire abated. So off they went. Was there a man dismayed? Yes, all of them, each heavily dismayed. Still, they went. Onward, onward, lurched the thirty-five.

Most of them made it to the hedgerow, sheltered in it, and tried to see through its density even as again gossamers of sheer radiance drifted overhead.

Archer had a sense of human figures fleeing on the other side of the bocage, but no targets presented themselves with enough clarity to fire at. Next to him, Goldberg was too winded to consider firing, as breathing was his current drama.

"Holy Christ," he said. "Can you believe we made it?"

"Gary, here, let me get your safety off." He took the weapon, though no Superman was strong enough to force the safety forward where sludge, dirt, and other filth had sealed it shut. The prospect of Goldberg with a hot M1 in his hands did not fill him with confidence, however.

"Be careful with that thing. Keep your finger off the trigger unless you aim at something."

Sergeant McKinney worked his line.

"Okay, guys, good work, stay low. Get ready to dig in if we get the order. You guys okay? Goldberg, good job, glad to see you up here with the big kids. Archer, watch out for your little buddy. He might need some help. Get his fucking gear on right, okay?"

Archer went to work reorganizing Goldberg's hopelessly tangled mess of straps and things and soon they reverted to their little game.

"How cool is McKinney?"

"Coolest so far," said Goldberg. "Much cooler than Malfo."

Cool, meaning somehow glamorous and capable at once and therefore intrinsically admirable, was part of the vocabulary of their own private Jack-Gary War, no one else permitted. Goldberg had picked it up from some colored musicians on a Harlem jazz expedition in 1943, and had brought it into play with Archer, who got it right away. Nobody else did.

"Cool enough to qualify as a war-god?"

This was the highest form of cool. They had yet to meet anyone that cool.

"I go with godlike. Almost there. Definitely deity class. Not way up there, but at least a lesser god, maybe a half god. Did you see the way the German tracers refused to get near him? They sensed his might."

"Maybe he's so Olympian he can actually keep us alive."

"Doubtful, but who can tell?"

A few minutes passed. A few guys smoked. In the meadow behind them, medics worked on the fallen. The sun was still out. Socks were burned, but not so intensely. The dry snap, pop, and crackle of infantry small-arms fire randomly provided background music, most of it from far away. It was all a movie, except it wasn't. From their position, neither Goldberg nor Archer could tell who had been hit or how bad. Was anybody actually dead?

A message was relayed down the line, man to man to man, under the "Pass it on" mandate.

"We're pulling out. Back to original positions. In five. Wait for the mortars for cover. Pass it on."

Archer passed it on to Goldberg, who passed it on to . . .

"All right, Jack," said Goldberg, "you tell me: What was the point?"

Not even Archer, who knew everything, could come up with an answer.

CHAPTER 21

Luftwaffe

"So if the Germans aren't using new technology, what are they using?" asked Brigadier Stacy.

"Men," said Swagger. "Certain men."

Bright day in London. Outside and far off, the now-moot barrage balloons drifted musically, riding as much wind as their cables would permit this way, that way. What trees could be seen were green with midsummer leaf, glittering as they wobbled in the same low breeze. Sun glints marked bombers en route to Germany not yet high enough to mark the sky with contrails, and the honk and squawk of traffic—muted, to be sure—nevertheless rose to the third floor and to Room 351.

"Not sure I—" the brigadier began, and Swagger cut him off, knowing him to be more interested in intelligence than etiquette.

"There are certain men with unusually good vision among those millions with solid but ordinary vision. A ballplayer like Ted Williams is one example. It's said he can read the rotation of the ball coming out of the pitcher's hand. That's how he hit .400."

"So you think the Germans have put together a squad of .400 hitters. They aren't that easy to find."

"Maybe if you know where to look, it gets easier," said Earl.

"Go ahead, Major. This is very interesting."

"I'm guessing these Germans started with the vision requirement. They knew they needed men who could see in the low light of dawn and nightfall when everyone else was still blind."

"I could see finding such men in routine eye exams. But an eye exam wouldn't tell you much about guts. Where would you find such men? There can't be many."

"Exactly. So, putting the two together, I'm figuring on a squad of former fighter pilots. You have to meet high vision requirements to hunt men fifteen thousand feet up at three hundred and fifty miles an hour, and you also have to understand the principles of marksmanship such as deflection, drop, and windage. But clearly you need guts in spades. And something else: mental strength. It's not easy work. You're mostly alone, and if it goes wrong, nobody can get you out of it, so you have to have resilience and high adaptability. Fighter pilot, dawn sniper. Pretty much the same thing."

"Seems credible."

"I'm thinking fighter pilots who've been injured. It takes a lot of refined skill to fly something as complex as a fighter plane well, to say nothing of reflexes, and coolness. A bullet, a bad burn, broken legs from a too-low parachute landing—all that can reduce aerial capability. So why not transfer Lieutenant Von Richthofen from the Eastern Front, where he's shot down fifty Yaks until one finally got him, to the Western, where his same batch of talents makes him an extremely dangerous sniper, except he doesn't have to have the reflexes or the ability to watch fifteen different dials while under fire. He'll get the same fifty kills damned fast."

"What does this tell us? How does this help us?"

"First off, it goes to tactics. Let's look hard at German fighter doctrine. How do they attack? What are their tendencies? If that's their core training, under pressure they'll revert to it. That can help us predict their moves."

"Excellent," said the brigadier. "I'll put it to my superiors and we'll get you talks with our air-to-air combat veterans. They'll know what the German does in the skies."

"Yes, sir, extremely helpful. But another aspect here is what you might call bureaucratic. This isn't happening by chance but in a highly organized structure, one that prides itself on record keeping, discipline, rigor, labor, and thoroughness. So it leaves tracks. To put such a thing together, someone has to go somewhere, propose it, get sponsorship for it, set it up organizationally. It was thoughtfully constructed, layer by layer, by someone who knew what the needs were but also how to slide it through the machine. A senior executive, you might say."

"One man."

"I see one man conceptualizing, knowing where to find his talent pool, selling someone with influence, and assembling the ace's sniper unit. That has to leave tracks. Therefore: a unit designation or operational code name, records of manpower requests, travel orders to collect the right personnel, a budget. As I said, this SS thing the Germans have would be the natural home for such a unit."

"SS," said Brigadier Stacy, "is at the center of most of their worst mischief."

"But they're also new, right, sir?" asked Swagger. "Meaning not tangled up in tradition, politics, rivalries, and grudges that never disappear. So these guys could set it up fast."

"They certainly could," said Stacy.

"We don't have high sources in the SS," said Colonel Bruce. "It's tight, and Himmler is a fanatic at security. But we do have radio intercepts."

"I'd advise having our analysts look hard at those intercepts again with a new focus: anything involving movement of fighter pilots, acquisition of telescopic sights and match-grade rifles, construction of shooting ranges near the front, transfers of senior instructors from sniper schools to Normandy, anything of that nature. I'd look for any unusual communications between Luftwaffe and SS HQs. Meanwhile, I'll send Leets out to some fighter bases to talk to our own aces about the Luftwaffe doctrines."

"I'll communicate this to SHAEF command and we'll all get behind it for a big push," said Brigadier Stacy.

"Lieutenant Leets, pack your bags."

CHAPTER 22

Coach & Horses

Overfed, overequipped, and over here, the Americans of the OSS variety had taken up a nearby pub as theirs till parade's end. It was called the Coach & Horses, and to anyone who cared—Earl did not—it was a mock-Tudor building a few blocks from Grosvenor at the edge of Mayfair. If he had cared—he did not—the Tudor connection would explain its white stucco sustained by struts of dark wood, its gabled roof, its wooden shingles, its Shakespearean melody in a district otherwise given to now-empty department stores, from the days when Mayfair was so chic even Vivien Leigh shopped there.

Earl only cared about the directions—gotten from Sebastian while Leets was out hanging with the Thunderbolt heroes in the hinterlands—and the address, No. 5, Bruton Street.

He entered, not to find a road show production of *Hamlet* unreeling, but about two dozen clearly American bodies that spilled or hunched or leaned everywhere amid a rippling Pacific of cigarette smoke and the clink and slosh of beer and harder being indiscriminately absorbed. Noise too, lots of it, for as a species your Yank cannot keep his mouth shut, even when another Yank is sounding off, and so in their race for dominance the effect is that of people shattering dishes in the back room of a large cafeteria.

No one paid him the slightest attention—just another American officer—as he slid in, found a space at the bar. The lone Brit barman, so used to Americans by now he could almost speak the lingo, landed quickly.

"Yes, sir?"

"Don't know your beers. Something with bite. You pick it."

"Yes, sir. I see no branch insignia. I know what that means. First one's on the Coach & Horses, for your help."

"There's inter-Allied cooperation for you. Bring it, and maybe I'll ask you for more help."

"Glad to oblige," said the barman.

If Earl noted such things, he might have been impressed by the late medieval buzz of the place, illuminated by flickering lanterns, all of the large and complicated room well fitted with wood, mostly buttress and panel, all with a walnut glow. Shields, a boar's head, crossed broadswords, and a helm or two suggested that knighthood had been in flower until yesterday.

The barman slid the brew across and Earl sampled and approved, though of course he found it a bit warm.

"Not being nosy, Major, but I've become expert on American accents. Can I try and place yours?"

"Go ahead," said Earl.

"All right, southern for sure. But not Texas, which is somehow broader and slower. I'd say mid-South, narrowing it to a belt running from North Carolina to Tennessee to Arkansas. Of the three, I'd pick Arkansas, as perhaps just as flavorful but less forceful than the others."

"Town called Blue Eye," said Earl. "West of Little Rock and Hot Springs, not far from Oklahoma. Good job."

"Thank you, sir."

"Now, since you're so good, I'm sure you can recognize a New York City accent."

The barman rolled his eyes.

"They sound like the IRA planning the bombing of a post office."

"Yeah, that's it. Irish, real Irish."

"I've no brief for the Irish, sir, nor am I opposed. But these chaps are indeed the loudest and most demanding. Are they bosses in America?"

"They seem to think so, I've noticed."

"Indeed."

"Is there a mob of them here tonight?"

"As always. The large table in the back then."

"And I'm betting the loudest is a Major Tyne."

"Seems to be their squadron leader. I can see him, looking over your shoulder. Back to wall, jacket off. Well bellied. Ginger turning gray. Face like a potato sack, and as usual needed an evening shave, which he didn't do. He's quite the loudest. The others seem to find his braying mesmerizing."

"Thank you, sir. I'll quietly finish this, then go conduct some business with Major Tyne."

Leets sat at a table at the 56th Fighter Group officers' club at AAF-150, until recently called RAF Boxted.

Behind the wall was a large white piece of painted wood with the insignia of the 56th at the center, a bolt of lightning bent to fill a blue chevron running across an orange shield. Below was a mysterious Latin inscription: *Cave Tonitrum.* Surrounding this emblem, arrayed row on row, small swastikas filled much but not all of the available space. The two men sharing tobacco and bourbon with him had put many of those swastikas up there.

They wore leather, crinkly and twisted yet still shiny brown, signifying newness, used not years but months. Underneath, open-necked khaki shirts well beaten by years and laundering so they looked all puckered like prehistoric lion skin. They wore—even indoors and in defiance of the rules and regs, as if *droit du roi*—officers' caps, though scrunched almost shapeless by the pressure of radio earphones. Nothing else of note.

It was a dark room, full of smoke and other men in leather. The leather, of course, was the Army Air Forces's Type A-2 flight jacket, which used to be an elite fighter pilot's signifier but was so attractive, it had been taken up by everyone, everywhere who could get their hands on one. Two hundred bucks on the London black market.

"So, Lieutenant, I notice you don't have any branch insignia on your lapel. What would that mean?"

"He can't tell you," said the other, the dry stick whose face communicated the spontaneity of marble. "It's top secret. He's with the spies."

"Something like that, sir."

"Well, then, let's move on. You also have a silver rifle on a blue plaque with a wreath on it atop your little array of decorations. What's that?"

"It's called the Combat Infantryman's Badge, sir."

"So you've been shot at?"

"Nowhere near as much as you guys."

"I saw you limping after the XO made the intros. Did someone hit you?" asked the one clearly classifiable as human.

"Yes, sir."

"Story, if you please," said the dry one, his eyes the color of the ball bearings that probably filled his dreams.

They were the champions, one voluble and sparkly, the other some kind of brainiac machine the War Department was rumored to have in its basement.

"Not much. I was part of a team that dropped into Normandy the night of the invasion. We were supposed to blow a bridge to slow down the arrival of German reinforcements. We blew it, but some very good people didn't make it out. I was the lucky one."

"What's your first name, young man?"

"Jim."

"Okay, Jim, Army Air Forces isn't Army, we don't make much of rank, only what's been earned. I'm Gabby. He's Bob. Now tell us what you need."

Earl found a small, empty table. The barmaid finally saw him and came over.

"You'd be having, then, sir?"

"Jameson. A bottle. Two shot glasses."

"Ooh, that's expensive, sir. It's not on the regular ticket."

"Take this. Keep whatever's left."

He slipped her a hundred. Her eyes went all goo-goo on him, since the dough meant so much more to her than him, maybe meat off the rationing for her youngsters. She smiled, showing standard Brit twisted teeth, and left. He lit a Camel, inhaled, enjoyed. The place had a nice buzz. A man could relax here.

She returned with the bottle, opened it, poured out a shot.

"One more thing," he said. "Go over to that big table."

"Them bloody micks?"

"That's it. The big guy, back to wall—"

"Major Tyne, that would be."

"You got it. Tell him Major Swagger would like to buy him a drink."

"He'd do near on anything for a taste of Jameson's, I'm betting."

"I'm making the same bet."

He watched. She went to Tyne, bent, whispered. Tyne looked over at Earl, seeing him for the first time. He nodded. Earl nodded back, affably. Tyne said something to the goon squad, and the table erupted in laughter. The guy was evidently quite a comedian.

Eventually, Tyne stood—a lot of belly wobbled against gravity—and lumbered over. Big guy, lots of meat. Red face, needed that shave, pug nose tilted up. The mug said Ireland everywhere, his ginger coils still seafoam frothy but now going north toward winter.

Earl stood, smiled.

"Major," he said, "thanks for joining me."

"Happy to oblige, Swagger. What's this all about?"

"I'm hoping we can talk out any problems."

"Sure," said Tyne. "Neater, happier that way. Stay friends, go drinking, enjoy London."

"My goal exactly. Please, tell me why I'm on your shit list," Swagger said, pouring him a shot of the J.

"I was a New York cop for fifteen years," Tyne said. "Walked a beat. It was the Tom Dewey era."

"The hero DA?"

"Hero my ass. Another pol, like all of them, only in it for himself. Publicity hound. Anyway, he was big on special squads. Anti-racket. Anti–Murder, Inc. Anti-dope. Anti-whore. All these little units with a favored guy in charge. They reported to nobody, didn't work in the squad room, had nothing to do with beat cops. So much better than beat cops. But in the end they did nothing. In the end they accounted for none of the money they spent, they didn't make any arrests, they busted no hoods. Lepke Buchalter went to the chair because of Lepke Buchalter, nothing Tom Dewey did. So every time I hear of some 'special squad' deal like you guys have going in your Room 351, with the MP outside and a direct line to Bruce and an unlimited budget, it gets me remembering what a joke 'special squads' are."

"And that's why you want us under you?"

"Oh, you know? You've seen the memo. It was supposed to be confidential."

"I heard about it."

"Listen, nothing personal here, pal. I just know how things work in this building."

"So what can I do to please you? Is there one thing to get you behind us instead of against us?"

The Irishman poured himself another slug of Jameson, finished it in a single gulp, and then another.

"One reason you're so golden at 70 G is because you've got a golden boy. The 'hero.' Leets. Everybody thinks he's the John Wayne of OSS. But he ain't. I've seen the photos. They didn't really blow the bridge; they just sort of twisted it. Only one buttress went down. SS Das Reich got it back up by the night of the ninth; they were funneling panzers to the front. So what did Leets accomplish to get a Silver Star and a CIB and all the gals in love with him? Not a goddamn thing. While guys like me, who set up the whole Jedburgh thing"—did he know this was a lie or had he come to believe it himself?—"we get nothing. A golden boy, a secret squad reporting to nobody—it's bad shit, Major. Everybody in 70 hates it. If you like your career, you'd better think of some way to deal with it."

"Where would I start?" asked Swagger.

"Get Leets transferred. There's a training camp outside D.C. in the Blue Ridge Mountains. I spent some time there. He could teach marksmanship, combat leadership, patrolling, radio contact. He'd do much better there than here. Hell, it would even be better for him. He'd be a star. He'd actually be John Wayne. Word would get around."

"I see," said Earl.

"Second, go to Bruce. Tell him you'd feel better if a senior executive was looking over your shoulder. Someone with field experience."

"You've been in the field?"

"It's a long story. I know my way around, believe me. So we move whatever is going on in Room 351 to Special Operations, where I'm vice-chief, under my direct command. Then I could judge what would be important, what not. I could take the important stuff to Bruce. He's got a lot on his mind, no sense in troubling him with detail. He's really a politician, not a military guy. Then I could take it to SHAEF. Make a presentation. I know how to do it. That place is a nightmare, believe me, I think you'd be lost over there. You'd get blindsided by some ambitious lieutenant colonel, he'd take credit for your work, and all rewards would go to him. If he was West Point, his pals would grease the tracks for him. Happens all the time. You've got to know the ropes like I do."

"They promised me no politics."

"I don't know what you're used to, but everything is politics. Look, I know you're really just a sergeant in the Marine Corps. But I'm trying not to be an asshole about this. You play ball with me, I'll see you keep that rank. Maybe join my staff. You seem like a good egg; maybe we can work it out so that we both benefit."

He poured himself another shot. The bottle was already three-quarters gone.

"Good whiskey," he said.

"Actually," said Earl, "I do have another proposal. Let me run it by you, just to see what you think of it."

"Sure, no harm done," said Tyne.

"We can't say anything bad about the German aviators we face," said Bob. "They are brave, resourceful, well-trained, and determined. They are the best, and how you win or lose has nothing to do with tactics, only with experience, luck, and maybe the fact that the Jug is a bit better than the 109, performance-wise."

The Jugs—official designation, P-47 Thunderbolts—that they flew were huge-engined tubes of steel not particularly designed for streamline but only for power. They attacked the atmosphere with a gigantic four-bladed propellor and a Pratt & Whitney R-2800 Double Wasp engine that cranked them up to 400. In a power dive, some had come close to

600. They were strong, impossible to bring down, and flown by men who got in close, held off till dead zero, then hammered the German kites with eight .50s. Nothing left but a smear of smoke in the sky.

Compared to the Me 109 that they flew against or the P-51 they flew with—both looked like sharks—they looked like the fat kid who lives down the block. The pilots sat atop all this engine in a little plastic bubble for a full 360-degree scan that would be the coming thing in fighter design. But for all their bluntness of design, they were the fastest airplane up there. They ate the sky.

"So you don't think—"

"I see some things that might help you, Jim." Friendly guy, next to Mr. Brain Machine. He seemed like a Wisconsin bartender.

"Yes, sir."

"I'm Gabby, not sir. Have another sip. That's an order."

He laughed at his own joke. But Leets took the bourbon, savored and enjoyed it, but not as much as he enjoyed sitting like a kid in the presence of Joe DiMaggio and Ted Williams.

"They do have some peculiarities that might bear on your sniper theory," said Bob. "For one thing, they're willing to stay and fight within the bomber stream itself. That is a very risky proposition. There are planes everywhere, they are moving, changing positions, and meanwhile us Jug jockeys are trying to get on their tails and flame them, so it's an incredibly uncomfortable situation. I'm equating that to the sniper's need to stay jacked in an uncomfortable position, especially when the targets are near. It takes a certain kind of concentration, maybe the same kind. No weak sisters need apply. The highly nervous wash out in flight school and sometimes even guys who can do everything lose their nerve and are quietly rotated home before fifty missions, so they don't kill themselves or anyone else."

"Guts," said Leets. "We figured that would be high on the list of similarities."

"Second in both cases," Gabby continued. "You're either a hero or dead. Nothing in between. Fighter pilots rarely go home because of wounds. If the plane is hit, it burns, and if he gets out—he doesn't always—he goes into a POW camp, if he's not shot on sight."

"That's sniper stuff," said Leets. "Occasionally but not always they're taken prisoner. Their job is to show no mercy so they know that mercy isn't coming to them. They also know that from most hides—say, a tree, a church steeple, a hill—there's no getting out. You're stuck there. So they live with that, just like the pilot."

"Good," said Bob. "Here's another one. I'd call it tactical selection. Against our big birds, the Germans prefer the twelve o'clock approach— that is, straight on at the front. They come right at the big birds because they know that way they're in less danger of retaliatory fire. The top turret of the Fort can't crank low enough, and on the G model, that chin turret looks good, but it's mostly for morale purposes. It's run by the navigator, but he's not behind the gun, he's behind the bombardier in the fuselage, and the thing is a robot servo-mechanism. I don't know of a single German that's been shot down by the chin gun."

"So how does that equate to a sniper—"

"There's another reason for a twelve o'clock angle: that's his easiest angle to the cockpit. He knows if he kills the brain, the animal dies. No pilot, no airplane. His whole thing is based on getting the brain shot, because you can fill a Fort with holes so that it looks like Fearless Fosdick, but it stays up there. Kill the boys flying it and down she goes. No sadder sight than a Fort going in. You pray for chutes and sometimes you get 'em, but usually you don't."

"Maybe an ex-fighter pilot sniper," said Gabby, "is choosing his variation of the Fort-killing shot. Tactical selection. Back of the head—there's the parallel there. The cockpit. That's what he's trained to do, and on the ground, in the low light, he probably goes back to that training."

"That's very good," said Leets.

160

"The other stuff—the eyesight, the awareness of shooting realities, including deflection, trajectory, and velocity—all that lines up nicely," said Gabby.

"Yeah," said Bob. "It's almost a shame it's baloney."

"See, here's how I'd handle it," said Swagger. "Let's you and me go outside, find a nice alley, and square off. Just so you know, I'm the three-time light-heavyweight champion of the Pacific Fleet. In '39, I won my last fight on the deck of the *Arizona* in Manila Bay in front of two thousand gobs and marines. Fifteen rounds. A long, hard night's work. Negro cook; he was a good fighter. You're not."

Tyne swallowed air hard.

"So I'll punch you so hard in the mouth, you'll shit teeth for a month." He smiled. The red vanished from Tyne's face as if his carotid had just been cut and he was emptying fast. A pasty white swept across his features.

Swagger lit another cigarette, just to show the big man how tremorless his scarred hands were. Meanwhile he kept a steady glare on the guy, watching him melt under its power.

"Y-you're making a big mistake, pal," said Tyne finally.

"I don't think so. I think I just ran over a cop who thinks he's still wearing a badge when in fact he's not wearing anything but a belly."

"You can't talk to me like that."

"Sure I can, Fatso. Anytime I want."

"I have friends, I have connections . . . When this gets around, you are dead, pal, and I mean *dead.*"

"You tell 'em and I'd bet they'd wonder why big, tough ex-cop Tyne let some Arkansas cracker push him so hard he pissed three pairs of pants."

"I—I—I—"

"You, you, you—my ass. See, I had someone who knows how to do it pull your OSS file. You haven't seen any action, mick. You haven't been in spitting distance of the Germans. You haven't been in howitzer distance of the Germans. You've always had an ocean or a channel between you and them. In my book, lying about combat is as lowdown trash as it gets. I've seen too many good young men die to let an ass-licking, politics-playing, potato-sucking monkey like you get away with it. You come after my people again and I will chop you up for Irish stew. Now get your fat carcass out of here. I have a bottle to finish. Only men with guts allowed at this table."

CHAPTER 23

Television

Archer and Goldberg were having an important discussion. They were also digging an important hole. Aerial photos had revealed that the Germans never returned to their positions, so the entire company moved one hundred yards eastward to the next hedgerow, theirs by right of conquest and German disinterest. However, it would remain theirs only by right of fortification.

Thus, the hole. It was for two men, as the entire hedgerow line would now be staffed by two-man foxholes. To occupy a hole, you have to dig it first. Neither of the young men enjoyed this part of the infantry life, while on the other hand they despised all the other parts of the infantry life too.

The Model 1910 T-handled entrenching tool each G.I. carried with him was basically worthless. It wasn't an actual shovel, being too short and light. It provided no leverage. Its main use was for tossing French apples into the air and batting them into atomic particles, always a good time killer. As a tool rather than a recreational device, it was calculated to do maximum damage to the lower lumbar region while doing minimum damage to the ground. It took a massive effort to cram it into the earth, twist it free, and hoist the load out, and for all of that, you got about a spoonful of dirt. Evidently it had been designed and adapted by the Army before anyone noticed soldiers all had backs, particularly those unused to physical labor of any kind, like comedy writers and engineering students. So the hole did not progress at any meaningful speed, while all up and down the line, men had finished theirs, having cut gaps in the actual wall of dirt before them so that they could fire on the next hedgerow, which was exactly like this one and exactly like the last one. The bullet garden was forever.

But the time digging was not wasted, as nothing less than the future was discussed. "I'm telling you, it's the next big thing," said Goldberg between teaspoonfuls of earth. "And the point is, you have to get in on the ground floor. Once they have it built, the only way in is via connections. And my only connection is my uncle Max, the cabbie, who once drove Fred Allen to the Bronx."

"Gary," said Archer, patiently explaining the reality of the situation, "the American people go to their radios every night and listen to news, music, comedy, and drama. *Gang Busters*, *Dick Tracy*, *The Goldbergs*, *The Pepsodent Show* with Bob Hope, *The Mercury Theatre on the Air*—it's entirely satisfying to them. They like a theater of pure sound. They don't want to change. If they want pictures, they go to the movies. To them, pictures are people twelve to twenty-five feet high, sometimes in color, with teeth the size of hubcaps and eyes the size of oil tanks. That's the rhythm. That's what they're used to, that's what they love. They're not going to chuck that to watch shows no better than the radio with pictures, what, ten inches high, if that, blurry black-and-white, no less. Why would they do that? What's in it for them?"

"Jack, they say the big networks are already pouring the bucks into the television kaboodle. They're betting on it being big. You'll have a million G.I.s coming home—"

"Not us, because we'll be dead."

"Of course. But let's skip the dead part. It's too depressing. Let's go to New York, 1948, the miracle of the television, and the one thing it's going to need more than anything which is—"

"Dames with huge kabongas."

"Besides that. Hell, everybody needs dames with huge kabongas. No, what they'll need is writers. Someone has to figure out what the dames will say. They can't just say, 'Hey, look at my kabongas!'"

"That would be enough for me."

"No, they need skits, lines, little stories, segue lines to the commercials, jokes, they need jokes, and the bigger it gets, the more jokes it needs."

"And that's how Gary cracks the big time."

"Yeah, and—"

"All right, take ten, smoke if you got 'em," yelled McKinney, the god sergeant, walking down the line. "Well, except you guys, you two geniuses, finish your goddamn hole, for Christ's sake. Archer, can't you teach him how to fasten his canteen to his cartridge belt?"

"He refuses to learn," Archer said, but by that time the sergeant was gone, on to the next few boys, and then the next.

So the two guys actually applied themselves and got the hole dug at least deep enough to protect them from—

But suddenly McKinney was back.

"Okay, you jokers, you're off the line. CO just radioed. He wants you guys back at the bivouac area at Battalion Headquarters."

"Us?" said Archer, astounded that anybody had noticed them.

"Yeah, you. Take a shower, shave, get a good night's sleep in a tent instead of that sorry hole, crap in a latrine, not the mud, put on some clean clothes. He wants you sharp tomorrow."

"What's tomorrow?"

"Is it our cover shoot for *Life* as 'G.I.s of the Year'?" asked Goldberg.

"One of these days your wisecracks aren't going to make me laugh, Goldberg, and then you'll be up shit creek. No, for some reason some hotshot intelligence guys are coming in to talk with you. Archer, make sure his straps are on right."

Part Two

UP FRONT

CHAPTER 24

Milton Hall

On the day of, Leets just back from his journey to the Thunderbolt gods, Sebastian drove them to Milton Hall, ninety minutes north of London, where the OSS and SOE lads had trained to form up into Jed teams. Jed teams that hadn't gone in yet were still much in evidence.

There, the two kitted up, drawing what was necessary from the supply rooms in the cellar of the big, fancy house where Leets had bunked for a couple of months. They were issued battle gear in the paratrooper style, which meant everything was slightly more raffish than the usual G.I. gear, as the paratroopers were the most stylish of the invading forces.

The only trouble came at the arms room, where both men presumed to require Thompson submachine guns, because both had fought with them before. The NCOIC was surly. Thompsons, especially the newish military-only M1A1 variant, were a treasure and he hated to issue them to guys not of a Jed team, no matter what OSS command demanded.

He tried to stick them with something called a UD-42. It was a 9mm replacement for the Thompson that the Army didn't like and never went anywhere, so the first and only run of manufactured guns were dumped on OSS. The thing looked like a toy and was so delicate it would disassemble itself at the threat of combat. Then there was that little Mickey Mouse caliber, the 9, which by Swagger's thinking was something that belonged in a boy's club, not a war.

"Thompsons," said Leets. "M1A1s, not '28s."

So, after much drama, the sergeant issued them the guns, each battered enough to suggest tales could be told, plus ten thirty-round magazines, a Remington Rand 1911A1 pistol with two mags, a pull-over tanker's shoulder holster, and five boxes of .45 ACP.

"We'll fill mags on the way to the airfield," Swagger said.

For him, sitting in the back of the car with the big gun across his knees, busting his thumb sliding .45s into the long magazines, it was like old-home week. He'd fought his wars with Thompsons since 1934 and had drawn blood with each iteration, the first Colt-manufactured 1921s, glorious royal blue almost too beautiful for rough usage. G-men and marines and gangsters loved it for the same reason moviemakers did: it was so sweet. It was never clear who was copying whom. Then came the '28, less polished, less finished. And now the M1A1, a blunt wartime expedience, stripped of glamour and thus more glamorous, in gray phosphate with all flashy touches banished in favor of the rugged, the reliable, the easier to manufacture—exactly as a sergeant hoped the men in his platoon would be. The signature vertical foregrip, which paralleled the sculpted angle of the pistol grip on the preceding generations, was one such. In its place, a utilitarian forestock lay under the barrel. The sight was a prong with a hole in it, the bolt a knob now on the side instead of the top, the elegant muzzle compensator devolved into a pig's snout.

It didn't matter. The damned thing was still a choreography in steel and walnut furniture of angles, planes, sweeps and streamlines that achieved spontaneous, perhaps accidental perfection, art deco on the way to pure classicism. Of its beauty, he was quiet, as that was private, between man and gun. On its utility he could be eloquent. It was heavy, solid, reliable. More than once Swagger had used his to save his or others' lives, and it never let him down, always issuing destruction with urgent precision to those who would do harm. He couldn't imagine going to war without one.

The plane—now called a C-47 in place of its *nom du temps de paix* DC-3, with the giant letters *CU* in white against the dark green just under the cockpit—clearly had just barely survived a rough D-Day night. Rocked back on its tail wheel, nose up pugnaciously, it displayed battle dress of black and white stripes on its fuselage, tail, and wings. That scheme had been adopted as identifiers to keep it from being shot down by its own side's fighters. Nevertheless, the Germans had not been confused and managed to fill this one with holes and rips.

But CU, under the guidance of its teenaged captain, got them there, despite the roaring currents that poured through its tattered fuselage. It was late afternoon when they finally set down at Deux-Jumeaux, one of the dozens of hasty airfields erected on the Cotentin Peninsula primarily by bulldozing a farm field flat, and then laying down a thousand feet of steel plating.

On the ground they encountered few surprises. Both knew that war was squalor. Wherever it touches, it leaves mess, litter, destruction, discarded or damaged equipment, knots of listless men who seem to have nothing to do, a few earnest heroes trying to make sense of it all and keep things going, and junk everywhere, plus more junk, and then some junk. That is what they expected; that is what they got at Deux-Jumeaux.

They hustled off the plane and out of the way of the guys in T-shirts who would be unloading stuff and soon found a jeep with a First Army intelligence officer, who ferried them quickly to First Army HQ for that night's bunking.

"You guys must be exhausted," he said, maneuvering his way through a misery of mud around dead tanks, some turretless, some burned to husks, some upended like toys by a child's rage. It seemed the metallic

171

corpses were equally of German or American affiliation. The roads were bordered with telephone wires, which looked like thick, twisted vines in the jungle; dozens of wires draped and hung over what trees remained or simply trailed on the ground. Sullen squads of infantrymen, looking like used machinery, moved aside for the vehicle but were uncurious about its contents. They just wanted to get where they had to be and sack out. Now and then the major had to sideline the jeep as a column of Shermans ground along the road, pulling up a coughing fit's worth of dust as well as releasing spumes of octane consumption and more noise than could be easily borne. They sounded like radiators clattering down a marble staircase. Meanwhile, too far off, artillery landed, small-arms fire cracked, buildings burned, men squatted and shat, crawled and died, became heroes or cowards, sometime the same man in the same five minutes.

"We're fine," Swagger said. "Just checking here, but you've got the names and units of the men we're here to see and transportation to and from?"

"It's laid on, more or less. You know the units are always moving, depending on the local situation, so you may have to improvise."

"I think we can do that. Any luck with my request to interrogate a captured German sniper?"

"We're still looking, but things here are confused and if and when we take snipers, they're in no hurry to tell us what they did. They think we're going to torture or execute them."

"We're not here to torture or execute anyone," said Swagger. "We just need information."

The First Army HQ officers' mess, third tent on the right after a left turn at the intersection of Tent and Tent, was unsurprisingly sodden, a bigger tent with a food line, overhead bulbs, and the smell of musty canvas obliterating the smell of the food, which might have been a blessing. The chow was basic field Army: corn beef, canned corn, a teaspoon of watery mashed potatoes, and all the thinned milk or coffee or powdered lemonade you could drink. At least, unlike the K rations that would sustain them from now on, it was reasonably warm and salted up.

They sat alone, but eventually a known face emerged from the background. It was Colonel McBain, of First Army S-2, who'd received the 70 Gros briefing. They rose but he gestured them down, dispensing with the etiquette required but usually ignored in a war zone.

"The general wanted me to tell you he found your analysis of our sniper problem first-class work."

"Thank you, sir," said Swagger.

The general, of course—the "G.I.'s General," as the press had fashioned the First Army commander—had a widely known aversion to actual G.I.s of any rank below field grade. He was a work-haunted technocrat who kept to his own tent and quarters and communicated with the world through a cadre of colonels, like McBain.

"We're hoping for the same quality in your next phase."

"We'll do our best, sir."

"If you have any difficulties, just radio call sign Master-2-Alpha. That's G-2, Army-level. The message will get to us and the difficulty will go away."

"Good to know, sir."

"Enjoy your meals, pick up a beer or two at the officers' club and sack out. You meet your driver at 0430. Sergeant Major McElroy. He's old Army, knows everything and everybody."

"Yes, sir."

That was it. First Army, after its leader, was an entity of few words.

The officers' bar—another tent, two tents down from the original tent but on the other side of the tent street, not far from another intersection of Tent and Tent—was stocked with tables and chairs and held little charm. It looked just like the inside of a tent. It was pretty empty except for cigarette smoke and the odor of a nearby latrine, and Swagger and Leets found a place quickly enough. They each had a beer.

"All set for tomorrow, Leets?"

"Yes, sir," Leets said.

"Okay, Leets," Swagger said. "Normally, I don't pay mind to what the people under me say or think. It's bad leadership to get too close to a subordinate. But since it's only the two of us and I am dependent on your skills and enthusiasm, I'm going to break my policy. I've been around this business enough to know when someone's got the snoot on. It's not that I miss your chatter or want to hear about how your girlfriend broke up with you, but I need to know what's eating you and whether it's going to fuck us up. Did you figure out the Luftwaffe fighter pilot theory was bullshit?"

CHAPTER 25

Confidential

NFIDENTIAL CONFIDENTIAL CONFIDENTIAL CONFIDENTIAL CONFIDENTIAL CONFID

5JUL44

To: MAJ Maurice Buckmaster
Section Chief
Section F
Special Operations Executive
64 Baker Street
Marylebone, London

From: COL David Bruce
CO London Station
United States Office of Strategic Services
70 Grosvenor Street
Mayfair, London

Dear Buck,

Hoping you don't find this note and the request it contains intrusive. Over here at 70 Grosvenor, we understand how hard you've been working and appreciate that the war is a 24-hour business. Equally, we appreciate your good counsel in some of the situations we've encountered.

I'm hoping for more of the same, particularly the latter. I've just had something new put on my plate and it's an area where F has had some great successes. I'm hoping to meet informally with you and perhaps your Miss Atkins—lunch, drinks, dinner, whatever works for the two of you—sometime in the next few days and chat this up. Any insights will be most appreciated.

The new direction comes directly from Mr. Hopkins, President Roosevelt's closest advisor. He speaks with the President's voice and so we assume he speaks for the President. At the same time, I'm inclined to believe that Mrs. Roosevelt had a hand in the matter. It seems to reflect her interests and perhaps blind spots as well. Mr. Hopkins sent it to General Donovan in Washington and the General has forwarded it to all station chiefs, so we are to take it as marching orders.

Mr. Hopkins suggests that we incorporate women into our operations—that is, not just as radio operators but as actual field agents. They would of course be required to penetrate enemy entities, lead other agents and guerrilla movements, plan and execute enterprises, and perhaps even kill—or worse! No doubt they have skills and talents the men don't share, and in certain circumstances I can see how their appraisal and solution to a mission conundrum might be just the thing.

However that may be, I'm still a Puritan by heart and a father of a ten-year-old daughter by chance, and it would pain me to send Audrey—or anyone's daughter—into situations of either danger or sexual compromise. It just doesn't sit well with me.

Thus it would be most helpful if—

A shadow fell across her typewriter. Millie looked up to see the unwelcome figure of Major Frank Tyne looming over her. He wore his full

Class As, not just his less formal Ike jacket, with his decorations, all three of them, pinned to his chest.

"Major Tyne. Oh, you surprised me."

"Sorry, didn't mean to sneak in. The door was open and—"

It was late on a Thursday afternoon. She was alone in the office, and after her typing still had to make mimeo copies of the SHAEF daily sitrep to go to all division chiefs, go over the colonel's weekend schedule, and make arrangements for his transportation.

"It's all right," she said. "I'm just finishing up some typing."

"I came by because I have something for the colonel. I hoped to get it to him right away. I don't want it going into the circular file, where most of my other—"

"Oh, Frank, don't be silly. Your memoranda go into his in-box the same as everybody's. He sets the priorities, and if he doesn't get back to you, it simply means he sees other concerns as more important."

"Well, I'd like to give this to him personally."

"He left for Scotland this morning. We had a dust-up between one of our training cadre and a local policeman. Alcohol and fisticuffs were involved. Lots of ill feelings were unleashed. It called for someone of Colonel Bruce's diplomatic skill."

"Oh. Well, then, I guess I'll have to take it to SHAEF. Maybe they'll act quickly as the law requires."

"What does the law have to do with it?"

"By law, military entities are required to respond to these inside of twenty-four hours."

He handed over a manila envelope. It bore the impressive seal in one corner that declared it to be an official document from the United States Congress.

"Frank, this is so unnecessary. I'm so disappointed in you, Frank."

"Millie, your boyfriend, Leets? Get ready to kiss him good-bye. He's on his way to Burma."

CHAPTER 26

Talk

"They said—" began Leets.

"I'll tell you what they said," said Swagger. "They said that the similarities between fighter pilots and snipers are superficial. They don't mean a thing."

"Something like that," said Leets, trying to figure an angle on this development. It hadn't occurred to him that Swagger *knew* the fighter thing was bogus.

"The sniper is oriented to achieve stillness," said Swagger. "He's got a simple yet refined thing to do. But its microscopic: a single tremor of finger or wisp of breath and he misses. Maybe he gives up his position and his life for nothing."

"Yes, I see. That seemed to be what they were getting at."

The major lit a Camel, took a drag, enjoyed, expelled a cloud that hung in the stale air, captured under canvas like everyone else's smoke.

"The fighter pilot," he said, "has to be an eyes-everywhere guy. He's got a 360 to monitor. He's got calculations to perform, meaning his own direction and how it relates to other objects in the immediate vicinity, friends or enemy, all moving at three hundred and fifty miles an hour in three-dimensional space. Plus, he's got fifteen gauges, twenty-one lights, and thirty-five switches to monitor. Oh, and folks are shooting at him and big airplanes are all around. Did I mention flak? Did I mention the pull of gravity? Did I mention a tiny gunsight in all that expanse of canopy? Did I mention cramps from sitting, chill from the altitude, mask discomfort, anxiety about the oxygen flow from it?"

"They were more gentle in their explanation."

"I'll add something they didn't think of. That is, 3D versus 2D. The fighter pilot is *in* space, the sniper is *on* space. The fighter pilot has to operate up, down, and sideways, among other folks operating up, down, and sideways. So it's not only important what's happening now, but how all those things will be happening, and where, in five seconds, ten seconds, and so on. Meanwhile the sniper's on a table-top called planet Earth, and up or down means nothing, not really. The elevation is measured in feet, not thousands of feet. He's got to concentrate and minimalize. The pilot's got to get with the rhythm of motion, his own and everybody else's. Seems I forgot weather. Clouds, the position of the sun, on and on."

"I didn't realize you could write a book on this stuff."

"So if I knew all that up front, what the hell did I sell it to the brass hats and send you on a wild-goose chase for?"

"Now that you mention it, yeah, that would seem like the next question."

"Leets, if I send you to do something, it's for a reason. I may not tell you that reason. I may need you believing something else. I would believe it to be better for you, not just me. If I'd told you the pilot-sniper deal was phony, the Thunderbolt boys would have seen through you in a second. They had to believe you, because you believed you."

"Okay, I get that."

"So here's why. Listen hard, then tell me I had another choice."

Leets leaned forward.

"Basically, it's two things. Number one, you and I know how bad the building leaks. It spills secrets like a busted sewer. All those smart people talking, bickering, plotting, screwing, smoking, running around, going to parties, a third of 'em red, another third FBI, and a final third, maybe the worst, just plain career scum. You can't trust 'em any further than you could toss 'em. But I don't want no one—excuse me, *any*one knowing what I'm thinking. And I am thinking something. But it's not fighter pilots as snipers. I'd tell you, but then that's what you look for as you investigate. So I keep it secret from everybody but me, and I put out this crazy airplane shit, just logical enough for the brass hats to believe, because for now I'm the emperor that nobody's yet got the guts to say has no clothes. They *want* to believe me."

"I see that."

"And to sell it, I send you out on a wild-goose chase. That puts the stamp on it, for damn sure. So if somehow word leaks via this or that channel and ends up in German hands, the Germans would then have a good laugh at how stupid we are. 'These bozos don't know a damn thing. Americans are idiots. Ha, watch us kill their night patrol leaders and tie up the Normandy front for months.'"

"You said there was a second reason."

"Yep. I had to move against somebody. Move hard, move fast, blind-side block him, bump him into making a stupid move. Whatever, just get rid of him."

"Tyne, I'm guessing."

"You got it."

"That bastard has it in for me, and he's got all that Irish blood— a good thing if the boss is named Donovan."

"Shouldn't matter, but it does. That's the way the world works. Real-politik, someone told me."

"Is that why I heard you showed up at SHAEF commo two nights ago and sent a confidential radioteletype to someone in the Naval Annex in Washington?"

"Maybe so, maybe not. If you need to know, I'll tell you. I will tell you this: I wanted you out of the building. The timing was an accident but it was perfect. You gone, you can't be blamed. What happens will have nothing to do with you. No one can say, 'Leets got rid of Tyne because Tyne liked the Fenwick girl too much. Leets won the war of Fenwick.' I don't want that shit in the air, giving people stuff to talk and wonder about, secretly being a factor in every decision they make regarding us."

"I didn't know Millie and I were a problem."

"Only to Tyne, which is why I've got to get rid of him."

"You don't mess around."

"If a guy's after your scalp, get him now. Tomorrow is too late. You don't want to look back after you've been fucked and think, 'Gee, if only I'd done something *then.*' "

"So—"

"So nothing. You bunk out now: 0430 we're on the road. We got some hard days ahead. I need you rested and ready. Besides all this bullshit, we've got a war to fight, or so I read in the funny papers. And on top of that, I think it's going to rain."

CHAPTER 27

Karen

Karen was never beautiful.

Even in her best picture, standing with a light smile on her face next to and holding hands with her beloved brother in a frock of the early twenties, there was something in her that forbade beauty.

He thought of that picture often. The frock had ruffles, as was the fashion then, even where Karen was. She wore a kind of bucket hat of the same white linen as the dress, meant to cool but unsuccessful in that attempt in the unforgiving climate of a farm.

Still, the distance from the lens and the total joy she took in the presence of the man who stood beside her—and would always, no matter the distance between them—occluded perceptions of the face. She looked like any hausfrau or milkmaid of rural declension with a difficult path in life.

Other pictures, other memories, showed more precisely the nature of the woman.

Why, oh why, did I lose you? Oh, why did I drive you from me?

The melancholy of it would never leave him. How could it? She loved him, so he destroyed that love out of his wantonness of appetite, his love of liquor and the company of other men, his need to play harder than he worked, and his inability, in most crucial areas of human intercourse, to exhibit a twitch of discipline.

Gone, gone, gone. Forever. Nothing would get her back. It was over, finished, gone. You stupid bastard.

The hunter shook his head, not quickly but powerfully, trying to knock the past from his brain and confront the present as it lay before him.

The smell of rain in the air—soon. The dim forms of the land, not yet illuminated. The warmth that was near July—or maybe it was July; he didn't know. A smell of vegetable and flower—and cow shit. Some breeze, but not enough to matter. Before him, a gully. Or more: a fold in the meadow, not deep but definite and exactly where the beast by natural instinct would rest.

And soon the beast would arrive. He'd heard him already, for by nature it was not a nocturnal animal, it feared the dark and was awkward in it, making bad decisions and ratcheting into panic at the slightest disturbance.

And tonight was special. Such plans had been laid, such traps had been set. This was no routine hunt. This was special, given the possibilities of the landforms. He could not fumble it and let all that planning go to waste.

But still: Karen. Tonight, for some reason, it was peculiarly hurtful, a species of pain that rotted the soul. If he could just reach through time and do this differently or that, such small things, it might never have come to what it had come to.

Her face was that of an ascetic. For she was an ascetic, but he had never had the patience to read what she wrote, and even if he had, it would have meant nothing, for that was not how his mind worked. Her face had sharp cheekbones, a sign of what one would call "good upbringing" or "good family," meaning it went way back. Her eyes pierced. She missed nothing, and when she settled on something, her eyes registered it with precision and seriousness. She would stare at it—whatever—for a long time, appraising its nuances, memorizing its shape and shade, seeing how the sun played off it, how the wind affected it, if at all. She made no rash decisions, she made no wrong decisions. Well, save one.

Why did you marry me?

They were young. The Great War and the Great Dying of the Influenza were over. It seemed to be spring everywhere, but dying old Europe still reeked of corpse rot and the same old men still ruled with iron wills and fists and self-deception amid piles of skulls and miles of graves. Both he and Karen were by nature adventurous, if each nature took "adventure" to have a different meaning.

For her, adventure meant learning, seeing, experiencing, recording exactly. Her adventure was fuel for her artistic nature. She needed provocation to function fully and express what she had.

For him, adventure meant conquest, dominion, wealth. It meant subjugating all, but preferably nature, in the form of agriculture or large beasts whose ways were to be learned and whose deaths were to be administered. It made him feel so very alive to see an immense thing crumple without noise, thump to earth in a cloud of dust. It meant something primal: The village elders will sing my praises at the council fire, my children will go to bed with full bellies, and I will fuck my wife.

It didn't matter that he was of no village, had no children, and upon return would indeed most assuredly *not* fuck her.

Thus it was doomed. Their courses took them in different directions, farther as the years passed, and what joy had been shared between them alchemized into something else, perhaps not hatred or even dislike, but at least a willed disinterest in each other's lives.

In such parched soil, how could anything last?

Noise.

It was here. It slashed him back to reality. He squirmed into the shot, checking his always-precise watch. Yes, near dawn. The sun's light had begun to infiltrate the eastern sky. Still too dark to see except vaguely, but the magic few minutes were approaching.

Movement, generalized, not specific, accompanied by, as usual, heavy groaning and grunting, a sense of clumsiness and uncertainty, halts and then irrational spurts, the movement of something that didn't want to be doing what it was doing.

It filled the hollow 250 meters before him. He saw its components in stumbling ecstasy, eager for rest and what it believed to be safety. The beast at rest. Like any organism, it spreads, seeks comfort, experiments with postures until it finds one, then finally settles in.

A whisper of sun. The edge of the star 93 million miles away. It pierces, at least to him but not the beast, who is too low to see it and hasn't noticed its presence at the tips of trees, nor the oozing glow of those precious minutes before the fullness of the disk has emerged to present itself.

To scope now. As always, a few twitches and adjustments, getting body and rifle and eye and finger aligned and in coordination, the structure beneath stable, the breathing measured, achieving that utter sensation of calm that is at the root of the entire art.

In the world of the magnified, he could now make out his target. It was the head, though bent, consulting or thinking or possibly—not probably—praying.

More light. Enough. The head came up and settled precisely in the three prongs of the reticle, and without willing it, for at this level will had been vanquished, to be replaced by pure if cultivated instinct, the trigger seemed to fire itself, the rifle jumped—a bit, not much, such were the glories of the cartridge—and resettled, the flash subsumed itself at atomic speed, the noise echoed, diffusing, amid trees and leaves and embankments shrouded in ground cover, and he could see his target hinge to earth, toppling like a statue in a revolution.

The American boys panicked. He knew they would. The death of their leader—sergeant, lieutenant, major?—terrified them. In seconds they had vanished and would by instinct race across the meadow to the streambed where there was more cover and a deeper trough. There they would gather, a second-in-command would settle them down, and a new course would be set.

The Germans had set their machine gun well. He himself had picked the spot. It was an MG-42. Only one burst was needed.

CHAPTER 28

Rain

The rain came. And it stayed. Unusually for this or most years, it rained and howled for four days. The world became a swamp, a green bog not fully on land, not quite underwater. No planes dared fly, ships lay far off, away from the potential wreckage of the littorals. Most patrolling halted.

The fucking Germans, of course, would endure it better. They'd had plenty of time to prepare and were by inclination war beavers, always building sophisticated, watertight fortifications, caparisoned under wet-weather gear that actually worked—their fucking garment engineers out-designing the Americans again—and saw the rain as a godsend, a vacation from war. If they were laughing earlier, by now they'd be positively in the aisles with joy and delight, as well as warm and toasty.

For Leets and Swagger, it turned the tour of the front and the interviews with the sniper survivors into an ordeal by mud—it looked like churned brown cement—and crappy American rain gear. The rubberized poncho was so poorly put together that it leaked everywhere, ripped if you turned or got up or down in it, kept coming unsnapped, and, no matter what, allowed a funnel of cold water to sluice perfectly into the neck of the shirt it meant to protect.

At least the guns were dry. The Thompsons were secured in green canvas zip-up carry bags that, given the irregular shape of the weapons, looked like giant worms a giant person had squished on a giant sidewalk. They lay in the well of the driver's-side rear seat, next to Leets, who always kept a protective hand on them. They were the most efficient part of the enterprise: the guns were in better shape than the two men who might use them and who spent their time hunched in misery as the spectacle of America at war unspooled beyond the heavy transparency of the plasticine jeep windows.

Even with the banty old First Sergeant McElroy behind the wheel—his face looked like leather pounded by rocks and stretched hard over bones—progress was slow, sometimes impossible. Before them on every road, the great machines of war foundered, slip-sliding into gullies, rooted in a gravy of earth and rain, clogging the roads, turning the Normandy front into a version of Times Square on a rainy rush-hour Tuesday when the subway workers were on strike. Nobody got anywhere fast, or sometimes even slow, or sometimes even at all.

"Uhhh!" screamed Leets, shoving desperately against the back angle of the vehicle—Major Swagger was on the other rear corner—hoping against hope to somehow nudge it onto ground dry enough for traction. No luck. He slipped, driving his knee into the cold French sludge that crept and oozed everywhere.

"Come on, Leets," called Swagger, who'd largely ignored the inclemency. "Give it another shot." Then he called, "Top, almost ready, as soon as the lieutenant gets his ass out of the mud."

"It's my fucking hip," Leets clarified, "for about the ten thousandth time today. It hurts like hell."

Somehow the tires bit, spewing spurts of wet slop upon each man, the bantam car leaped ahead, and Leets and Swagger managed to get aboard, seeking shelter under the vehicle's canvas canopy, though it too was so poorly designed and constructed, rivulets of cold rain slipped in, and there was no position in which one or more of them didn't land upon and penetrate the passengers. Meanwhile, the windshield fogged, the wipers cranked sluggishly, and the thing made signals of defeat, as if its plugs had drowned, screaming, in the surf.

"Okay, Major," said the old sergeant, "just a few more miles to the 4th Infantry. We'd best bunk there tonight. By night these roads are going to be impossible."

"That would push the 9th to tomorrow and then on to VIII Corps not until day after," Leets said. "Even if it stops pouring tomorrow, the roads will still be a wreck."

"Okay," said Swagger glumly. "I don't want to get mashed by a Sherman in the dark. Who'd that help except the Germans? And Major Tyne."

Yesterday, a runner caught up with them at the VII Corps tent village and delivered two top secret radio teletypes.

The first was from SHAEF HQ in Bushy Park, subdivision G-2, from the notoriously well-connected "Colonel" Sebastian.

"Is there a closed door in England that kid can't talk his way through?" wondered Leets, opening it.

SIR, it said,

RUMOR HAS IT TYNE HAS BROUGHT CONGRESSIONAL HEAT TO 70 GROS. SOME NY POLITICO HAS AUTHORIZED HIM TO CONDUCT AN INQUIRY INTO ROGUE OSS UNITS, BUDGET OVERRUNS, LACK OF ACCOUNTABILITY WITHOUT TANGIBLE ACCOMPLISHMENTS. COULD LEAD TO BIG TROUBLE; COL BRUCE CAN PROTECT YOU FROM EVERYBODY BUT US CONGRESS.

SEBASTIAN

"Tyne is a bigger fuck than I thought," said Swagger.

"Can he do this?" wondered Leets.

"Only if we let him," said Swagger, opening the second. It had arrived, of course, three hours after the initial one from Sebastian and was from Colonel Bruce himself, warning of the same impending catastrophe, and closing with the worried admonition, I'LL DO ALL I CAN BUT NOT EVEN IKE CAN STAND AGAINST CONGRESSIONAL AUTHORITY.

"What do we do?" Leets asked.

"Our jobs," said Swagger.

"Hope we come up with something big in the next few days," said Leets.

That seemed unlikely. What they had so far found was far from the anticipated intelligence gold mine. The survivors of the sniper attacks had jangled memories, often contradictory. They couldn't locate the sites of the incidents. Even if they could, the rain had obliterated any tracks, swept away spent shell casings, rearranged foliage that might have been prearranged for a shooting position. No one was even sure where the shots had come from.

The stories were the same. A sergeant or second lieutenant's head suddenly devastated by a bullet out of the dark, hitting just under the lip of the helmet. Panic, confusion, abject flight on the part of the suddenly leaderless patrol.

Sometimes most or even all made it back, sometimes not many. A rumor was currently circulating that an entire squad had been annihilated by a machine-gun team working with a sniper who'd put down the leader and, presumably realizing where the men had to go for shelter, had arranged for the MG-42 team.

"This is the first sophisticated thing they've done," said Swagger. "They're working in tune with other units. They're learning."

He paused.

"It also means—possibly—they have very good intelligence up front."

Leets said nothing. He had no opinion. He simply nodded, as if gravely considering the situation but had no read on the possibilities.

Just to provoke him, Swagger said, "Could the Germans have a spy in SHAEF?" when they got settled that night at the 4th Infantry HQ tent compound. The rain beat down, a cold wind turned the night to frozen misery, and all sane men were under cover.

"My guess," Leets finally said, "is probably not at this level. Planning at the squad patrol level is all improvisation. The CO looks at a map, consults with the XO over which company to send on that night's patrol, and the company commander decides which platoon and the platoon leader decides which squad. Or maybe they mix 'em up, combine them. Or maybe they've got special guys who like the patrol game because they get to sleep late and it's a lot more fun than shivering in a hole on the line."

"Go on."

"So that info is ripe for just a few hours, and only in company quarters. It probably doesn't even exist at SHAEF HQ. Why would General Eisenhower have to know that 3rd Squad, 2nd Platoon, Baker Company, 3rd Battalion, 4th Infantry, was heading out a thousand yards to an unnamed creek on a map, following it for one mile, then setting up a watch post on Old MacDonald Road to see if there were any night panzer rearrangements ongoing? Third Squad does its job and gets back at 0600, and at that point the info is moot. To get it into play, someone in Baker would have to know and have secret communications across the line to the Krauts, who in turn would have to be set up to move fast."

"That's solid," said the major.

"Not enough time," said Leets. "And since it's happening all over, they'd have to have spies in every platoon in Normandy. Ridiculous. It's gotta be radio intercepts. It's a game they're really good at. Somehow they're reading our sector orders and getting the info to these specialized night snipers fast. Maybe it's some new technology."

"So I guess we'll forget that tangent. We're not in the spy-catching business, are we? We don't know jack about radio games. We can just send memos when we get back. For now, we'll just settle on what's in front of us."

What was in front of them, next day, were nine bodies. Yes, the rumors were true. An entire squad plus the platoon leader, a Second Lieutenant McMurchison, had been wiped out. That afternoon, a patrol in force, complete with mortar crews, two .30 machine-gun teams, and a couple of bazookas, had recovered the bodies, though not without incident. A brisk firefight erupted, nobody in olive drab got seriously hurt; maybe some of the players in *Feldgrau* did, but who knew?

By the time Leets and Swagger got there—they had to retrack their journey back to the VII Corps sector and the 4th Infantry area of operations—all nine lay under ponchos. Some guys from Graves Registration were due in to take them onto the next step of their voyage into the earth, but for now it was peaceful. The rain had stopped at last, a wan sun reluctantly pushed wan light through wan clouds, and the world was mud-gushy, sporting puddles and foot and tire tracks everywhere in the goo.

The CO, a Captain Melville, met them.

"You're the G-2 experts?"

"We're not expert yet," said Swagger. "We're still trying to make sense of all this ourselves. Maybe they can tell us something."

"Well, I wish I'd had time to put them in a tent. I don't want our guys to see you poking around with the bodies. Bad for morale."

"Got it, Captain," said Swagger. "Nothing unseemly. Just want to look at the wounds. Maybe you have a sergeant who can briefly pull back each poncho for our check, then cover up. Be done fast."

That made some sense and the captain seemed to appreciate the offer.

It went quickly. The men had been stripped to G.I. underwear, as no army in the history of armies can allow its dead to be buried in reusable uniform and gear, and lay behind the headquarters tent. Swagger and

Leets did their work, aided by an unnamed staff sergeant while the captain and his XO stood by.

The sergeant snapped off the poncho halfway, to reveal each dead kid. All so young. Most died with eyes closed, faces at rest. The wounds were high-velocity, chest or belly, leaving small trace except for raspberry sherbet–soaked G.I. undershirts, since the German 8mm Mauser moved so fast, it usually produced a through-and-through smallish entry and exit punctures, massive blood loss, but not much in the way of blown-off limbs or blown-out chests.

Swagger merely said, "Mauser. Okay, next," and moved the train along until at last they came upon Second Lieutenant McMurchison.

Different. Headshot from behind, the bullet producing a tidal wave of pressure as it passed through the skull, and it was the pressure that erupted on the other side, the face, not so much the bullet. Looking at the face was not easy; it had been rearranged, all features now askew and unrelated to other features, identifiable by shape but not location. A cavity, disclosing hideous gobbits in unnameable colors, frags of bone, an eye missing entirely, tatters, blobs, and noodles of tissue, also in odd colors, the remaining eye drained of meaning and spark.

"Have to look harder here," he yelled back to the CO. Then, to the sergeant: "Lift the head, please."

The sergeant did, and Swagger bent to push through the hair. Entry wound, seemingly dime-sized, small, black, hidden in tufts. If you wanted, you could have put something narrow, like a pen, through it, into the skull. Swagger bent, and examined yet more closely.

"Leets, take a look."

Leets did. Saw nothing out of expectation, from a few blood rivulets disappearing into the young officer's hair to a slight inward beveling of the wound itself, signifying its direction and identifying it comprehensively as entry, not exit.

"What do you see?" asked Swagger.

"Straight-up entry."

"Tell me if I'm going blind or not. Is it possible that hole is of lesser diameter than we might expect? Smaller than 8mm Mauser, I'm thinking. The 8 runs .324 in diameter, a little bigger than our .30, which goes .308. That's looking to me just a bit smaller, maybe 6 or 7 millimeters. Smaller than the Jap 7.7, which is a .312, like a Brit .303. I've seen a lot of Jap 7.7 holes"—one in his own chest from Tarawa, he didn't mention—"and they were bigger. Or am I imagining it? You don't see anything like that?"

"Sir, now that you mention it and I'm looking for it, yeah, possibly. You'd have to have calipers to tell for sure."

"You could also pick out little bits of metal from the skull," Swagger said. "And do an FBI spectrum analysis on it, to see if it was composed of the metals of the 8 Mauser, and if not, what? But we're not FBI, we don't have tweezers, a spectrum analyzer, a laboratory. We don't even have a—"

"Sir," said the staff sergeant. "Pardon here, but I'm thinking if you tried to insert an M1 .30 caliber into the hole, you'd at least get some idea of the diameter—rough, but in its way a good indicator."

"Good thought, Sergeant. Why is it always the sergeants who figure shit out, Leets? Do you know?"

"By rights, the true noblemen of the world?"

"Or just damn good shop foremen. Let's get us an M1 cartridge. Take a break, Sergeant. Smoke one if you got it; if not, smoke one of mine."

Smokes done, cartridge obtained, all four men—the captain and the XO joining—watched as Swagger ran the test. He did it delicately, out of respect to the dead lieutenant.

No, the .308 diameter of the U.S. .30-caliber ball cartridge, suitable for the Garand rifle, the BAR, and the Browning machine gun, water- or air-cooled, would not fit the entry wound. It was close—it could have been forced—but it hung up just before the furthest expansion of what only Swagger knew was called the ogive; to the others, it was just where the bullet got fatter.

"Does that tell you anything?" asked the captain.

"It suggests whoever's doing this is using some kind of new-to-inventory cartridge. Maybe a better-performing one, chosen for ballistic reasons, chosen because that's what he was used to shooting, chosen out of some kind of bureaucratic or supply chain necessity. I don't know of any military using a main battle cartridge under .30 caliber."

"Maybe a varmint round?" said the XO. "I'm from Pennsylvania, and the shooters there do a lot of groundhog work with high-speed wildcats in weird calibers like .22-250, .22 Hornet, even one Mr. Ackley called a '.22 Earsplittin' Loudenboomer.' Fast, flat shooting, little recoil, highly accurate, especially with the long scopes they use. Just exactly what a sniper might need. He's a kind of groundhog hunter, after all."

"Damn good thought," said Swagger. "Even so, I'd have to say, this one looks too big for that. Maybe .240? Some kind of .264? Two-seventy, even: Jack O'Connor's big-elk medicine?"

Nobody had an answer.

CHAPTER 29

Maps

For Goldberg and Archer, the rainy weather got them something rare in wartime infantry service: a weekend off. Well, maybe it wasn't a weekend, since neither was entirely sure of the day, much less the month—it was still 1944, though, wasn't it?—but the effect on morale was the same. The captain didn't want to send them back to the line when word came the First Army G-2 aces would be late, owing to conditions. This was out of extreme empathy—to himself, not them. He thought it would impress important folks if the G.I.s he presented appeared to have stepped off the cover of *Yank* and knew that another few days on the line, unlikely to be attacked so their absence had no strategic importance, would wilt them hard. He wanted them sharp, not looking like the sodden, weary, hobo dogfaces of Mauldin cartoon fame, Willie and Joe. No, Jack and Gary would be smart, trim, clean-shaven, and spiffed up. Thus, he found them meaningless indoor tasks and required a sergeant to check each night that they had hung up their uniforms, cleaned any mud off their boots, and shaved clean. Basically their job was hygiene.

So he was disappointed when at last the celebrities showed up: two sodden paratroopers, by the gear and weapons, each with a tommy gun and a .45 in a shoulder holster, each in green herringbone twill that had of late seen much rain and was therefore more grocery bag than garment. He might have doubted their identity if Major Jackson, the Hawthorne expert, of Battalion G-2, hadn't been their escort, or maybe chaperone.

Intros, brief, professional, quick transit to the G-2 tent where the boys would be delivered shortly. The two sloshed through the mud indifferently. They were so sodden, it hardly mattered.

"Major Swagger," asked Jackson, "do you want the captain and me here for this? It might relax the men."

"Thanks, good offer. But I may have to get stuff out of them they haven't told you. Guys always know a lot more than they pretend to. They may even know stuff they don't know they know."

"Understood," said the other major.

"Do you have any doubts about them, either of you?" asked Swagger.

"I try not to hold ASTP against them," said the captain. "Yeah, they're smart, but not in a way that is helpful to the Army. Too much imagination, too keen to see through our games, too quick on the wisecrack. To me, the lost weapons were a red flag. I guess I buy the story. They panicked after the death of Malfo and took off to God knows where. They're not by nature soldiers, so I suppose I can get it that they didn't notice until the next day. But that happening to *both* of them?"

"I found them typical ASTP kids. Smart in the abstract, unable to figure out the shovel in the practical," said the G-2. "They did note the presence of a 503rd Battalion Tiger moving through the sector, and I'm told that was forwarded to the Brits, where I hope it did some good. They got back in one piece somehow. They're not in the ten percent who'll win the war for us, they're the ten percent who'll complain about winning the war."

· · ·

"I'm sure they're here for an update on the miracle of television," said Archer. "Or was it radio vision? Or tele radio? Or atom vision?"

"Jack, could it be about our bananas with the Tiger guys?"

"No way they could know about that. Unless they have spies in the 503rd Heavy Tank Battalion, German Army Division No. 6, or whatever it is."

"Tell me again: We didn't do anything wrong?"

"Nothing. We actually did right. We ID'd the tank. I'm sure it's all about the tank, yeah, more on what camouflage it had, which way was it headed, could we find that road on a map—"

"And the rifles?"

"It's an okay story. Stick to it. When Malfo got socked, we took off like jackrabbits. Ran like hell for six hours. Then we noticed they were gone, but we didn't have any idea where we were, much less them. Who can say otherwise?"

"Kurt."

"Kurt's busy blowing up British Cromwells and eating bananas. I doubt he remembers. Just be cool. Cool, cool, cool."

So with cool in mind, they were taken to Major Something and Lieutenant Something, who actually looked very cool: unshaven yet dignified, utterly calm, totally focused. Tommy guns leaning in a corner, cool-guy paratroop jackets, .45s in shoulder holsters, fast to hand. They looked like gangsters of war, clearly a different category of officer than the bumblers who led them. By contrast, the two privates were soldiers out of a backlot musical, all spick-and-span, unwrinkled, clean-shaven. What kind of nutty movie was this?

"Where did the shot come from, Goldberg?" was the question the major got to sooner rather than later, after hurrying him through the preliminaries.

To Goldberg, in a tent partition alone with the man, both in rickety chair over a rickety table, he was another war god. He scared Goldberg, but at the same time Goldberg loved him, just as he would have loved Bugsy, knowing that Bugsy's way was far from his, but nevertheless accepting that it was cool beyond words. The major's own skin seemed to satisfy him very much. He smoked, listened hard, didn't poke or twist, never smiled, never frowned, took earnest notes, but always circled back to this one moment: the death of Sergeant Malfo.

"Behind, sir."

"Behind relative to what?"

"Ah, I guess the gully. We'd set up there and sent some guys out to listen. I think it was twenty or so yards long, just one of those depressions or hollows you get. Next to the stream in a sort of glade of trees. So that's where Jack and I were at the end of the line. The sergeant came along to get Jack's report. Then his head—"

"Was he standing?"

"Yes, sir. He'd sort of risen, as if to go. And wham, no face."

"And you heard the shot?"

"I think so. It's hard to remember, it all happened so fast. I think there was a shot."

"Loud, soft? Close, far?"

"I'd have to say sort of far."

"You heard German rifle fire in the assault in the bocage a week ago. Those were Mauser K98s. Can you compare or contrast?"

"Maybe softer. But then, farther away too, so . . . but still, maybe didn't have the huge crack of the Mauser."

"What was the light condition at the time?"

"Not pitch-dark. Maybe a little glow from the sun, which hadn't quite risen but was starting to. No direct sunlight, for sure."

"You thought the Germans could see in the dark?"

"I did. But in thinking about it, I'm not sure it was totally dark. Shapes were beginning to come clear. Distance vision was starting to improve. He could have . . . well, I suppose, he could have just seen us."

199

"Sunrise on that day was 0541 British war time. Sound about right?"

"Just about perfect, sir."

"Now, I noticed in your report, although you didn't mention it when you told me about it, an interesting phenomenon. You started sneezing."

Wow! The guy had read very closely. Plus, he'd come all this distance to the front to ask about sneezing!

"Yes, sir."

"Any idea why?"

"Ah—" A new one. He'd forgotten it. It seemed to have taken place in a world that no longer existed. He tried to re-create the moment but could come up with nothing, only a memory of uncontrollable sneezing for a few seconds or so. He did remember that Jack had teased him about it later, slightly pissing him off. But that had nothing to do with anything.

"No idea."

"Big sneeze? Little sneeze? An *ah-choo!* or more like a stifled, wet thing? Uncontrollable? A series? A single, or did it come in the dozens?"

"It lasted for a few seconds, sir. Less than a minute."

The sneeze! What the—

"Why, typically, do you sneeze? Medical condition? Asthma? Allergies?"

"Nothing that I—"

"Try and think of another time you sneezed."

He ransacked his memory. Coney Island with Sylvia Grossman? Running from the Italian kids on Columbus Day? Sneaking down to Times Square to the dirty bookstores? Basketball in gym class and on the playground? Ebbets Field?

The memory reassembled in his mind. It arrived in sepia, as if out of a scrapbook, golden-hued, under the magic sky of towering clouds, the expanse of the green field rolling out to forever, or the Bronx at least. He remembered his father that day, so proud to have the tickets. He remembered the smells of popcorn and Cracker Jack and fresh, cold beer out of brown bottles, carried and sold by men in white uniforms. He remembered how sticky the cement had been, from generations of tobacco and chewing gum, the way his shoes stuck to it and crackled when they came loose. He remembered how weirdly mythical it seemed, as if animated by the Disney guys after the fashion of *Snow White*. He remembered how happy he'd been. Nobody was trying to kill him. And he thought nobody ever would.

"Ebbets Field. We had really good seats. My dad got them from his boss. Good game. Play at the plate, late in game. Wham, guy slides just as ball gets there, they collide, dust all over the place, and—I don't know why—I begin to sneeze. 'Gary,' Dad said, 'you missed the most important play! The Dodgers won!' That's the last time, sir."

"Dust," said the major. "Dust."

When it was over, the two were told to go to the mess tent and chow down while the big G-2 guys consulted and discussed and then brought in the battalion G-2 and the company commander.

Dinner: meat that had once been flesh of a mystery animal, possibly a gnu or an ibex. Green beans soaked in water, so limp you could tie them around your fingers. All of it heated ever so slightly, more an imitation of heat than actual heat. Powdered milk, an apple, a flattened sludge of what was rumored to be pineapple upside down cake, lacking only pineapple and cake. Coffee that almost remembered that it was coffee.

Plus, interesting discussion:

Today's dispute, over the upside down cake and the near-coffee coffee, was in regards to this significant issue: How cool was Swagger?

"Cooler than McKinney?"

"By far!!"

"Cooler than Robert Taylor in *Bataan*?"

"Robert Taylor has fifty people to make him cool," said Archer. "Swagger just *is* cool. Clearly, cool enough to be a war god."

"But which war god? Just any war god?" responded Goldberg.

"I think he'd have to be Mars himself."

"No, no," said Goldberg. "Mars is Patton. Both generals, see? This has to be some other war god."

"Then he'd be Achilles. Achilles was a major. Swagger's a major. Seems more like a sergeant than a major, but he is a major."

"I agree, but Achilles was a man, wasn't he?"

"He was a man-god. Half god. Mothered by somebody important. Dipped in magic stuff to be invulnerable except for his heel. That's god enough. Moreover, Achilles did his own killing. Ask Hector about that one."

"Fair enough," said Goldberg. "The next time I see him, I'll run it by him."

"Okay, you guys," said a strange sergeant, leaning in from nowhere, "they want you back at G-2."

They slipped into the tent, and the sergeant led them to the connecting tent—tents, tents, tents!—in which the original interrogations had taken place. They looked to formally report and salute as per regulation, but the major gestured them to the table where two chairs awaited.

"Chow good?"

"Delicious, sir."

"Wonderful," added Gary. "The best! I did have a question about the pineapple cake. They said it was upside-down. How could they tell?"

"I take it that's a joke," said Swagger and flamed him with a melting stare.

"Yes, sir," said Goldberg. "Sorry, sir."

"You know, I told a joke once. Think it was '37 or '38. Folks seemed to like it. I may yell another one too. But until then, Private, no more jokes. There's a war on. Have you noticed?"

The moment seemed to last a thousand years.

"All right," said Swagger. "Here's the deal. Go to the officers' bar and you will be permitted a couple of beers. Then go back to quarters, sleep late. Take a hot shower. Have a nice lunch. Then go to the HQ tent and pick up your new gear. Battalion is shipping it out specially for you on my request, most importantly each a roll of duck tape. Duck tape is your new best friend, your mother, your cousin from someplace interesting. You'll get two grenades. Tape the levers down, tape the pins flat. They go in your pants pockets. You'll get an angle-head flashlight, TL-122, OD with a hook. Check the batteries. Then hook it to your pistol belt and then what, Goldberg?"

"Tape it, sir."

"You're catching on, Goldberg. No M41 field jacket, no helmet and helmet liner, no cartridge belt, no combat suspenders. You don't need a cartridge belt because you won't be carrying Garand rifles. You'd just lose them. You're each getting an M3 grease gun, five magazines, three boxes of fifty rounds. Load the magazines to a capacity of twenty-eight. Don't lose them, all right? They could come in handy. You'll have a bandolier for the grease gun mags, each in a pouch purpose-built to the shape and width of the mags. Hang it over your shoulder. Tape it to your shirt. You'll have a bayonet. Hook it to your pistol belt. Tape that down too. When you get the belt fastened, tape the latch. Tape the bayonet so it doesn't rattle. You will have a canteen. Tape the little chain that holds the cap to the mouth. Tape the buckles on the straps of your combat boots. For cover, you'll be issued a paratrooper knit cap, A-4, OD, winter wear, quite warm. Pull it down over your ears. Goldberg, tape your glasses on. When you're done, you should be mostly tape. Have you got all that?"

Both men nodded.

"Can you handle a grease gun, Goldberg?"

"Er, point it, pull the trigger? Is that it, sir?"

"That'll do for now. Lieutenant Leets will show you more specifically. Archer, pay attention to your pal. Make sure he can run it, got it?"

"Yes, sir."

"Report to the company yard at 1830. We'll travel to the lines by truck and at dark, around 1915, we head out. Lieutenant Leets will navigate; he's in the lead. Goldberg, you'll be after him. Then you, Archer. I'll take up the rear. No chatter. No cigarettes, no gum or candy. You do not discard anything. Try to walk lightly. Go through brush sideways. Don't cough, wheeze, or sneeze. Don't fart or burp. Pretend you're on a date. Any questions?"

"Ah, sir," said Archer, "if you're counting on us to lead you back to the spot where Sergeant Malfo got killed, I don't think we can do it. It was dark, he did the navigating, we just followed his directions and—"

"Someone ASTP-smart recovered his map pack, Archer. Any idea who?"

CHAPTER 30

Mr. Hedgepath

The one thing you could say about Limehouse Chinatown was that it had so far escaped destruction, from either the German bombing of 1940–41 or from the county council slum clearance initiative of 1938. Well, yes, the random five-hundred-pounder, or the council bulldozer, flattened a building here or there, leaving what looked like a gap in a set of very dull teeth, but no big damage as had crushed the East India docks a mile or so down the road.

The cabbie wasn't even that familiar with it, as few in the East End, either coming or going, could afford a cab. It was gotten to and from almost entirely by tube. And, never having been there—in fact, never having been anywhere east of Aldgate Pump—Mr. Hedgepath was of no use to him. Most of the streetlights were out; few roamed the dark streets; few celebrated. It was a town of ghosts, as most of the thousand chink restaurants had closed down, men off to war as cannon fodder for the crown, women living on the army checks, the children scabby ragamuffins in tatters, with big, hollow eyes, going to scurvy on the ration card. They'd do anything for a piece of candy.

"Here, sir?" asked the cabbie.

"Well, possibly," Mr. Hedgepath said. He wore his silly army suit on the principle that an American out of uniform was more memorable than one in uniform. He was technically a lieutenant colonel or something like that. Major colonel? Lieutenant brigadier? It didn't really matter. He was serving in the Office of War Information's London station, where army rank was viewed as rather amusing but nothing to be troubled with; his job was to vet scripts before broadcast to make certain they didn't divulge anything unnecessarily, as if he had any idea what was necessary and what was not. He had been a senior radio public relations executive at CBS before the war and knew all the broadcast people quite well. This got him an office, a secretary, a small section of earnest young women who did most of the work, and a kind of roving commission to do this or that socially, at Mr. Sherwood's pleasure, the latter being the head of the overseas division of OWI in Washington. Fortunately, Mr. Sherwood didn't have much pleasure; he generally left things alone, as he too had a busy and demanding social life in America's capital. Plus a play to work on.

Mr. Hedgepath got out. He saw the sign, though no light illuminated it. WING CHOW RESTAURANT, it said. The windows had been boarded over, then covered with grating. Only a dim light above the transom signified that it was more or less open.

"Yes, this is the spot. Well done."

"Sir, beggin' pardon, this ain't a neighborhood where a Yank of high officer class ought to be caught. Not just the Judys lookin' for a quid for a quick stand-up in the alley, but all kinds of devious Chinamen, opium hounds the lot, plus wogs, Jews and Russians, seamen and fishmongers, all ready to take a cosh to the head and disappear with a gentleman's wallet."

"I assure you," said Mr. Hedgepath, "I am to be well protected."

"As you say, then, sir."

He entered, finding it as dark inside as out, at least in appearance.

It was colorful in scent, however, as from an unseen kitchen poured a rainbow of odors, a far reach from anything his delicate nose had ever encountered. No chop suey house in Manhattan smelled like this. Fireworks of various sorts seemed to explode in his mind.

"Sir, a table?" said a fellow of oriental aspect in white. Thank God he spoke clearly and not in that jibber-jabber Chinese English of the Chan movies.

"Actually, have we a bar? I'm to meet a man, sooner or later. A quiet table there would do nicely and not take up space set aside for diners."

"No bar, sir," said the man, "but no diners either. You may sit without worry."

He was taken to a table in a darker part of the darkness, a corner, and while his eyes found the proper exposure setting, he ordered a pot of tea. It came. Chinese, of course, and though he'd only had a Chinese tea a few times, he judged this one as quite well done.

Some cookies came as well. Curled crispy, slightly sweet, one crunched open to his fingers, ejecting a message on a white strip of tissue. He peered at it, could see nothing, put on glasses.

A TIME FOR NEW ENTERPRISE, it said.

Quite nice, actually, not that he believed in such nonsense. Outside, far away, a doodle hit. The building shook, some dust drifted about, and the vibration lasted a second. But he judged it to have hit no closer than Brixton at least, on the other side of the river.

Time floated by. A candle was brought, flickering gamely even if its reach was not impressive. The odors seemed to constantly reorganize themselves; he imagined a tapestry, undone, forever being respun to new design and hue. It was actually quite nice. A fellow came in, left with a bag of food. Then another. A couple of racial peculiarity—very brown but white in feature, nothing at all Negro to them—came in, sat far away, and ordered and ate quietly.

He's checking, Mr. Hedgepath thought. A man in his profession must be very careful. One assumed one would be observed leaving the cab and the street studied to ascertain if followers were present. Possibly, then, he had a spyhole, and was watching at this exact moment, searching for an odd giveaway that might suggest inauthenticity. And, actually, Hedgepath did feel inauthentic. This sort of thing wasn't his specialty. He was far more valuable in other offerings, and his handkerchief was slightly ruffled over being sent on such a crude mission. But in for a penny, in for a pound.

At last, a figure materialized in front of him and slid to a seat. Even so, Hedgepath couldn't get a fix on him. He was as dark as the place, maybe darker, dark in low hat, dark in coat wrapped full about neck, dark in scarf about the lower face. He appeared as a character out of Conrad or some lower form of amusement.

"Join you, Mr. Hedgepath? That's it, eh? Hedgepath?"

"Hedgepath, yes," said Mr. H. "And you are . . . ? I was not given a name. Only the number I called."

"Raven."

"As in *the* Raven, from a radio serial or such?"

"No, Raven, as in Phillip Raven. Just a name. It'll do for now."

Mr. Hedgepath was relieved. So far, so good. Nothing tricky here. Seemed straightforward. No code words, signals, secret handshakes, shoelace codes; just everyday practices.

"Are we ready to proceed?" he asked.

"You seem nervous."

"I am not used to business such as this."

"It's quite commonplace, I assure you. Please, finish the tea, order more. The chinks know how to brew tea, eh?"

He nodded, seemingly to no one, but instantly another pot was delivered and his cup was placed.

"Not sure how this works," said Mr. Hedgepath. "Do you start or do I?"

"You, I think. But not the issue for tonight. Instead, speak generally as to who and what you do by day. I may check some things."

"Of course," said Hedgepath. He launched into a rather tedious account of his career, its various ignominies and failures, the plots against him, the taunts he had to endure from those who suggested he was not quite right. Finally, he got to his favorite time, the drift to radio after the newspaper and publishing house miscues. There, nothing was held against him and he flourished, meeting the cultured artistic set of the big town, writers, artists, film people, all of whom welcomed him for what he could get them. Some of them may have actually liked him. Then he saw the light. Gave him purpose, and when a chance to join the true elite came along, he could not have said no.

"And now," said Mr. Raven, "high-power Yank officer."

"Hardly. Nobody pays us much mind. But it's fine. I can help in many ways and this gives me a chance."

"All right," said Mr. Raven. He paused, poured tea, sugared it, creamed it, had it. Took a fortune cookie.

"Let's see what the Chinese predict."

A TIME FOR NEW ENTERPRISE, it said.

"Excellent. You may proceed."

"I think they all say that," said Mr. Hedgepath.

"Be that as it may, we shall take it as a blessing from the Buddha himself. So. Proceed, please."

"There is a fellow who seems to be stirring up trouble for us in certain areas. I have his name written down. He is at the front now but will return shortly."

He took a folded piece of paper out.

"To remove him administratively would take time, energy, finesse, all of which are in short supply. It would also be ugly. Therefore, we turn to other means. You are the other means. Highly recommended, I might add."

"He is American?"

"Yes. An officer, a hero, a man with a bright future ahead. Handsome too."

"I do so love working with the handsome ones. They have too much. More, they have no idea of how the ugly or maimed suffer. Their destruction is always a satisfaction."

He pushed down his scarf and leaned into the flickering circle of candlelight.

It explained everything—or perhaps nothing. Deviated septum. Man with a crack in his face. Exiled forever from daylight. The discontinuity of the upper lip under the nose exposed a ragged dark delta of teeth and gums. It was hard to look at. Harelip, it was so cruelly called. It meant a life without love.

The scarf came back up.

"So the doing of it will be no problem morally," he said. "The only problems are technical. Well, and the fee. You know of it?"

"I do," said Mr. Hedgepath.

He pushed an envelope across.

Mr. Raven opened it, counted the notes inside without removing them—much practice at this, it seemed—and said, "Bought and paid for."

CHAPTER 31

Commando

I t turned out to be the crank that had him so worried. So worried, he
made no jokes about the phallic nature of all this war stuff, which he'd
already filed away for his first television script. Anyhow, the gun itself was
considerably lighter than his nine-and-a-half-pound Garand rifle, shorter
too, easier to handle, especially with the stock retracted.

A wartime rush job built actually by an automobile manufacturer,
it was just an assortment of stamped metal parts welded more or less
together in a hurry. It had a Hey-kids-let's-build-a-machine-gun! look
to it, the complexion of a hand grenade and the grace of a coat hanger.
Lieutenant Leets had shown him how to make it go bang, or rather
bang-bang-bang: first, pop the ejection cover; second, grab and rotate the
crank, pulling it back and down until it locked; third, pull out the stock.
Then point and bang-bang-bang, bursts of .45 sent downrange, probably
best to hold to three-round sprays, as the gun, like any other automatic,
rose higher and higher with sustained bursts.

Yes, fine. Yes, all commando, ears covered by watch cap, glasses taped
on, everything else taped so that he felt like the Mummy: he made almost

no noise at all, looked cooler than he'd ever hoped to look, his M3 grease gun sling looped over his shoulder, one hand on the pistol grip, the other on the thirty-round magazine filled with twenty-eight rounds, his face smeared with a commando's burnt cork.

"But what if I'm not strong enough to crank the crank?"

"Pretend like you're cranking your other crank," said Archer, always willing to go low for a laugh in the cheap seats.

"Ha-ha," said Goldberg. Then he turned to the lieutenant.

"I'm not exactly football material, sir. I'm not sure it—"

"Let's see how you do."

So he tried it, under the lieutenant's gaze.

Ooof! Acchhh! Ughhh!

Not the easiest thing but, with effort, doable, he supposed.

"I think that, if it comes to a firefight, you'll find your muscles fill with energy. You'll be much stronger, Goldberg. Don't worry, it'll be all right."

"Maybe crank it now?"

"Not a good idea," said the lieutenant, who, unlike Achilles/Swagger, seemed somewhat human despite the authority and experience. "You could trip, a branch could catch inside the trigger guard, you might have an involuntary seizure or flinch—even one of those famous sneezes—and suddenly you're hosing down the bullet garden with .45s, maybe hitting me just ahead of you, and certainly you notifying the Krauts that they've got trespassers."

"Yes, sir."

"Goldberg, you can do this thing. I know you can."

"He's got stage fright," said Archer. "This is a new role for him. He doesn't have any material for it."

"In the Army," Goldberg said, improvising for his debut as "Kid Commando" on the Bob Hope television show on NBC, "when they told me I was getting a grease gun, I thought that meant I'd be working in a garage. Instead, I ended up in a war!"

"That's a start, Goldberg," said the lieutenant, giving him the ghost of a smile, real or just a fake morale builder; who could tell?

So now they crept through darkness, trying to be silent and efficient. Leets led, Goldberg was second, next came Archer, and finally that sphinx of masculinity, taciturnity, and implacability, the war god Swagger, who said nothing to anybody and looked as familiar with his Thompson as a golfer would with a club.

They moved along in the dark, close to a hedgerow, and—upon reaching its termination in another hedgerow—slithered through and over carefully, fighting to keep breath low and effort minimal. No grunting, heaving, sighing. The key was noise, which was death, was to be avoided at all costs.

"These guys work off of noise," the major had said. "That's how they initially make contact. No noise, no contact, no sniper. Get it, guys?"

"Got it, sir," both kids had said.

Was the route familiar? Ah, hard to tell in the dark. It was like invading a dreamscape, taking a tour of a nightmare. They confronted the maze of field and hedgerow made more baffling by the shield of darkness, under a moonless sky, a vault full of stars, now and then a sunken road or a creek, both to be negotiated carefully. A small roll of hill, a zone of rocks, the ghostly specters here and there of cattle standing in the dark, some low cow sounds or shuffling, the stench of their shit. Occasionally, from the universe next door, the brisk sputter of small-arms fire, muted by distance. A flash, a rumble, not the weather of nature but the weather of man. Nature was gentler tonight, providing a soft breeze, a temperate climate, all sorts of niceties that unfortunately had to be ignored due to the exigencies of the situation.

Now and then the lieutenant would call a halt. Not for smoking or resting or drinking from a canteen but for map-and-compass check. The major would scoot forward, he and Leets would bend low to the ground and consult their instrument and document under the carefully disciplined light of the angle-head flashlight held close to both, they would chat briefly, then the major would return to his tail gunner's position and the group would begin its travels again.

Goldberg kept thinking, When, exactly, did I volunteer for this?

It made no sense, it made no sense, and then, suddenly, it made sense.

Archer achieved the same insight and tapped him on the shoulder. The lieutenant's fist came up, stopping the parade.

Yes, it was just ahead now as things organized themselves and in so doing clarified and provoked images long thought gone.

A glade of low trees and, barely visible in the dark, what seemed to be a kind of trench bulked up on one side. It touched some chord in his memory, as if from a dream or another life recalled. Beyond that would be the creek. Listening now, all heard the slow gurgle of the water. They were there, but that also meant that, by the index of a month ago, the German lines were four hundred yards or so beyond them, once over the creek.

The major kept them still for what seemed like hours. He listened, he looked. Then he gave Leets the nod, and the lieutenant edged through the trees and slipped into the gully. Then Goldberg, then Archer, then the major. The officers kept them at the farther end of the gully—*depression* was more like it, Goldberg saw, realized it had acquired depth and length in his dreams—and kept the no-talking discipline. The major stationed himself behind and took watch. He had good eyes. He could see stuff nobody could. He was looking for movement, listening hard for ding or clink or cough, and it occurred to Goldberg that he had diagnosed the sniper's method as based on following in the dark, not waiting for an interception. That would explain the emphasis on noise discipline too.

Evidently satisfied nobody was on them, he turned and the four folded back down the gully. They halted two-thirds of the way down and went into infantry squat.

"Okay," whispered the major. "Where, exactly, was the sergeant standing when hit? Can you remember?"

It was Archer who scooted down a bit, hunching near the end of the depression.

"I'd say here. Gary, right?"

"That's it," said Goldberg.

"So like this?" asked the major, and he put himself in the late sergeant's position, standing.

"Yes, sir," said Archer. Like Goldberg, he was wondering what the fuck this was all about.

"And you were . . . ?"

Each man re-created his position on that night. What was this macabre bit of war theater about?

"So that's where you were when you started sneezing, is that right, Goldberg?"

"Yes, sir."

"Sure?"

"Well, maybe more like this," he said, and squirmed backwards, relocating about a foot.

Leets's flashlight startled the infantrymen. He held the cone of light tight to the ground, defining a certain space of raw earth, finally to a slight uphill to an edge, and then the trees took over.

"That would be it," said the major.

He called them together.

"Dust," he explained. "That dust made you sneeze, Goldberg. It hadn't rained in a month. That means the bullet that hit the sergeant probably deflected downward and struck the dry dirt. It yanked a cloud of dust in the air. We're here for that bullet."

That was enough talk for the major. He grew bored with talking easily, it seemed. Lieutenant Leets took over.

"Okay, carefully lay down your weapons. Carefully untape and withdraw your bayonets. Then carefully creep to the area just defined. Each of us will take a quarter of the sector. We believe that, having traveled through the head and two walls of skull, it has lost a lot of velocity, and so, when it hit, it probably didn't go that deep. No use looking for disruptions in the dirt where it struck, as the rain turned all this to mush over the last week. Slow, smooth scrapes, like a road grader. You're probably looking for something very un-bullet-like. It'll be crunched, ripped, maybe even blossomed into a kind of flower. It may have broken into smaller chunks. That's what happens when bullet meets bone, and this one did it twice. Also, it might have shattered, even blown up. Look for particulate. Archer, define 'particulate.'"

"Tiny pieces. Fragments. Little slivers or crumbs of metal. Possibly shiny in the light."

"Good job. *Comprenez*, Goldberg?"

"*J'entre dans la salle de classe*," said Goldberg.

"Another joke, Goldberg," said the major, who might have been exposed to high school French as well, "and I'll *J'entre dans* your *salle de* ass with my boot."

The lieutenant set up his light, low enough so the Krauts couldn't see.

It was not easy. Well, it was easier than getting shot at or yelled at, but still . . . it was not easy. Hunched, knees going numb, fingers bleeding, small of back hurting, running surprisingly low on energy after the long trek in, anxious about Germans moving about in the dark, they toiled and toiled and—

"Something?" asked Archer.

He displayed a grimy little curlicue of metal, looking like a gilded fingernail, in the center of his hand. The major's light came onto it.

"Possibly. We'll keep it."

He removed a cellophane bag from his pocket and held it open for the deposit.

What could anyone do with anything that small?

216

Next, Goldberg's turn. Should he, should he not? It was hardly anything. But he made a noise, the major's light came onto his palm, displaying another sliver, this time not curled but straight, as if of ice.

It went into the bag.

On and on they went. More slivers, more flakes, more curlicues, in all for the work at least 0.005 of an ounce accumulation. Was this trip really necessary?

Three hours in, they were done, at least with the designated area. Still, nothing that was or could have been a bullet.

"Take a break," said the major.

The two guys slid back, taking breaths, shaking pain out of their crabbed hands and easing off their cramped haunches, but they could hear the officers' whispers.

"Do we have enough to send to the FBI lab?" asked Lieutenant Leets.

"As I understand the process, the answer would be yes. But that would just tell us metals. We'd then have to assemble a baseline of metals in all the other service cartridges for comparative purposes. Plus, who knows how long the Bureau deal would be. They see us as competitors. It doesn't matter if Ike gets on the horn and screams his lungs out. They're not going to hurry. We jump all that if we can find the goddamn bullet."

"Sir," said Archer, "maybe we could work till dawn, then just go prone here until tomorrow night. We could get the whole gully done."

"Good thought, Archer, but the longer we're out here, the more likely some Kraut-head bumps into us. We don't know how active they tend to be in the daylight. We all get killed or taken, we haven't accomplished anything."

"Yes, sir."

"Okay, Lieutenant Leets, you pick the most likely areas. We'll go over them, only deeper."

Much work. Harder, deeper, more demanding. More back pain, more finger numbness. Goldberg cut his pinky on his bayonet but manfully kept going, pausing for only seconds for a quick suction application, then returning. Everybody worked, everybody sweated, nobody talked. And nobody had any luck.

"Okay, relax for a few," said the major. "Then we'll haul ass. I want to be gone well before the sun comes up."

Without any explanation, he took himself to the rear of the gully and set up shop. Those great eyes. If there was a sniper out there, all believed and took relief from, he would see him.

In five minutes, he slid back.

"Nobody there. Okay, let's—"

"Here's an idea," said Leets. "It rained hard, right? If the bullet wasn't deeper but shallower, only half buried, maybe the water would have swept it away. Where's it going to go? Down the trench to the lowest point, where it would collect. Let's—"

But Goldberg and Archer were already at the single significant puddle of the gully, halfway down. Kneeling, they plunged hands into the water and began to explore the muck. Leets and the major joined them.

Anyone observing this ritual would have thought it religious in nature. Four supplicants worshipping the church of the puddle, bent in the concentration of total prayer, their wet, cold fingers sliding through the subsurface goop, trying to do it without disturbing the placid surface. There was no need for orders here; all knew by instinct that too much disturbance could destroy the thing's delicate resting point, drive it deeper, out of touch or reach. It just went on and on and on—

"Hey," said Goldberg. "I think I got—"

He lifted his treasure. It was a piece of gravel.

"Nice try," said the major.

"Okay," said Archer "Okay, I got—shit, it slipped, it's got to be . . . yeah, yeah, here it is."

He pulled it out and, yes, there it was.

Even before the major's light hit it, they could make out an abstraction of destruction, yet sustaining an odd sense of density, of being heavier than it looked, as did all bullets, its streamlines vanished in the drama of its impact.

The light hit it, showing that it had somehow sheared in two upon the hit, the newly exposed face displaying its inner core of lead, the gilded jacketing cracked into slashing petals, like a lethal rose, the point flat as a boxer's snout. The base was totally gone, in some other puddle, perhaps, or flung whimsically into the trees.

"Good work," said the major. "That little bit of scrap metal is going to tell us a lot. Now let's get out of here."

He deposited it in the cellophane bag, the bag into his pocket as all rose into a crouch, quickly wiped wet, dead hands on their pants, and gathered their weapons. Leets led them, same formation, out of the gully to the edge of the trees, checked his compass, and they set off through the darkness, disappearing into the dark maze again.

All, but particularly Goldberg and Archer, felt the amphetamine of success coursing through them. They'd done it! They were headed in now! Another adventure of The War successfully survived! Another day off at Battalion tomorrow, a sleep-in excuse for at least a day, and since it was a dogface habit to count the future in twenty-four-hour segments, that meant a lot.

The hedgerows fled by as if in a blur, each field navigated and crossed, each row penetrated and passed, streams leaped, sunken roads crossed, the odd fence or clump of mute, bored cows passed. It would be light soon. They were getting closer and closer.

The lieutenant's fist came up.

All stilled, went quiet.

Nothing at first. Then from far away, though drawing nearer and nearer, came the sound of a German tank.

CHAPTER 32

The Admiral Duncan

He deserved it. He'd earned it. He had performed heroically, lived up to his deep creed, once again proven his worth. Who could begrudge him? Not even his most severe critic, himself, could begrudge him.

It was allowed. It was convenient. It was appropriate. Plus, he'd filched a fiver from the money due Mr. Raven, and it was therefore affordable.

The cab dropped him at his quarters, the May Fair hotel, where all Office of War Information officers stayed, but he did not enter. He watched the vehicle pull away and quickly disappear in the night's fog. It had stopped raining, but the true London curse, that density of vapor that somehow turned yellow in the lights of occasional lamps, was everywhere. For Mr. Hedgepath's purposes, that was good, not bad. It was another sign that tonight's indulgence was meant to happen.

He crossed the street, took a block down, then turned east, toward Soho. Occasionally a cab sailed by, less occasionally a private vehicle or somebody's military lorry, but nothing of note. No American staff cars. Excellent. He felt secure in the cloak of anonymity the fog, the late hour, and the threat of a doodle dropping on one's head, which kept things quiet.

Soho still stood, though, like all of London, it had its gaps from bomb or doodle. Tonight, however, there was no danger, as the doodles had fallen on the other side of the river, where poor Brixton was getting hammered flat by the cunning little pulse-jet bomb.

No crowds, no outdoor lights, no buzz of rush and dither that suggested the presence of civilization, but still the club district of London purred on, war or not. He knew exactly where he was going.

It was called the Admiral Duncan, after a navy chap who'd sunk a lot of Dutchmen, and it had been in the trade since 1832, with all sorts of dreadful business in its sordid past. At 54 Old Compton Street, it looked to him rather like dear Judy's Oz, where most others saw a commonplace storefront dive.

He stood there watching for a few minutes. He'd seen it before, of course, on pretend random walks. But he'd never quite mastered the nerve to enter. Nerve was not a strong point of his. Doubts whirled through his now tightly focused mind, but then they always did when one gave in and did what one needed so desperately. Suppose there are other Yanks in there, or someone from the BBC whom he knew from official intercourse regarding broadcast policies? Or someone far more mundane, a driver, an MP, a janitor, even? But he thought the chance small this late, a weeknight, foggy, doodles dropping randomly. Besides, the fiver burned in his pocket.

"Bold, then, are we? Out for a blag?" a voice next to him suddenly inquired. He jumped and turned. The fellow was a boy, eighteen by the look of him, cockney by the sound of him, available by the posture of him.

"Upf, er, ah, no, by no means, no, of course not," Hedgepath gibbered in response, completely nonplussed by the nakedness of it, knowing what the slang had to mean.

"I'm trade," said the youth. "Dilly boy. Knows a nice alley. Safe from rozzers. Get you dolly soon enough."

"Please, no," he said. "I'm not here for that."

"No, and Jerry ain't dropping buzzies on our arses neither, is he?" said the boy. "Only a quid. You'd be wasting time and gelt at the Duncan finding a lad to molly."

"Please, sir," Hedgepath begged.

"All right, then, Yank. Hope you get your cottaging done," said the boy, smiled and disappeared quickly into the fog. "You're passing up the best queen in the town."

Hedgepath was shaking, his confidence suddenly vanished. He wiped his brow of perspiration, took deep breaths, and tried to talk his way out of the tremors that assailed his limbs. It's nothing, he said. It means nothing. Why am I so frightened? Nobody saw, nobody knows, it's all dandy. His superior officer didn't know, nobody knew. His secret was safe.

Bravely, he crossed the street and entered the Duncan.

An hour later he emerged, feeling quite spiffy. It had gone well, for a first time. Who knew what paradise lurked in such dark places? He tasted air uncontaminated by the rude English Ovals they all smoked and felt it purifying and gratifying. For once his need had vanished. It would of course return tomorrow, as it always did, but for now he felt composed, undistracted, able to face his duties with vigor.

He walked the block, bent almost into a huddle, as now and then a cab passed in the fog, and shortly he had arrived at his own Mayfair block, saw the hotel ahead, and knew that—

"Oh, hullo."

It was Mr. Raven, stepping smartly from some Edwardian crevice.

"Imagine meeting you here, chum," said the man with the cracked face from behind the dark scarf that shielded his face from prying eyes.

Utterly befuddling for Mr. Hedgepath. He was a genius at compartmentalizing. He kept his many separate lives indeed separate. There was no sloppy sloshing in deportment, and whichever of them he had to live, he exiled the others from mind totally. That was his true gift, though having accommodated the one called NEED, he had yet to find another one into which he could insert himself.

Thus he fell into paralysis.

"What are you doing here?" he asked after a few seconds of sorting through various responses.

"It seems our business is not quite finished."

"I assure you, it is. You have your fee, you have your assignment. Nothing more should be necessary. It is understood that we shall never again meet unless absolutely—"

"I'm happy to tell you that the job shall be done. Raven always delivers. That's why his fee is so high."

"Look, if it's about the fiver, I do so apologize. It was a moment of weakness. I can get it back to you shortly."

"Well spent, was it, in the Duncan? You're satisfied, then? That's superior. Your officer told me that's where I'd find you. To each his own, says a man with a ripsawed face."

"Please. My weaknesses should be no part of this conversation."

"And they won't. But it does seem that your officer values that which you are sworn to protect rather more than he values your ability to protect it. He views you now as a liability. Life can be cruel, eh?"

With that, he drove the murderously sharpened edge of a nine-inch recurve Gurkha cutting blade (called a kukri, brought back from the East by one of Her Majesty's boys in red half a century ago and picked up for a song at a West End pawnshop) into Mr. Hedgepath's raw neck, an inch below the jaw, an inch above the collarbone. It was the Ripper chop. It instantly sundered both carotid artery and entwined jugular vein. The blood spurted like a spritz from a seltzer bottle, driven by pressure from the perfectly healthy heart. The brain drained before the poor fellow hit the ground. He went down like a Whitechapel whore, graceless and loose as a rag doll, hitting the pavement with a bit of thud, a spot of splash from the lake of his own black fluid. Drops flew through the air. His eyeballs rolled up into his head, leaving blankness to spook his discoverers the next morning.

It was a silent operation, perfectly executed, another reason for Mr. Raven's higher fee structure. He was worth every penny.

He checked the deserted streets, and no witnesses lurked in the sulfurous fog. He bent, plucked the wallet from the body's rear pocket, for the necessary fiction pushing the line that the fellow had run into robbers. He was most pleased to see that the remaining bills amounted to the fiver invested in chicken gelt. It was his, after all.

CHAPTER 33

IV

Possibly the only field-grade officer in the U.S. Army to perform his own recon, Major Swagger slithered back to his boys shielding in the lee of a hedgerow about two hundred yards off the sunken road.

"Leets, map."

The lieutenant got it, unfolded it, held the flashlight low to it, and he and the major bent to see.

"Okay," said the major. "Panzer IV, maybe thirty-five *Panzergrenadiers* in support, all in that autumn-color dot camouflage, so that means SS. Heavily armed. Unusual number of MG-42s among them. Das Reich, Leets, your old buddies."

"Can we get by them, sir?" asked Archer.

"That's not the question. The question is: *Should* we get by them?"

He let it sink in. It did.

"Okay, the fact is, we have to kill this fucker. Why? Two reasons, Well, three. The first is, if we divert, we go off the map. It's Malfo's map, tight, restricted to patrol route. We go around, we enter the wilderness of the

225

bullet garden. Who knows where we end up? Maybe Berlin, maybe San Francisco, maybe hell."

He waited. Nothing. Not even from Leets. No joke from Goldberg.

"Number two: this is setting up like some kind of killing raid on your company, which is dug in about a thousand yards due west. It's not a major attack, aimed at retaking ground; it's too machine-gun-heavy and man-light. I think what they'll do at dawn is take the panzer on a beeline hard cross-country, close in to three hundred, and then open up. Tank 75s, four or five MG-42s. They'll just hose down Dog Company, kill as many as possible, then withdraw before artillery or air support can do a thing about it. A probing attack. Just part of the war of harassment. They know we're not night patrolling because of the sniper, so this is a free shot for them."

"Number three?" asked Goldberg timidly.

"It's fun to blow up tanks," said the major. "Goldberg, get that bazooka out of your pocket."

"Sir, it's in my other pants."

They squat-walked 150 yards, pausing every few seconds, following the line of the hedgerow—it was a border-line hedgerow, not as thick as those that hid paths—to the bushes that marked the presence of the sunken road. This time Swagger led, followed by Goldberg, then Archer, then the lieutenant.

Archer carried the—what? Device? Bomb? Demolition? Anti-tank thingamajig? Okay, "baseball" seemed to be the term of art.

It was strictly improvised. Swagger had directed them all to lay their pineapple grenades on the ground. Then, taking his watch cap off and opening it up to form a pouch, he untaped each lever, unscrewed each Mk 2 fuse cap, and poured from each of the eight 1.5 ounces of flaked TNT, making for a total of twelve ounces of explosive, which he carefully poured into the cap, then gathered it up into a ball. Then, of course, duck tape, the war's most efficient weapon. He wound it about the clump of explosive and wool adroitly until it was about the size of and could therefore be called a baseball. Not enough to blow a tank in the sense of destroy, but enough, if placed carefully, to disable.

"They've run some barbed wire around the thing," he explained. "I'll squirm through and get up on its back. Weakest point of any tank is the side of the turret. I'll tape the baseball to the turret low, left side. The armor's only about fourteen millimeters—"

How does he know all this shit? Goldberg and Archer wondered, but not Leets, who knew that in his off-hours Swagger went to the 70 Gros library and read technical intelligence manuals on German weapons and tactics.

"—and it'll blow right through. More important, that's where the turret traverse motor is located. It rotates the turret. I'm going to blow it to shreds. Without that, they can't aim the big gun; with no big gun, they are dead if they run into anything from thirty-seven millimeters up. That means they will withdraw to make repairs."

"How to detonate, sir?" asked Leets.

"I'll push one of these grenade fuses through the tape and material of the hat, jamming it down into the shit. I'll pull the pin, then roll off and cover low to its tracks. It'll go in four seconds. Should rip open the turret, send the traverse motor to the shithouse, seriously maim the seventy-five gun, tear out wiring and stuff, set small fires everywhere, produce a lot of smoke."

"Earl," said Leets, "I don't think the Germans are going to let you do that."

"That's where you come in. When I move to the tank, you go with me and get to the other side of the road and cover up. After the blast, you turn your attention to the Kraut bivouac a few yards out. Should be lots of confusion there, but to make it more confusing, you open up and spray the area with suppressive. That gives me cover to get across to you, and when I get there, we take off. Gotta move fast. They'll eventually get around to sending people after us, but I'm guessing we have too much lead time. Questions?"

"What about sentries?"

"Aren't any. They know there's no patrol activity in this zone tonight."

"How do they—"

"Never mind," said Swagger. "They have no idea we're out here."

"How do you—"

"Lieutenant, you're asking too many questions. Let's concentrate on making this IV a piece of scrap iron. Okay?"

They low-crawled the last fifty yards, a good ten yards apart. They made no noise, as they were taped up everywhere: no clinks, no rattles, no jingle-jangle. They came eventually to a tangle of low trees just above the descent to the road. And there it was.

Panzer Mk IV, or PzKpfw IV, Ausf. H, in the clinically insane Wehrmacht nomenclature. Twenty-six tons of tank, a little bit more than half of its younger brother the Tiger. It didn't so much resemble the Tiger as give clear evidence of emerging from the same gene pool—that Guderian touch! Squared off at all angles, contemptuous of streamline, it was an all-Krupp production number from the heart of the heart of German industrial power and brilliance. It definitely made the Teutonic all-star team, dictated by iron logic, driven by cold ambition, solid as the ingots from which it came. It moreover acquired a certain spook charisma by virtue of a convincing camouflage scheme that reduced it to waves of brown, beige, and green dots on what had to be a late-autumn background, its details lost in the rhythms of the dots and colors. Somebody knew what he was doing.

That same capable person—obviously Panzer star Generaloberst Heinz Guderian again—had to be responsible for the long tube of 75mm barrel protruding from the Gothic cathedral of the turret, a replacement for the stubbier version on earlier models made inevitable by the persistence of enemy steel. It didn't compare with the velocity and delivery power of the mighty 88 on younger brother Tiger, a legend in its own time, but it was still a formidable weapon, as all too many burning Shermans littering the beautiful countryside made clear. The MG-42 in pintle mount at the commander's hatch spoke to the same need. One could dispatch death at hyper-speed with such a weapon, easily the best machine gun of the war: Goldberg still believed it fired five thousand rounds a minute. Another machine gun lurked under the front hatch, right side. More hyper-speed death. Fuck the Germans! Why did they have such good shit?

But the problem became instantly clear. The barbed wire laid around it wasn't unspooled in U.S. Army amateur indifference but tightly strung, staked deep into the ground, extremely dense. Again, somebody who knew what he was doing had set it up, maybe the generaloberst himself. As usual, superb warcraft.

Swagger stared at it. Getting through it was going to cut the hell out of him. Well, okay, nothing deep, maybe a lot of blood. Tomorrow—assuming it arrived on schedule—there'd be stitches, bandages, alcohol smears, maybe some plasma, and plenty of penicillin. Oddly, he feared that the most. He hated shots.

"Sir," whispered someone in Goldberg's body, though by no theory should it have come from Goldberg's mouth, "you'll never get through that wire. Neither will anybody else. It's too tight. It'll hang you up and cut you to pieces."

Swagger looked hard at the wire. The kid was right. It was more a hedgerow of barbed wire than a roll of the stuff. And you just knew that the German barbed wire would be sharper, cut deeper, hurt more, grip more savagely, than any barbed wire in the world. It was probably Krupp barbed wire, fucking Krupp!

"He's right," said Lieutenant Leets. "Sir, that stuff will eat you alive."

"Fuck," said Swagger. "So what do we do, throw the baseball at it?"

"Sir," said the other person inside Goldberg, "I can get through it."

"Gary, are you nuts?" said Archer. "He can't do that," he said to the officers. "He's 115 pounds soaking wet, so scrawny no uniform or piece of gear fits him. He can't even chock his gun." He turned back. "Gary, I'm not going to let you."

Bicker-bicker-bicker.

"I can do it," said Goldberg, "*because* I'm a scrawny runt. No big guy—"

"Do you even know what a turret is?"

"Yeah, it's that thing up top with the broomstick sticking out."

"Shut up," said the lieutenant. Then: "He's right, Major. He's the only one here."

"So *there*, Jack. The lieutenant agrees with me!"

"Okay, Goldberg," said Swagger, "you're onto something. Give your grease gun to the lieutenant and dump your pistol belt, bayonet, and canteen. You're going to approach from dead rear once you're through. Carry the baseball in your teeth. Just squish it on the turret and tape it, left side, two-thirds of the way down—"

"I can do that."

"The armor is angled as it rises, to deflect shells, so don't let it throw you off. Archer, cut some tape for him. Wrap it around his thigh. Goldberg, peel the tape off, just stick the baseball on there. Neatness doesn't count. Then jam the fuse prong into the explosive. Secure the fuse housing in your other hand, but do not cover the lever. Pull the pin. We'll loosen it up so it's no problem. Pull the pin; when the lever pops off, you roll hard off the tank, and when you hit ground, roll even closer to the tank. The blast won't hit you. When it goes, you get up and—"

"Yeah, the hard part!" said Archer. "How is he going to get back through the wire? The Germans are not exactly going to be pleased the little comic from Brooklyn just blew up their nice tank. That's going to be a long ten minutes with Germans shooting at him."

"I will lie on the wire and flatten it," said the major. "Goldberg, you trample over me. Or crawl, or whatever. Then you guys pull me out, and we disappear."

"He's my buddy!" said Archer. "*I'll* lie on the fucking wire. I'm taller: there's more of me." Then he remembered it was an officer he was snapping at and he started to add, "With all due—"

"Forget it, Archer. You want the job, you have the job. Is everybody square?"

It seemed they all were.

"Goldberg," said Swagger, with what might have been his first recorded half smile in twenty-three years, "when I asked you if you had a bazooka in your pants, I had no idea you *were* the bazooka."

CHAPTER 34

Wire

It didn't hurt like he thought it would. It hurt much worse. Goldberg made it through the barbed wire hedge with wounds only to neck, back, both arms, chest, ears, hands, fingers, pelvis, thighs (both sides), calves, and shins, even one through his boot into the top of his foot. He bled about fourteen gallons. In fact, he was in so much agony, he forgot to worry about the Germans.

The worst one was a particularly deep jab on the right upper arm, so deep that it hung him up. It felt like a spike, not a barb. At a certain point he determined that he'd probably die of starvation, not German action. But then he reconsidered and recommitted to death by German.

And then he was out. He lay on the dirt of the road, breathing raggedly, gathering strength, will, and nerve. The weight of the baseball clasped between his teeth began to administer a new form of pain, to the muscle on the underside of the jaw. He'd never clamped before, so this one was a new sensation. He removed the bomb, coughing, gagging a bit, rotated his jaw to bring some life to the deadness it was currently registering, then regripped the thing. Ugh, tasted awful. Who said TNT wrapped in wool and tape made a good appetizer?

He slowly low-crawled forward. He could hear laughter coming from the Germans camping out a few dozen yards beyond the tank as if they were in the Catskills. Maybe they were feasting on bananas and about to break into a hearty round of SS banana songs. *"Yes, ve kill no bananas today / but lots of Jews to make them pay,"* something like that, to accordion, tuba and deep, rumbling belches.

Then he bumped into the tank's tread. Viewed from half an inch away, it was quite alarming. Steel, much scarred and scratched from crushing all before it, including gravel, stone, trees, dirt, and skulls. It looked the sole of the devil's boot. It stood for everything German: unmalleable, expressionless, brutish, nasty, and smeared with shit. He blinked his eyes. Yep, still there. No dream this, but reality.

Do it do it do it!

He dragged himself up, realized how gigantic this steel beast actually was, particularly when you're five foot six and 117 pounds and never made a basket in your life. Crouching, then standing, he searched for a handhold, found one, planted his left boot against the nearest available tank wheel, and hoisted. Not quite enough. Try again, more upward thrust. This time he got almost aboard, was slipping, grabbed something he hoped wouldn't explode, and pulled himself up.

More breath catching, more sweat on his face, maybe some aroma of Nazi wieners and sauerkraut from a cooking fire. Could that really be what they ate? *Really?* He kind of swam forward, across the flat back of the thing, encountering tidbits of German efficiency. Spare wheels were bolted to a rack, a grille let the engine breathe, some shovels were held in place by stout metal locks, everything was hard, metallic, awkward, all angles sharp, not a nuance of softness to be found. It's a *tank*, you idiot. What did you expect: feather pillows, teddy bears, knishes, egg creams?

He arrived, finally, at the turret. Angled, as the major had instructed.

Again, seeming gigantic. It could have used some face cream. Its raw metal complexion was rough under the handsome dappling of autumn's tapestry of color, and as he ran his fingers across it, he felt its smelted waves in the steel, its accumulations of melted seams where the welder's torch had turned it briefly liquid in the joinery of plates. Rough beast. Where did that come from? Yeah, a rough beast. Now, time to kill the rough beast.

Move slow. The eye is attracted to fast movements, so if you hurry some Kraut may just catch a trace of blur in his peripheral, turn, and you're dead. Wisdom of Swagger. What made Swagger run? Swagger made Swagger run. Always right. Knew everything. Feared nothing. Six foot, one eighty, all *goyische* rectitude and duty, boxer's scarred knuckles, eyes like ball bearings out of Warner's George Raft Department. He never felt a pimple of fear in his whole life. He was born so brave bullets were afraid of him.

Hating Swagger, loving Swagger, wishing he were a war god like Swagger, he oozed ahead, trying to keep himself both slow and flat to the turret. Funny, the thing was so rough against his chest, it kind of soothed him. Didn't feel bad at all. Who'd have thought that would happen?

The world didn't end. Nobody cried out in German, *Achtung! Eine Jude!* Instead, a loud chorus of laughter broke out. Someone must have told a really funny fart joke.

He was there, three-quarters down the turret. He took the baseball from his jaws and squashed it against the steel, feeling it mush somewhat. Pinning it with his left hand, he reached down with his right and unpeeled a strip of duck tape that had been wrapped around his thigh by Archer. It crackled off easily and he got it planted next to, around, and on the other side of the baseball, holding it tight. One more to go. Ach, when peeled, it somehow flitted back on itself like Scotch tape and the two sticky sides meshed. It added seconds to his ordeal as he carefully separated the connection, then got the strip oriented around the baseball. Seemed pretty solid. Now only the fucking fuse.

He reached in his shirt pocket, opened it, pulled the thing out. Bad news. Evidently he'd picked up some mud on his shirt somewhere in the ordeal. It had dried. Pulling the fuse free cracked a little hunk of solidified mud.

Solid mud + stress = ?

= dust.

He sneezed.

Crouched at just outside the circle of wire at the front right bogey wheel of the IV, they heard it.

Ah-choo!

Then that gulping, perhaps drowning sound of someone trying not to sneeze, but the sneeze won, and broke from him in a wet splutter of high velocity and violence. Sneezed, sneezed again, sneezed a third time, serial sneezes, a machine-gun burst of sneezes.

Someone heard it in SS tent city. The man rose, fearsome in camouflage the color of nature itself, unleashed some kind of big black gun, looked hard at his big machine, trying to figure out what the hell was happening, and then screamed, *"Amerikanische Pionier! Amerik—"* before Swagger cut him down with a burst of Thompson.

"Kill 'em," Swagger yelled, and all three Americans went into full auto mag dumps. Flashes like small stars exploding, pinwheels of brass spitting free, the noise of hell's chariots on cobblestone, the guns hammering and leaping, and each could see—not much. The fire streams hit the tents, tore up so much dust that most details were obliterated. Then it was quiet. The three reloaded, seeking targets.

"Could we have gotten them all?" asked Archer, sliding another long box into the mag well of his grease gun, pulling the cocking lever, almost exactly as the snaps and clicks signifying mags, breeches, bolts, rounds all doing in concert what they were supposed to do from the others. Lots of smoke, lots of dust. Then flashes began to explode from the obscured target area as the Germans, most unhurt, quickly slithered from the target zone, found positions at the margins of the road, and began to counterfire.

"He better blow that thing before they get their machine gun into play or we are fucked," said Swagger, then raised his weapon as German bullets began to rip the dust near them—too near them—and started tracking Kraut muzzle flashes for destruction.

The noise was so terrific and terrifying that Goldberg, atop the tank, almost dropped the grenade fuse. But he didn't. He knew from the nearness of the gunfire his pals were hosing down Camp Nazi but that he'd better get the lead out or somebody in gray would get the lead in—*him.*

But now he was surprisingly concentrated, surprisingly not neurotic, surprisingly bereft of comedy. Combat does that sometimes. He mastered the geography of the grenade fuse, a kind of metal gizmo the size of a lighter, with a tube descending from the center and a curved lever bending down one side. It looked disturbingly primitive. Still, he plunged the tube into the heart of the baseball and it penetrated and sunk with no difficulty.

A bullet hit the tank turret—it sounded like somebody hitting a pipe with a wrench—and then another. More dust, or more likely metallic particulate, but this time no sneezes. Too busy. He secured the fuse with his left hand, making certain to leave clearance for the lever to spring, and pulled the pin—surprisingly easy—with his right. The lever popped off, reminding him of toast in an MGM comedy short about goofy husbands in the kitchen. The thing began to sizzle.

Go! Go!

He launched sideways, felt gravity claim him, fell six feet to the ground, where the thump of arrival was considerable but not so much that he didn't remember to roll back to the tank, not away from it, and—

. . .

It went.

The effect, so close, was experienced more as pressure than noise, for it seemed to release violent tremors, the earth itself shivering, vibrations bouncing crazily, new oceans of superheated gas sent spurting into the atmosphere, maybe the twenty-six tons of Krupp war steel even rocked on the springs that supported it.

"Archer, get back there and into the wire. Give him something to climb on. Leets, cover him. I'm going to move in a little and burn some more ammo."

Crazy major. Was he nuts? Everybody wanted to run, except for Swagger, who saw more damage to do. He scooted forward, set up in a kneeling position about fifteen yards ahead, and started squeezing off bursts. For Archer, who saw him as he landed in a jungle of wire, he was definitely Achilles outside Troy, his darkened face lit by muzzle flash, the empties pouring from the breech of the weapon, which he held in tight control against his shoulder. Done with one submachine gun, he let it drop on its sling and pulled another, Goldberg's grease gun, also slung about him. He thus lost no time on a reload but kept up the fire, spewing dust and death at the German encampment.

Archer felt a thud, then another; he had been so fascinated by the heroics of Swagger, he hadn't seen Goldberg approach at a dead run, leap aboard his back, plant another stride just as forcefully, then leap off. It was Leets then, pulling him out of his entanglement. He felt a hundred little stabs, but they hadn't begun to hurt yet.

"You okay?"

"Yes, sir," he lied as one by one the punctures lit up.

"Goldberg, help him," said Leets as he himself turned to assist the major in killing as many SS monsters as time and ammo and opportunity allowed.

But in seconds they were both back.

"You guys okay?" the major asked.

"Yes, sir."

"You can move, right? Nothing broken, no veins bleeding out, no broken bones?"

"All good," said Goldberg.

"Okay, same as before. Leets on the compass, then Goldberg, then Archer. I'm on the rear. Only double-time this time. Let's get the hell out of here. These boys are seriously pissed."

CHAPTER 35

Vivien

For once, Millie wasn't the most beautiful woman in the room. That honor went to Miss Vivien Leigh, the film star, who commanded fealty as had the Hamilton woman she so recently played; exquisite in face and bearing, her eyes alight with the fires of wit and mischief, her form, which was long as winter and slim as a flower's stalk, shown so lovingly by a clinging green chiffon dress. Its emerald hues made the alabaster of her skin shine in glorious contrast.

She was on the arm of her husband, Larry, who would elsewise be Laurence Olivier, the other film star, and easily the handsomest man not only in the room but in the world. Cleft chin, glossy black hair, trim as a blade, dapper, charming, cleft chin, beautifully tailored tweed suit, eyes intense and passionate, and, of course, cleft chin.

Each attracted worshippers. She was recently back from a Middle Eastern tour, three months of sleeping on cots in tents, scorpions, lice, sand everywhere and water nowhere; he was editing his *Henry V*, shot in Ireland where a rousing battle of Agincourt had been re-created, to do for the home island what Miss Leigh had done for the Desert Rats. Everyone

239

had to do his bit, but Mr. and Mrs. Larry were doing so much more than their bit, it was hard, perhaps even wrong, not to adore them.

So Millie just stood smiling at the colonel's arm, filling in for his tired, ritzy wife. It was one of her duties. You could say—though she never would, as she was far too classy for such nonsense—she was therefore doing her bit too.

About her, rank, style, decadence swirled, as did pink faces, thin bodies, beauty and its by-products lust, envy, hatred and awe, which were so palpable one could but touch them, feel them, rub them. Cigarette smoke, diamonds and furs, silk and chiffon, the indefinable thing called glamour, particularly when set against a glistening style moderne of simplicity, planarity, symmetry, and unvaried repetition of elements, expressed in sweeps of streamline and shimmer that suggested the speed with which the future was sought, all driven by the beat beat of an authentic Negro jazz trio from Harlem, U.S.A. Despite the jive, the larger thing was a waltz called "The Fancy at Play," war or no war. Everyone had a tribal identity: the Smart Set, the Children of the Sun, the Colonels and Missuses Blimp, the occasional hero, the occasional genius, the spies. Chatter, gossip and slander, bitterness and eagerness, floated on air, moved about by zephyrs of ambition, small or large. Sex lurked. Well, the illusion of sex. No actual fucking with this lot. Too old, too smug, too much of a bother, all that snapping, unfastening, unbuttoning to the forties wardrobe, whichever gender.

The colonel was there at the invitation of Sir Colin Gubbins, who was impresario of Special Operations Executive, which was the British coequal to OSS. Sir Colin was there *avec fils* via his subordinate Maurice Buckmaster, head of F Section, and Buckmaster was there because his wife liked the high life. So it all occurred on the whim of one silly woman, but then, how often is that not the way of the world?

"Millie," the colonel said, "if I look at my watch, it'll seem I'm bored. Can you check yours, discreetly that is, please?"

Her neck a long and elegant porcelain vase well shown by Madame Chanel's plunging neckline, the hot thing of 1939, there having been no collections since, she had no difficulty in rotating it slightly as she reached as if to check her auburn hair and got a glimpse of the tiny Cartier face.

"Eleven twenty, sir," she whispered in his pink ear.

"Another ten minutes," he said, "and this ordeal has passed. I must canoodle now with both Colin and Buck, make my thanks and farewells to our hosts, the, uh—"

"Fitzreillys, sir. He supplies Supermarine with oil filters, she's a minor poet. Quite minor."

"They always are, aren't they? At any rate, you needn't bother to come. Just look beautiful and mysterious and all will pay tribute by genuflection but otherwise not be of bother. I've circulated a rumor that you're our office's top assassin, so that should keep the rich old pinchers at bay."

She laughed. He was always a good companion, charming, so witty and unpretentious, with that politician's gift to speak easily to anyone anywhere on the ladder. She watched him vanish deftly in the social pavane, took a sip of her excellent wine, shifted weight from one beautiful leg to another and—

"Hi, darling."

She turned.

"Miss Leigh! Oh, my goodness, what an honor it is to meet you! Why I—"

"Shush. Among us girls, it's always Vivien. Even Viv, if you like it. I had to come over. My goodness, what a beautiful girl you are. Have you any interest in cinema?"

"Actually," blushed Millie, "I was screen-tested by RKO. I just stood there like a tree stump. They gave me some lines to read and I just, you know, *read* them. I was incapable of making them come to life."

"Nonsense. I could teach you all you need to know about screen acting in an afternoon."

"They did offer me a contract. But it wasn't for me, even if I do so love movies. Obviously, *Gone with the Wind* is my favorite."

"Right. That one turned out. Not all do. Some go straight into the loo, which is where they belong. It's an uncertain thing, and perhaps you're wiser to steer clear. And what is it we do now?"

"I'm personal assistant to Colonel Bruce. I suppose I can tell you he's of the spies. There's a lot of spy people here tonight."

"So I've been told. I'm sure they're the same as the chaps who actually wear uniforms. Here in London, it's a game. All these generals and, one supposes, spymasters just want to pinch your bum. What do they think that's going to get them? And how much of a thrill can it be? I mean, good heavens, an arse's an arse, whether it belongs to Scarlett O'Hara or Lulu-Jane the fishmonger."

Millie laughed. Vivien Leigh was quite a character! How could she be so famous, so gifted, so successful, and yet so much fun?

"Oh, God," Viv suddenly said. "Darling, here comes Larry. Not to see me but actually you. If he's had a third champagne cocktail, he could be feeling quite sure of himself. He's rather ecumenical when it comes to bed partners."

"I would never—"

"Of course you wouldn't. But he can be, shall we say, difficult to un-horse in these matters. I'd brace myself for a run-up."

But at that moment, who should ride to the rescue but Colonel Bruce?

"Miss Leigh, I'm afraid I must steal my assistant back from you. Come please, Millie, it's time to go."

"Of course, Colonel. Do take care of her, as she's quite marvelous. I love a pretty one with a sense of how mad it all is," said Vivien behind a 9,000-watt smile.

He deftly plucked her from the girl star, neatly avoided the onrush of the boy star, and steered her to door and stairway all without a tremor.

Yet just the shadow of upset drifted across his patrician features. "Is something wrong, Colonel? You look upset."

"Not an emergency but a situation. I've just had word that an American officer has been murdered. In Mayfair, for God's sake. Seems to be some sort of poof incident. He was that way inclined."

Millie said nothing. Her face darkened.

"His name was Alan Hedgepath. OWI, broadcast specialist. Can't be war related, as he held no secrets, other than what Eddie Murrow was leading with. Did you by chance know him?"

"I think I met him at a party in New York."

"My dear, I must say, you look shattered."

CHAPTER 36

The Hunter

Karen, in white. She never tanned like the British women but instead freckled, so that in high summer she looked like a boy on a raft in a vast American river under her strawberry hair, her body lithe and swift, her eyes dark and luminous. Except her Negroes were everywhere about her, in love and awe, living for her smiles, for that was her affect.

Then bright sun. The umber earth. The crush of heat, the song of the insects, the crackle of the dried brush. The spoor. The tracks. The smell of blood exciting the boys. Their eagerness, his rectitude and care. The process demanded care. You do not rush when—

Gunfire pulled him back.

He blinked awake in the darkness, hearing the roar from close by. Suddenly the tent canvas shrouding him shivered as fire laced through it—a burst of submachine gun, he reckoned—and as part of the same phenomenon it left a sweep of punctures curving across the canvas where the bullets had sought him.

He grabbed his long rifle, rolled left, pushed his way out from under the edge of shelter half pegged into the earth. He emerged at exactly the moment the tank exploded. The noise was a spike to the ears of even one as experienced as he. A stab of incandescence pierced the night as the turret of the beast twisted under the strength of the blast, seemed to rise a bit, then fell back, hopelessly askew. The proud gun was useless, smoke and some flame began to bleed from the wounded steel, the smell of burning rubber as the hoses melted in what turned into conflagration.

Someone was still shooting. The air was full of the whine and whisper of bullets overhead or striking nearby, plucking dust to float and haunt the night air. Screams, echoes, wild shots, yells in German as Scharführer Ubrecht tried to impose some sort of order.

The raiders quit shooting, but for another full minute the *Panzergrenadiers* of SS Das Reich kept their fire up. Eventually it dawned on them they were shooting at memories. Everyone lay quiet, waiting for someone to take initiative, but the only initiative demonstrated was by the flame-eating SS-Obersturmführer Rothmann's beautiful machine, an ace T-34 killer that had met its ignominious end somewhere in France. Eventually the dust settled, the smoke and gas drifted, the wind blew clarity across the scene, and it revealed the chaos of post-attack: many of the tents felled, men either clutching wounds or dead, a few urgently seeking equipment in fallen tents. The air stunk of spent powder and blood.

He rose, found Rothmann in command of five men gearing up for pursuit.

"*Herr Obersturmführer*, no, don't go," he said.

"Did you see what the bastards did?" replied the young officer, his face in pain. "I lost eleven men killed outright, another ten wounded, plus the vehicle. And fucking intelligence said no activity tonight. Nothing like this ever happened in Russia!"

"These are different people," he said. "Normally, it's not like the American soldier to be so aggressive—the paratroopers, perhaps, but these are now line soldiers with no interest in heroics. So this bunch is quite proficient."

Rothmann quit fiddling with his MP-40 and lit a cigarette; the flare of his match displayed five hard-core Waffen-SS storm troopers, weapons and harnesses in place, their combat tunics wearing the dapple of the woods, faces grim with sweat and dirt and anger. It was a scene from the movie Leni Riefenstahl had yet to make.

"Whatever, they tore us up terribly and the attack is off. It's back to the lines on foot, with wounded on stretcher. God, what a fucking mess. But first we must catch—"

"You cannot catch them," he said. "They're too far gone. You'll lose control of your men in the dark. You'll make noise. Maybe they'll set up an ambush and you'll lose yet more."

"But, *Herr Sturmbannführer*, we cannot just slink away. I cannot report to our officers that we were ambushed by American devils in baggy pants or whatever who destroyed us and went home to bacon and pancakes."

"Of course not. Get your wounded to Medical. I will track them in the dark and I will make them pay."

The young officer looked at him.

"Go ahead. *Heil Hitler*, or whatever you prefer. Just kill them. Kill them all."

"Unlikely. But I will kill their leader."

He was alone now, preferring it that way. He knew the land, having daily explored and mapped it for over a year, rain, shine, night, day, fall, winter, spring, summer. He knew each hedgerow by shape and height, where its soft, penetrable places were, the organization and sequence of the checkerboard units of the meadows, how the sunken roads crossed the land, how deep the streams were, how thick the trees were in the small patches of forest that still survived from medieval times.

He didn't need a moon to hunt. He didn't need any scientific apparatus, as rumor predicted. He needed only his five senses, his ability to look at a landform and project from that a map, his understanding of how an animal in flight would read that land instinctively and make certain choices inevitably.

But mostly he needed his vision. It was and always had been remarkable. He could see at a level of detail in low light as no one but a few he had ever met. He could identify airplanes at ten thousand feet, the spin on a football traveling at him—he had been a top goalie off this gift—so as to understand how it would curve as it flew at him. But the rifle was his natural métier, the most perfect expression of his gifts.

His father was a hunter and had the gift of vision too, but it had eroded long before the old man died.

"You will surpass me," his father had told him at the age of twelve. "Every small gift I have, you have twice as large. Every strength I have, you have twice as much. You can track all day and never miss a sign. You can memorize the land and the habits of your prey, and you have the hunter's calm at the moment of the kill."

"What, then, should I do, Papa?" he had asked.

"You must leave. You will never be happy here, nor express a tenth of your gifts. Your gifts will destroy you here. All gifted men lack humility. They understand their superiority. It's hard for them to show patience, solemnity, and dignity when among the inferior. That is to be expected. Thus you must travel. This place cannot contain you. You must go where others of your skill will go, and only among them will you feel comfort. You cannot be responsible for idiots as you would be here. Go elsewhere, where the land teems with animals. Learn the ways of the most dangerous of them. Only in testing yourself against death at its rawest will you become who you can be. You will draw their blood, but if they have not drawn yours, you will not have had a full life."

He had had a full life, as his scars signified. Ripped, raked, trampled, nearly drowned (twice), his body looked like a big-cat scratch pole, which in some ways it was. But he had survived grievous wounds, secretly enjoying the agony, the blood, the urgent gravity of the surgeons sewing him back together, the life-giving relief of the penicillin. Pain was life. Death was life. He was the apex predator.

And his proudest accomplishment: a thousand! Only a few had reached that toll. It took years, it took dangers undreamed of, it took discipline, knowledge, an unrelenting sense of mission, and most of all will. You hunt the strongest, you must be the strongest. Otherwise he smashes you and your guts are eaten with glee by birds and hopefully you are dead by that point.

He heard them. These men were far more skillful than any before. They made no extraneous noise, they left no track, they traveled swiftly without pause for drink or rest. They were, as he was, professional.

Paratroopers? Perhaps they had returned. Or the Rangers who'd climbed the rock face against fire at Pointe du Hoc? Those were soldiers! It could be either or neither. Who else would the Americans have capable of such daring and skill? They were not a warlike folk and would be only victorious on an immense tide of supply that could not be stopped. But these, he thought, these were interesting.

His ears told him probably four, no more than five. Moving in a vertical line, at the lee of the hedgerow two units over. They would leave no sign, for whoever led them knew about sign, just as he knew about noise, and did not fear the night. His eyes too must be superb.

He knew pursuit was not an option. If he followed them, they would arrive at their own lines before he could close the distance for a shot. That would not do.

Thus he had to arrive before them and wait, not by any means his favored tactic. Still, one must adjust. Knowing the land, he knew the meadow the raiders traversed was aligned to take them off to the right, and if they stayed on that line, where the travel was easier and the security of the wall of brush to the left more attractive, they would travel one thousand yards to cover five hundred. His solution was simple: he would just travel the five hundred.

He raced ahead, veering off to the left, plunging centrally across a meadow, unconcerned with security. A sniper could take him, a machine-gun position could finish him, a fusillade from a patrol could down him. But there was no sniper, no machine-gun position, no patrol. He reached a road, dashed across, climbed the other embankment to find trees, but rather than detouring around the trees, as most would have done on a dark night, he charged ahead, knowing there to be little undergrowth among the scrub pines whose layers of fallen needles closed other vegetation out, and he emerged a minute or so later into a wider field. Ahead lay a line of trees, which suggested a creek, and just behind that the American line. Having examined the line with binoculars, he understood where the most likely approach would be, where they'd close in enough to issue the password, and be admitted without gunfire. There was no shot from cover. From the trees where he was, it was too far, in what would be low light. From either edge of the field, the angle was too extreme, and he'd be shooting at a moving target, in the dark from way out, the angle of deflection being all but impossible to read.

The solution: he would lie flat in the field, still as death. In their joy at being so close, they'd pass him by. A fatal mistake. But they'd halt at the streambed, feeling themselves safe. They'd put out the password and one by one slither across to that breakfast of pancakes and bacon.

But the sun was beginning its rise. A glow had begun to suffuse the eastern sky. He checked his watch and knew that it would break just about perfectly, giving him light to shoot.

CHAPTER 37

Happy

I t might have been the happiest day of his life. Better than Coney Island. Better than the top of the Empire State Building. Better than hearing his first joke on *The Izzy Morton Radio Music and Comedy Hour.*

I blew up a German tank!

That was the totality of it. He, Gary, who had never made a basket in his life, 117 pounds, five six, freckly, frizzy redheaded, 20/10 in both eyes, avoided fights like a crazy man, mocked even by Ma and Pa, to say nothing of Uncle Max and Aunt Sylvia, scared of the roar of the subway downtown, scared even of downtown, joke writer (sort of: actually, three jokes sold, total income off of comedy $12.50): little Gary, *he had blown up a German tank.*

Hero? Well, sort of. Alone on the turret, the Germans shooting at him, he'd stuck to the job long enough to get the baseball taped up and insert the fuse, and recalled remembering how to manipulate the fuse. The pin came out, the lever sprung away, he dove for cover.

The noise. Who would have thought it would be so loud? It was *so* loud. Cowering shakily under the thing, he swore he felt the earth move, heard the rip of steel rupturing, experienced the bright light of noon in the vividness of the flash, smelled the smoke, felt the heat. Maybe he was inventing a few sensations? It hadn't really started burning for a while, so maybe there was no heat. Smoke? Sure, probably, but did it actually smell?

Well, whatever. Next he was up and there was good pal Jack stretched across the barbed wire like an overcoat across the sofa. He felt fleet and graceful, hit Jack full speed, and was over in two bounds. Then he and the lieutenant had pulled Jack off the wire.

"Nice going, Gary," said Jack.

"Are you all right?"

"The only thing that hurts is my whole body, so no big deal."

Suddenly, Major War-God was there, calm, southern, fully godful in all respects.

"Let's go before they figure out we're not the 101st Airborne."

Of the next, he had only vague impressions of following the major through the dark fields, squirming through holes in the bocage, dipping down into the troughs of roads, sliding through belts of trees. He had no idea where they were going because he was replaying his heroism (Heroism? Yeah, maybe. Bravery? Suppose so. Capability? Definitely!) in his mind, and trying to figure out how he could work the experience into a routine without seeming obvious. Something like that is so much better, he understood, if *someone else* tells the story and it just gets known.

"Say, are you the guy—"

"Oh, that. It was so long ago; I can hardly remember it."

Actually, he did, and would forever remember *every single thing* about it. He remembered how high the tank felt and how he stretched to climb up off the step of the drive wheel. He remembered how sharp the steel of the rear of it was as he squirmed along. It cut his knees, bruised his shins. He remembered how slanted the turret was. He remembered the waves in the steel, the crudity of the welding, the smell of the gasoline that drove the thing. All those details . . . yet, oddly, he had no picture of the tank itself. So he replaced it with some memory shifting with the Tiger he'd seen under more opportune circumstances. It was pretty much like a Tiger, wasn't it? What did the major call it? Yeah, a Panzer IV. *Oy vey*, so much bigger than a III. I'm telling you, a Four is one giant piece of *goyische* machine. It's as big as a subway car, only with a gun!

"Hold up," said Leets.

The four stopped, as on a darkling plain. Maybe a glow to the east, where soon enough the sun would peek above the rim of the earth. Cool wind, almost soundless, no cows, little rustle to brush or trees. Gary stopped, was surprised how much he hurt. He hurt *everywhere*! Memo to self: in future, avoid barbed wire.

Major Swagger slid to him.

"Hear anything?"

"Uh, no, sir."

He asked Archer the same question, then reached Leets and the two had a whispered conversation. He gestured for them to join.

"Okay, we're about five hundred yards out. See that line of trees? Can you make it out? That's our line. How do you guys feel?"

"I'm okay," said Archer.

"How about you, Killer?"

"Holes everywhere, but I've got at least five hundred yards left."

"Sir, did you hear anything?" Archer asked.

"I don't think so. I think we made it clean out of there. Okay, listen up. In case there's shooting, I'll move on an angle to the right; then, when you hit the trees, work your way back to your outfit."

"D-do you think there'll be shooting?" old Gary blurted.

"No patrols on our heels. We'd hear them coming. One guy? I don't see how he could have gotten here so fast. But Germans, who knows? So we play it calm and slow. No sudden moves. He might not see us, but he'd see movement, and that's enough target for him. Stay low. High is death, low is life. Just this last little bit, got it? I want to get this done before the sun."

"Yes, sir."

"Leets, I'll take point. You herd these dogies along."

"Yes, sir."

They went, low, bent onward. In the lee of a hedgerow, the last one for this adventure. Ahead the trees, the stream that ran through it, and the happy arms of Dog 2-2. No fatigue. Pain dulled by the morphine of survival. A whole new world awaited, and it would be a good place for all of them.

A last bit of naked field. A little like crawling across a bull's-eye, but everywhere in all the universe, it seemed, stillness prevailed. They were completely alone with the fading night, the dimming stars, the rising sun, the softness of France in high summer before the day's heat clamped down. Even the birds were quiet.

Made it.

Got to the tree line.

"Incoming," Swagger announced, in what could only be called the paradox of a "loud whisper."

"Password?"

"Boise. Countersign?"

"Idaho."

"Okay, Leets, you first."

The lieutenant, a big man, made like he was small. As low to earth as he could get and yet still be bipedal, he crouch-walked through the stream to the sandbag revetment and toppled over. Appearing in one second behind his Thompson, he was safe. Now Archer. Same drill. No problem.

"Ready, Goldberg?"

"Yes, sir."

"No comedy, got it?"

"Got it, sir."

But comedy was gold. A line hit Goldberg. It was too good a line to let lie, and it had to be delivered at this moment or the timing would be all fucked up, and in comedy and war, timing is everything.

In midstream he rose, not far, just a bit, and proclaimed, "Toto, there's no place like—"

The bullet hit him two inches to the right of his left ear.

CHAPTER 38

Pistol

He knew nothing about guns. On its barrel the thing said MAUSER and then 7.65. He thought the first was the maker, obviously, German or Dutch or something, and the numerical must be a size designation. It was a hunchbacked thing, its wooden grip curved around the handle. Short, blunt barrel, most angles squared or somewhat squared. Surprisingly heavy for the smallness of the package.

He'd bought it from a dissolute soldier in an alley in Lambeth in 1934 at a quid ten for the tattered box of ammunition, pale brown, on which the script read SELBSTLADE-PISTOLEN and above that KAL. 7,65 m/m. That box, designed for twenty-five, only held nineteen. Perhaps an earlier owner had his own professional needs. The bullets were perfect little sparrow's eggs, each in its separate partition. Again, heavy for size, the bullets had a pleasing solidity to them. They rested heavily in the hand, and it only took a few minutes in the daylight of his rooms the next day to figure out how the system fit together, the bullets sliding into a spring-driven box which slid into the handle and locked, then another sliding enterprise, this time of a kind of cover to the thing. Draw back, let pop forward on yet more springs. A satisfying mechanistic click as the whole thing reached full potential. He had tested it on a sleeping vagabond near the river, saw enough blood to know it worked admirably.

Since then he had fired it seven times, leaving eleven more bullets. Each time it had worked perfectly and his target had been felled fast, stilled forever. His technique was simple: Get close. Then get closer. Point to head or heart, pull trigger. Then depart. It had never failed.

It wasn't always by pistol, of course, but when it could be so done, he had done so. Easier than the knife, no mess or spatter, as in poor Hedgepath's case. Much easier than the strangler's knotted scarf, no struggle, no hideous festival of choking and gagging, no bowel release at the ultimate second, no nightmares afterwards.

It was now in his mackintosh pocket and his hand had closed about it, learning its contours. Was he to use it today? Unlikely. Still it gave him comfort, and as he knew its deployment was upcoming, he wanted to re-familiarize his fingers with it.

But today would not be about killing, only watching and following, learning and plotting. He wasn't sure if the target had returned from the front yet, and until and if Hedgepath's replacement made contact, he could only go on what instructions were found in the paper that the late Hedgepath had provided in the Chinese restaurant:

He can be identified by the presence of a beautiful woman in well-tailored American uniform. She is tall and willowy. She could be in cinema. You cannot miss her. He is also tall, well-built, in the uniform of the American Army, where he is a lieutenant. He will have one bar on his shoulder epaulet, either gold or silver. He may have a bit of limp from a recent war injury. His name is Leets.

You will probably encounter him leaving 70 Grosvenor around 8 p.m. They go to dinner, or at least have gone to dinner, twice a week, when their schedules permit. Usually they walk, being young and robust still, and usually they choose a close-by Mayfair pub for repast, nothing fancy. He will then walk her to her rooms at Claridge's, where women of her position are quartered, and then return to his quarters at the Connaught. That segment of the journey would seem to be the most propitious for your enterprise.

In time, the service across the street let out. It was held in an ancient church of Anglican denomination, not far from the headquarters, here in American Mayfair. The spot was well chosen: it had that British dignity the Yanks always think is so fabulous. The get-together was a farewell to the same Mr. Hedgepath he had helped along the path to heaven. Mostly Americans in attendance, but a smattering of English, boys from the spy game and coppers, perhaps a mucky-muck or two.

She was easy to spot. That would have been so in any crowd, but in this one particularly. She was accompanied by an older gentleman, quite dapper, himself in uniform, who was quite oblivious to her charms. But Raven's eyes went to her and lingered, as would anybody's. And as did everybody, he fell instantly in love with her, and that kind beauty of hers. Yes, beautiful, yes, decent. So naturally the love was infused with and driven by hate. It pleased him to take her lover from her. It was what all the beautiful ones deserved. Her tears would be many and bitter. She would know his pain.

CHAPTER 39

Field Hospital

The jeep was ready. Leets and Swagger said their farewells to Dog Company, Second Battalion, 60th Regiment, 4th Infantry Division, VII Corps, First Army. To everyone on the outside, it seemed they had a rousing success. A German tank destroyed, a German attack prevented, intelligence obtained that pointed to success in the overarching mission that had brought the OSS officers to Dog 2-2's little part of the war in the first place. And now home by the same methods as arrival, only backward, to pursue newly uncovered leads.

Yet neither Swagger nor Leets felt sanguine about it. People die: that's why it's called a war. Even worse, people die for stupid reasons. But to die for a funny line?

"It wasn't even that funny," said Archer, before they evacuated him to the battalion field hospital.

Upon the shot, Swagger had pivoted, emptied his last two magazines into the dawn at the far bank of hedgerow, where all evidence would have suggested the shot had originated. Meanwhile, all up and down the line, Dog had joined in. The hedgerow briefly disappeared

258

in a blitz of impact dust. But a nervous recon that afternoon—Swagger led it—found no blood trails, no tracks, no spent shells, no other indications that the sniper had been there. It was as if the man had vanished.

"Was he invisible?" Leets had asked.

"No. He just knows a little about this sort of thing. Advanced field-craft. Lots of miles on this boy. He can move without leaving a sign. A dog might be able to track him, not a man."

"I thought we might find a shell casing at least."

"Doubtful. There was no shell, because he didn't eject one. They only fire once. They do not recycle the weapon, even if they have secondary targets. They have shooting discipline. They do not want us finding a spent shell. That would indicate what rifle they're using, which might tell us who they are, which might tell us how to kill them. Same thing on the headshot. Given the velocity of the bullet, the headshot will certainly exit, deviate, and disappear. No evidence. This thing has been put together very carefully."

Leets mulled Swagger's information. The major didn't give it up easily. He'd only tell you what you had to know. Who knew what was cooking away in that USMC brain?

Now the jeep was about to pull out, but Swagger told the sergeant major to hold it a few minutes.

"What's going on, sir?"

"I'm waiting for Archer to come through for me. He's torn, but he knows the right thing to do. He'll do it. He owes Goldberg."

Leets looked up to see Major Jackson, the battalion intel officer, racing to them from the company HQ tent.

"Major Swagger?"

"What is it, Major?"

"I just got a call. Private Archer said he'd like to see you. He's got something he has to tell you."

259

"Okay. Did you hear that, Sergeant Major?"

"Yes, sir," said the salty old driver.

"What's this about?" said Leets on the way over.

"He's going to tell us how they really lost the rifles. There's something funny about it, but he wouldn't spill because he was afraid it would get Goldberg in trouble, and Goldberg was *always* in trouble. Now it's time to spill."

"Sir, you knew and you didn't say a thing?"

"I've been around enlisted men enough to know when they're covering something up. But I also knew that if I poked them on it, they'd go silent and get defensive. I thought they needed room to rethink."

"You don't miss a thing, do you?"

"Wish I didn't. But I missed the German sniper," said Swagger. "I only figured it out last night. He was SS and he was with the tank because he knows the territory so well. He was going to guide the panzer and the machine-gun crews in. He was in that encampment. Too bad our suppressive didn't finish him. But once we left, he realized that he knew the ground better than we did and he could beat us back. He did."

"He was waiting for us?"

"We walked right by him. He was prone in the field, maybe fifty yards out."

"But when you fired at him, you fired at the hedgerow two hundred yards out."

"That was the one smart thing I did. If I'd fired into the field, my chances of hitting him were minimal. More importantly, he would figure I knew where he was and was onto him. So it was a little misdirection on my part. He thinks we don't know a goddamned thing. In fact, we're breathing down his neck."

"Do you know who and what he is?"

"I believe I do. I'll tell you when you need to know."

. . .

A fifty-cot tent filled with one hundred cots, a nurses' station, some low-hanging light bulbs, sides up to vent in summer, sides down to heat in winter, a red cross emblazoned on the tent's roof. Wounded men, white as sheets, their nostrils tight, their eyes rolled back. Wide bleeding lacerations, shattered limbs, internal injuries, faces in shreds, some alert, some out cold, some clenched in pain so extreme, they had to be loaded with morphine, some dead but as yet unnoticed. Nurses wandered what aisles were available, monitoring. Occasionally a doctor poked his head in. Occasionally a corpse was removed. The patient inflow and outflow seemed about right. It smelled of chloroform, alcohol, and blood.

Swagger checked with the head nurse and found his way to Private Archer, staring blankly at the canvas above him. Since it was warm, the sides were up; the drama outside of men coming and going supplied a steady roar of noise plus the continual traffic of patients in and out as the facility struggled with its duties.

"Archer."

His words jolted the young soldier, who had at least four visible bandages, two on his neck, one on each arm.

"Sir," said Archer.

"How are you?"

"If Gary were here, he'd say, 'Holier than thou.'"

"How many?"

"Nineteen, sir. None too deep. All hurt, though. A few needed stitches. Also, I think they gave me at least as many penicillin shots. I'll be okay soon enough."

"Good man."

"Sir, I heard you nominated Gary for a Silver Star."

"I did. For his parents. He won't get it, though. Maybe he'll get a bronze. All the silvers are reserved for West Point grads or generals' nephews. That's the way it works."

"I wanted to thank you. He would have liked that."

"It felt right to me too. But, Archer, that isn't why you asked to see me. I know that, you know that."

"I wanted to set the record straight. If you have to put me on report, that's your decis—"

"I don't give a damn about report. Just tell me what you need to. It's about the rifles, right?"

"Yes, sir."

"I never heard of two men losing both rifles, all six grenades, and both bandoliers of ammo. I hope you traded them for whores and whiskey."

"No, sir. We were, uh, 'captured.' The Germans threw them in a pond. Very strange tank crew. That Tiger we reported. But they didn't shoot us. They, uh, gave us bananas."

He told the story, Swagger listening hard, nodding here and there, concentrating so hard, you'd have thought his eyes would pop.

When Archer was done, Swagger said, "The Krauts pick up troops wherever they can. These guys weren't German. Maybe Latvian, Estonian, maybe Ukrainian, I don't know. But maybe their commitment to the cause was less pure. Getting you to a POW pickup point was off mission. They didn't feel like executing you. They thought Goldberg was about nine. You caught a break, I'd say."

"Yes, sir. I just thought—"

"One thing. Let's go back. You said when they released you, they had a big joke that made them all laugh."

"The guy that spoke English. He told us the joke. They thought it was so funny."

"Can you focus on that?"

"Ahhh . . ." Archer made a show of concentrating, when the word at the center of *funny* had never really left his consciousness.

"He said, 'Kurt says, beware of the'—well, that's the odd part. He didn't put it in English, though his English was good. Somehow, in his language, it was funny. It was something like *nah-jez-nik-ee*."

"Sounds like he was warning you against the boogeyman. The ghost. The vampire. Some force that wasn't part of routine army stuff."

"I thought so too, sir."

"Spell it out."

"Ummm, mostly *n*'s and *z*'s with a big *k* and *y* at the end. I guess *N-A*, then *J-E-Z*, then *N-I-K*, then *EE*. Maybe Russian? Russian guys who hated Stalin and went over. *NIK-EE* sounds Russian."

"My Russian's a little weak, Archer. But I'll find somebody who knows."

"Yes, sir."

CHAPTER 40

The 266th

Of course he had a name. Administrative protocols of the Waffen-SS demanded one, and so, appropriate to this time and place, he became Martin Tausend, that is, SS-Sturmbannführer Martin Tausend, of Sturmgruppe Tausend, attached to SS Das Reich, the armored division that supplied muscle in 88- and 75mm dosages to the German Normandy effort. Thus, as Sturmbannführer Tausend, he sat with a fellow officer at a table as the two picked over recent developments. Far off, small-arms fire stuttered, the occasional big one detonated, men fought and died, another day in the bocage, Wehrmacht-style. It was warm and friendly; birds sang, cheese ripened, wine aged, and professionals Sturmbannführer Tausend and Oberst Pfefferkorn worked things out.

"*Herr Oberst,*" he said, "Das Reich has lost a tank and eleven men killed. Worse, it failed in its objective to harass the Americans, who as we know are basically flighty troops anyhow. Such harassment was designed to make them flightier and destabilize them for any new assault formations."

"I understand that, Tausend," said Pfefferkorn, battalion commander of Grenadier Regiment 897 of 266th Infanterie, now attached to 353. Infanterie-Division of LXXXIV. Armeekorps especially for *Bushkrieg*. He was a hard-as-Krupp-steel professional, *Feldgrau* to the cellular level, a First War veteran who had stayed in the army after the betrayal of 1918, fought Bolsheviks in the streets of Munich in 1919, trained secretly using broomsticks for rifles in the Soviet Union when the two nations cooperated throughout the twenties, came into the light in the thirties during brazen rearmament, and had spent two years (three wounds) in Ukraine and eastward.

"Help me please to understand," asked Tausend, in SS camouflage, all brown spots—they looked like peas—and melancholy black waves. "As I see it, the whole escapade came about due to faulty intelligence. I was told there was no American patrol activity that night. As a consequence, I advised Das Reich no actions were necessary and his men should get a good night's sleep before the morning's fun. We were then raided, the panzer was destroyed, eleven men died."

"I must therefore apologize but equally explain with regret that some things are at play here that I do not myself fully understand. I do appreciate the fact that you have not sent screaming, accusatory telegrams to Berlin demanding my return to the Eastern Front, which I have no desire to revisit. That shows a willingness to accommodate."

"I prefer accommodation. It is my nature. And as you know, and since we are in private—"

They were in 266's No. 3 Battalion's HQ tent, twenty miles north of still defiant Saint-Lô, five miles east of the front, and between them on the table was not a Luger but a bottle of schnapps, nicely toasted, a little licorice bite to it, after the German fashion.

"—you know that I am purely military, and not the kind of political who spouts mad nonsense and worships little men in little mustaches."

He was a mild enough specimen of Aryan features himself, blond though a bit pudgy, blue-eyed but reasonably calm. He had no appearance of craziness, malevolence, even turbulence. His slightly bulky body suggested prosperity, not strength.

"I admit there was a mistake, *Herr Sturmbannführer*. But there are always mistakes, you see?" said Pfefferkorn. He had a radical scar running from left eye to ear. A Russian chap at Stalingrad had tried to bayonet him in the head and not quite gotten the job done. Pfefferkorn had finished him with three bullets from his P-38 and continued to lead his men until he passed out from loss of blood. Even 133 stitches had not knit the wound sufficiently. It looked like an open sewer. As he said laughingly to his wife, "Such is war!" He was that kind of soldier.

"I have myself been assured that our source is extremely reliable," he explained. "I do not even know who and what it is: radio intercepts, code-breaking, or possibly a wretched believer in our superheated Aryan master race pornography. Or someone with a weakness for Nietzsche. But whatever, however, whichever, his information can never be one hundred percent accurate. The complexity of modern organization sees to that."

"You are saying, *Herr Oberst*, that the American war machine is rickety, feeble, occasionally stupid. Thus, one component may not know what the other component is doing and things never happen in coordination or even for a reason? In other words, just like our own?"

"Exactly. To require perfection, Tausend, is to court tragic disappointment. You are to be commended on your success so far. Their night patrolling has stopped. Kudos to Attack Group Tausend and to Operation Tausend—your creation, I understand. We are therefore able to maneuver and fortify almost at will. It is a great tactical advantage and it is one reason that, while our armies retreat everywhere else, they do not do so in the bocage, and Saint-Lô is still ours."

"You would then recommend I view that day's activities as an aberration?"

"Please do. As I have no authority over SS, I cannot insist. So I plead: do pursue your efforts aggressively. We of the regular army are in your attack group's debt. Assure your men the intelligence blunder was a rare, statistically insignificant occurrence—an anomaly, if you will."

"I am reassured and will return. To believe otherwise would not be healthy."

"Meaning?"

"If those Americans were there by accident or coincidence or bureaucratic incompetence, then, yes, it can be dismissed. The other explanation is bad for morale. Mine especially."

"And that is?"

"That they were there for me."

CHAPTER 41

Old Man

The word reached them before they reached an airfield. Plans had changed. Now they would report ASAP to First Army headquarters at Vouilly, four miles southeast of Isigny-sur-Mer. Someone there wanted to talk with them.

It turned out to be the big guy himself, Major General Omar N. Bradley, commanding officer of First Army. Though it was late when they arrived after another stop-start adventure on the turnpike of American vehicles that ran behind the front lines, the general saw them immediately.

A lieutenant colonel of G-2 took them to his command trailer, knocked, and yelled in, "Sir, the OSS people are here."

"Okay, show 'em in. I wasn't sleeping anyway."

Shock number one: general in old West Point bathrobe, smoking a cigarette.

Shock number two: no fire-breathing, boot-stomping, rah-rah, give 'em hell guy like some. Looked like a teacher: tall, thin, bald, lower jaw slightly oversize, eyes small but fiercely intelligent. No trace of gifted ballplayer he'd once been. Only a haggard elder with big problems. The circles under his eyes looked like monsoons, the newly cracked wrinkles like arroyos in the Mojave, the slight palsy suggesting soul-deep fatigue and tons of pressure. It had been a long time since the G.I.'s general had smiled, because too many of his G.I.s were corpses.

Both Leets and Swagger came to, but the ceremony of courtesy was waved off by the old man, who had no interest in it. Behind him on the wall was an eight-foot-high map of southwestern Normandy, his army's positions on it designated by pins. It looked as if it had been stared at so hard, its colors had faded.

"Gentlemen, sit, smoke if you want. Need coffee? Long, hard pull over here, I'm told."

"We're fine, sir," said Swagger.

"I know your background, Major," he said. "How many islands again?"

"Three, sir. Guadalcanal, Bougainville, and Tarawa."

"Hard fights out there. Clearly you know your business."

"Thank you, sir."

"I'm told you men destroyed an enemy tank with improvised explosives on night patrol a few days ago. Decorations should be presented."

"No need for us, sir. I've nominated the two enlisted men with us, one posthumous for Silver, the other for Bronze. I'd be most pleased to see those go through."

"I'll make a note of it."

"Thank you, sir."

"I like initiative. It's lacking, alas, in the goddamned bocage. The first time I saw bocage, I couldn't imagine it. Remind you of anything, Major?"

"Guadalcanal."

"So I'm told. Anyhow, I wanted this face-to-face, not for an update or a mid-operation briefing, anything like that. I'll let you do your job. I just want you to know how important it is."

"Yes, sir."

"Here's the bigger situation. Ike is furious. The Brits are furious. The

President is furious. General Marshall is furious. No one anywhere anticipated being hung up the way we are and taking the casualties we are taking."

"Yes, sir."

"Worst of all, in my view, is the toll it's taking on our troops. One in four of our infantry casualties, First Army–wide, is neuropsychiatric. We have more than five hundred cases of self-inflicted wounds. Marines could take this pressure, as I'm sure you know, Major, and so could paratroopers and Rangers. But draftees who were behind a plow or a soda fountain six months ago are finding it difficult."

"Yes, sir."

"Sniper fear is everywhere. There are many ways to die in battle, gentlemen, but for some reason the sniper causes particular terror, particularly among fresh troops. I almost issued an order to execute any enemy snipers on capture, that's how serious I am and how badly they are hurting us. Did you hear of that?"

"I did, sir."

"So I'm just saying to you, if you've been going one hundred miles an hour, now you have to go one hundred and fifty. If you're working twenty hours a day, now you have to work twenty-two. If you need any logistics support—travel, firepower, cooperation from other commands, ours or the Brits'—let me know and I'll see it happens fast. But I need some sort of sniper victory—not sure yet what form it'll take—to give to my people."

"Yes, sir."

"I won't trouble you with details, but we've got a big breakout operation coming, new strategy, new weapons, new cooperation with the Air Forces, a whole new ball game. But all that comes unglued unless the line troops believe they're not about to be shot in the head by a mystery man who can see in the dark."

"We'll get it done, sir," said Swagger.

. . .

As they walked to that night's quarters, Swagger said, "Assuming we get back tomorrow on sked, you take that girl of yours out to dinner or something. Then, the next morning, have Sebastian drive you to Scotland Yard's ballistics lab and see what they can tell you about the composition of the round we recovered."

"Yes, sir."

"Do you have a friend in Brit intel? One of those fancy guys who's a duke or a lord or something?"

"I know a lieutenant named Tony Outhwaithe. Another Jed. Smart guy. Trained with him. He's back in London at MI6."

"Good. Get him to take you to some kind of foreign language department in Oxford or that other one. I'll have a word for you to translate. Not sure which language. Have to know what it means not just exactly but casually, in a joke, an old wives' tale, a fairy tale, something like that. Can you do that?"

"The etymology. Yes, Major. Of course."

"In private, drop the 'Major' bullshit. 'Earl' is fine. By the way, you did real good out there. You're a good officer, Leets."

"Thank you, Earl. But can I ask something?"

"Sure."

"Here's what I don't understand. You could have told General Bradley about the business with Tyne, and Tyne would be on his way to India tomorrow at dawn. Yet you didn't."

"Because if I do that, then I'm Bradley's boy. No idea how that plays. Maybe there's a Patton faction that hates Bradley, wants him out, and so their cooperation with us goes away. Maybe his reputation scares people so much that they hide rather than risk screwing up. We'll take care of Tyne ourselves when the time comes."

The time had come. Upon reaching their quarters, a runner brought by three radioteletypes. At 2342 hours, Colonel Bruce had informed Swagger to report to his office at 10 a.m. two days hence. At 2117, Lieutenant Fenwick told Lieutenant Leets that Tyne had "photos" and was boasting they would doom his career. And at 1722, "Colonel" Sebastian told them not only what Fenwick and Bruce told them later but that Congressman Mulrooney had flown in as the enforcer.

Part Three

AIRSTRIP ONE

CHAPTER 42

Coach & Horses (II)

The man with the cracked face watched them emerge from her hotel. They walked slowly, as lovers do, shoulders rubbing, heads down, voices low and intimate; he seemed to loom over her, as if offering protection. He, particularly, looked exhausted; his fatigue could be read in the tentativeness of his gestures, the suggestion of infirmity in his step. The front had therefore been an ordeal for him.

This was all to the good, thought Mr. Raven. His reflexes would be slower, his attention less persistent, his energy much lower. In the aftermath, Mr. Raven would disappear into Mayfair's alleys, find a tube station, and head back to his rooms in Limehouse, enjoying the imagery of the beautiful woman's grief. He expected there might be a service for this Leets, as there had been for poor Mr. Hedgepath. He might attend, just to view from across the street the delicious ruin that afflicted her. How nice that would be!

He stayed well back, on the other side of the street, as they drifted, though not without destination. It was a certain pub not far away. They entered. A nice glass of stout for relaxation, perhaps something light to eat, then he'd walk her back to the hotel, and hence to his own hotel. That was where the intercept would take place. He'd scouted it already, worked the details in his head. He'd be beyond the big building, but not by much. Leets could only arrive on Grosvenor from one direction and would be spotted a block away.

Mr. Raven would time it perfectly. He was clever with details such as this. He'd walk toward him, head down, a dowdy little Englishman in bowler and absurd overcoat, and they'd pass on the sidewalk. Maybe a "Sir"/"Guv'nor" exchange in homage to the affinity of America for Britain would pass between them. One step past, he'd spin as the Mauser came out of his pocket, lurch forward to place it near the back of Leets's head, and fire. Then it was another quick spin, a departure down an alley off Grosvenor and then into the greater maze of London. Job done, money earned, a victory for himself over the whole world in the sense of the world of the undamaged.

He headed for Leets's hotel, the Connaught, to put himself in position well in advance of the action. It was always better to be early than late.

Since it was always OSS night at this particular pub, that's where Leets took Millie. No Irish tribal gathering in the rear tonight, no waves of gossip riding the smoky air, just a lot of tired spies hoping for a brew and a plate of chips to drown their troubles before another tough four-hour day tomorrow, plotting, plotting, plotting. Oh So was only so so Social tonight.

Each had a warm brown phlegm the Brits comically called beer, fought its brackish thickness to get a bit of relaxing buzz going.

In the low light she looked, if anything, more beautiful. Those luminous eyes, generally closed off to the world, were alive with . . . sparkle? Glitter? Light? Something like that. How do lashes grow so long? How is skin so smooth? How is symmetry so geometrically precise? How are lips so . . . what? Red? Plump? Kissable? He didn't know the word, if even there was one.

"Gosh, you look great tonight."

"You look tired, Lieutenant. Blowing up tanks must be so fatiguing."

He laughed.

"That was the major's show. I was a supernumerary with a tommy gun."

"It's got the whole place abuzz. More heroics from Leets."

"A kid got killed out of it. Nice little guy. Funny. Nobody tells that part. Or if they do, they say, 'Hey, that's war.' But still—haven't felt so blue since Basil caught it."

"What I love, Jim," she said, taking his hand in both of hers, "is that through all the ugly, you've stayed compassionate and sensitive. His death hurts you, which means the war hasn't crushed you as it has so many."

"I suppose," he said.

"So tell me about Swagger. He's the mystery man. Every girl in the office wants a date with him and he doesn't go out, go to parties, go for walks. He's just duty eight days a week."

"With Earl it's nine. On his off time, he reads technical intelligence reports on German tanks. Great soldier. The best. Smart as they come. The interesting thing is, he's bilingual. Really."

"French would be his second language? From Arkansas?"

"No, his second language is 'NCO.' In the Marine Corps, he was profane, gruff, tough, what you might call super-okie. Heavy southern accent. Enemy of grammar, but nevertheless unusually vivid in expression. Exactly the sort of sergeant warrior king any kid would follow up a hill. I had worries with how he'd fit in here on Society Hill."

"And . . . ?"

"And he fits like a glove. I've never heard him bust a verb or crack an 'ain't' or an 'it don't.' He stays not only with but a little ahead of every conversation. And the war, the sniper stuff—he can see into it. He figures out answers where nobody else even had questions."

"You know, the colonel ordered an FBI check on him. He's clean as they come. But here's the odd thing: it examined his family, but it said of his father, Charles, 'We have no information on this subject.' I've seen a lot of FBI reports and I've never seen that before."

"Hmm," said Leets, calling for another glass of the brown beer-like sludge.

"We did get War Department records too," she went on. "His father had three years of teachers college, so Earl grew up in a home where correct English was spoken. But then Charles went off to war. Not in 1917 but in 1914! He fought with the Canadian Army for three years. Then he transferred to ours, where he was highly decorated. Led trench raids, it was said; got out a major. He went on to become the sheriff of Polk County, Arkansas. Famous gunfighter. Died in 1941, shot in a meaningless robbery in some tiny town."

"Maybe losing his dad to something stupid is why Earl never talks about his past, his family, his childhood, Arkansas. Hurts too much. The old man gets plugged in a heist after four years in the trenches? That's a rough one."

"I have a feeling it's more complicated than that. Earl left home in 1931 to join the Marine Corps. Who knows why?"

"All I can say is, I'm glad he's on our side."

The food came, they nibbled, and then he could no longer stifle his yawns.

"You've got to get some shut-eye, Lieutenant."

"I know."

"The Tyne thing is tomorrow."

"The major has made it certain I'm not a part of it. He's got me out on errands."

"Frank Tyne is a dog," she said. "I wouldn't trust him to run a lemonade stand. I couldn't bear it if—"

"The major doesn't seem worried. Maybe he's got it figured out."

"Frankly, I worry about Colonel Bruce. He's a wonderful man, but a politician. He'll go the way the breeze is blowing."

They left, began a slow walk back to her hotel. This time, a little softened up by the stout, they drifted together, arms touching. Not much was said. Leets enjoyed her closeness, her smell, her face in profile, perfect and precise. He'd never seen such a beautiful woman.

Mr. Raven watched them standing close outside the hotel. Neither seemed in a hurry to depart, even though duties beckoned tomorrow. Would they kiss? He hoped. It would be a sort of *l'envoi* for the young officer, almost a movie scene, as much like the embrace of Mr. Taylor and Miss Leigh in *Waterloo Bridge* as could be imagined. These two might even be more attractive than the cinema performers. But where was the background music? Mr. Raven had to imagine that for himself, and he felt it surge through him, rather jolly as in the flickers.

Duty—his, not theirs—beckoned. It was time. He knew exactly the moment. He had timed it. It would take him four minutes through two alleys to get to Leets's residence and another to find his selected post in the alleyway just past it where he could linger in the shadows, unseen. Leets, walking a less secretive path, would arrive in six.

All auspices were positive. No coppers, few cabs, now and then a soldier or two, winding home from a night at the bar, but nowhere in this little universe was observation, much less detailed memory, probable. It would be clean, the snap of the pistol so unexpected here among the trees and the august stone buildings that any who heard would immediately deny it, roll over, and try to get back to sleep.

He fondled the German pistol in his pocket. He was so ready for this.

• • •

"Oh, God," he said, holding her, "how I dreamed of this in the mud, with the Krauts shooting."

"You shouldn't have been thinking of me, Jim. You should have been thinking about not getting killed."

The taste of her lips, the feel of her thin yet taut muscularity, the softness of her breasts against him, his need to crush her to him, to make her part of him forever.

"Please, please, please," she said, "tell me you'll be careful. No more heroics. Let Swagger be the hero. You just take the notes."

"I'm hoping there's no more cowboy stuff. But you just never know how it's going to happen. If—"

"Don't say it."

"All right. I was going to be so MGM-noble too. 'Duty,' all that stuff."

"I just want Leets in bed with me for the rest of my life."

"Won't that be fun?"

"And how. Soon, darling. Now go home, go to bed. Big day tomorrow."

"Too big a day. I'm actually going to the office. I can bunk on the sofa. That gets me about an hour's extra sleep."

"What a smart soldier," she said.

CHAPTER 43

The Flap

With turbulence in the forecast, everyone was tight. No eye contact, no handshakes, no joshing or fake collegiality. Just the four, in the colonel's office: Swagger, the colonel, Tyne, all in fresh Class As, freshly shaved, crisp as cornflakes. And Tyne's pet congressman.

Mulrooney (N.Y., D., Fifth) looked like a crossbred fifty-five-year-old leprechaun and gigolo. Irish in face and dress, complete to black suit and tie, white shirt, dark but shaven jowls, eyebrows like black swallow's wings, nose like a tiny ski jump, he was nevertheless rather handsome, even dashing. It was in a single harmony of dark Irish beauty. He had a big face like a movie dolt. His hair was sleek, wore its sheathing of pomade well, and boasted always-desirable tinges of gray at the temples. One could see why, if not movies, the next best thing would be politics.

"Millie, coffee, please," said the colonel, shooing them to his circle of chairs at the fireplace, under the portrait of some wonder dog or other. "Now, gentlemen," he said, "I do realize there is some contention here, but I'm a great believer in the 'casual meeting.' If we can chat in a friendly

281

way over coffee on a beautiful London summer day, I'm sure we can work all this out."

Millie brought a pot, steaming, and four cups on a tray. As she bent, asked about cream or sugar, she found the grace to turn to Swagger and mouth the words *Good luck*. He nodded.

"Sir," said Tyne, "I'm just wanting to go on record here saying none of this is calculated as an attack on either Major Swagger or yourself. You're both fine, exemplary officers with great records. I am only concerned with certain administrative tendencies that could attract undue attention in the middle, alas, of an election season. I know Tom Dewey and how he operates. I wouldn't be surprised if he had spies in the building right now, rooting for anything that could be called 'corruption' or 'misman-agement.' They could be used in the fall against the President."

"I wish we could keep politics at bay," said the congressman. "But that's only in a pretend world. Here in this one, as I'm sure you realize, Colonel, politics are everywhere. November will be upon us soon, and Thomas Dewey means to take over. You would know this, being of our breed yourself. House of Delegates, Maryland, Virginia. You would know it's not possible to say, 'Forget politics, win the war.' To win the war, you have to win the politics."

"Anything to add, Major Swagger?" asked Colonel Bruce.

"I don't know or care anything about politics," said Swagger. "Never have, never will."

"Believe me, young man, you may not be interested in politics, but they are interested in you," said the congressman. It was a treasured line, drawn from Trotsky, and everybody laughed except Swagger, whose face remained almost disinterested.

Tyne then launched into his tirade, since practiced and polished, somewhat condensed, but basically the same. "Special groups," un-accountable budget overruns, blurred standards of success, morale crisis for others in the building, all of it leading to lessened efficiency.

"I can see Tom wanting to know why in a strategic global war we're frittering away men, talent, and money on ridiculous enterprises like blowing up small bridges that will have almost no impact on the war," said Mulrooney. "Or funding secret groups with no professional supervision, no endgame, no reliable gauge of their success, and increasing resentment from a rank and file held to more stringent standards."

"Major Swagger?"

"I'm just doing the job as it was explained to me. As I understood it, they wanted me to be outside of all that. No politics. Just a hard sprint toward an end. I made the calls, right or wrong. It's got nothing to do with anybody else."

"I have to ask, then, Major," said Congressman Mulrooney, "can you perhaps define or elucidate your progress so far? Can you, in other words, justify what's been done?"

"No, sir. That just opens me up to sniping, second-guessing, the involvement of too many folks who want to stir the pot, too many bosses to please. It never works; it always hurts."

That brought things to a momentary halt.

"Well," said Mulrooney, "that's the sort of attitude that could bring on a congressional inquiry, even a hearing. You would have to answer under subpoena. So you gain nothing—"

"Congressman Mulrooney," said the colonel, "I'm sure we all want to avoid that. Tell us, what would you see as some gesture of responsibility that would have the effect of turning everyone's eyes elsewhere?"

Glances flew between Mulrooney and Tyne, but Tyne was the lead dog on this adventure in barking.

"Sir, it's my contention, and I've asked around quite a bit to support it, that as capable as Major Swagger is, he's fallen under the sway of an underling, his staffer Lieutenant Leets. That is, First Lieutenant James Leets, transferred in from the 101st Airborne because of his fluent French. Leets is one of those careerists, shall we say, who sees the war as an opportunity to rise, not as a global conflict for survival to win."

"Can you be more specific, Major?" asked Colonel Bruce.

Tyne unleashed his Leets smear. It was like sitting through the movie again. He added some new touches: he had supervised the Jeds and so he knew of what he was talking. Next, the day's stall over the Bren guns, and he gave himself credit again for straightening that out.

He dispensed with the attack quickly: "It was a total catastrophe. Captain St. Florian, an able, even legendary British agent, was killed, along with perhaps dozens of French fighters. And while Casey did detonate charges at the bridge, they did not knock it down. German engineers quickly got it—"

"How quickly?" asked Colonel Bruce.

"Very quickly. Meaningless overall."

"I don't think SHAEF would agree."

"Sir, let me show you." The pièce de résistance. "I have obtained top secret Eighth Air Force recon photos that will document the supposed 'destruction' of this bridge."

He opened his briefcase, took out several heavy sheets of paper rolls, unspooled them to display the imagery, and proceeded to point out that the bridge was indeed not flattened but only twisted and that a solid effort by the Organisation Todt had it up and permitting passage to the beach area within two working days. Swagger wondered how much it had cost him.

"But no Tigers?" said the colonel.

"No, sir, but Tigers are irrelevant. The Panzer IVs and the Panthers raised hell with our Shermans."

"Major Swagger?"

"I have nothing to say. Wasn't here for that. Wouldn't know a thing about it."

"Sir," said Major Tyne, "the point is that Leets and his pals promoted his little misadventure into a major success here in 70 Grosvenor when it wasn't. They have a clique thing going where each boosts the other. And that false reputation for success is what got him to Room 351 with its unlimited budget and its complete lack of accountability and its potential for being publicized as an OSS waste, directly attributable to the President. This photo"—he held up the picture of the twisted, droopy bridge, which did in fact look rather pathetic against all the other landscapes of vast ruin the war had produced—"could cost President Roosevelt the White House. That's all I'm saying."

"And your recommendation?"

"Well, certainly Lieutenant Leets has to go. Immediately if not sooner. Then the Room 351 operation should be moved from Special Projects to my own Operations team. I'll be able to supervise directly all of Major Swagger's findings and make the proper presentations to SHAEF when the time comes and—"

The phone rang.

"Dammit," snapped Colonel Bruce. No one in history had ever seen him nonplussed before. "I told her," he explained, rising, "no interruptions."

He went to his desk, picked up.

"Millie, I thought I told you—" Whatever it was, it stopped him as cold as a bazooka rocket stops a tank. Then he blustered, "Can't they wait? What is so important? What? Oh, God. The Army. All right, send them in. Let's get this over with."

He went to the door, explaining, "I apologize, gentlemen, but I'm told this is urgent SHAEF business: can't wait. I'll take care of it in just a second." He opened the door.

There were four of them. They looked like the Notre Dame backfield outlined against a blue-gray November sky. Meat, lots of it, well distributed. Those brutality-inured faces, flat, almost phlegmatic, not registering much. The white caps, the white armbands, the white belts, the white holsters, the gray .45 automatics, the white lanyards, the white leggings, the black billy clubs. Every note sounded MP. *Cheese it, the cops!* A lieutenant, two sergeants, and a corporal.

"Sir, Lieutenant Green, 130th Military Police, attached to SHAEF. This is a felony arrest and I have to advise you that, during the performance of our duties, military protocol is temporarily suspended."

"Lieutenant, what on earth—"

"Which one here is Tyne?"

The looks of the others identified Frank.

"I don't—" he started.

Cops do not let perps dominate the transaction. That's the point of being a cop.

"Mr. Tyne—"

"Major Tyne."

"Mr. Tyne, you have been indicted by grand jury hearing on one count of felony murder committed against the person of one Reginald Bowie, known as 'Hot Fingers,' of Harlem, New York, 15 November 1935. You are hereby remanded to arrest and incarceration and will be transported immediately to the First Army stockade at Bushy Park until transportation can be arranged for your return."

"But—"

"You are also hereby informed that all courtesies, protocols, special rights, and considerations due a major in the United States Army are considered rescinded. Please remove all signifiers of rank before we cuff you. You are as of now a prisoner."

"Leo," Tyne said, "this is outrageous. You can't let them—"

Congressman Mulrooney rose to launch an eloquent and shaming defense of his ally. It lasted somewhere between one and four-tenths of a second before he brilliantly executed a 180 so graceful it's still talked about today, riding and driven by the pure diesel of the four most powerful words in the English language: *on the other hand.*

"On the other hand, Frank," he said smoothly, "I'm sure this can all be settled at some future date." He added, "I wouldn't want to interfere with the law."

How swift the wind doth change; how swift the politician doth read, absorb, process, develop new policy, in the black blink of a smiling Irish eye upon what prevails.

"Prisoner Tyne," said the lieutenant, "if you don't get that shit off your uniform, my men will do it for you, and they won't be gentle about it."

CHAPTER 44

Childish Fantasies

After the brief stop at the Scotland Yard ballistics lab, where the twisted bullet remnants were dropped off for analysis, Outhwaithe said, "I say, what's the driver's name?"

"Sebastian."

"And that thing on his arm?" He meant the double striped chevrons over the *T*.

"Tech five, meaning corporal in our army."

"Excellent." He leaned forward. "Corporal Sebastian, your boss here has decided to give you the afternoon off. Can you spend it wisely, rob no banks, cane no Irishmen or bobbies, nor be caught naked at Trafalgar Square?"

"I believe I can," said Sebastian.

"He's good at that," said Leets.

"Excellent. Deposit us, please, at No. 5, Lancaster, Crouch End. Can you find it?"

"Near Archway, sir?"

"Indeed."

And why wouldn't Sebastian know London that well? He was king of it, after all.

In short order, he maneuvered the staff Ford through traffic to the North End and beyond, and located No. 5, Lancaster, which turned out to be a modest place of brick and wooden struts, undamaged as yet by doodle or four-hundred-pounder, called Ned's Garage.

There, Ned himself brought out Tony's car, which was a small dark green Morris sportster, a miniature thing that repeated the British design aesthetic of boxiness. One could say it looked like a steel essay arguing against the streamline. It was distilled and diluted from the twenties trope of the cube and thus presented an assembly of tinier cubes to the world, all in the career of adding as much wind resistance as possible. All angles, all fenders, all windshields, were squared up to the breeze. The "tyres" would have been square if possible, their spokes homage to the nineteenth century, and even the headlamps had the aspect of upside down teakettles welded to each fender. It was as aerodynamic as a coffin. Its canopy was down, the cockpit looking quite Sopwith Camel, and Ned had taken care to rub it to its highest green gloss.

"It's a Tickford drophead coupe," Tony said. "One of two hundred and fifty-one ever built. Got it for a song from a major off to Burma. It's a dolly to drive. Care to take us to Oxford, chum?"

"Ah," said Leets, "the left-hand driving will get us both squashed under a truck before we get out of town. I'll just sit on the right and hold on to my hat."

Off the boys went in the dashing toy car, which indeed, under Tony's effortless expertise, snaked around curves, opened up wide on flats, all while ruffling hair and raising dust. It was, as they coursed through the rolling and soon enough Oxfordshire hills and greens, almost as if there were no war on, the sun bright, the sky cloudless and unmarked by Bf 109 or Spitfire contrails, and not a barrage balloon or a bomb crater in sight. One would have expected them to discuss poetry.

Outhwaithe had a mysterious fondness for Leets. You wouldn't think his type would go for Yanks. They'd met at training at Milton Hall after Leets had been seconded from the 101st. He was by no means as unflappably insouciant as Basil but might have been called a fetal Basil. Give him time, and if he lived long enough (doubtful), he might even become the new Basil. However, as for now, he'd returned from his Jed foray—a nicely done job on a railway line south of Paris, keeping Jerry from shipping yet more armor to Normandy—to MI6, not SOE.

In time, the medieval university town arrived. Well, they arrived, but to them, so effortless was the motoring, it felt as if it had arrived to them. It lay before them, steeples and domes, rather mauve in the haze of pollen and agricultural dust. Entered, it had the aspect of an intaglio etching, so many and varied were the textures, particularly as one buzzed through town and on to the seat of learning, a collection of cathedrals to knowledge, one might say, though arranged horizontally rather than vertically. The Bodleian sandstone was everywhere, each building seeming to present a different degree of weathering to the world. Since it was summer, flower life had everywhere invaded and vanquished, curling and spiraling up the odd stairways, brightening the greens between or fronting the colleges and the quads, all of it so alive under the radiance of an Oxford summer sun that one half expected a meandering Dodgson to come out to enjoy the toasting rays. The chestnut was a-blossom, discordant to the cobbles, the cupolas, and the gables. Scholastic quiet? Hardly. Bells banging away, celebrating the passage of time, one supposed, or just that noise equated to life as only the living could make it and only the optimistic could want to make it. The crowd was mostly women now, however.

"The girls have taken over. Actually, the government has taken over and it's largely girls now. Brasenose completely. Most of the other colleges are just office buildings, though bravely a few dons hold out against the deluge. Look quickly, you might spot an authentic undergraduate."

There were a few as yet spared the rigors of desert, jungle, or bocage, all with that languid undergrad posture that suggested power and wealth inherited, adored or abjured as the case might be, who seemed to poke their way through the distaff mob.

"Squint and make all the clerks go away and it's still beautiful, eh?" said Outhwaithe.

"Sure is," said Leets, realizing that his own college, back in Evanston in the Midwest, had like so many others imitated the Oxonian cloistral hush, Gothic architecture, and vapors of both learning and yearning in its affect.

"Doomed, of course. Though the German bombs failed, the war in general will wipe it out. When we win, the common man takes over, doesn't matter the system in the end. No more poofs and eccentric geniuses and barefoot poets. No wits like Oscar. No aristos plowing the town girls untouched by shame, decency, or law, then loudly proclaiming their innocence. All gone, all drowned. Surprised this much remains."

Outhwaithe was, of course, addressing himself and required no answer from Leets, who in any case would not have had one.

Tony found a car park outside of the one called Balliol—this one vast like Xanadu, with gables and a central, if squared, tower proudly proclaiming the year 1282 and all that—parked, and led the American in.

"Leets, old man, look here. These lads can be snappish. They aspire to the worst expressions of English snobbery and will miss no chance to express it. He will be tart, dismissive, rather bored, and quite unwelcoming. And I don't even know who he is yet!"

"I'll be harmless," said Leets.

"Nothing personal. He's just playing a part these blokes have rehearsed for fifteen hundred or so years."

It was dark, musty, the Middle Ages in personification. Knighthood might still be in flower here, but so was urination, as it smelled of uncouth plumbing. Outhwaithe knew the way and took them to a third floor that proclaimed itself the Department of Classics. Entering, they met a secretary who got a rather vague dean out of a nap, and he took them still deeper in the bowels to another room, which for all of it didn't look all that different from a modern language department at Edina High in the suburbs of Minneapolis.

"Bowra's our polymath. Wizard on languages. Speaks and reads 'em all," said Dean Whatever. "So smart that many despise him. He's cheesed off now because he felt he'd be elected Oxford Professor of Poetry, to go with his other little university trophies. But the Day-Lewis bunch outmaneuvered him, and that post stays vacant till after the war. He broods and curses and plots and dreams. So if he's short, it's an example of what politics—faculty or any sort—can do to a chap."

Hence: Bowra. Tweedy, balding, fifties. Gravedigger face after a thousand or so holes and too many rotting corpses. Bad teeth, skin the color of parchment. Rather unsavory. No Mr. Chips. Mr. Chits, as if the world owed him and had not yet come clear.

"Professor Bowra, two chaps from Intelligence here. One's even a Yank, that's how important it is. Need some language help, something quite arcane. Can you have at the pitch?"

"I suppose one must," Bowra allowed, his face a dispatch of extreme annoyance.

They sat, and without provocation the professor said, "I'd offer tea, but that would elongate the experience. I'm quite busy today avoiding work and prefer to get back to that important task. Please do rush sloppily on, as time is too precious to be wasted on anything except wasting time."

"Excellent start," said Tony. Then he endeavored to explain it all. Bowra nodded as if he even cared. Then he said, "All right, then, gentlemen, unveil the mystery word."

Leets made a stab at it.

"Was that an expectoration, sir?" asked the professor. Good one! Oxford 1, Northwestern 0. Leets soldiered onward.

"I was trying for something that might be spelled *N-e-j-d-z-n-i-k-i*. Remember, the soldier heard it several times in German captivity, then waited a few weeks before telling my officer, who then told me. Obviously it's eroded, in his memory, in the major's, and then in mine, and it was never too clear to begin with."

"Like a stone in a stream, worn smooth by the water's passage," said Professor Bowra. "But enough remains. Actually, it's Czech."

"Czech!" said Tony.

"Indeed. Sudetan Czech, almost certainly. Contested land between Germany and the Czechs, the Germans taking it over in the Anschluss of 1938. Its residents thus became, no matter how reluctantly, German citizens, obligated to German law, vulnerable to German conscript. Czech or not, these lads couldn't say no to Nazi conscription. That's how they end up in a German tank, in France, fighting Americans, barely speaking German at all."

"Do you know the word, sir?" asked Leets.

"I do and I don't. I will specify the word, but not the meaning, as Czech is a language in which word order is quite flexible and that flexibility frequently dictates meaning. So the word's meaning might be useless without the sentence in which it was spoken. But one must do what one must. I will give you the word and many possible meanings. That is all I can do. It is up to you to carry it another step. I should think spies would find the game quite amusing. It's rather like a code."

"Men's lives are at stake, sir," said Leets, banking on midwestern literalism to carry the day. Bad move.

"But then it's a war, and men's lives are always at stake, are they not, young man?" was the swift response.

Leets surrendered. What else was there?

"Unfortunately."

"Well, let us try and save some, shall we? *Nejdzniki*, the final *i* rendering it to the plural. Immediate meaning, then, 'raiders.' Metaphorical possibilities, depending on context. 'Invaders,' 'road agents,' 'bandits,' 'highwaymen,' 'thieves,' 'pirates,' 'any random group of nasties,' 'brigands'—"

"They were joking," said Leets. "They'd joke about something German that seemed particularly absurd to them."

"Plausible, I suppose," said the professor. "Not quite conclusive, though, may I offer another approach? 'Raiders': Accepting the literal, who would the Czechs see as raiders? Not the Nazis: too recent. Not the Huns: too ancient. You'd have to know of something in between in Czech history or more, its folklore. That is, its children's tales. Perhaps there's an aspect of raiders out of children's stories that these very tough men would share and find amusing."

Silence.

"Where on earth would we go for *that*?" asked Tony.

"I know just the chap for you," said the professor. "He was in the trenches in the First War. The Somme, all that. Possibly it affected him. He's quite brilliant. He's also barking mad."

CHAPTER 45

The Thin Man

What a good boy he was. Instead of spending the afternoon trolling for shopgirls in the pubs, Sebastian returned to duty at 351. He had to know the outcome of the Tyne drama.

"Uh," said one of his informers, another T/5, "they took him out of here in handcuffs and a T-shirt about 1100. It's said Colonel Bruce seemed quite happy in the canteen. Major Swagger, as usual, went back to 351 without a word."

"Man, is he good," said Sebastian.

"That seems to be the consensus," said the fellow.

But if Sebastian expected gloating and celebrating, Swagger didn't get the general order. Same dour concentration as he was looking through what appeared to be decrypts from some code-breaking operation of Brit origin.

"Sir," Sebastian said, announcing his presence. "The lieutenant went on to Oxford by car with the British officer. He released me. Here I am."

The major looked up.

"Okay, Sebastian. I've actually got something for you other than waxing the car. You used a word to me, to keep me from sending you to the 1st Ranger Battalion, remember? I'd never heard it before. Because I went to college at the University of Banana Wars. It wasn't on the reading list."

Sebastian knew right away.

"'Realpolitik'?"

"That's it. Define again, please."

"Uh, the way it really is, as opposed to the way everybody thinks it is or everybody thinks it should be. For example: we are holy crusaders against evil. Realpolitik: we are just another batch of scramblers, hustlers, con men, consumed by grudges, petty politics, ambition, some of us really stupid, some of us—"

"Okay. Now, who would know about this stuff?"

"I'm sorry?"

"Who could look at a situation and give me a read on it from the angle of this 'Realpolitik'?"

"I would say you, sir. Major Tyne comes against you, he ends up in handcuffs. That's as Realpolitik as it gets."

"Forget that."

"May I ask, sir, what is this in regard to?"

"Sure you can ask. And just as sure, I'm not answering. It's not for tech fives. Or even major generals—yet."

"Yes, sir."

"Back on point: In London, who? Where?"

Sebastian concentrated.

"Not in service. Not in spies? Journalism? Edward R. Murrow? William L. Shirer? Hem—"

"I think he'd have to be British. That is, to know the politics. Not parties, districts, that sort of thing, but, um, operating principles."

"Culture."

"I suppose."

Sebastian came up with a name.

"Never heard of him."

"On BBC. Lots of people hate him. Seems to call it straight. Not really the college type; he was a cop in Burma, went on the hobo in Paris and London, spent time in coal mines, always trying to write stuff. Finally managed to get it published. Now he's well-known."

"Call BBC. Say you're me. Use your most polished voice. Get me in to see this guy. Tell him it's for the war effort."

They met at a pub not far from Broadcasting House, the odd ship-like building that was BBC headquarters that had made its port of call Marylebone, a few streets away. The pub bore the name the Lion & Unicorn, but inside it turned out to most resemble the Pub That Looks Like All the Other Pubs. Its banality was only bearable by virtue of its darkness and the power of its hooch.

Swagger entered, feeling completely out of place in such a dark English burrow, but a tall Englishman stood and gestured. He looked like a Brit variation on Abraham Lincoln, the string bean with the tragic face in tweeds so baggy he'd slept in them for sure, dark shirt, dark tie with stripes, a kind of rhapsody in brown-indigo. Cadaverous, 150 pounds dripping wet, fag hanging from mouth, its syrupy smoke drifting up into his smudge of mustache, cheekbones like bayonets, a shock of thatch hair. And of course he had a bad cough, a hack that sent tremors of damage through his scrawny, elongated frame. It spoke of heatless rooms, thin coats, an icy wind cutting everything, being down and out in cities of full and plenty. He looked like he'd gone native in his own country.

"Major, I'm Blair. That is, my real name. The radio name's just a fraud."

"Sir, I'm Swagger."

"After the stick? I carried one in Burma."

"Nobody knows. Old family name. A mystery. Anyhow, thanks so much for this, Mr. Blair."

"Thanks so much for coming over and winning our war for us."

"I'm the sort who finds that sort of thing fun."

"As you so appear. Anyhow, politics? However may I assist you? Wait, do let me get us a jar."

"Please," said Swagger.

He himself lit a Camel, laid a couple of packs down on the table as an offering to new friend Blair, and looked up to see the man with two glasses filled to the brim with brown amber, about one-tenth of an inch of foam as surface flotsam.

"Ciggies?" said Blair, sitting. "So appreciated. Now, how can I be of aid?"

"I've got a situation where the sides aren't clear. Not sure who represents who. As I apply myself to it, nothing makes sense. I was hoping you'd see something in it that might clarify it for me."

"Fascinating."

"It has to do with this thing called Realpolitik."

"Hmmm," said Blair. "Might have an idea or two. Realpolitik almost got me killed in Spain. But do proceed."

"I'm trying to solve a problem but the only answer I can come up with makes no sense. It boils down to one problem: How do you win by doing harm to your own side? Is it possible?"

"Could you be more specific?"

"Suppose someone on our side is giving information to their side. Seems straight-up treason, for whatever reason. Maybe the traitor is crazy, maybe a lot of money has been paid, maybe he's got a thing for secrets."

"Wouldn't an investigator figure that out?"

"Here's the strange part: This person doesn't consider himself doing wrong. He thinks it's right. But what normal person could think giving dope to the Nazis was right unless they were cooked in Nazi cow shit for the past ten years and didn't know better or were some kind of trained professional agent."

"And those two possibilities are out?"

"Completely."

"Now it's coming clear," said Blair. Deep puff, the orange of the oxygenated burn suffusing his prematurely aged face, the drifting penumbra of smoke obscuring it, but still his brow went scrunchy, his eyes went narrow, as he put full brain into fourth gear.

"All right," he said. "Maybe there's a third player on the board. A secret player."

News to Swagger. Had no meaning in any part of his life. Couldn't fix on it. Third player?

"I'm baffled, Mr. Blair," he allowed.

"Here's the dynamic. Your traitor hates the Nazis as much as anyone and would give nothing to them. However, this person's alliances are not to you but to another anti-Nazi. A supposed ally of yours whom too many take to represent the hope of the world."

No names, nothing spoken. But now Swagger grasped it.

"So you're saying he gives it to this third party. And the third party . . ." He paused.

"The third party is the party of Realpolitik. It sees an advantage on forwarding the information to the Germans. That's because it's not looking at tomorrow or next year but at twenty years on. It knows that harm done to you in this war will reverberate far in the future and sees its own benefit in it."

Swagger stewed, parsing, holding pieces up to the light, turning them, seeing how it played out.

"Here's an example. I know it well, as it almost got me killed."

Blair smiled. This was such fun for him. He liked this story. It explained so much.

"In 1936, there was a war in Spain. Straightforward thing: believers in democracy on one side, believers in authoritarian rule on the other. Stalin rushed to the aid of the Spanish republic, the democratic side, the 'good' side, with men and supplies. So one would say, 'Hooray for Stalin for supporting the republic. What a good chap!' And that's what many vegetarian freethinkers and intellectual chrysanthemums and bad poets said."

Swagger nodded.

"Stalin, as it turned out, didn't give a rat's shit for Spain. The only thing he cared about was the future of Russia, particularly of his enemies there, do you see?"

"I do."

"He used the Spanish war to draw them out. Fools and dreamers— I count myself among them, maybe the biggest fool—they were drawn like flies to rot. But to his mind they were unreliable. They were too undisciplined and therefore too likely to be driven by passion over loyalty. He knew what would become of them, how they would turn out. At the same time, in Spain as in Russia, he was consolidating power over the secret police. He who controls the machine guns controls the present and thus the future. You see, here's the brilliance of the bloody bastard: he saw his enemies of the future. He saw beyond tactics, beyond strategy. That's Realpolitik for you. He knew that even if they weren't guilty yet, they inevitably *would* be. So he destroyed them, his allies, those on his side, in all their foolish innocence, and as they faced the firing squads, they screamed, 'But we are innocent!' 'Yes, but you will be guilty soon enough' was the answer, followed by bullets."

"They came after you?"

"I had a date with a wall. Nothing personal. Just by classification. Lefty dreamer, in a silly militia called POUM, which I joined carelessly, not caring what the initials stood for. Turned out to be 'Party of Marxist Unification.' It represented Trotsky's dream of world revolution, not Stalin's dream of revolution in one country. The Stalinists suppressed it, arrested all, shot them. Learned my lesson, did I. Just barely made it out, last train from Barcelona after the purge. I didn't think ahead. You must."

"So that means if I want to make sense of my situation, I ought to consider not the short-term effects but the long-term. The results twenty years down the road and what is necessary to achieve them."

"Your talent for grasping the core is vivid and sure. I'm guessing you're a splendid soldier."

"I'm still around, if that's anything."

"That's the fellow!" said Mr. Blair, interrupted briefly by a spasm that ripped him from lung to head. "I'll now give you an adage to help you. When dealing with certain kinds of chaps, don't think 1944, think 1984."

CHAPTER 46

20 Northmoor

Tony slid the MG to the curb, killed its purring kitty-cat motor, and said to Leets, "They can be so trying. But are you ready for another Oxonian? If this boy's been in the trenches, perhaps he'll have a bit more humility to him."

Wearily, Leets said, "Let's give it a shot."

"Good man! The brigade shall advance!"

They approached one more stately mansion. At least, *mansion* is what Leets would have called it, for it resembled those in both Edina and Paris: a gabled, shingled, chimneyed indulgence of home, it had to have at least six bedrooms and yet at the same time seemed to reflect the prototype English country bungalow of children's books. Lawns lay about it so that no building interfered with its visage, and they were greened up to an emerald hue. Like many playthings of the rich and established, it was in fact rather childish in its straightforwardness, its symmetry expressed in units of window spread about harmoniously, like notes on a score. Vines engulfed its front, suggesting a permanence out of olden time.

"He's a writer?" Leets said.

"So Bowra said. Of what, I don't know. Hasn't made the Sunday rags yet."

They knocked, and Miss Marple answered, not that Leets had ever read Dame Agatha. She had what might be called character, wise eyes, and only a slightly crinkled face under a frost of hair. She was not the sort to slobber over strangers, even heroes in uniform. She knew enough of life to understand what bounders they could be.

"Madam, hullo," said Tony. "Sorry to drop in unannounced—"

"Bowra rang up," she said. "I'm Edith. Edie, if you prefer."

"Ah, splendid, but as humble pilgrims to the shrine, we'll stick with 'ma'am.' So you know we're from the intelligence services and would like to borrow the professor's brain. Wouldn't be here unless it wasn't rather sticky."

"Yes, yes," she said. "Tea's on. I'll get Ronnie. Hard to tear him away from his project. Silliest fool thing I ever heard of. If my mother—no matter, this way."

She led them to a comfortable living room, furnished in pillows and books, and got them seated, then went to fetch Ronnie and tea, in that order.

He entered. No infantry bucko to him. Signal Corps, one would have thought, accurately. Gangly of body, boney of face, dressed as one would expect, in corduroy bags bagged out over brogues that looked equally as if they'd suffered a war or two, a blue shirt uncinched by tie, hair askew from much running of fingers through it in despair over the perfect adjective. Writer's hair, Leets would have supposed, not knowing any writers.

"Hullo, hullo," he sang out, "stay put, no need to stand, no ceremony at 20 Northmoor."

But they stood anyway. "We stand for the Somme, sir," said Leets.

"I just got in the way in that one. No heroics here. I am a man whose life was saved by a flea, so what do you expect?"

"A flea?" said Tony.

"Bit me, the little bugger, one of millions. This one gave me three bags full of trench fever. Six months in hospital. Then judged too feeble for battle. Spent the rest of the war supervising men who needed no supervision in loading crates on lorries in Sheffield."

"Being at the Somme was enough," said Leets. "And being there is far more important than leading bayonet charges into machine-gun fire."

"How nicely said. American, young man?"

"I am, sir."

"Yet you've spent time in Paris. I note a rogue Parisian vowel occasionally declaring itself."

"Ten years. I was schooled there. I speak it quite fluently."

"It helped him become a hero," Tony said.

"He's joking," said Leets. "Like you, I was mostly in the way."

The professor laughed.

"Do sit, I insist."

Edie brought tea and some kind of biscuit thing that looked beyond the strength of anyone's dentition. The Brits loaded up on lumps and cream, while Leets used the condiments more sparingly.

"We do apologize for interrupting your project," said Tony. "Good of you to give us time."

"Not sure if it's a project or a monstrosity," the professor said. "I wrote a children's tale in '37 and it was well received. I could not let it go. I decided on a follow-on. And yet, dark times have turned it dark itself. It seems to be full of battles, betrayals, secret weapons and missions. No child could stay with it and any adult would find it silly. It only has one natural reader, otherwise totally lacking an audience. That one would be me, and I already know how it ends!"

They laughed. Not stuffy, this one, nor arrogant. But neither ignorant.

"Now you have a riddle," he said, "and you think a philologist and folklorist could help. That's what the beastly Bowra said."

"Something like that," said Outhwaithe. "I would—"

"Please, Leftenant, let the American explain. I find his accent so delightful. Yours I hear every day. It's mine, brummy/Oxford/public school/ touch of military."

"Yes, sir."

Leets ran through it, hitting all the stations of the cross in his midwestern soda-water voice and occasional French twist of lemon.

"Minnesota," said the professor.

"Yes, sir," said Leets.

"I treasure accents. I'm the Henry Higgins of Oxford."

They laughed.

"But this isn't Shaw, this is war. All right, then. The riddle is: Whom would Czech soldiers refer to when they found humor in the word 'raiders' in reference, you believe, to another group among their own? Correctly surmised that the subgroup would differ from the group, hence 'raiders' would not be the Huns themselves."

"That's our thought."

"Whom do the Czechs remember? They've had many raiders, you see: Germans, of course, Hungarians, Turks, even Russians, all trying to nick a bit of land off, here or there. Yet, possibly among the many, one has settled in the Czech imagination and lasted there through the generations. Do we have any descriptions of these Czechs? Handsome people, yes. I strolled through in 1911. If you can give me a description, perhaps it will help me understand, as one tends to note those who look like oneself and forget the others."

"The G.I. was struck by the tank commander. He said—soldiers' memories perhaps can't be trusted, but this guy was pretty solid, I thought—he said he was large, thick crown of hair, blond, perhaps. The most amazing thing, he had a beard. A thick blond beard. So he's a fellow who would go his own way. And he must be good at the tank business, because his German bosses have seen fit to leave him alone."

"Blonds are not difficult to find in Czechoslovakia. Many of that complexion, complete to the pale skin, the blue eyes, the steely temperament, are to be found in the north reaches of the country. In some ways, it's far more of Hitler's nonsensical 'Aryan fantasy' than Germany. The dirty little beggar doesn't seem to realize that Aryan is a language, not a gene group."

"I doubt these boys spoke Aryan," said Tony.

"Or had even heard of it. But, yes, I can answer your question. Your tank sergeant notes what reminds him of himself. He's seen a batch of them doing something rather odd in German territory, so odd that it's become part of the folklore of his own little troop."

"We're baffled."

"That's because you have no idea, nor does the world, of how successful this group of 'raiders' was in their heyday. They not only came and saw and conquered, they intermarried, even as far south and east as what is now Czechoslovakia. Hence the sergeant is one of them, and he was only noticing his kin. Do you see it yet?"

"No, sir."

"Not merely did they visit as far south and east of Czechoslovakia but possibly as far to the west as America. They certainly had their innings in Great Britain as well. I know that because both of you bear their imprint. You two, a British and an American lieutenant, are blond, solid, and brave. Why, it's all from the same source. You and the tank sergeant and the men you seek: you're Vikings."

CHAPTER 47

The New Friend

The little man with the cracked face was nothing if not indefatigable and he logged his many hours on watch. He was also cunning. He would not station himself at any location twice in a row. Rather, he rotated, cutting the chances of arousing curiosity by permanence, sometimes at 70 Grosvenor, sometimes at the man's hotel, sometimes at the woman's. And he changed wardrobes and hats as well. Sometimes a mac, sometimes a tweed balmacaan, sometimes a waterproof; up top, sometimes a bowler, sometimes a fedora, and sometimes a derby. He did or didn't carry a brolly. But always he had a scarf (plaid, black, sometimes green, sometimes pale yellow) about the fissure that dominated his face and made it unforgettable, and always he had his little pistol. Sooner or later, by the odds, the American lieutenant would appear, the street would be empty, and the contract would be dispatched.

However, this night was proving particular. Indeed the young beauty emerged, though not with Lancelot but with another female, this one also in uniform. Tall, angular, American by that uniform but exotic as to face. He wondered who she might be and in what American department she

307

might serve, but it didn't really concern him, and knowing would mean nothing as far as ultimate ends were concerned.

Still, he pondered. He could not help it. Miss Fenwick, after all, was the major part of his life now. Perhaps the two women were office chums, perhaps the stranger a newcomer to the shop needing special counseling, perhaps an old friend from home, though the disparity in facial structure rendered that one unlikely. He tried to read body positions and found no symptom of affection, only banal professional distance. There seemed to be no attraction save via subjects being discussed, and that discussion was rather professional as well.

They walked, finding a place likely not to be full of drunken, sexually aroused soldiers, and settled in for a private chat in a dark corner. He waited from across the street, thinking perhaps Lieutenant Leets might join them. Not tonight. The two left after a bit and headed back to the hotel. It seemed odd to Mr. Raven that, of the two, it was the newcomer who seemed to dominate. It wasn't just the height, or the ten-to-one ratio of her words to Miss Fenwick's, but also a slight posture of control, of looming. Sexual? Doubtful. He had heard of such things even if he'd never witnessed them, but in their style of contact, no sexual information was conveyed. It was more of a governess instructing her charge, a teacher lecturing her student. Odd, what?

They disappeared into the hotel. Mr. Raven checked his watch: 10:30 British summer war time. Being diligent, he hastened via two alleys and a cut-through to the hotel that housed the American men and again set up a discreet watch, shifting his weight from foot to foot every few minutes to keep them from going to pins and needles. Tick-tock, tick-tock, it went faster if one didn't think about time or comfort or circumstances.

What did Mr. Raven think of? Recent professional successes? How he got in this strange game? The three times in his life he had had sex, all with prostitutes, two women and a man? A dog he kept as a boy? The way his face had driven his father out? His mother's despair? The poverty, the sense of exile as his face clearly marked him of a different species.

None of that. A neighbor, Mr. Garland, had taken him to Brighton Pier in 1923. He'd seen the vast onion of the Royal Pavilion, the West Pier jutting proudly into the blue water, the throngs of bathers, the open-air cafés. Mr. Garland bought him a lemonade. Mr. Garland was the only man in the world—or woman or child also—who seemed not to notice the magenta crevice that ran from septum to lip, the teeth it exposed, the drool it allowed, the blubber it brought to speech. It was as if, in Mr. Garland's care, he was just another boy. Remarkable, so long ago. At the end of that summer—Raven's best, with an actual pal—he was told that Mr. Garland had hung himself and overheard some neighbor women say the poor fellow had worked in hospital, in a ward for men who'd suffered facial wounds in the Great War. He'd grown used to the atrocities done to flesh by steel, and to him disfigurements were quite meaningless. He just took the young boy because he seemed so lonely and it was so little to do to bring an extra whisper of joy to the world. Alas, the terrible depression created by haunted eyes and ruined physiognomies had become too much to bear. With his death, of course, the Brighton excursions went away. But huzzah, then, to Mr. Garland and all like him who—

There he was, the American lieutenant. Getting out of a little car, one of those sporty things one saw around occasionally, a boxy little sprite of a car with an open cockpit and spoked tires. Seemed to be another lieutenant, this one English, at the wheel. The two men were friends. They had a last laugh, the American's louder, and parted. The American turned and headed inside with an unprecedented bounce to his step.

There would be no killing tonight.

CHAPTER 48

SHAEF

Sebastian drove them to Bushy Park the next morning, scooting around the occasional closed streets where bombs had fallen, pressing hard across the Thames through Lambeth to find a southwestern tangent toward Teddington and then on to the place itself. Once 1,100 acres of green beauty, it was now home to a war town and even a short airstrip behind barbed wire and a full battalion of heavily armed MPs.

But in the interim after Lambeth, when traffic as well as Sebastian's driving ceased to be a drama and the roads and land opened some, Leets had to use this first opportunity to ask a question.

"Sir," he said, "I heard all about the, uh, disposition of Major Tyne—"

"We can drop in on him, Leets, if you want. He's in the Bushy Park stockade, as I understand."

"Actually, no, thanks. But could you tell me how you—"

"Oh, that? Yeah, I needed him out of our hair."

"There must be a story."

"A little one. In 1935, when Tyne was busy cracking colored folks in the head in Harlem, I happened to pull a new second lieutenant out of a burning hut in the middle of a firefight in Honduras. He was pleased at the outcome."

"I'd say."

"But he learned from that incident that maybe leading Marine infantry patrols in jungle fights against guerrillas for a big banana company wasn't quite his cup of tea. So he left the Corps, went to law school, and from there joined the Manhattan district attorney's office. Became a big racket buster for Tom Dewey. He kept in touch over the years. For some reason he thought I was some kind of hero."

"I wonder why."

"Yeah, yeah. So, anyway, I put through a radiotelegram to him, saying a certain ex–New York cop was giving me a rough time on a temporary duty assignment in London. He said he'd take care of it, no problem, because there's always something in the files on a New York cop. He did, faster than I expected. That's all there was to it."

"Wow," said Leets.

"I don't like people thinking I was born yesterday. Tyne and his congressman thought they were cocks of the walk, but it turned out I had a bigger—well, you get the picture."

"That is so smooth," said Sebastian from the front.

"Keep your eye on the road, Sebastian," said the major.

Entered after a laborious ordeal of identification at the gate off Sandy Lane, SHAEF HQ at Bushy Park resembled a western town from poverty row moviemakers: muddy, makeshift, low, rather shabby. It was a little less populated now, because another SHAEF had been set up on the invaded continent, and many had already moved there. So figure in a ghost-town look to this Old West: no lean-tos, exactly, but huts of cinder block and shingles, Quonsets of aluminum, some larger units that appeared to be all wooden. Gene Autry wasn't around and no horses were tied at its

311

hitching posts, but a few jeeps seemed to have been abandoned, quietly grazing at the mud and what little uncrushed grass remained. The sparse population was mostly young men with non-crucial office careers.

Sebastian found Building B, which differed from A and C in that it had eight windows instead of six, and left his passengers off.

"You stay here, Sebastian," said the major, "in case we have to make a quick getaway."

"Motor running, sir?"

"Not a bad idea."

They reported to a tech at a desk, who promptly alerted a second lieutenant of the headquarters variety, who informed them there would be a slight delay—hurry up and wait, of course—until the cast was assembled. He led them to a canteen, got them coffee, and abandoned them amid tables full of huddled conspirators.

It wasn't long, only two cups' worth, before he fetched them and led them to a certain room unidentifiable from any other rooms, housing a conference table and a spew of chairs, and as common as aspirin. Normandy was planned here?

Well, maybe not. But something was, and they were joined by the same Colonel McBain and the brigadier from before.

"Gentlemen."

"Sir," each OSS officer said, initiating salutes only to be waved down.

"He's landed," said the colonel. "Should be just a few minutes. He'll jeep over by himself. Believe me, he knows the way."

"Sir," asked Major Swagger, "may I—"

"No, you may not," said the colonel. "On top of that, you are to make no report to anyone, including Colonel Bruce, of your attendance at this briefing, to say nothing of its contents. As far as anyone else is concerned, it didn't happen."

"You didn't even dream it," said the general, and at that moment the door opened and a thin but solid bald officer entered, dressed in the jacket he had invented and that was named after him. His tie and his shirt were the same color of OD that most would call "brown," and though his accumulation of chest-displayed fruit salad was modest, the four asterisks on his epaulets seemed to weigh a ton each. His face, though immaculately shaven, didn't look as if it had worn a smile in a decade. Wary. Weary. Maybe even sad, at all the death everywhere, every day, over and over. But still crisp and hungry to do his duty, which was to Finish the Fucking Thing.

Again, Swagger and Leets jumped to, and again were waved off.

"Please, gentlemen," said the newcomer in a flat midwestern affect, as if he too had stepped out of a Republic western, this one set in Abilene, "no ceremony. Sit and report, that's what you're here for. I will listen. I may ask some questions. Smoke if you want. I certainly will."

They sat, the SHAEF and First Army fellows up front, the marshal from Abilene a few chairs back. Death-mask face aside, he was rather athletic in body deportment, eyes blue as sky, but no sign of that famous smile. He had quickly plucked out a pack of Camels, plucked one out, and was enjoying it as if it were the only pleasure left in his very long day.

"Major?" said Colonel McBain, "you have the floor."

Earl stood.

"Gentlemen, we can identify the means and the weapons of a special SS unit designated to kill American patrol leaders in near darkness in the Norman bocage," he said. "In short order, I will have tactical suggestions, accompanied by my own request to lead the response in the bocage. Lieutenant Leets wants to go too, of course."

This was news to Leets, although he sure as hell wanted to go. Of course the major had shared nothing of this with him: "I'll tell you what you need to know when you need to know it." Evidently, this was the time at last.

"The first thing you should know," said Major Swagger, "is that you can forget the fighter pilot idea of mine. I sent Leets to talk to the Eighth's leading Jug aces, and they shot that one down fast. But that freed us to pursue other directions, and we have concluded that while, yes, these men are of Waffen-SS—Das Reich, to be exact—and they even have a code name, which is Sturmgruppe Tausend, or Attack Group Tausend, not only aren't they pilots but, more importantly, they aren't German and they aren't snipers."

CHAPTER 49

Escape

Everything had to be planned and prepared. It was not in Sturmgruppe Tausend to improvise. Improvising was for amateurs. The morning after all had voted to follow Sturmbannführer Tausend's plans, serious work began.

He sent the twins, as they were nicknamed—Matthias and Brendt—who were the youngest members of Sturmgruppe Tausend. Blond, remarkably similar, rather attractive in any sense of the word, they were both the sons of clients and friends of Brix, Brix being the *Sturmbann-führer's* nickname in his native tongue, as derived from his true name. Being not elder but second elder sons, they wanted to emulate their father's success so that he might notice them instead of merely giving them large amounts of money to go away and not bother him. Like many second sons, they were earnest and reasonably effective at their tasks.

They departed that night on a southwestern azimuth, using their superior night vision to navigate landforms and wetlands that would have halted others. Each was heavily laden, and instead of their sniper rifles, they carried the new StG 44 with six banana clips in the 7.92 Short caliber, which offered them ideal compromise between long-range accuracy and short-range firepower. Since they were quite young, they also liked that the guns looked so science fiction–like. They seemed straight out of the *Buck Rogers* serials that had been making it to their town since 1934. But their hope was to avoid contact, either American or German.

Their job was twofold. First, to recon the route so that it could be accomplished at speed under light pack when the time came. Second, to cache foodstuffs to a destination certain to be off the main axis of the American attack, where they could rest unscathed and unnoticed until the next phase.

They more or less paralleled the front as they vectored diagonally across southeastern France. Three times they went to earth as patrols passed, all of them German. The Americans were still not up to night patrolling. So much the better. Some marshes were difficult and slowed progress but at least made tracking them impossible, though in neither army was it plausible that a tracker of any skill would have been available.

They made it about a third of the way across the Cotentin Peninsula the first night. They slept soundly, in a farmer's otherwise untouched barn, because they knew that although the Americans were just a few miles away, between them and those Americans, Panzer Lehr, the great armored division, was in place. No American would visit them that night. The IVs and the Tigers precluded such a possibility, and Panzer Lehr, though depleted, would have to be attacked with at least a regiment-sized unit to make any headway.

But what lay beyond was less enticing. Between them and the last twenty miles to a coastal village called Lessay, the territory was controlled by the 2nd SS Division Das Reich. Though they themselves were nominally SS, they knew that line units of the Waffen corps were likely to be tough, salty, Russian-front veterans of the highest caliber, determination, and idealism. Moreover, they were the slaughterers of Oradour-sur-Glane, a village in Brittany they had wiped out in punishment for resistance activities on their trek to the bocage after D-Day. They had then hung 110 villagers in another village, Tulle, in retaliation for a bridge commandos had blown. They would, perforce, see obedience as an absolute and death as a mere technicality, nothing particularly profound. They could easily convince themselves that two fellows loaded with supplies and headed to the coast were deserters. A tree, a telephone pole—even a bridge—would do quite nicely in the application of justice to such criminals, no matter the double-lightning runes on their collar tabs. So the irony—not interesting to them, for they were not educated in the delights of irony—was that they had more to fear from the Germans than from the nearby Americans.

Using their night skills, the twins penetrated and passed through 2.SS, though not without a few tense moments when a patrol almost surprised them and then proceeded to pass within mere feet of their supine positions in the brush.

But they made it to Lessay, finding it picturesque and not quite on the coast but rather on a cove that emptied into the Channel. It was then no hard matter to find a barn to secure their loads beyond the eyes of anyone who wasn't looking for them. Thus, when the night of flight came, Sturmgruppe Tausend would find ample stores of nourishment to succor them on their journey home.

They traveled the route in reverse to return. It was a fraught journey, as had been the first one, but they were certainly up to such challenges. They made it back to the *jactstuga*, the hunting lodge, at about four in the afternoon, negotiating the last miles in daylight on the assurance that the Americans would still be timid. They got there in time for the evening meal. Just in time for Sturmbannführer Tausend's announcement.

"Perfect timing," he said. "Word has just come. Tonight the Americans patrol en masse. They send ten groups into the bocage, all from the entity they call 'Seven Corps.' They need the latest information for their big attack. Instead of information, they will find bullets. Tonight we finish the job. Tomorrow we head home."

CHAPTER 50

Theory

"Here's how a sniper works," said Swagger. "He finds a hide overlooking a field of fire. He ranges all the landmarks before him. If he's got time, he walks the target area, counting steps, taking notes. If not, he relies on his own judgment, which is certain to be good. If he weren't in a war, he'd dream of being a sniper. That's who he is.

"He waits for the targets to come to him. He's particular. He examines candidates through his scope. Officers first, NCOs next, machine gunners third, other snipers fourth, dogfaces last. Having made his pick, he settles in, gathers, calms, finds the position, makes the shot, follows through. He kills one, scatters the others. Now he waits. He knows some hero will rush to the fallen man. He takes that one. Result: fear, lack of aggression, collapse of morale, sense of victimization. Every man is in the crosshairs.

"The sniper withdraws. A good day's work. They do it to us, we do it to them. They did it to the Russians, the Russians did it to them. The Japs and the Marine Corps: same dance. It's how infantry wars are fought."

He paused, lit another cigarette, and thought he had them. Maybe too much detail. But it was a story, and color and detail made it more real. They wanted more.

"Sturmgruppe Tausend does nothing like that. No hide, no range information, no preset escape routes. Everything's fluid, based on where the patrol is going, which the sniper can't know. But his lack of knowledge doesn't deter him; that's the game, the sport. That's why he's here. That's what he loves.

"Instead, he lays up close to our lines, knowing where we're likely going to cross into no-man's-land on our patrolling. He's usually right, because we do tend to do things the same way. He lies flat as the patrol passes him. Then he follows. His extraordinary eyesight lets him see well enough in the dark. Plus, we make noise, we leave sign. We wear helmets, we carry shovels and bayonets, which bang and clank. We shit and piss; there's your smell. We smoke, throw away butts or packs, we eat our Baby Ruths and our K-ration meat loaf and toss it aside. We leave a track as wide as a highway. The sniper is never ahead of us; he's behind us. It's called stalking.

"His fieldcraft is superb. He knows how to move in total silence and he can freeze in a position and hold it for hours if he thinks eyes are coming his way. He doesn't rattle the brush, he never coughs or sneezes, he never falls, and if by some joke of fate he slips or runs into thorns, he doesn't curse. He is sealed up so deep, he's hardly there.

"He knows to the second when dawn comes that day. He's got a high-precision watch, wound and adjusted to inform him when that moment arrives. He'll have a window of a few minutes in which, to his eyes and through his scope, he can see what nobody else can. Possibly he's been close enough already to pick out the leader. More likely, he's figured out the tells. The leader will stand first if the boys are resting, or he'll be second in line if they're moving. He'll have a Thompson or a carbine, never a Garand. He'll have a .45 in a holster and maybe a tanker jacket instead of '41 field coat. He might have a bar on his helmet.

"The shooter makes his shot. He always shoots for the back of the head, because he knows the high-velocity round he's using will go through and the bullet will never be found. Then he freezes as the patrol panics and dissolves. What he doesn't do is equally a part of it. He doesn't eject a shell for us to find. He doesn't engage in a firefight. He doesn't continue the stalk. He goes still and closes down, knowing that nobody will encounter him. When our fellows are gone, lost, captured, or whatever, then he makes his withdrawal, carefully rubbing out signs of his presence, carefully making sure not to have made boot prints or disturbed the shrubbery in which he's hidden. He wants nobody tracking him and he knows exactly how a tracker's mind works. Any questions?"

"You're saying . . . not a sniper. So he's a hunter. I see the difference," said the general.

"Exactly, sir. But what kind of hunter, since we live in a world full of 'em? I'm one, Leets is one. And each of us, and everyone else, hunts different game in different ways, in different conditions, different seasons, different lands."

He paused, waited, letting it hang in the air like the dense smoke.

"Consider the game. Big, loud, stupid, leaves sign everywhere. Crashes through the brush. But very dangerous. Can unleash massive firepower in an instant. Takes a brain shot—the leader—to bring him down. That's the American infantry patrol, Normandy 1944. It's also the elephant."

A pause came to the world.

The general lit his fourth cigarette.

The other two officers blinked, swallowed, said nothing.

Even Leets, thinking himself beyond it, showed surprise.

"Did you see that coming, McBain?" the general asked.

"No, sir. Not in a million."

"Please continue, Major Swagger."

"Elephant hunters," said Swagger. "Same tactics, same risks, same demands, same thrills. It goes even to the same shot. A Scottish big-game hunter developed his own methods a few decades ago. He studied elephant anatomy and learned that there was a passage to the brain through thinner parts of the skull from the rear, and it could be hit—superb marksmanship necessary, of course—with a high-velocity, flat-shooting round, it could penetrate and bring the beast down immediately. No need to face him with an eighteen-pound double bore like a Kynoch .577 Nitro Express. You could do it with a .275 Rigby, a smaller, lighter rifle, with a magazine for follow-up if necessary. It's a discovery someone hunting the beasts for meat to feed a camp or to sell ivory would use, not something for rich safari guys guiding American millionaires."

"Elephant hunters," said the general. "And, sure, our guys are the elephants. I suppose you know which elephant hunters, correct, Major?"

"I do," said Swagger. He turned to Leets.

"The bullet," he said.

Leets opened the briefcase, took out the cellophane-wrapped twist of copper and lead, and handed it over. The officers passed it around.

When it came back to him, Swagger held it up.

"I won't trouble you with the adventures we had recovering this thing and what it cost. But this is the round that killed Sergeant First Class Samuel Malfo on the night of June 19, 1944, in the 9th Division sector of Normandy. It went through the sergeant's head, killing him instantly, but quite unusually deflected downward to the earth and turned up a couple weeks later, moved by rain into a puddle in the trench.

"We took it to the Scotland Yard forensics laboratory. They analyzed the metals and the proportions and concluded it could not have been any of the three common rounds of our campaign, the British .303, our own .30 Government, or the German 8-millimeter Mauser. The lead was of a much purer, higher quality. They could not get a caliber off it because it was, as you can see, so mangled as to preclude caliper measurement. But I asked them to predict, given the proportions available of the partial round, the weight of the total package. They came up with 140 grains, again lighter by considerable degree from English, American, or German service rounds.

"Who uses a 140-grain bullet, one much lighter than the standard weight? Well, the Italians. But their service rifle is basically junk and could never achieve this kind of accuracy. So there's really only one answer: a certain army follows its own way and had picked a cartridge designated a 6.5 x 55-millimeter round all the way back in 1894. A long bullet for ballistic stability but light enough to be driven at high velocity for excellent accuracy and penetration. It has moderate to light recoil, so it can be fired in practice for weeks on end without damaging or dispiriting its shooters. It's a widely used hunting cartridge, by the way, though with lead-tipped bullets, not the pure copper casing of this military round. Who are they?"

He tortured them with another pause.

"Let's cross-check. From another source, we learned that some Czechoslovakian tankers in the area made jokes about the presence of *nejdzniki*, pardon my Czech, in the combat theater. The word means 'raiders.' Who would the Czechs call raiders? Look at Czech history for the answer and wonder why there are so many blonds in Czechoslovakia or here in Great Britain or in the American upper Midwest, Lieutenant Leets being a fine example. Same answer to the cartridge question: Vikings.

"That is, Swedes. The 6.5 x 55-millimeter cartridge, in its 140-grain, full-metal-jacket variant, is the Swedish military round, for the rifle they've used since 1894, maybe the best-made service bolt anywhere—the Swedish Mauser. They're firing out of a Swedish Model 1941 sniper rifle, a tuned and improved '96, with a German Ajack four-power scope. By all reports it is far and away the best sniper rifle in the world, far superior to the ones in our war.

"Adding it all together, you've got a small group of Swedish professional elephant hunters working the bocage against your people, doing damage far out of scale to their numbers. These are exceedingly capable men."

"Major, any speculation on who is behind this?"

"Yes, sir. I believe they are led by a man calling himself, for military purposes, 'Tausend.' The other day, while Leets was at Oxford chasing down Vikings, among other errands, I went through piles of mysterious decrypts the Brits provided, at my request, looking for a bill of lading and shipping destination to which they attached no significance. I was looking for precision watches to the supply battalion of SS Das Reich. I found one, from February 1944, for fifteen Luftwaffe Fliegler chronographs. Model 1941. The Brits could make nothing of the destination, which was sub-notated 'Sturmgruppe Tausend.' The Brits had never heard of it, either before or since. The Germans, I'm told, name special units for their commanders, as in Skorzeny Gruppe for the Mussolini rescue at Grano Sasso d'Italia. So it seems fair to conclude the guy's name is Tausend. Tausend meaning thousand. What's the significance? He's proud of it. It's his best accomplishment. He's one of few men in the world who's killed over a thousand elephants."

CHAPTER 51

The Chief

"Millie, would you come in for a while," asked Colonel Bruce.

She jumped up, of course, pulling the door closed behind her, leaving a personal letter to Harry Hopkins, FDR's closest advisor and good friend of the colonel, unfinished.

She was lovely all days, but this day she was incredibly lovely. Flaubert said, "Sometimes beauty strikes like a knife," and that's what was going on here. It just cut your throat.

She came, she sat. The older man—who was of course hopelessly in love with her, although it was well hidden behind that diplomat's professional personality of discretion and understatement—took a look, finished up with a smile, and said, "You know, Millie, I have never and will never ask about your personal life."

"Yes, sir. It's appreciated. Not that it's particularly interesting or re-markable."

"I do, however, know from many sources that you're seeing First Lieutenant Leets."

"Jim is a very close friend, sir."

"A fine officer, a fine young man. Medical school after the war—splendid. If it matters, and if I were your father, I would certainly encourage you."

"Thank you, sir."

"And, of course, I want you to know that I bought into none of that nonsense that Frank Tyne cooked up. We are well quit of him; I'm quite sure you'd agree."

"Yes, sir. He bothered many of the young women with offers of nylons in exchange for dates. No one will miss him."

"But I do have a certain concern, and though I'm hesitant, I feel I must probe something here. Again, no private details are requested or even sought by deflection."

"I understand, sir."

"I am concerned with Major Swagger. It seems to me that of late he's resigned from our outfit. He's gone over entirely to First Army G-2. I thought it passing strange that he insisted on his latest briefing being held at Bushy Park, not here at 70 Grosvenor."

"Yes, sir."

"Quite honestly, I'm a little put out over not being included on the briefing list, and if he files a report, I'm sure it'll be anodyne. I do feel cut out. So my question for you is simply: Is something going on? Has Lieutenant Leets ever suggested there's some problem with Major Swagger's assignment to OSS?"

She took a deep breath.

"I only know, not from conversation but from observation, that Lieutenant Leets thinks very highly of the major. He believes furthermore that they are onto something and making excellent progress. But I also sense that Major Swagger is very tight with information. Jim doesn't even know what the major thinks or is planning or what the schedule is. The major keeps it all in his head and has very emphatic ideas about how to proceed. I guarantee you that whatever Major Swagger tells the generals at Bushy Park, it will be the first time Jim has heard any of it."

"I see," said the colonel. He seemed troubled. That far-off stare signi-fying ships on the horizon, too far to identify. Then he looked back at her.

"It's as if he doesn't trust the office. *This* office. He thinks there are spies among us. Could that be possible?"

"Nazi spies?" she said.

"Well, who else would spy on us?"

CHAPTER 52

Building 9-King

They got in the car, Sebastian jacked the Ford into gear, and they began to creep toward the exit and the drive back to 70 Grosvenor. Leets was buttoned up solid. He looked like he'd just swallowed a doorknob.

"Don't leave yet, Sebastian," said the major.

Sebastian pulled over.

Silence floated through the car like a vapor.

Finally, Swagger said, "I get it, Leets. You're pissed because everything I told them I was also telling you. You didn't know about the watches, you didn't know about the Swedes, you didn't know about the M42 6.5 sniper rifle, you didn't know about elephants. Fair enough."

"Sir, it's just that it's hard to do what I'm supposed to do if I'm always a day late, a step behind. I could have told you about the brain shot on the elephant. I went on a safari with my father when I was fourteen, ten years ago, and I learned all about that stuff. It's called the Bell shot, after the Scottish hunter who perfected it, another thousand-elephant guy: Karamojo Bell. Actually, Walter Bell."

"Yeah, that would have helped," said Swagger. "Little details like that help hold their interest."

"Sebastian knows more than I do," Leets went on. "I know he's been acting as your agent behind my back, doing things I should do."

"Leets, I have been in a military at war since 1931. I know how it operates and I know how to protect myself from stupidities, politics, and follies. I have to carry everything in my head and never commit it to reports or schedules or outside observation. I use the resources at my reach as best I can. Between us three, I think that 70 Grosvenor is a fucking sieve. The boss is charming as hell but as ineffectual as a clown. He just wants everybody happy. Here's a way to fuck up an operation or a war: keep everybody happy. Do you get it?"

"Yes, sir."

"Okay, let's move on. I told them I'd have a plan in two days, but, yes, in fact I already have a very solid tactical operation in mind. Nobody gets to hear it until I decide, and then it has to happen fast, according to certain guidelines I will set up. Do you get that?"

"Yes, sir."

"Any other questions, while I'm answering? Leets?"

"Only—what's next, sir?"

"We have to find a guy. He would be a big-game hunter of the thirties, the Africa-Kenya safari part. I'm counting on you, because, yes, I know you were on safari. I need an elephant guy if possible, but maybe just big cat and plains if we can find him. I know most of the professional hunters are off playing soldiers with the King's African Rifles. But we have to find a guy fast because we need to know about the Swedes. Maybe Mr. Bell."

"Bell is retired to his estate in northern Scotland, as I understand it," said Leets. "Anyway, he left Africa in 1921. No good for us. He'd only know hearsay and gossip."

"Sir, if I may?" said Sebastian.

"Sure, kick in here, Sebastian. You'll go to prison with us if this fails; you might as well put some money in the pot."

"A guy who's been there is very big on the posh party circuit here in London. The war is the best thing that ever happened to him. He's a foreign correspondent, supposedly screwing the hottest of the girl correspondents, a busty little blonde from *Life*. Meanwhile, his real wife is in Normandy, doing a man's work covering the real war.'"

"Skip the gossip, Sebastian."

"Well, he's been on safari. Written stories and books about it. 'The Short, Happy Life of Francis Macomber,' *The Green Hills of Africa*. He's really a novelist, very famous guy. Big outdoor guy, boxes, hunts all over, fishes for marlin."

"What's his name?"

"Ernest Hemingway. His last bestseller was *For Whom the Bell Tolls*. He was in Spain. He was also blown up in Italy in 1918. Wrote about that too."

"Never heard of him," said Swagger. "Not sure I want to now."

"He'd be perfect," said Sebastian. "Don't you agree, Lieutenant?"

"I have to say I do."

Swagger made up his mind fast.

"Nope. Not interested."

"Sir," said Sebastian, "if—"

"I don't want anybody who's written books. He'll tell the story but fix it as he's going so that it's better. That's what they do. The simple, messy crap isn't good enough for them; they've got to 'fix' it so things happen in a certain order. Plus, he'll find a way to make the story about himself. We'd have to sift through the bullshit for weeks to get to the real stuff. We don't have the time. Come on, Leets. Want to telegraph your father for advice?"

"That's not a bad idea. My dad was a superb hunter and he did in fact know all the—"

And then it struck him. Wham, right in the forehead, sitting there in the backseat of the staff car on the muddy road out of Bushy Park.

"Okay, here's something. See, these guys are all rich and they like nice things. One thing I remember from that trip is that everyone had a very nice rifle. I mean *very* nice. Mostly they had these huge double-barreled short-range cannons in calibers that began with a 4, maybe a 5. I even heard of a 6. Beautifully put together, regulated so that both barrels hit dead on at thirty yards, held to be charge distance. They were called 'Best Guns.' There's about four or five makers in the world capable of turning out rifles of that beauty, power, and reliability, and they're not cheap because they're built by hand, one at a time. My dad had a Holland & Holland .470 Nitro Express that was a piece of art. He waited four years for it."

"Like to see it sometime," said Swagger. "But where are you taking us?"

"Most of those shops are in London. They all sent men out to Africa to hand-fit their clients to the gun. That's what one hundred pounds for a rifle does for you. My thought: go to one of these places now, find the boss, he probably knows a lot of these guys. He might know of one or two in their fifties, too old for the war, who're sitting it out in London. That would be our guy."

"They must have a commo building here," said Major Swagger. "We'll go there, Leets, call your MI6 friend Outhwaithe, get him to pitch in, and get the Brits to open up to us American cowboys. Then we've got something. Where is this Holland & Holland?"

"That's the funny part. London. The factory is northwest of Mayfair. About three miles from our office."

CHAPTER 53

Nowhere

The world had emptied. Rather, *his* world had emptied. All the boys and girls had gone to bed, or at least to ground. Leets had not been back to the Connaught in two nights. He had vanished. The beautiful girl who was his paramour worked late, walked unerringly back to Claridge's, and went up to her room straightaway. He never saw her new female friend again and began to worry if perhaps he'd dreamed of such a thing.

But worst of all, nobody had contacted him. With the unfortunate death of Mr. Hedgepath, he was sure that Mr. Hedgepath's successor would reach out to him, if for no other reason than to maintain contact, to assure him that things were as they had been, that the job intended was still the job to be done. These things did change, he knew, depending on this, depending on that. That was the nature of the spies, and that was why he preferred straight business dealings with gamblers and gangsters and the occasional outraged husband. Their minds were so unsophisticated, their needs so urgent, that they only had one direction, which was straight ahead.

Not so clear with spies. Everything was fluid. Allegiances were always in flow, friendships came and went, loyalties were gossamer, the need to keep it all hushed sometimes generated ruthless disposal. Regimes changed, ministers changed, policies changed, all in a blinding flash of time, fast as a telegram from Europe. Codes were broken, arrests were made, confessions tortured out of suspects; all that came to bear or at least could bear weight on the mission as originally contracted. They hired you as an ally and in a trice you became an enemy.

He could only soldier on. After each night's sentinel duty, he would check for the landlady's notes and, no, there were never any messages for him. That being the case, he resolved to continue the course, finish the job, and collect the second part of his fee.

It was not easy. Engaged, he knew he was vulnerable. Sooner or later someone would notice a man so singular as he emerging from the Bond Street or Green Park tube stations or the No. 22 bus and begin walking an uncertain few blocks' walk to Mayfair. Nobody would notice him casually, because, sensibly, each walk varied. He'd loop around Berkeley Square, he'd head over to Mayfair, then veer back down and enter from the north. He'd go to Piccadilly and come up through St. James's Park. He never repeated himself within the week.

But, of course, the absence of pattern was pattern. If he were being watched by someone from the spies, the care with which he avoided repeating himself would be evidence of his conspiratorial intent, for no other reason would explain such wanderings, save adultery, and no one would ever confuse him for an adulterer.

It seemed even the weather had turned against him. All moisture had left the air, which meant no fog arose. Fog was his friend, and with his knowledge of the city he could penetrate and evade with almost magical ease. What a Ripper he would have made if his game had been cutting tarts!

And damn Jerry, he had by this late date given up dropping bombs on London. That meant the night was organized, quiet, observable, and that the coppers were all walking beats, looking for something to do. It would just be like one of them to note him using two routes to converge on the same spot, nick him, and find the little pistol. Nothing good could come of that one.

Then it happened. Just the littlest thing. But it arrived like a burst of sunlight from an occluded gray sky. He got home and found a note from Mrs. Pitchett-Crumpers.

"Call Brumley 2445," it said.

CHAPTER 54

908 Harrow Road

Less than two miles northwest of 70 Grosvenor lay 908 Harrow Road, backing on a large cemetery whose rolling greenery in the bright July sun made the old building stand forth like a single black tooth. A structure from the century before, it thrust upward as a composition of squared-up brick fronted by windows that hadn't admitted light since the queen died, dirty as the brick itself. Dickens could have toiled at the lathe in years gone by, for the firm had been around since 1835. One presumed a loading dock lay behind, but what lay in front was nothing to be noticed by any except those of the trade.

Outhwaithe had beaten them there. He lounged, smoking, on the fender of his little green toy car, but tossed the ciggie, drew up tight when Sebastian pulled in. He snapped to, saluted the major.

"Sir, Lieutenant Outhwaithe, at your service."

Swagger threw a loose American salute back at him and said, "That'll do it for ceremony, Lieutenant, but I will take you up on the service."

"I believe I can accommodate, sir. I have made some calls. The chap is called Wilson, Robert Wilson. Spent the last forty-odd years in Kenya; in

335

fact, he was there when it was still called British East Africa. He escorted your first President Roosevelt before the Great War, sir. Quite highly thought of among the professional hunters and has guided maharajahs, film stars, and even the odd famous novelist."

"I take it there's no hunting in Kenya now?"

"That's right, sir. Most of the lads are off officering somewhere or other; the others have fallen back on work for the big coffee planters. Wilson was so highly admired that Holland & Holland offered him a job back here supervising their sniper rifle contract with the army."

"Sounds like just the man. Let's go."

Outhwaithe led them to the door. Next to it, a much-weathered brass plaque still announced the names of Harris Holland, the uncle, and Henry Holland, the nephew, though you had to squint to read it.

Outhwaithe knocked, and in time a man—so bent and wrinkled, he might have worked on that lathe with a youthful Dickens—pulled the door inward and peeked out.

"Hullo. Lieutenant Outhwaithe of military intelligence, along with two others of the American department to see Mr. Wilson. I believe we are expected."

"Yes, sir. Please do follow me now. Mind the steps, mind the machines on the darkened factory floor. We're going into the long room."

He led them through a dimmed factory floor haunted by ghostly apparitions, which would have been the tooling so important for turning out rifles among the world's best and the world's most expensive. Now they were shrouded and mute and gave a funereal aspect to the transit through.

A door then led to the "long room," which by contrast was brightly lit, and at a long table five men were bent and working on what, it was clear to all present, was the British Lee-Enfield, No. 4 variation, with which the men of the empire now faced enemies across the globe. But this wasn't just routine inspection and reassembly. This crew was hand-fitting machined parts back together after a filing to improve the fit or the trigger pull; applying a wooden cheek piece to support the shooter's face and therefore eye at the same spot with regard to the scope; attaching a rather formidable optical mount to the piece (it looked like a tractor in fact, with two large screw heads that tightened it to the receiver so big as to resemble wheels, being mightily over-engineered as if from Victorian steel out of the Victorian imagination); and, as a final touch, laying a telescopic sight to the lower half rings of the scope mount, applying the upper half rings to enclose, then tightening all these components together with screws, screwdriver, and good English muscle. The scope itself looked rather Victorian as well: short, steel, mostly painted brass. It could cosh your jaw to splinters, properly launched. It was the famous (to some) No. 32, originally designed for the Vickers machine gun. Why that scope, ancient as it was? Because the Ministry of Defense must have had hundreds of them lying about, which is the way of ministries of defense.

In the back of the room, in a glass-walled cube of office, a man sat at a desk, clearly annoyed by the phone conversation that kept him anchored. As the old fellow brought them closer, the man on the phone nodded, waved, put up a finger to suggest this call was a major nuisance. They heard him say, "Yes, yes, Colonel, I fully agree, but to meet that deadline I . . . Yes, I suppose . . . Yes, sir, I'll certainly see to it. Good day, sir."

He stood and rushed out to meet them. A ruddy-looking man, with sandy hair and a stubby mustache, temples beginning to show silver. What you noticed was the color of a face baked in four decades' worth of sun; however, being light complected, it had allowed itself to turn not brown but instead almost auburn.

"Hullo, so sorry about that: every bloody colonel wants his rifles now, you see. How are you? I'm Wilson." He smiled, and that rearranged his face slightly, opening up the wrinkled crevices around his eyes, displaying their virgin whiteness. That meant he'd never smiled in the field over those four decades.

"Sir, I'm Outhwaithe. These are our American guests, Major Swagger, Lieutenant Leets, here to chat about elephant hunters."

"Indeed, I'll do my best. Happy to chip in. Tried to join the African Rifles but they told me I was too bloody infirm. Trampled by a buff some years back, and my hip's never been the same."

"We sympathize, sir," said Outhwaithe. "All present, then, have been wounded in one sort of way or other in action."

"May I suggest the tearoom? I've had it cleared and nobody will bother. The chaps here don't really need me. I more or less take care of the bookkeeping and get yelled at by the various angry colonels on the phone and make sure every shipment is properly addressed."

"Excellent," said Major Swagger. "Please lead on."

"I've had Mr. Laughlin brew up some tea. I know the Yanks prefer their coffee, but it's hard to get in wartime."

"Tea is fine," said Swagger.

It was a green room, shabby-gentile, with worn leather sofas and arm-chairs and various heads of exotic beasts arranged to look down indifferently. It was, as are most man-only chambers, a mess, with old newspapers and half-full ashtrays everywhere. The stench of tobacco filled the air.

They arranged themselves, old Mr. Laughlin brought the tea, everyone fumbled and sweetened to taste, and then got to it.

"Please smoke if you care to, gentlemen. Everyone else here does. I'll prepare a pipeful myself if nobody minds."

Everyone except Leets broke out cigarettes and in seconds the room had the added appeal of the first battle of Ypres, when the Germans unleashed mustard gas.

"Lieutenant Leets," said Swagger, "will you explain to Mr. Wilson why we're bothering him?"

"Yes, sir."

Leets went through it, synopsizing vigorously, stripping the narrative to its essentials: sniper kills targeting patrol leadership at early dawn, what appeared to be elephant-hunting tactics complete to the preferred Bell shot, superior fieldcraft amounting to seeming invisibility, silence and no trace or track, the inevitable stasis at the front, which had to be broken.

"I suppose if we were Russians or Japanese," said Leets, "we'd just let our soldiers die and chalk it off to the cost of war. But it doesn't work that way for us."

"Nor should it," said Wilson. "We learned that lesson the hard way in the first do with these fellows. But I believe you've left a lot of details out."

"For a good reason," said Swagger. "We've decided the best way to do this is to play a little game with you. Lacking those details, you will confront the issue in the abstract, rather than being influenced by them. The lieutenant will explain as acutely as possible the attributes of the fellow we believe developed, organized, and now leads this operation. We'll see if you can ID him on traits alone."

"Actually, I already know who it is. But do proceed, Lieutenant, as this is quite fascinating."

"Okay," Leets said. "Begin with the shooting. He is a superior marksman. No doubt about it; he—and most of his guys, though they are not as good, really—can hit a quarter-sized target through a scope in near darkness from two hundred yards out from a field position time after time after time. He doesn't miss, and it doesn't matter if you're standing still or moving: if he fires you're dead."

Wilson enjoyed a mouthful of hot tobacco ingest, then expelled it, bringing the scent of cherry vanilla to the room. Swagger fought this aggression with a counter-blast of LS/MFT and the two vapors mingled and chemically mutated into something harsh yet sweet and simultaneously sweet yet harsh.

"Fieldcraft superb, as said," continued Leets. "Plus, we infer leadership skills. He can get men to follow him. He has the gift of conviction and persuasion. We believe this makes him 'charming,' in some way, magnetic, big in personality and grandiosity."

"When this chap and your Hemingway were together," said Wilson, "it was like Barnum & Bailey or Gilbert and Sullivan, each trying to outdo the other in the role of happy king of all men."

"If you know, should I continue?"

"Do, yes. I find this really fascinating."

"The politics don't matter. He knows how vile the Nazis are, what crap they spew. He's beyond that. He just wants to do what he does best, for whatever reason. Maybe it offers freedom from his regrets. But now that the hunting is over, he's turned to war. He went German, we think, because he had a connection. He could just as easily have ended up in this room, converting No. 4s to snipers."

"It could be either Brix or Ernest, in fact, although their conditions are of different sorts. Ernest fears that he's a coward. Who knows? Even I don't. Even he doesn't. But he at least has his art to consume him, though I believe he'll eventually turn on himself, as he's turned on everyone else. Brix has only his hunting."

"Brix, then?" said Outhwaithe.

"Yes, quite. You couldn't know his appetites, which are legendary, his sins, which are endless, and the rage he feels, which he expresses on you but means for himself. He was in love. Desperately, honestly, totally. But he couldn't leave the oh-so-willing African girls and the bloody client wives alone. And thus he drove his wife away, to an Englishman and a divorce. I forgot to mention, he gave her syphilis. That's why, under it all, he's quite mad. Mad at himself, mad at you, mad at me—we were briefly partners—mad at the world, and simply mad."

CHAPTER 55

Secret Mission

It wasn't as if Sebastian was now off duty and could simply relax while the big boys did their business. He had a mission. It was time to go behind enemy lines.

He drove a mile south down Harrow Road, toward London's center, and came at last to a pub called the King William IV. It had been there for centuries and from outside appeared not to have been refurbed since Lord Cardigan complained about the claret.

The young man parked on a side street, went to the trunk, opened it, peeled off his T/5 jacket, and slipped on another jacket, almost identical, except that it wore the oakleaf of a major and its rainbow of dillydangles on the chest indicated a heroic careen through war localities, with distinction at every front. He popped on an overseas cap, that little envelope of a cap known to everyone who's ever seen it as a—well, never mind. It too announced a major, not a tech 5. Now he was fully costumed in the uniform of the enemy. Apprehension meant instant execution—well, probably not, but at least mild remonstrance from someone who frankly didn't give a damn. Still, undercover is undercover.

He crossed Harrow, entered William IV's hangout, a typically dark space with typical posters urging victory, observed all that was typical for any four-hundred-year-old beer joint and that which was not. Which was not included another American officer sitting at a table, pretending to enjoy a glass of the brown petroleum by-product the Brits call beer. Ugh.

Waves, typically American, smiles the same, handshakes even more so, then sit down.

A cankled maid from the J. Arthur Rank British Frump department approached, and he pointed to the disturbing tower of foamless, gelid aspic his countryman was drinking and reluctantly agreed to the same.

"Have you gotten used to their beer, Jack?" he asked his companion, Jack Middleton, Major, attached to OSS at Milton Hall, which trained and supplied all the hugger mugger stuff various commando types were charged with bringing off, including Jeds.

"This batch tastes like they at least pushed it through the filter down at the Shell refinery," Jack said, "so I don't think you could run a tank on it like most of the other."

"Better not get too close to it with your cigarette. 'Mystery Blast' Kills 17 on Harrow Road,' that sort of thing."

"I don't think it would explode," said Jack, "but it might burp. Anyhow, got the you-know?"

"You know I've got the you-know. Do you have the you-know?"

"You know I have the you-know."

The twelve-stone-five lass brought the glass. Sebastian steeled himself for a courtesy gulp, fearing anti-American riots would break out if he left it untouched.

It took its time allowing itself to move, but—finally propelled by the gravity of a tipped glass—an ounce or so passed into his fearful mouth. It tasted like the Battle of Culloden from the mud's point of view.

"Yummy," he said. "I might take another sip in the fifties, if we're still here. Now, how about some nice fish shit? They do a great fish shit here."

"Thanks, I'm saving room for my two hundred and forty-third consecutive pineapple upside down cake at the officers' mess tonight."

"Okay," said Sebastian, mindful of the time, "maybe now we know no MPs are around, we could do the transfer."

Jack kicked a briefcase over. Sebastian pretended to drop something, maybe a piece of beer, and bent over. Peering in, he saw exactly what he needed to see.

"Tell me how that stuff is going to win the war," said Jack.

"I can't. I don't know."

"Then tell me why the guy doesn't just requisition it out of 70 Grosvenor supply? It's not exactly a city-busting bomb. I'm sure they've got it."

"He's odd that way. Doesn't want anybody to know what he's up to."

"So it's as big a mystery as 'Who the hell was William IV?' and 'Is Major Swagger really a major?' "

"Can't answer the first one," said Sebastian. "I never heard of him either. As for number two, here's your answer."

With his right hand, he pushed over a folded batch of bills. Hardly the crime of the century: a hundred bucks.

A few more ingestions of the, er, "beer," and it was time to go. Again, it went smooth as syrup on nylon, and each went his merry way back to other duties.

But Sebastian couldn't get over it.

What the *fuck* could Major Swagger want with ten one-ounce bottles of LePage glue and ten ordinary G.I.-issue Bulova wristwatches?

CHAPTER 56

Brix

"Minor Swedish aristocracy," said Wilson. "Nine hundred fifty-third in succession for the crown, that was his joke. Some, not a lot, of family money. Natural hunter. Hunting father, grew up the in the north, amid rifles and heads on the wall. Had killed all his Swedish game by the age of twelve. Met Karen at eighteen, married her at twenty-one, went to Africa at twenty-two, supposedly to run a coffee plantation. That failed; he was no businessman.

"Odd thing here is that she herself was quite distinguished—not as a hunter, though she did, but as a writer. You may know her by her pen name, you may have heard of her books. In certain circles, highly regarded. In certain circles, he's only her first husband, known as the 'Mistake.' So you have a strange combination of superb hunting skill, crushed romanticism, bitter, perhaps crippling, loss all hidden behind a convincing outer mask of joviality, collegiality, and damned fun. And everybody in the circle loved Brix."

"The name is—" asked Leets.

"Yes, of course. Briks von Osterlund. Called Brix by all. Solid, strong, handsome, but not in that prissy film-star way. Handsome in solid, dependable ways. Flynn could never play him. Maybe Gary, though I'd have to see some lurking darkness in Gary."

"Please proceed, Mr. Wilson," said Swagger.

"Well, not much to tell. For a while, as a professional hunter, fantastically successful. Everyone in the client circle had to have a safari with Brix, then had to do gin fizzes with him at the Norfolk Hotel. Became used to being loved, admired, even adored—by both men and women. I do believe when they write the history of empires, they will leave out the true motivation. Not profit, not land, not power, but sexual license. Certain men—maybe all, but only certain have the means—yearn to escape the homeland's propriety and are drawn to the edges, the frontiers, there to pretend at one thing while pursuing another."

"So there was a lot of—" started Leets, to be interrupted by Wilson's, "Yes. Quite."

"Brix among the worst. It cost him gravely. It cost him Karen, for a few paltry orgasms with unworthy women. Hence, his epic regret. However, let me press on. Major, I suspect your real and only question would be: Is Brix capable of putting such a thing as you describe together? My answer, without qualm or remorse, is: Absolutely. He cannot sit in Stockholm and rot out in pain. Like any man of action, he is at his best when he has a mission. The stalk and kill would release him from memory. He must proceed. He cannot stultify. Action is life; inaction is death. And don't forget, a certain infection is eating away at his brain, making it far more emotional, far less sensible. I saw a lot of that among the old African hands. And, of course, he had drinking problems already. Conceiving and engineering of this would save his life."

"There are other hunters," asked Swagger. "Do you have any thoughts on them?"

"You can see how his brand of capability, charm, and adventurousness would appeal to the young. I can give you the names of several of the

345

younger Swedes, possibly sons of former clients, rich-second-son adventurers who came to be his boys, if you like."

"Probably not necessary," said Swagger.

"Have you solved the mystery of his rifle?" asked Wilson. "It would be a key here."

"We believe it's a Swedish Mauser sniper rifle; they call it a Model 41, 6.5x55. I'd put it the number one sniper rifle in the world, with apologies to your Enfield No. 4 (T)."

"The Swede is a superb cartridge, a superb rifle. When they are finally surplussed, many customs will be built on them. As for the cartridge, one cannot do better for thin-skinned animals."

"I do have one basic question left," Swagger said. "What are his flaws? What mistakes will he make? What can he be counted on to do wrong?"

"Have you hunted, Major? I'd bet you have."

"I grew up with rifles and heads also. The heads were white-tail deer, occasional black bear, some big mountain cats. I went with my father every year to camp. I hope to take a son to the same camp when this is over and teach him the same lessons."

"Then you know the hunter's way, his patience, his need for boundaries and rules. Those make the chase ethical and meaningful. Those are so deep in us."

"Yes, sir."

"Brix will play by those rules, in all except for one circumstance. It's something only the Germans have a term for. Only the Germans, connoisseur of the grotesque, *would* have a word for. But I've seen it, I've had it, I've defeated it. I'm guessing you have as well. The term is *Blut verrückt*."

He drew more cherry vanilla into his throat, then expelled it into pungent, moistened, clinging vapor. He thought the concept deserved such ceremony.

"Meaning 'blood-crazy,'" he explained. "It happens. One shoots the animal, but it does not go down. It bolts. One must pursue into the brush, as honor demands. One follows, knowing that brush hunting is highly dangerous. At last a dribble of blood. Then another. Each is bigger until 'dribble' no longer applies. Finally it's a puddle, a lake. You are elated. You have lived up to the standard of the one-shot kill. You are saved from your malfeasance, lifted from your purgatory, elated with your success. You see a clearing ahead and the blood leads you there. You know what you will find: the creature, dead. Or in the last stages of bleeding out, so that your coup de grâce is a necessary mercy. Boldly, confidently, you step into the clearing. Of course he is there. But not down. Men's vanities preclude them from being realistic about how much blood circulates, especially in an elephant. He is no dying beast but the fully enraged bull, and he knows it's you who've slain him. Now it's his turn."

"Had it happen with a cat once," said Swagger. "I saw the big pool of blood and was sure I had him. I rushed in and there he was. I got him in mid-leap, feeling his breath. When he hit me, he was dead. You think this Brix is inclined to blood-craziness?"

"I've seen him fall prey to it more than he should. I have to say, it was my Holland .570 Nitro Express that saved him once. Had I not fired, perhaps we would not be here and all those boys would not be dead."

"You had to fire," said Swagger. "That's the point, after all."

"If you face him, perhaps knowing of *Blut verrückt* and his weakness for it will be of help. I do wish you luck," said Wilson. "I'm sure you're a capable man, but Brix is the best in the world."

"No, sir," said Leets. "Major Swagger is the best in the world."

CHAPTER 57

Deceptions

Back in the car again, prowling through a fair London evening at twilight, Major Swagger said, "All right, Sebastian. You take Lieutenant Leets back to the hotel, then you drop me at the office. I want to belt out a draft on my tactical plan. Leets, see that girl of yours tonight. It might be a while before you get another chance."

"Sir, she's off with Colonel Bruce tonight at some shindig. I'd happily help on the draft."

"No, I need you alert. Have a drink in the bar, get some sleep. You too, Sebastian. That's an order."

"Yes, sir," said Leets.

After he was dropped, Swagger said to Sebastian, "You got the stuff from the Milton Hall guy?"

"Yes, sir."

"Good. Now forget everything I said to Leets. Drop me at the office. I've got a phone call to make. Then, I hope, you drive me to Bushy Park. I'll be there all night. You'll have to catch your shut-eye in the car. Or maybe they can find you a cot."

"Yes, sir," said Sebastian. "No problem, but . . . I have to ask: Is there some reason you're not informing Lieutenant Leets that—"

"Yes," said Swagger, "and if you needed to know, you'd know."

"Yes, sir," said the young man.

In his office, Swagger got a card out of his wallet with a phone number and made his call.

"Bushy Park Headquarters," came the answer.

"First Army liaison, please," he said.

"One moment, sir."

It was close to ten, but he assumed they were running a twenty-four-hour shop: it was a war, after all, and it went on all the time. And they were.

"First Army, Sergeant Guthrie."

"Guthrie, this is Major Swagger, Grosvenor Street. I need to speak to Colonel McBain as quickly as possible."

"Sir, he's—"

"Wherever he is, Guthrie, find him. He'll want to take this call. I'm at London, Lincoln 5990. That's a direct line, no need to go through the switchboard."

"Yes, sir."

It took ten minutes until the phone rang.

"Swagger," he said.

"Yes, Major. McBain here."

"Yes, sir. In about an hour, possibly two, I'm going to arrive. I would like a dictationist to take down the tactical plan I'm going to relate and hoping for you to move it up the chain ASAP. It has to go up fast for General Bradley's approval so that it'll come down fast. I looked at the long-term forecasts and I believe heavy weather is due on 22, 23, 24 July. I'd like to get this done quickly because in the rain everything is paralyzed, nothing happens, and I know we're getting closer and closer to whatever big operation you have planned."

"Good judgment, Swagger. Obviously the details are embargoed but indeed something of that nature is on the schedule, and it's imperative that your operation precede it."

"I should add, sir, that there are some things for your ears only that I don't want on paper. Some contingencies have to be planned for on a security basis, and that whole initiative is defeated if the plans are put on paper and circulated to SHAEF and all others on the normal distribution routes."

"There's no such thing as too much security," said the colonel.

CHAPTER 58

Wilson

Would this be the night? It felt like it.

Before him, Wilson had two tools. One was a half-full bottle of Haig Scotch—he'd already knocked back the first half—and the other was the Webley Mark IV .455 revolver his brother had carried at the Somme, only to die in 1924 of esophageal cancer. Funny, what? The German Empire killed twenty thousand that day, but it missed Captain James Morley Wilson. A cluster of insane cells, invisible to all except men with microscopes, does the job better eight years later. Jamie was philosophical. He said from the hospital bed where his wife and brother had come to support him, "I suppose one owes God a death, eh? He takes it when he wants it, nothing a chap can do. So do remember me around the campfires and do now and again take a taste of something stronger than water to conjure me, if only for the second, out of the night into which I have passed. That's all one can ask."

Jamie was the bravest man he'd ever known, and he'd known many brave men. He supposed he himself was among them, for the lions that had taken him down, the buffs that had stomped him, the crocs that had ripped slashes into his leg (thank God for the Webley that day!). Survived it all. And for what?

That was this evening's question, to be answered in the depths of the bottle or the muzzle energy of the Webley. *What has it all meant?* He had reached the conclusion it had meant nothing: he was useless. Now, with a war, he had so much to contribute of skills and courage and shooting, to bring the hunting imperative to the battlefield, and inspire. Yet he could not. They would not let him. They laughed at him: old man, buggered hip, muttering about Africa, even getting retired officers to call in and vouch for him. He was officially useless. If this was the night he chose the Webley's half-inch wad of lead, the *Times* would give him a paragraph. Some millionaires and their wives in New York or Mayfair or Hollywood or Baghdad would say, "I say, old Wilson did himself in. Imagine that! The fellow seemed so hardy on the last hunt. Just goes to show, you don't know a damned thing, really, do you?" and return to their vodka tonics or martinis or whatever.

The job he had was meaningless. It gave H&H license to use his name and evoke the old Kenya in hopes that after the war, the hunting would return, and Robert Wilson—worked for H&H during the war, didn't he, on their sniper rifles? Yes, good sport—would restore some luster to the sport and perhaps attract some of his formerly glamorous friends, on the illusion they'd still be glamorous.

Wilson knew what silliness that was. Most of the rich ones he cliented about were quite stupid. They had no idea what they were doing, no appreciation for the creatures they hunted. They were only there because going safari was one of the things a certain set had to do, out of the fashion of the thing, not the meaning, to show off immense disposable income, not courage or character.

This was another argument in favor of nothingness. Helping some dim cinema star or ancient banker's idle son pot a lion did the lion, the only honorable participant in the ceremony, no good. In fact, all clients were Frances Macomber, fatuous shells with wet-loined, formerly beautiful wives who needed (both of them) to tell other meaningless swells at Cap d'Antibes. It had really just been a stunt for publicity, but its only true meaning was that Ernest's father-in-law was rich.

So many years ago with President Teddy, it was different. Teddy was far and above the best of the Americans. Superb shot, unflinchingly brave, without complaint, the stamina of a plow horse, he shot his dreadful rifle brilliantly, the last out of loyalty to the American marque Winchester, which had produced a lever action behemoth of sharp corners and wretched angles and fearsome recoil in a far-too-powerful iteration called .405.

"Mr. President, I'd happily make loan of my .570 Nitro from H&H; it's engineered in such a way as to not butcher you when you fire."

"Thanks, Wilson, but one thing I mean to prove out here is the superiority of our American gun, even if it's a fantasy. I'm sworn to Winchester and told Thomas Gray Bennett, the sahib of the firm, the same. So I'll shoot the damned thing, no matter if my damned arm falls off and my damned shoulder turns the color of a grapefruit left for rot in the Florida sun for two damned weeks. Just have the boys bring something wet, warm, and soft, preferably not a woman, as I am married, to apply to my arm."

So that one had some meaning. Was it the last? He searched but could only remember various degrees of Frances Macombers and would-be Hemingways among the Americans and even more piggish behaviors among the damned Feringhees. No, wait. Gary was fine. More cowboy than actor. Behaved, realized his good fortune, a disciplined shot, and a chap who got the code that Hemingway only blathered about.

He made another dent in the Scotch. It burned—it was a good burn—going down. The blur was commendable, the way everything fell from focus, as was the further distancing of cause from effect. This enabled him to pick up the gigantic revolver.

Not a good thing to play with a loaded revolver when one is mostly potted. Accidents that weren't quite accidents had a way of happening. If he were to do it, he wanted to do it hard and real, not haphazardly, cajoling himself into oblivion and pretending to be surprised in the moment the bullet entered his brain.

The revolver was a stout British concoction, and its over-engineered Victorian solutions to problems others had solved far more elegantly gave it a particularly clumsy affect. It broke down the middle for access to the cylinder, and one then inserted six .455 cartridges, big as duck's eggs they were, into the chambers. It was snapped shut.

To fire, one had to draw back the hammer until it clicked or draw back on the strength of one finger on the trigger, which was like pulling a rake through gravel. Could be done in haste, if Zulus or Huns were upon one, but most people preferred to use the off hand for setting the hammer first, perhaps enjoying the smoothness of the rearward draw of the spur and the satisfying click as it locked into place. Thus was the revolver made ready to fire.

He flicked a lever behind the cylinder, opened the revolver. Six yawning holes faced him. From a yellowish box at least ten years old he withdrew, one after another, six of the duck's eggs and slid them in place. Again they found their position with a satisfying thump. He closed the thing. Satisfying click. His thumb went to hammer, drew it back. Solid, impressive click, perhaps a little vibration as it locked back.

Now it was lethal and volatile at once. The drama of the loaded and more-than-loaded, cocked gun sent a buzz through him. It would take but a moment to press it to his temple and, with the slightest pressure to the trigger, let the hammer fly. A hundredth of a second would remain in the short, unhappy life of Robert Wilson, professional hunter, failed brother, useless drunk; then the hammer would strike a primer, which would ignite the powder, which would produce a tidal wave of pressure and drive the bullet into the—

What was it?

A signal attempted to reach him from far off. What could it be? He could not die without knowing. He had to find the source of this last personal Nile. He uncocked the revolver, restoring the hammer to its supine situation, opened the thing, thereby ejecting (one magical touch of Webley's otherwise thunderous clumsiness) all six deadly duck's eggs from the chamber, three landing on the table, three on the floor.

What?

From where?

He looked at the bloody thing. What was it trying to tell him? Well, more Scotch, obviously. He obliged—obviously.

The revolver was broken almost totally in half, joined only at a certain low point by a hinge. It had been for all intents and purposes sundered. What was in that, what could it mean, what on earth . . . ?

It was almost like a take-apart, a take-apart being a rifle that could itself be taken apart into two halves, unlatched and unscrewed, for the hunter's convenience in travel or other possible applications. Why was this suddenly resonant to him?

Take-apart? Why in God's name was he suddenly consumed with an image of a take-apart rifle.

And then he had it.

A salvation. A meaning.

CHAPTER 59

Flares

Gary was shaking him awake.

"Jesus, they're here!" he was yelling. "They're coming!"

Archer fought the fog of sleep and Gary disappeared, but they were still here. They were Germans.

The man shaking him was named Rossi. Archer was sleeping in a hole wrapped in a blanket, filthy, unshaven, basically miserable. It was dead fucking night, and the fatigue gurgled through every vein and artery in his body. He was hungry. He was cold. Then he figured it out.

He bolted upright, hearing the percussion of small-arms fire, most of it automatic, coming at him. Fuck fuck fuck fuck *oh, fuck!*

He grabbed the grease gun—somehow, he'd never quite gotten around to shipping it back to battalion—and rolled to the line.

He saw tracers floating in from a far hedgerow. They looked like New Year's Eve streamers sheathed in pixie dust, separating into burning blimps as they approached. He saw bubbles, sparks, embers, pinwheels. He saw ghosts—apparitions, phantoms, miasmas, haunts, whatever— seeming to float through the field.

A mortar shell detonated behind him, then three more as the Germans diddled with the range, each blast turning his ears to ding-dong hell, each one releasing a devil wind of shock and grit.

He looked up and down the Dog Company line. No McKinney.

Then he remembered. McKinney sickbay, twisted ankle, needed to wrap it and stay off it for forty-eight. He looked for Blikowicz, the corporal, now in command, but saw him trying to assemble the BAR he had been cleaning. Who the fuck was in charge? The lieutenant was somewhere else, wherever, but not here. Were there other sergeants? He couldn't remember. It was all messy in his mind, which was basically occupied with controlling the I-do-not-want-to-die panic.

"Shit, let's get out of here!" someone screamed.

Mortar.

"There's thousands of 'em!"

Mortar.

"Come on, for Christ's sakes, retreat."

Mortar.

"Get to your foxholes!" Archer heard someone yelling, amazed next to discover it was him. "Get the fuck up, get to your foxholes. Radio, call Battalion, ask for artillery. You guys, come the fuck ON!"

As if to lead by example, he threw himself at the lip of his own ragged hole, cranked the bolt on the grease gun, felt it snap to readiness, and fired a long burst. It bucked, it flashed, it spat empty shells, it rattled the leaves of the trees in which they'd dug their line of foxholes. Who knew if it hit anything but air, but it cleared his mind.

"O'Malley, get that gun in action," he yelled to the machine-gun pit nearby on the left. "Have your assistant gunner get flares up! We need illumination now! God dammit, now, get off your ass."

One by one, Dog Company's reluctant warriors seemed to come to the firing line.

A flare popped finally, turning all to orange, wobbly surrealism as it descended, swinging, on its parachute. In its lurid glow it seemed the whole German army came at him. He fired again, saw targets go down.

"Come ON, god dammit."

"I'm up," said Blikowicz.

"Blik, take that gun down the line and set up. They may have run another squad down behind that hedgerow and it's going to jump us."

"On it, guy," said Blik, and turned, pulling his gunner along.

Still, the Germans came.

Still, the mortars fell.

Still, the air was alive with the sound of extremely nasty humming-birds with ARCHER written on every single one of them. Dust and atomized bark flew where they connected with the natural world. It got crazy.

Still, smoke drifted.

Still a flare popped, brighter this time.

"Open up. Come on, god dammit, lay down your fire. Throw a grenade."

At that point, the machine gunner, O'Malley, joined the circus. He let off a long burst, traversing the meadow full of Germans. Counter-fire drifted at him, looping German tracer, ripsawing the dirt where they struck. Close, they ran across the American .30 position, shutting it down, but O'Malley was up and back on his gun. He hit a tight cluster of dark shapes, spinning them outward like pins after a meet-up with a bowler's ball.

The Dogs had finally achieved some sort of coherent firebase. The smack of Garands, the snap of dink-ass carbines rolled like waves. A few yards down, Blik's BAR found targets attempting to flank. Nobody stood up to Blik.

And then it was over.

Another flare.

Where had they gone? In this field, the sprawled or bunched bodies of Germans lay thick, like some dark, shapeless vegetable. Gun smoke hazed the air, smelling of sulfur and burning leaves. Shadows danced a crazy jitterbug and everything wobbled because the flare wobbled.

Someone next to him put a radio phone in his hands.

"Dog Two, this is White Six. Come in, Dog Two."

"Dog Two," Archer said.

"Sitrep, Dog Two."

"They hit us in company strength. We managed to drive them back. I see bodies all over. We may have taken some casualties, not sure yet."

"Dog Two, get your wounded to pickup point, keep the flares burning all night, stay on the line. We'll come up with artillery fire mission if they come back."

"Wilco, White Six."

"Good job, Dog Two."

He put the phone down.

"Casualties?" he cried.

"One dead, four wounded, two pretty bad."

"Okay, four guys on stretcher crews, any four. Get the bad wounded back to the pickup point ASAP. Ambulance on the way."

"Yes, sir," said someone.

"Hey, College," said the guy named Rossi, from some scary city in the east, "who the fuck put you in charge?"

"Your dago ass breathing air and not dirt puts him in charge," said Blikowicz. "And if you don't like it, come see me and we'll discuss it."

Blikowicz: 190 pounds of cast-iron coal miner from western Pennsylvania. Hands like hammers, arms like axles, full of guts to the eyebrows. Needless to say, nobody cared to discuss it.

CHAPTER 60

Questions

They sat in the colonel's office. Late, so very late. Cigarette smoke, dead butts in an overflowing ashtray, dead mugs of coffee making rings on furniture. Two tired men trying to finish it up, desperate to finish it up.

The clerk typist sat in the next room, hoping he was done for the night. But for now, forgotten, he merely sat in the indifference of officers.

"All right, Major," said the colonel, "I've gone through it, made some notes. I will now play devil's advocate, as I'm sure General Bradley, or more likely certain ambitious members of his staff, will play with me when I present it."

"Go ahead, sir," said Swagger.

"First and most obvious, why go to all this trouble and deception? Seems easier to give a Mustang recon squadron the job of low-level photo missions over the Norman forests. Then interpretation officers could locate the site under the trees, particularly as you believe it to be between Saint-Gilles and Marigny, just beyond VII Corps sector. Next step: a squadron of B-17s each with eight five-hundred-pounders. Next step:

360

a squadron of Jugs, each with eight .50s and twelve 2.5-inch rockets. Mission accomplished. Wouldn't that be faster and more efficient?"

"In my opinion, sir, no, sir. I hate to keep repeating myself, but—"

"Go ahead, repeat away. Consider me an idiot who needs everything explained twice. I'd rather you think me an idiot than General Bradley."

"Yes, sir. To repeat, these men have spent most of their lives and all of their imaginations hunting, and all of its skills are instinctive to them. They will camouflage so effectively that no Mustang jock is going to see them and no photo interp genius is going to pick them out. Instead, the planes will hit less well-camouflaged German field hospitals, kitchen units, logistics dumps, fuel tanks, the sort of auxiliary structure any army needs. You'll destroy them, thinking you've accomplished something, and you've accomplished nothing except to alert the hunters that you've got an idea they're there, so perhaps they change their tactics. Maybe they infiltrate our positions and take out a lot of field-grade officers. Maybe they form a murder squad and go after either Eisenhower or Bradley. Think what that does to troop morale, just when you need it for your big attack."

The colonel sighed.

"Okay, good. Now, next, weapon choice. Our experience has been that our most effective weapon against the sniper has been the rifle grenade, then the bazooka. No direct hit or skilled marksmanship needed. You, against doctrine, plan to deploy the Browning automatic rifle."

"Yes, sir. With tracer. Both the bazooka and the rifle grenade have crude aiming systems and it'll still be quite dark. Both distance and even windage—both the rocket and the grenade, being slow movers, are prone to wind deflection—are factors best handled in full daylight, so it all adds up to mean I have no confidence in their ability to get on the target. A good BAR man can walk his tracers onto it in three shots and continue to fire for effect when he gets there. The assistant hands him a mag, he puts another twenty there. Might as well get out of the .30-caliber all that it offers, which is high accuracy, high velocity, high penetration. It'll chew through any vegetation, even trees. Unless our bad guy is behind concrete, he's going to get tagged in the swarm of .30s we lay on him."

"Last, given the breadth of the problem, why launch from the VII Corps sector? Why not more men, go wider, bring in troops from VIII Corps?"

"I want to make it easy on them. No logistics, no travel, meaning no transportation. If we put ten patrols out over a narrow front into the no-man's-land before VII Corps, we draw the hunters. There are only ten of them. They've never hit more than ten targets in a single night. So I'm putting together something that's too tempting to resist. Hunters have a nose for the herd."

"All right. Now, about this other stuff: the distribution, the speed, the—"

"It relates to certain realities in OSS, sir. I only want tactical plans going there via one source. Easier to control."

"All right, you know it, it's your call. I'm going to grab some shut-eye, then hop an L-4 and see the general personally. I hope to have your authorization by tomorrow by 1500. I'd stand ready to move."

CHAPTER 61

The Rifle

"Matthias, Brendt. Clean your rifles as I clean mine."

"Brix, we cleaned them before our journey and have not fired them since," said Matthias—or was it Brendt? All these months, he still wasn't sure.

"I don't care. Clean again. You will engage tonight and you do not want to die because of a filthy rifle. If you die, it should be because of bad luck and enemy skill, not your own idiocy."

"Yes, sir."

"Watch me. Emulate me. I have all responsibilities on my shoulders: to you, to your fathers, to the others, to the Germans, to duty, to survival. Yet, amid that, I clean my rifle. Do you see? Do you understand? Come, join me, we shall have a little party here."

Each had before him a Swedish Mauser Model 1896, though hand-selected for accuracy at the factory. It was a long, slender weapon, without the hulk of other rifles used by snipers most of the world over. It fired a bullet not of .308 or .312 or .324 dimension, as did the Garand and Springfield, the Enfield .303 and the Gewehr 98, but of .264. The physics to that reality meant that, its weight much reduced, it was propelled through the air much faster. The bullet was also, compared to them, quite long, which meant the barrel rifling grooves spun it more rigorously, which made it more accurate. At the same time, all things being equal, it had a much lighter recoil signature, so that no one feared it, dreaded shooting it, grew to hate it.

That was the cartridge, which, superb though it was, was nevertheless meaningless without a rifle with which to shoot. Hence the Mauser of 1896, said to be among the most ingenious of Herr Mauser's many variations of bolt-actions over the years when the world was arming up for its first big dance. But it was also long and, in comparison to the sturdier conceits of the service rifle 1939 on, rather old-fashioned in appearance. Only the Russian weapon, the Mosin-Nagent, rivaled it as seeming to come from an entirely different design aesthetic as well as an earlier century.

Swedish steel, German design, German optics—four-power Ajack, probably the best in the war—it was a rifle that was clearly intended for marksmanship from behind cover and implicitly suggested the Swedish contentment with self and lack of ambition to invade others. It was designed to shoot enemy officers—Danes, Norwegians, Russians, Germans, whichever—at three hundred meters, and the long steel-cored bullet had been designed to penetrate the heavy wool layers that winter warfare would mandate, search out and puncture those juicy little bags full of blood in the dark interior of the body. The rifles having been constructed with loving care by the anal-retentives of the Carl Gustav Arsenal (in business since 1812), it was a superb instrument of long-range death, though not so much fun for climbing hills under fire.

As with all Mausers, the bolt slid out with the simple manipulation of a lever on the left of the receiver. No more disassembly required. The barrel was then reamed with cotton swabs soaked in solvent, which dissolved any residue from previous firings. The swab was replaced with a steel brush, any stubborn residue was vanquished, and another swab removed all traces. Bore: shiny bright. The rails of the bolt were then scabbed with a brush, again in search of residue. No worry of burrs or cracks, for the steel was too high in quality. A squirt of oil into the trigger mechanism distributed the lubricity of that unguent to all necessary surfaces. The bolt was slid back into place with that satisfying click so seductive to the people of the gun, and the weapon was ready to do any job its agent was capable of doing.

"All screws, make certain they're tightened. Nothing can be loose. Check the elevation dial under the scope. Easy for it to slip, and then you have a miss. Check your notebooks to make certain it's properly adjusted. Check the tape on the sling so you have no rattle. Do one hundred snap fires to make certain your trigger finger has recovered its discipline from the long time between shots. Do stretching exercises so that you are limber for the journey. Check your packs, make certain you have foodstuffs for a longer trip if something should preclude your return to the *jactstuga*. Say your prayers to our Lord and Savior. Swear allegiance to our fine king, Gustav V. Genuflect to the wonder of our extraordinary country. Sing hymns of praise to your fathers, who raised you in splendor and freedom and encouraged you to become what you became. Save a special thanks for the fine woman who birthed you and nursed you and to any siblings who came before or after you and in either case helped you to become what you became."

The boys rolled eyes and shuffled to show their mild annoyance, slightly upset that they were still boys and not yet soldiers, but obeyed.

"Now, sleep," commanded Brix. "It will be a busy night. And tomorrow, having done our job, we shall begin our return."

CHAPTER 62

The Apex

The call wasn't the one they'd been hoping for, not yet. It came at 1400 hours from Outhwaithe at MI6, for Leets, who then handed it to Swagger.

"Sir?"

"Yes, Lieutenant?"

"Ah, I've had a call from Mr. Wilson. He's thought of something else and would most urgently like to see you."

"It's a little late, Lieutenant. We're on standby for orders."

"Actually, I suggested that he motor over. He's now at Berkeley Square, two streets away. West bench. Perhaps you've time to meet him there. I know what this is about, and I do think it's of merit."

Swagger looked at his watch.

"Okay, I'll head over there quickly. But we may get the call-out at any second."

"Yes, sir."

Swagger hung up. "Sebastian, if we get the nod before I get back, you and Leets pick me up. I'll be at Berkeley Square with Mr. Wilson."

366

"Yes, sir."

"It's Wilson. Needs to see me," he told Leets. "Not sure why but should check it out."

He covered the two streets to the square rapidly. London, mid July: maybe weather was incoming, but no sign of it yet. Sky blue and mild, a sweet breeze, some sway to every branch and leaf in sight, no damage visible on the way over, so it was like the old London, the London of All That, which the First War had said good-bye to. Swagger passed a bobby; a couple of American airmen; someone who had to have been either a Spitfire pilot, a dam buster, or an actor playing either; women, all attractive, though he'd exiled that part of his brain to China or possibly even Pluto until The War was over.

He entered the park, saw Wilson sitting alone on a bench down the walk, and noted the place otherwise to be empty. He walked over.

"Mr. Wilson."

"Major, hullo, hullo, so glad you could join me," Wilson said, rising. He was in a droopy tweed suit the color of the heather, and a bucket hat picked in its own tweed to clash riotously with the suit. A dingy plaid tie held an otherwise indifferent shirt together. "I do appreciate the pressures you're under, but possibly I have some aid for you."

When they both sat on the bench, under the splendid shade of a splendid plane tree, Swagger noted that a leather case, perhaps twelve inches by twenty-four, had been lifted to the man's lap. By the burnish of it and the sparkle of the brass fittings, he suspected it was something at the higher end.

"I believe, or so I have inferred, you are going on a hunt after the sniper."

"That seems to be the general direction," said Swagger.

"Well, though I've witnessed the building of four thousand Enfield Ts, I'm not sold on it for that sort of work. It's heavy, the screws can easily slip a bit, the telescope and mount were designed for a machine gun, and our .303 is not by nature any sort of target finder. Nor can I quite get on the Garand rifle thing your chaps have come up with."

"It's an abomination," said Swagger. "I tried to find a scoped Springfield, but they're mostly in Marine hands these days."

"I thought, 'If the major is bush-hunting Brix, who's already got leverage on account of the accuracy of his weapon, why make things worse? Why not make them better? And, indeed, better is what Holland & Holland does quite well."

He unbuttoned the case and lifted the lid. In two pieces, a bolt-action rifle lay in compartments well secured against a red velvet cushioning. The raised lid displayed three labels, the most prominent of which bore the heraldic imprint of the maker, its shop address at 98, New Bond Street, London, W.1., which actually was but a few streets away from where they sat under the Berkeley Square trees.

"We call it a take-apart. You see the convenience. Instead of wearing it on a sling about the shoulder, an impediment to fast movement in tight places and also in the way as you should surely have a Thompson along for closer matters, you can withdraw from your rucksack the stock and the action, fit them together by an ingenious hook action our chaps have invented. There, suddenly, from nowhere, you would have what I'm certain is the best stalking rifle in the world: light, handy, eerily accurate."

Two red-yellow boxes of Kynoch ammunition were included in the box's treasures, among the cleaning rod, a tin of oil, and some rags and patches. Swagger bent to read the information.

"We call it the .240 Apex," said Wilson. "As a man of the rifle, you'll appreciate it. In actual caliber, .245, in shell a flanged magnum, in bullet one hundred grains of soft-nose, in velocity around—I think this will please you—three thousand feet per second."

"Wow," said Swagger, indeed pleased.

"We came up with it in 1920 for thin-skinned African plains game. The heavier guns were difficult to snap-shoot well. Reports from Africa have been enthusiastic, and I have dropped and seen many drop an impala at range with just that rifle."

"What's the scope?"

"The scope is our own, extremely well-made from German glass and Birmingham steel. Four times magnification. As you can see it is already locked in place, hence no need to adjust each time in and out of the box. I've zeroed in on our range to my eye; perhaps in the field you'll have time to dial it to yours. But it can put five in an inch at one hundred yards with the Kynoch."

"Seems just about perfect."

"This is what we call a Best Gun. Much care has been put into it by men who've been doing this sort of thing for half a century. Thus the wood is exhibition grade, with gorgeous figure running through it at high shine, the checkering perfect in execution, the metal highly polished, and every single piece hand-placed to assure perfect fit and function."

Swagger's eyes ate the thing up. He knew a fine rifle when he saw one, and with its mellow rhythms of blond woven through the wood, its precision of construction, and its perfect grace of design, he understood in a second he was seeing the extraordinary. As would any rifleman, he thought: *I want to shoot it.*

"Far from cheap at thirty-five pounds to the customer and he's happy to wait a year for his to arrive. This is yours now, as my contribution to the war. My morale is not your responsibility, but the idea of pitching in with more than imprecations to king and country, plus checking shipping labels and dealing with the odd buggered-off lieutenant colonel, has great meaning to me."

"Mr. Wilson, I'd happily accept this as a loan. In certain circumstances, including the one I'm headed into, it could be the absolutely right medicine. But only on the proviso that afterwards, if both it and I are still around, you let me return it."

"That sir," said the old hunter, "would be a privilege. This one is new, one of the last civilian orders the factory completed before the war. Its original owner, I'm afraid to say, has perished. North African desert, tanks. So it has been sitting in our gun vault since then, waiting for the war to end and a well-heeled American cinema star to appear. It has not yet been blooded."

"I hear you," said Swagger.

"Do blood it, please, Major."

CHAPTER 63

Pisser

r. Raven waited. Nothing.

But he was not waiting for Leets and the girl. He was not in Mayfair. He was actually in the Cheltenham tube station, there by order of direction from a strange voice on the Brompton exchange.

The bloke had said: "Men's loo, Cheltenham tube, red hat, between six and seven p.m. Urinal." Then he hung up.

He had investigated the loo, to find it the usual slime hole caped in Anglican squalor, complete to the countervailingly nauseous odors of urine and those chemical cakes they place in the urinals to keep the smell from overwhelming but in actuality only magnifying it. Grotesque.

Seeing no red hat at any of the installations, he'd abandoned an in-room observation point for a bench outside, near the gigantic, endless moving stairway that took travelers up and down to street level. He sat, obsequious and uncharismatic, one of London's endless accumulation of gray men with gray lives and gray pasts and gray futures. Nearby a news kiosk was still open and the leaderboard for the *Mail* announced, YANKS TANGLED IN VINES, over a four-column shot of a disgruntled G.I.

crouched in some thick vegetation as, presumably, Jerry's snipers owned the air above his head. He looked grim, bored, doomed.

You and me too, mate, thought Raven.

The seconds slithered by. At one time, a doodle went off somewhere far away. Hitler was still launching them, hoping, one presumed, for a lucky hit on Parliament or No. 10. Sirens followed, louder, then softer. It meant ten blokes and their missuses and kiddies had gone to vapors when the flat went up. A tragedy, of course, and all involved in the bomb flying should be hung. But at the same time Raven felt outrage fatigue. How angry can one be for how long before it wears thin? He thought he noted the same grim desperation in the faces of others as well, even on the BBC or in the rags. When was this fucking thing to be finished? How much longer? Whatever it is, tragedy or atrocity or royal crusade for all good and holy, it had much worn out its welcome.

Hello.

Yes, red hat, sock-like thing, chap wearing it along with a pale, back-belted jacket, all the rage ten years past, headed into the loo. At last. Raven hoisted his weary legs up, weaved through the beyond-early, not-yet-late crowd, entered, felt the smack of piss in the face. Ugh, so loathsome and filthy.

Man in red hat at urinal. One next to him on left open. Raven went to it, made play at unlimbering but actually did not, simply stood, awaiting. He felt the fellow's eyes pass to him.

"Face, please, chum."

Raven dipped head, reached up and for one second hooked the scarf, lowered it, and exposed the fissure that cleft his lip like a rip in the wall of the universe, then re-scarfed.

"No faking that, then," said the chap.

The man with the cracked face had a moment of scalding anger, and into his brain popped the image of pulling the kukri and cutting this slithery snake hard and deep just for the brief pleasure of seeing him die in his own blood in puddles of stranger-piss. But he just clenched his teeth.

"The Yank has gone back to the front, they told me to tell you. He'll be there for nobody knows how bloody long. You'd best steer clear of his digs, then, on the off chance some copper gets wind of you. They'll tell you when he's back and you've got to go hard and get it done."

Raven nodded.

"Good fellow," said the go-between. "Now, any chance you'd suck my bone for a quid?"

"None," said Raven, took a quick look around, saw that the place had gone deserted, then cut him deep across the face with the knife, opening a long, lasting gash. Blood fell out of it like marbles rolling off a table. He went down into the piss with a splash.

Raven then unzipped and urinated on him, taking his time. If anyone came in, seeing the spectacle, they left in a split second.

"Do stay down or I'll open you wide knob to nipple, you cunt wyrm," Raven said, then put himself away, turned, and headed out to the moving stairs.

Part Four

NIGHT SHOOTERS

CHAPTER 64

Young Guy

They met at 1700 at the 9th Infantry HQ, about a mile behind the lines. There were about thirty of them, highest rank a second lieutenant, the rest sergeants and corporals, from 4th and 9th Infantry Divisions, that is, VII Corps. They were either BAR men or assistants or patrol leaders designated for the evening's work.

They sat, ragged and G.I.-tired, in their folds and swoops of ill-fitting olive drab twill, all of it the same, all of it different. Most wore the M41 field jacket, some wore paratrooper boots, some wore boondockers, all wore the canvas leggings laced tight. Straps ran across, around, and off them at various angles and looped over various appendages running in various directions over their torsos. Some had grenades, some had bayonets, some had .45s, one had a Luger in a shoulder holster. Some had day-old beards, some week-old beards. Pants were bloused or not, depending on nothing. Since various contractors had various ideas about the meanings of olive drab and Shade No. 2, the variety of hues of the largely improvised khaki universe tended to devolve into a cascade. It looked like an explosion in a khaki factory. Add wear, distress, patching, multiple washings in lye soap, and it became clinically insane. Whoever heard of an army where nothing matched? Wasn't "matching" in some sense the point of an army?

But the guys so costumed had acquired, to the last of them, the languid beauty of men who lived close to and worked with danger, even if it never occurred to them. They self-segregated by unit but were not hostile to each other. They'd all been through too much shit for hostility and suspected the forecast for tonight was more shit, heavy at times.

At 1705, six officers entered, more or less similarly dressed, though cleaner. Some creases were even observed, and fresh shaves. No ties, of course, no decorations, nothing but the foreman's watchful look.

"TEN-hut!" came a call, and the infantries cranked to, but before getting fully upright, a younger fellow said, "At ease. Sit down, men, relax. Smoke 'em if you got 'em. Remember to peel your butts."

He went to the head of the room, while behind him the other five found wooden chairs.

"My name is Collins," he said. "You work for me. I work for General Bradley. He works for General Eisenhower, who works for President Roosevelt, who works for the American people. I wouldn't be here and you wouldn't be here if those bosses didn't think it important. I for one think it is so goddamned important, I drove myself in a jeep through a rainstorm to get here. Are we square?"

A murmur of assent swept the audience as it dawned on them they were looking at one of the stars of The War, their corps commander (youngest in history), Major General "Lightning Joe" Collins. The general's presence itself carried the message of: Do not fuck this up. They therefore resolved to not fuck this up.

"I'll be short. You're about to be briefed on an operation by Major Swagger of Intelligence. He was on Guadalcanal same time I was. They're still talking about his work there, all over the Pacific. You listen to what he says. I think it's a terrific plan. It'll get us back in the war and pave the way for getting the hell out of the bullet garden. Major Swagger?"

Swagger stood.

"Thank you, sir," he said.

He turned to face the men.

"Tonight, we're going to kill some snipers."

CHAPTER 65

News of the World

The bulletin arrived, as usual, at 1600, teletyped from First Army. She opened it, read it quickly, understood therefore where Leets had vanished to, and set to work.

"Sir," she said over the intercom, "the 1600 is here. It seems to contain information about our missing boys."

Colonel Bruce came out and quickly looked at it.

"I fear we've lost them," he said. "They're now a part of First Army. They're not even reporting to me anymore."

"Maybe this happened so fast they didn't have time. You know what they say, hurry up—"

"And wait. Except this time it's wait, wait, wait and then suddenly 'Hurry up.' I also suspect that Major Swagger's usual paranoia is at play here. The fellow simply does not want anyone looking over his shoulder."

"As I said, Lieutenant Leets says he's very capable."

"I hear the same. I feel like the father of the star football player who has no idea what football is! Well, get it mimeoed and distributed and we'll see how it turns out."

"Yes, sir."

She inserted a mimeo paper into her Underwood, scrolled to find the right starting spot, and began to type.

Taptaptap.

PSECRET TOPSECRET TOPSECRET TOPSECRET TOPSECRET TOPSECRET TOPSECRE

BY ORDER OF GEN BRADLEY

AUTHORIZED MAJGEN SMITH

FIRST ARMY STRATEGIC SUMMARY NO 43, 22JULY1944.

The same as usual: broken down and summarized by Corps sector of responsibility, the news of the day on the European Theater of Operations, same as it had been since a little after D-Day.

Stasis at the front but for incremental progress as the troops were regrouping after the long-awaited capture of Saint-Lô, with German counterattacks expected. Enemy activity, beginning with the usual question: Where was the elusive SS Das Reich? Otherwise, unconfirmed sightings of panzer divisions moving here or there, coming and going, combining and recombining like amoeba on a microscope slide. First Army activity: same for American units as designation of corps and then division meant less and less while maneuvers made regrouping mandatory. Units, it seemed, were liquid, and they squirted and puddled this way and that, sometimes by design, sometimes by accident. You could wake up and find the guys the next bivouac over were completely different today. Update on deployment of Sherman tanks with improvised "bocage busters" engineered to their snouts to crush through the medieval barricades with minimal loss of life. Bad news on the artillery shell shortage: no quick end in sight. Reports on Army Air Forces attacks on enemy bridgeheads and supply depots, which, the USAAF claimed, were going fantastically, although they always said they were doing a fantastic job. Combat reports: routine, except for a larger-than-usual counterattack near Saint-Lô, resulting in heavier-than-usual casualties. An 88 barrage near another French town, casualty figures unusually high. Shoptalk: command changes and then finally updates from the four corps, three of which declared: NO ACTIVITY PLANNED. But not so for one of them.

VII CORPS

Night patrol activities to resume in frontal sectors, in and around St. Gilles. 4th and 9th INFDIV units will patrol in strength night of 22/23 to ascertain enemy artillery strength and panzer relocations.

Taptaptaptap.

CHAPTER 66

The Sergeant

Archer sat in the fourth row. He was now a buck sergeant and would be leading his people on the deal tonight, because, after all, he knew the territory. He'd learned it the hard way.

He sat, listening, as Major Swagger, still a war god to him even if Gary wasn't around to share such amusing trifles, briefed the guys on what would be going on, called Operation Toto. It seemed easy enough and he liked the way it ended.

"Okay," said Swagger, "that's it. Questions?"

Of course a silence, and then somebody said, "Sir, just curious. Seen a lot of operation names, usually places, but nothing like Toto. Is there some story there?"

"Archer," said Swagger, who seemingly hadn't noticed him, "tell them."

"A few weeks back, Private Gary Goldberg went with us on a patrol to develop intelligence for tonight. On the way back, he blew up a tank. But he always had a wisecrack, and when he raised his head to say a gag line, one of these guys we're after nailed him coming over the line. Gary was a good man. Very good man. He was quoting Judy from *Oz*: 'Toto, there's no place like—' and that's when he got nailed. The idea is to salute him. He earned it."

"Any others?"

A hand went up.

"Go," said Swagger.

"Prisoners, sir?"

"I'll take that, Major," said General Collins. "I don't want any reports, official or otherwise, of prisoner executions. That's not our policy, never has been, never will be. At the same time, the point here isn't to take prisoners, it's to kill snipers. If you have the shot on the German, you must take it. No one should die, nor should any extra effort be made to acquire prisoners. If they are taken, it's by-product, not product. That's on patrol leadership. You NCOs, keep control of your men."

Another hand.

"Sir, I've been on the BAR since North Africa, first as an assistant gunner and now I'm the gunner. Have done a lot of shooting with it. I love it. I may marry it."

There was some laughter.

"If you maintain it, you won't get a Dear John from it," Swagger said, to more laughter.

"Yes, sir. But shooting it at night always involves more or less guessing where the rounds go. Tracers help, but still we have to walk the fire into the target. That takes time. If these guys are as salted up as you say, they won't panic but they could easily roll behind or drop into cover they're sure to have found. If we miss 'em, we scare 'em, but since they're professional, they'll just be back tomorrow night."

"Good question," said Swagger. "BAR men, raise your hands."

Twelve hands came up.

"Lieutenant Leets."

Leets rose and with a briefcase went to the audience and gave each gunner two objects.

"You've just been handed a brand-new G.I. wristwatch and a one-ounce bottle of LePage's glue. The watch isn't a souvenir. The Army doesn't give souvenirs. You'll have to steal those on your own. When you get back to your outfit, you take a bayonet and you very carefully break the crystal and shake out all the fragments. Then you take the LePage's and you squirt a dab of it onto your BAR front sight. Then very carefully—you may need tweezers for this—you peel off the minute hand of the watch and you plant it in the LePage's, exactly tracing the front sight. The hands of the watch are painted in radium by the young ladies of the Waterbury Clock Company of Connecticut. The hands glow in the dark.

"What that means is that you'll always have your front sight marked. You put the marked sight on your target and you dump your mag of tracers. Shouldn't take but a second or two, depending on the breaks. Your assistant gunner hands you another mag and you dump another twenty. You let the .30 tracer do its work."

"Anything else?"

No. Questions answered.

"Okay," said Swagger. "Just remember the key principle here: They think they're hunting us. We're hunting them."

CHAPTER 67

The Stalk

The Americans were loud tonight. Perhaps it was that they were so out of practice, as Sturmgruppe Tausend had been so effective it had all but closed down night activities.

Matthias could hear them coming, he could hear them going. Six, in pot helmets—sometimes they went in knit caps, like socks—with the usual sound of a parade. Jingle jingle jangle, clank clunk crank, bing bang bong—it seemed like every piece of equipment they had crashed into every other piece, all the time, every step. Plus, they sighed, grunted, groaned, cursed, even chided each other. It was a clown show.

That was fine with the young Swede. Truth was, like many of his age, he'd gotten bored with this whole thing some weeks ago. It was fun through June, sure, and when you knocked one down, it felt like you'd done something more or less important. But still: it was an army, even if it was a Swedish distillation of a German actuality, and while he appreciated that Brix kept the actual German soldiers away and out of everyone's hair, it was still an army. He had to write up a report for each kill. He had to locate it on a map. He had to clean his rifle, again and again.

He had to keep his laundry in rotation. He had to watch his drinking, and while moderate in his appetites, the fact that a real blowout with aquavit was forbidden had made it so attractive.

And Brix. You think this was the pinnacle of his life, but the man's responsibilities seemed to be wearing him down. So charming, so vivacious, so charismatic—but here, week six of summer camp in the middle of a world war—he'd been ground down out of anxiety, overwork, pressure to maneuver with or against the Germans, fears of some kind of big American counterattack, which all knew had to be coming but not when or where. All of that had crushed the man whom everybody loved.

"I'd say Brix needs a vacation," he'd said to Brendt that afternoon before they set out for the sector.

"I'd say *I* need a vacation," said Brendt. "Why don't we just disappear now and head back along the path that we found out of here."

"Brix would tell your pappa. Your pappa would be so disappointed. This was to teach you discipline without actually having to be in a real army. It was a fabulous opportunity."

"But a few more Americans? What difference could it make?"

"You'd never know. For want of a nail, the shoe was lost. For want of a shoe, the horse was lost. For want of—"

"I've heard that so many times, I may get ill."

"Well, that's the official line and it's not without its wisdom."

"Tomorrow, thank God, we leave. Not soon enough."

"I'm with you there, brother."

Now he let the Americans build a good lead, perhaps a quarter of a mile. He moved silently in their wake, on the balls of his feet. At his age, strong and lithe, with his superb vision and coordination, it was quite easy. He didn't understand why the Americans were so bad at it. What of red Indians, all those silent creepers from the two-reelers that made it to Stockholm on a regular basis. Nothing at all like that. Instead, big, stupid men, always seemed to be complaining. He spoke English and he'd hear snatches of conversation.

"Bring it up, god dammit."

"No, compass says we turn left here, by the stream."

"I don't care what the map says."

"I told you to change your socks, god dammit. *Now* you get a blister."

"Okay, light 'em up, but stay low."

"Jefferson, you take the point. When we get to the sunken road, we'll take a break and a map check."

Such imbeciles. He'd been to Africa twice and had killed nine buff and six elephants. That hunting was so much harder than this. It was as if these elephants had gotten drunk, so they could be counted on to do stupid things, get lost, meander in circles. Sometimes they actually never went anywhere. They just got a mile outside their lines and hunkered down for the night, figuring it wasn't worth the effort to get any closer to the German lines.

And when you culled one of them, they panicked like children. Not so in Africa. Even the herds stayed together after a cull. In fact, generally they paid it no attention and went about their business while the boys took the ivory and what meat they could for the campfire, leaving the rest for the hyenas that moved in the shadows, waiting for the safety of dark so they could close on the carcass for the evening meal.

Americans scattered, running like ninnies or little children through the night, bumping and tripping and whining. Twice, soldiers had run so close to him he could smell their perspiration as they lumbered by, more or less in the direction of their own lines.

But he knew that, for them, the night was a terror, an ordeal. For him, it was a bounty of possibility, never truly dark but just a melody of darker tones. You could always see enough; the stars or a moon made that certain. It was almost too easy. What could go wrong?

.   .   .

He told them to bumble, but these guys bumbled even more than they had to. They sounded like a silent film comedy with a soundtrack.

"Too much noise, Lieutenant?" asked Sergeant McKinney.

"I guess there's no such thing as too much noise. Not tonight," said Leets.

"I'm going to have to rest them soon."

"Of course. But in the rest we revoke to discipline. No smoking, no noise, no moving around. Disperse 'em. We don't want this guy shooting until we're set up."

"Got it, sir."

McKinney gave them hand signals, close enough to see, and the clown parade suddenly acquired some professional style, halted, and melted to earth. No cigarettes were lit, nobody complained about the CO or how stupid this shit was. They got it.

Leets scooted back along the column of hunched and hard-breathing G.I.s, all tensed up, eyes outward and alert. He got to the end, where the BAR man and his assistant gunner crouched.

"You guys all set?" he asked.

"No problem, sir," said the corporal on the BAR.

"How's that radium working out on the front sight? Still in place?"

"Looking good, sir," said the man. He lifted the big rifle, and Leets could see at the end of the barrel just a whisker of illumination. It was enough to get a good sight picture.

"You square, Private?" he asked the assistant.

"Yes, sir. Got the tracer mags on the left and the straight ball on the right. Won't mix 'em up."

"Okay, when we set up, you know you go to bipod. We want the gun secure and to hold the shots into a tight area."

"I put the bipod back on this afternoon," said the corporal. "Good thing I could find it."

"I know they're a pain in the ass and mostly useless, but tonight it's mandatory."

"We're locked in, sir."

Leets checked his watch. It was about 0615, a quiet night in the middle of a battle. All was still, nothing was bright. Stars above, indifferent, a cool wind pressing its nose through the branches.

He clapped the gunner on the shoulder.

"We'll move soon. Another hour of trampling. Then time to go to work."

He was surprised how hearty this bunch was. They usually went to break about every twenty minutes, exhausted and spent. You could always hear them breathe, the heavy in-out of the lungs, the occasional squeak as some air was expelled through a dry, twisted pipe, the tinkle of urination—and the jokes about urination. They thought it was so funny. Don't spill! Watch your aim! Write your initials! He'd heard a hundred variations on the piss joke. Americans! Babies!

But soon dawn would crack and he'd have his magic minutes of seeing clearly when they could still see nothing. That was optimum shooting time and it worked so much better if the boys set themselves down then. He didn't want to be moving himself, shooting a moving target. If it had to be done, it had to be done, but it was so much better if everyone cooperated. Better even for the cull, for that meant the Bell shot, straight through the head, and for him it wasn't even like death, it was just a sudden cessation of all sensation. No pain, no regret, no contemplation of how a life had been spent, no human baggage; just sheer animal death, total and in its way merciful.

He checked his watch. Its radium hands, ever loyal, ever accurate, declared the time to be 0643 and still the Americans plunged ahead, louder than a parade of fire engines. They had to give up soon. It wasn't in them to make the kind of crazed physical effort that took them to the edge of collapse. He wondered if—

Oh! Sudden silence ahead. They had halted. He heard clanking and bonging as their pieces of metal banged against each other when they went down.

He saw they'd cut through some trees—not a forest, really; more a gathering, with plenty of room between the spindly trunks. He could make out shapes squatting, some comically collapsing backwards, having chosen a slight depression that sloped down to a stream. A match signified a cigarette being lit, then two or three more snapped briefly to light. He was too far to see the glow of the burning tobacco, but it didn't take long for the odor of it to reach him. Americans and their cigarettes.

He was in open ground, about 140 meters behind them. He went flat, squirmed this way and that in the grass, found a comfortable prone off of which to build his position. Looked at his Luftwaffe Fliegler watch: 0707.15. Two minutes until the sun cracked the horizon, turning the night to gray-blue-indigo as it took its sweet time rolling on toward the brighter colors in the spectrum.

The rifle came up, he looped himself into the sling, cranked it tight, slid behind the butt. He had in seconds constructed a superb platform, steady as a boulder. He closed his eyes, tried to will his heartbeat to settle.

He looked again at his watch. Less than a minute. He checked conditions: no wind, no humidity, temperature about 60, all quiet on the Western Front. He sunk stock against shoulder, manipulated his arms so that the rifle rested on bone, not muscle, with a thumb clicked off the Mauser safety, a milled flange at the end of the bolt. He found his cheek weld, took a calming breath, opened his right eye. At four-power the scope magnified the world fourfold, and the men went from blurs to shapes, recognizably human. They were at leisure and would now begin their journey homeward, having happily run into no Tiger tanks or Stuka airfields.

The reticle through which he viewed the domesticity of the American patrol was steady. It was basically three inward pointing bars at 3, 6, and 9 o'clock, almost but not quite intersecting dead center, allowing a gap that defined the hit. Superb optics, German, Ajack, the best, absorbed every last photon of light available and held it in perfect clarity.

He watched as a man rose, turned left and right as if to address his followers, then turned to lead them out. The light broke. Nothing dramatic, as if by cinema lamp magic, just a sudden sense of something halfway between blue and indigo descending smoothly on violet, massaging its hold on detail, defining the image to crispness and precision, and at last there was perfection, the man turned away, the others not yet back in the war, some not even done smoking, yes, perfection. As always, his finger made the decision, not his brain, and the rifle reported and jacked back into his shoulder, though neither phenomenon was particularly overwhelming, and in the return of the rifle to position he saw the head in tatters, and only confetti swirled about.

This is not as it should be, he thought.

In the thin woods, Leets watched as the squad set to work. Two two-by-fours, one four feet long and one two feet long, were screwed together in pre-drilled holes. A G.I. M41 field coat was tossed around the shorter span, scarecrow-like and buttoned tight, while a G.I. sock cap, crammed with newspapers, was taped to the shorter upper strut. Someone placed his helmet atop and the thing was ready to do its duty, if it only had a brain. Fortunately, the men who'd lift it had brains.

Leets low-crawled back to the gunner. He was prone behind the BAR, had the rifle stock hard in his shoulder. The gun was supported by two metal legs at the muzzle that held it solidly in place parallel to the earth.

Over the smear of green at its snout, the dark world of trees and fields loomed, where, somewhere, a man hid, waiting to kill.

Leets whispered, "Okay here?"

Nods arrived signifying the affirmative.

"Eyes open. Look hard. Corporal, this works best if you see the flash yourself. What's your name, by the way?"

"Dunn, sir. Pennsylvania."

"Okay, Corporal Dunn, let's make this work."

The corporal was into the part. His eyes peered hard at the blankness before, knowing that at a certain moment, for just a splinter of a second, the unburned powder of the sniper's cartridge would blossom in flame beyond the muzzle, yielding a plumage of billowing, shapeless radiance. Then it would be gone.

Leets checked his watch.

He let the second hand rotate through 0709.15.

16.

17.

18.

God let there be light—a little, at any rate. If you looked in a certain direction, you'd see the edge of blaze as a piercing announcement of day arriving, but nobody looked in that direction.

19.

20.

"Raise it," said Leets, and ten yards behind him two G.I.s hoisted the crucified dummy upward, held him steady at the zero-degree angle, though not absolutely still. His movement, in the blur of the scope, would signify life.

The bullet arrived before the sound, but only by a fraction of a second. It hit under the lip up the helmet and smashed into what should have been pure brain but was instead a cluster of wadded paper held in by knit wool. Still, it exploded, the helmet flying one way, the paper clumps blown outward in chunks like giant tufts, a vibration of velocity buzzing through the construction.

All three of the spotters saw the flash spurt in the night, and by the time Leets and the assistant would have issued instructions, Corporal Dunn had already pivoted the automatic rifle onto it, by virtue of the radium minute hand broadcasting guidance.

He dumped the mag.

The BAR—Browning automatic rifle—was the infantry's squad automatic weapon, one of the last weapons designed by John M. Browning himself. It was solid, heavy, reliable, powerful, and accurate, like all the other machine guns the old Mormon imagined. Nobody wanted to carry it, but when the lead started flying, everyone wanted it in the fight. Nobody argued with it, as the Germans twice and the Japanese once discovered, and neither of them had a gun in the inventory that brought so much death off so much portability.

The tracers flew like neon arrows to the target exactly, and nowhere else so skilled was Dunn's gun hand. They rushed outward, streaks of sheer incandescence.

Leets could see them arc explicitly into the target area and dissolve it into a smear of generic, detail-free destruction, which was whipped dust, frags of vegetable matter, grass mowed hard, bits of rock and mud, a symphony of destruction by velocity and energy in a small area.

The gun ran dry.

The gunner had the dead mag out and the fresh one in in about two-tenths of a second.

"Area fire now," said Leets. "Soak it."

To Matthias, it seemed the wall of hell had sprung a leak, so dense was the incoming rush of flame. For each of his sins a point of light roared Matthias-ward, a cluster of livid destruction, sparks of death. Then, on the power of visual association and at a speed that had no place in time, he thought of Christmas candles, of Sweden in December, crisp and cold, of Pappa and Muti and his laughing siblings in the big house in the woods outside Stockholm. He thought he'd live there forever.

He was wrong.

CHAPTER 68

Nutmeg

The first call over the SCR-300 came into Operation HQ—the 60th Regiment, 2nd Battalion G-2 tent at 9th Division Headquarters at 0755.

"Nutmeg Leader, this is Nutmeg Two George One, do you read?"

The voice arrived over the blocky receiver in a soup of fogging static and blur, with odd squeaks from the atmosphere or screeches from random radio demons, yet they galvanized the crew of operators, the clerks standing by, and Colonel McBain, running the op.

A tech sergeant responded, "Nutmeg Two George One, we have you. Proceed, over."

"Nutmeg Leader, we have a good kill. Repeat, we have a good kill."

Cheers broke out; everyone there knew what was going on and that the reports of successes or failures would now be coming in.

"Ask him to summarize," said McBain.

"Nutmeg One, can you give specifics, over?"

"Nutmeg Leader, worked like a charm. He took his shot at the dummy, our BAR team nailed him hard. I'm standing over him now. About thirty-five, blond guy, SS camo, all messed up by the fire."

"Rifle recovered?" said McBain, and the message was repeated.

"Nutmeg Leader, affirmative. Nice scoped piece, but not German. Will bring in."

McBain took the microphone.

"Good work, Nutmeg One, now get your people back here."

"Sir, that's one," said the radio operator. "Do you want me to relay to Notorious, Jayhawk, or Master?" meaning division, corps, or army.

"Let's wait on that and see if—"

But another radio crackled to life, this one from another 9th component, "This is Nudge Fox Two, over."

"Go ahead Fox Two, over."

"Nutmeg Leader, we got one. Still alive, shot up pretty bad. Rifle all busted to hell. Don't know how much longer he'll last. Bring him in or let him bleed out? Over."

"Tell 'em to make every attempt to get the guy in," said the colonel, even as still another call came through.

It went so fast. All the 9th Division Ns reporting success to Nutmeg, all with kills or captures. On its own set of SCR-300s, the 4th Infantry Division patrols called in similar successes.

"Sir, relay?"

"Yes, yes, do it," said the colonel, so the word went up as well as out, to Notorious, then to Jayhawk, Master and from Master to Liberty, which was SHAEF itself: "Operation Toto reports eight SS snipers killed, two wounded and in captivity, though there's no optimism on one of the wounded."

"Casualties?"

"None, sir."

"Tell the boys: well done," someone very important said.

"We will, sir."

But one patrol hadn't reported. It was Red King Three.

Major Swagger.

CHAPTER 69

Red King Three

What wasn't right?

Something? Many things? One thing? What, what? *What?*

He felt like the crazy man on the Norwegian Munch's bridge, hands to ears and head, a scream of dread exploding from his lips in a blue world under an orange sky, the point being the pointlessness of it all. Why should it matter? It's only me. *Who am I?*

The answer, of course, was: *I am I.*

He could see the officer's head in the tiny space defined by the three near-intercepting posts as gray light washed across the scene, increment by increment, yielding details, such as the rakish tilt of the helmet, the stiffness of carriage, the slight apprehension expressed in the backward and forward twists of torso.

Based on the size of the man, the range was 175 meters.

No wind, little (though increasing) light, his finger on this trigger, the reticle crucifying the officer as steady as a brick in mortar.

His finger caressed the trigger, yearned to trip it and send another—his last—to hell. Not this chap himself, nothing personal, but all, all of them, the rich ones, the suave ones, the condescending ones, the ones who loved him but not quite enough, the ones who were not man enough to keep their wives out of his bed. Fuck them all, he thought, and fired.

Except he didn't. His finger would not let him.

Look again, it commanded.

And so he looked again and saw how the officer was not merely stiff through the neck but also the torso, and when he rotated—the light just revealed this last, saving detail—the jacket did not twist and stretch, it rotated exactly with him.

Nobody moves like that.

It's a trick, he realized.

Somebody—whoever—was onto him.

Swagger, next to the gun crew, used every last morsel of concentration as he peered into the dark. Nothing. Just varying shades and tones of night, perhaps a blackness here suggesting a bush, a mellower wave suggesting a tuft of grass, some verticals suggesting the trunks of the thin trees, and, farther back, the line of a hedgerow, effectively limiting the known universe.

He lifted his watch up into his line of vision.

Sunset seven seconds past, now eight, another with each snap of the second hand as it rotated around the dial, onto ten, then fifteen.

"He's not biting," he said. "This son of a bitch is smart. He saw something." He thought a second. Then he said, "Gunner, on my tracer, short bursts."

He stood and his eyes prowled through the darkness, looking for probable hides. A density of tone had to be a knot of brush and he peered through the peep on the Thompson and put five into it, the tracers flicking out to that place, perhaps devastating it. Then came the follow-up from the automatic rifle, its reports deafening in the otherwise silent night, its tracers moving faster and straighter, hitting, kicking up clouds of earth, one or two striking rock and vectoring off. But by that time Swagger had moved on to find another possible hide and marked it, to then be purified by the Browning gun.

They worked through both mags of BAR tracer that way, then hunched. Archer came up to them from behind.

"He never fired at the dummy," he said, perturbed.

"He saw through the game," said Leets. "He's probably halfway to Stockholm by now. But maybe we got him on the area fire. He couldn't have moved far. The son of a bitch."

"Shall we go after him?"

"Wait a bit," said Swagger. "If he's alive, he's got the advantage, both in longer reach and vision capabilities. We have firepower and manpower. But I don't want to lose any of your people stupidly, for nothing. We'll let it get brighter, then move out in two elements and see if we can pick up the trail—if there is one."

The world exploded. Had he not already decided it was a trap, he would not have rolled right as a burst of automatic fire, leaking blaze, struck into the earth he had so recently occupied, doing to it as it would have done to him. The stings of pellets of dirt, rock, organic matter made supersonic, sprayed him. Abruptly, pain announced itself from two vague places on his body.

The firing went on for quite some time. It lit the world, and where it pounced, it ruptured. Enough tracer bounced off rock to turn the spectacle incoherent, with zips of flame spinning or rushing this way or that amid the rising torrents of dust and the falling torrents of green fragment.

Then, just as abruptly, it stopped.

They know I'm here. They just don't know where. They fired where I could have been and only by the grace of a second's realization was I not where I should have been to meet my death. Now: Can I escape?

This, however, was not only a question of will, strength, and luck. It was a question of wounds. Broken bones meant he'd stay where he was and go into some kind of last-stand effort. Maybe take a few with him. But if he could move, it became a different world.

He willed his senses to settle down so that he could isolate the pain. Yes, thigh, deep and painful. But when he put hand to it, no blood, no puncture in the material of the SS camouflage. This meant a ricochet, probably, part of a broken bullet whizzing insanely through space, still packing massive energy but not quite in the killing range. No broken bone.

The other, however, did in fact bleed. It was a groove gouged down his arm, from elbow to shoulder on the pure horizontal, at which point the bullet and the body parted company. Too severe to be called a graze, too deep to be called a flesh wound, yet too far from important organs to be called a fatal. Moreover, no bone broken and, judging from the quantity of the blood, no veins or arteries sundered. But it would bleed continuously until swaddled and pressured into stillness. It was, fortunately, his left arm, not the limb that was the core of his shooting. He knew when he had time he could pull gauze from his med pack, wrap it tight, and recover possibly even without stitches. It would make an interesting scar to show around the safari fire in years to come. It would become part of his legend.

So on to the next: Would they come after him?

His thought was yes. They'd gone to so much trouble to kill him, they must be very disappointed that he hadn't fired and brought their little charade to a proper conclusion. Of course they'd come, if only to see if blood suggested wound, which suggested trail, at which point they'd pursue.

Next question: How would they pursue, since pursue they would? If they came en masse, they'd make too much noise. As well, the Germans, having heard the ruckus, might send their own troops to inspect, and a firefight that nobody particularly wanted would take place over stakes that nobody particularly cared about.

He concluded that only one man would pursue, if he found a blood trail. That would be whoever had worked this ploy out. Sharp fellow. Hunter himself, had to be, or at least blooded by much action. Interesting to chat with such a fellow. Surely one of Brix's few peers in this game. That teased Brix, and in his mind a plan began to form.

It was superb! It was wonderful! It played on the hunter's mind! It turned the hunter's instinct against him. It would be so much fun!

This is what I came for! he thought.

Now all I have to find is a rabbit.

"Blood, Major," someone yelled, and Swagger went to the call.

There it was: not an ocean's worth, but not a scratch's either. The dust was scuffled from where the man had rolled, risen, and started off, wounded badly or not, in what dark was left.

Where would he go?

Swagger looked up to the landscape. It was Norman to the bone, the rolling meadow, the scruffy, occasional spurts of scrawny trees, the random clots of bush, the array of gullies where a millennium of rains had forced the land to yield, the far hedgerows, a row of larger trees perhaps signifying a creek or a sunken road, and finally a patch of wood.

"He'll go there," he said, pointing to the woods.

A sniper needed cover but he also needed escape. He was not Japanese. There was a point to survival, not a shame. All the smaller knots of vegetation or the gullies that gave the seemingly flat land the complexity of a rolling sea offered no escape. He could shoot from any, but men would come at him from all points of the compass and there'd be no way out. Killing him would be a mess, but kill him they would.

The forest, in contrast, offered a continual process. Shoot, move, fall back, shoot again. He could maneuver under cover, from trunk to trunk, bush to bush, gully to gully. He could take a few, maybe more than a few, and the longer he held out and the more shooting there was, the more likely a German patrol would arrive.

Swagger knelt, pulled off his rucksack, and opened it. He took out the two halves, each wrapped in towel, of the Holland & Holland rifle. Almost too beautiful for words, its highly figured wood a symphonic complexity of tone and texture, its blue metal finished to silky blue perfection, it was meant for rich men; it would now serve in the infantry, the poor man's ultimate destiny in wartime, in a world of mud and crawling. Hence: military necessity, which in wartime trumped all, from humanitarian love of your fellow man to simple sentimentality to the beauty and singularity of the instrument. It was the creed of all soldiers.

He linked the two halves, pivoted them, felt them glide together over expertly machined and polished metal joinery, twisted tightly to align the one to the other, then threw two latches that completed the operation and made whole and potent the Hollands' African stalker in its scorching .240 Apex version. Above that, undisturbed by all the take-apart and put-together, ran the high tube of the scope, 4x, the finest German glass in the world as amplified by British engineering, which, as the Spitfire proved, yielded to none.

"Okay," he said to Archer, threading Kynoch's .240 cartridges into the magazine, "get your people out of here. If we all go after him, he kills at least half of us. Meanwhile, the Krauts will figure out there's a game on a thousand yards from their lines and send a patrol out to investigate. You guys could have a nice little gunfight, but what's the point? It would mean nothing, not with a big attack coming on soon. Get 'em out of here. I'll go after this bastard."

"Sir," said Archer, "you need another gun."

"Sergeant, I said get 'em out of here."

"He needs to be played between two men. He has the advantage of concealment, accuracy, and patience; we're the bumbling pursuers. If he thinks there's only one, that's what gives the other guy a chance."

"I wouldn't ask any man to draw fire for me," said Swagger.

"Sir, you are not asking. I am volunteering. We both know this is how it has to happen. Corporal Blikowicz can get the patrol back. I'll go with you. I'll make the noise. When he shoots, you'll see the flash, and you can put one of those fast-movers through his eye."

"At the expense of your life."

"Maybe he'll miss. It has to happen."

"Hasn't happened yet."

"You know it's the right move, sir."

Swagger paused. The reality: Archer was right. Chances for success went up exponentially with a two-man team. However, chances of the sergeant catching one also went up exponentially.

He handed his Thompson to the nearest kid.

"You keep that grease gun handy," he said to Archer. Then, "Blikowicz, get these boys back fast. We'll be in when we're done."

With his keen eyes and keener experience, Brix had no trouble finding them. In fact, he found four. But finding them wasn't enough. It couldn't be just any hole but a fat old guy's, the beast who was too jaded to dig deep for protection, who no longer had any kits and dams to protect, who had learned, over long years of survival, that just a few feet was enough—usually.

Brix plunged his hand in, was immediately bitten, drove forward despite the pain, got his hands around the buck's throat, and extracted him. People think bunnies are so cute and cuddly, for little girls to love. Not so. They are, as animals, quite savage by nature, and death fits easily into their worldview, either on the receiving or giving end of it. This old buck was huge for his species, clearly a warrior, and the scars he bore about his head and face marked him as the victor in many a fight to the death with the younger chaps for access to the old man's does.

The creature went about six pounds, was strong, his thighs muscled and his paws well equipped with ripping claws, as many a younger buck had learned to his regret. His two front teeth were yellow stalactites, engineered for pure chomping of animal, vegetable, or mineral. In Brix's strong grip, he squirmed powerfully, tried to bring either teeth or claws into play, meaning to rip his aggressor profoundly. In normal circumstances, any man so encumbered would have dropped the battling warrior, letting him scamper off. Brix did not have that luxury.

Instead, he adjusted his grip slightly for leverage, then, holding the thing entirely by its head, snapped it hard two or three times. Rabbits have committed many sins, but loquaciousness is not one of them. The neck went with a dry click, the animal died in the silence by which it had lived, and it hung from Brix's hand, dead meat.

He stuffed it into his shirt, feeling still the warmth that would remain in its body for an hour or so. That essential task completed, he turned to consider and saw that he was nearly a hundred yards deep in the Norman wood. It calmed him. He'd grown up in forests. He'd hunted in forests. He'd stalked elephants in forests, as well as buff and rhino and lion, all of them wounded and desperate. He'd spent a lot of his life in dangerous forests, where death was a whisper away and the careless were always invited to dinner—of themselves.

His thigh still signaled pain. It had betrayed him twice, giving out, tossing him to the ground. If anything, the pain had increased. The only thing that would help would be brandy and rest, neither immediately available and unlikely to be so for some time. The wound on his left arm still leaked blood—not in copious amounts but in spurts and squirts, too visible to miss. The Americans would have no trouble following such a trail, even if they were city-bred.

Trees closed the light off, to his benefit. He could see so much that others couldn't. Moreover, even better, it didn't look to be a bright day, with rain possibly moving through. He glanced at his watch, and it informed him that it was not yet 0700. Full light was still half an hour away, which gave him time to maneuver invisibly. He looked at the architecture of his little sector, searching for an arrangement of features that would best fit his plan.

Behind him, he saw what appeared to be a patch of light maybe two hundred meters out. That meant a clearing. Clearings were good. Most forest business finished in clearings, where one beast managed to lure another and settle up fast. That, then, would be the setting. To the clearing. To the quick finish. To the last shot. To the triumph.

This is what I was born for, he thought.

Swagger and Archer had reached the edge of the forest, but by different paths. Archer had come straight across the meadow, hunched low, dropping every few dozen yards. Swagger, meanwhile, had told him it was unlikely he'd get shot: the guy was too busy getting in deep and setting up. He wouldn't be hasty or improvisational unless forced. Taking him at his word, yet still feeling a valve of fear installed in his guts, he advanced steadily, finally making it to his destination. Swagger was already there.

Swagger had taken a different route. He'd gone through—it cut, it hurt, it ripped, but so what?—a hedgerow and in the adjacent postage stamp had double-timed it to the same forest line, where, he'd guessed correctly, the hedgerow would abate. He reached it and slid over to the right, seeing Archer's open field run. Had Archer played football like Leets?

Rejoined, the two conferred.

"There'll be a path. Not a gateway, not a sidewalk, but enough room for a single man or a single-file column. It was invented by cows. It's been there for six hundred years. You'll see blood. Not a lot. This guy isn't gut- or lung-shot but, from the blood, more likely winged in a limb. He's mobile but not fast; that's why he's got to settle in, anticipate your approach, quell the hurt with concentration, and lay down one well-placed bullet. Got that?"

"Yes, sir."

"That's your play. Don't rush or take stupid chances. I'll be in deep cover maybe thirty feet inside the woods. I'll move with you, but don't be yelling to me. You'll hear me more than see me. I'll be there."

"You can keep up with me?"

"I believe I can. You got the gist of the plan already. Your job is to draw his fire. When I see the flash, my job is to put one through his eye. I just won't know how it's going to play until I see the spot he's picked."

"Suppose you don't see it?"

"Every July 22 for the rest of my life, I'll think of the heroic—what was the name again?"

"Ha ha," said Archer.

"I'm glad you got a promotion," said Swagger. "This is sergeant's work."

Archer scooted the wood line and indeed quickly found a path. He peered into a dark tunnel, the ground worn barren, where countless herdsmen had trod to get their cattle home the quick way.

He knelt.

"Got it. Yeah, there's blood here. Not much, a dribble. I only see it because it's bright against the dark."

"You only see it because he wants you to see it," said Swagger, not far off, but invisible. "He's got to recon before he takes a shot. He doesn't yet know if it's one guy or an entire mechanized infantry regiment on his tail.

As I say, he's settled in, has his shooting lane picked, is waiting for you to step in it. But he'll be patient. Hunter's nature, sniper's nature."

"Okay, I'm set."

"Take a deep breath. Not too much longer now."

"Got it."

"All set?"

"All set."

Archer began his slow, cautious trek into the woods.

It had worked so much better than he anticipated. Now he had made it to his shooting site and was well set, prone in undergrowth but with a clear line to the target area. All the parts of his plan were exactly as he had foreseen, all in perfect relation to each other, the distances precise and more than manageable. He had checked the rifle to see if any of the knock-about had upset it and found that it still held true, twenty-eight notches of elevation, at four notches per minute of angle precise on point of impact at about 140 meters. No wind to deflect or calculate against, the rifle alive and supple in his hands. No need to go to position yet, as he knew that positions only degraded over time. When his target emerged and he went to position and scope, he wanted those muscles full of strength and energy.

It wouldn't be a blue day. Ripples of pewter and silver occluded the sky, low-hanging clouds sure to bring rain shortly. That was better. He'd conclude his business, then begin the limp back, sure to run into Germans from the 353rd Infantry checking on the disturbances. They could carry him back. Then he and the boys would unite at the *jactstuga* and depart by nightfall. It was almost ov—

He heard him.

Something of the dampness in the air amplified each sound. He heard the rattle of metal parts clanging—why did they make so much noise?

Didn't they learn?—and (possibly this was his imagination) some dry, heavy breathing. The man was scared, and why wouldn't he be? But he was game, give him that. He would be their best man, of much experience.

Brix concentrated. Then he saw him moving along, still in shadow. That ridiculous helmet they wore, so round against a nature that never in a billion or so years had produced anything so round. The details gave themselves up to Brix's hard eyes.

Khaki swaddles, nothing fitting, again so American. Too much equipment, all those things carried on straps and belts. Baggy pants. Some kind of Schmeisser-type submachine gun, presumably for spraying the suspected piece of sniper-infested forest; grenades, little checkered ovals calling up the baseball so important to the American imagination.

The rifle came up, and for just a second, before the target dropped and disappeared, he saw the young, rather handsome face. Square, earnest, duty-driven, so American. As if from a cookie factory; they all seemed to look alike. But he was all soldier, at least at this penultimate point of his life.

A lesser man than Brix would have fired, but there really wasn't enough time for the certainty Brix demanded. To do so would mean a lunge at the trigger, sure to throw off the shot. Brix's patience and utter trust in his gifts compelled him to rest, wait, relax.

Could there be more? He hadn't seen or heard any. A patrol would have made much more noise. There was no sign of another man anywhere. No birds stirred in the forest, no low muffled sounds of passage arrived on the cool, moist air. No sign of anything except the boy, the passage into the clearing, the hesitancy.

Brix knew why he was hesitant. He had designed it as such. The boy perched on indecision, awkward, his jubilation at what he beheld in deep conflict with the sniper fear that no man at war ever overcomes. He could see the boy again. He'd taken his helmet off, held the submachine gun at the ready for fast use, its wire stock hard against his shoulder for stability. He was mustering courage. He was convincing himself. He was on the cusp of action.

Brix found his position. The world leaped into clarity, four times the size it had been, the details more exact. The boy had not shaven; he could not keep his left hand still on the submachine gun's lengthy magazine as his fingers pressed the keys of an imaginary piano involuntarily, fearful of danger.

Brix knew what had to happen. It was willed in the perfection of his plan. *Blut verrückt.* Who could deny its allure, its call, its offer of salvation? Brix cranked right a bit, to the space the boy would soon occupy. He was ready.

The boy stood.

He was exactly in the intersection of the three posts of Brix's scope.

Brix's finger was faster than his mind. He fired, perfectly.

CHAPTER 70

SCR-300

Leets was on the SCR-300.

"Nutmeg Red Leader, this is Nutmeg Blue George One, over."

"Receiving, George One, let me put Colonel on, over."

Leets was in the G Company area HQ, a rude assemblage in the hobo army crossing France, well protected by sandbags, machine guns, and soldiers. He was just in. But so was someone else.

"Nutmeg George One, this is Six, over."

"Yes, sir. We made it back, but I thought you should know: Red King Three just came in. That is, most of them. Swagger and Sergeant Archer are still out there."

"What's going on, George One?"

"Their guy didn't bite, never took a shot. They area-fired on his proximate location, and found blood traces. Major Swagger and Sergeant Archer went after him. They sent the other guys in, worried they might get bounced by a Jerry patrol."

"Christ," said the colonel. "No need for that. Seven kills, two captures. We won. Another guy, who cares?"

"Swagger cares," said Leets.

From far off, there came the dry, disassociated sound of a rifle shot.

CHAPTER 71

Blut Verrückt

Blood everywhere, red-black even in the feeble sun.

"We got him!" shouted Archer. His voice reverbed with ecstasy. "Sir, we killed him. I'm going to—"

"NO!" screamed Swagger. "You hold up there, Archer. You freeze, you go still, you don't do a goddamn thing."

"Sir, I—"

"Archer, you calm down, you hear? You just stay there, god dammit."

"I . . . sir, it's—"

"Archer, listen to me. What do you see?"

"I can see into the clearing. There's lots of blood. Blood everywhere. He got hit in the area fire, he got a rag on it or something, he wrapped it, then he staggered out. He kept going for, what, a mile, but finally the rag slipped, he fainted or fell, he lost control, and it all came roaring out. Jesus, there's blood everywhere. He got to the clearing, dying, he staggered, he fell. He's there, he's down, he's dead. No man could lose that much blood and still be breathing. I'm going to—"

"Archer, it ain't his blood." It was the first grammatical mistake he had made in two months, not that he noticed, not that he cared.

"Major, I—I—No, he's there, we hit him, it's all over."

"It ain't even started, Archer. That's a dog, a cat, I don't know. Gutted, squeezed dry of blood. It's supposed to make you crazy—it *did* make you crazy. The second you step into that clearing to check, he puts the bullet through your left nostril from two hundred meters out, then goes home to pork chops and beer."

Archer said nothing. The great war had gotten very tiny.

"Here's the game. I'm moving forward to the forest line, setting up. I'll check the landscape and figure where he is. When I give you the okay, you come around. You come fast, looking for the body, the grease gun ready to put a mag into it. But one second later, you go hard, flat, prone. You cannot stand still but for one second. That's as he eases the last bit of wiggle out of his sight picture, even as his finger is applying pressure against the break. If you're late, he kills you. Got me?"

"Yes, sir."

"I'll zero on his flash."

"Suppose he shoots when he sees me?"

"Not how his mind works. He's already seen you. He knows you're here, trying to figure it out. He wants you to see the animal carcass. He wants you to know he's fooled you. He wants you to know he's out-hunted you."

"Yes, sir."

"You hold tight now."

Swagger eased forward, squirming through the rough brush as easily as possible, trying to squeeze around bushes, to slide by saplings, to move without alerting this little piece of Normandy that he was here. He made it within five feet of the sunlight and considered what he saw.

Clearing, yellowed thatch, not grass, more like a kind of ragweed cut here and there by clumps of wildflowers, patches of low brush. A stump lay off-center, a hundred years' worth of raw, dead wood, now gone gray with age and rot. Beyond the forest, its nuances hidden in shadow, its color not really green but a riot of greens and shades and hues controlled not by rhythm but by nature's need of nonsense. Murky areas were abundant in the forest line.

Which one?

And then Swagger knew.

Not across the clearing.

He was behind them.

He'd ripped the animal, he'd spread the blood, he'd backtracked and let Archer pass. He wanted to shoot from behind. He wanted the Bell shot, into the back of the head, his favorite, his professional elephant hunter's signature of excellence.

Swagger rolled, squirmed to the left. Peered back along the trail that Archer had traveled. He found a pit of darkness 130 meters back. He eased this way, then that, finally finding a vantage under some bushes. He locked into his prone, the rifle so light and easy to manipulate, wanting, somehow, to come to his shoulder.

He squinted through the scope, finding the center of the darkness. Then he moved his eye up half an inch so that he looked over the tube.

"Archer, move into the clearing. Turn on that hard left as if looking for the body. Freeze. It's an animal. One second. Then go down hard. Are you ready?"

"Yes, sir," said Archer.

"Count three and go."

Swagger counted three internally, heard the clank of metal as the boy raised himself, lurched into the field, turned.

The shot was a spasm of light, a fraction of a second's worth, a nova that was born and died faster than a blink, from the low center of the pit of blackness, and fixing it in his vision, he raised the rifle, saw exactly the almost-intersection of the three posts at the vanished nova's site, and his finger took the relay at light speed from his brain, bypassing consciousness altogether.

In the report he heard it, a kind of addendum to the months of effort, to the very long stalk: it was the punch of bullet in flesh. It was a smack, a slap, a snap. It was the meat shot.

CHAPTER 72

Bad News

She had never disappointed him before. She had been perfect, in all things and in all ways, and in fact he was in love with her, as were all men, and he so looked forward to their parties together. But not tonight.

"I'm so sorry, Colonel Bruce," she said. "I have a friend in OWI. Her name is Zora; she's big in pamphlets. She was involved with a flyer, a P-51 pilot. She learned today that he'd been shot down over Germany on bomber escort. She's shattered."

"I'm so sorry," said Colonel Bruce. "When will it ever end?"

"I know we were supposed to go to Maltby's tonight," said Millie. "But I just can't. I have to be with her. You understand."

Actually, understood too well. Maltby was some horse's ass big in MI6 via wealth, not brains or talent, and all the tribes would be gathering tonight to drink his whisky and laugh behind his back. Wives, girlfriends, probably some crazed beauties who were weirdly drawn to the spy world, that sort of thing. Possibly an actress or two. Vivien had a nose for such events; maybe she'd show up with that handsome dolt husband of hers.

Sir Colin had pushed the invitation on him, but the colonel was convinced it was only because Sir Colin, when he wasn't dispatching cutthroats into Europe, had the woof-woof for Millie and, like so many others, knew her to be unobtainable, but nevertheless, even with his dreadnought of a wife, HMS *Devastator*, along, he yearned to look, to sniff, to brush, perchance to dream. So Sir Colin would be quite disappointed.

Such is war. They also serve who only dream of Millie but then go home to empty cots or possibly empty wives. Whoever said war is hell certainly knew what he was talking about.

"Would it be appropriate to send flowers?" he asked.

"She was so destroyed, I doubt she'd notice. But they're quite liberal in that office, so I expect she'll have no trouble taking time off to reassemble and go forth."

"It occurs to me, my dear, you have *never* asked for a day off. And the pressure on you must be extraordinary. Would this be time for you to spend with your friend, who seems to need you more than I do today or the next three or four days, perhaps?"

"Oh, thank you, sir. But I'd prefer not to. When Lieutenant Leets gets back from the front, possibly then. We were thinking about going to Scotland for a weekend."

"Oh, wouldn't that be fun," he said, though the mention of Leets was somewhat depressing, since the whole Room 351 crew had vanished and he had no idea what they were up to. Or even where. The front? And then there was the fuss over their driver's transfer. The name was . . . yes, Sebastian, Ozzie Sebastian's boy, Deaf Sebastian's nephew, wanting out so suddenly. Demanding it, pulling every string he had, and he had many strings! What could that have been about?

But he knew in all circumstances it was best never to acknowledge ignorance, so he made no mention of the situation. Did he know anybody at First Army who could straighten him out? Well, there was that Colonel

McBain who— No, he'd gone to Europe too. Was anybody left at Bushy Park these days?

"Why don't you go to her now, Millie. I'll bumble through the Maltby thing on my own, though I'm sure the entire staff of MI6 will miss you deeply."

"Thank you so much, sir," she said, smiled one of those I'd-die-for-it Millie smiles, and left.

CHAPTER 73

Felled

Silence after the shot. The forest was empty. All life had gone mute to the particle level. The flowers dared not bud, the leaves not unfurl, the wind not whisper. No birds sang, nor peeped, nor hatched.

"Archer. Are you okay?"

He thought the boy must be. No sound of a hit affiliated with the sniper's shot.

A stir, a rustle, a clank of canteen on steel buckle.

"Sort of."

"Wounded?"

"No, sir. But I felt the cemetery wind as it passed. He wasn't but two inches off. Did you get him?"

"Dead solid."

"Yahoo!" said Archer.

"I'm moving in from the right. You move in from the left. Keep that gun ready. You may still have to dump a mag."

"Got it."

They rose and in awkward tandem approached the theoretical chamber of the theoretically dead sniper through the brush on either side of the path. Swagger took the lead, his rifle on sling. He had his .45 in his hand, cocked, unlocked.

Not a creature was stirring, not even a rabbit. Except for the random slosh of the leaves through which they passed, no noise. Swagger pushed ahead but was weary of being *Blut verrückt* himself and didn't want to blow it now with an ill-considered rush into a waiting gun. This prick might still be alive.

He was. But just barely.

He had been hurt before. He'd been thrown three times by buff, breaking a total of seven ribs. His left arm had been chewed badly by a wounded leopard, which Robert had killed with a brain shot from 150 meters with a Mannlicher-Schönauer. One season a croc had broken his leg. Various husbands had socked him in the jaw at the bar of the Norfolk in Nairobi. Hemingway, one of those I-love-you-when-I'm-sober-I-hate-you-when-I'm-drunk chappies, had thrown a roundhouse; Brix had slipped it easily but gone arse-up on a lime twist on the floor—the hotel bar again—and thrown his back out. The next morning Hemingway apologized but his back wasn't interested. It hurt for months.

Nothing like this. The bullet hit with the force of a sledge, blowing him back into the tree, off the tree, into the path, and quite unconscious. He awoke seven or so seconds later to find himself soaked in blood and already dead from the waist down.

The bullet had struck above and a little to the right of the heart, blowing through the left lung, exiting under the shoulder blade on the yaw, pulling mottled tablespoons of lung tissue through an exit three times larger than the entrance. Breathing, not easy but necessary, produced a broken-accordion effect as wind leaked from the wound, exciting odd vibrations that were somewhere between whistle and gargle. It was the sucking chest wound.

Instinctively he crawled, the rifle sling looped around his wrist. But quickly enough he saw how pointless that was and was realistic about his chances, which no longer existed. Death, a black leopard in a tree, watched him with yellow eyes.

Hello, old friend, he said. Gotten around to me, have you? Well, at least I gave you a run for the money.

He rolled over, freed of the rifle, and squirmed, dragging the dead cargo of the lower half of his body behind, to the trunk of a tree. Somehow he willed himself semi-upright, as if on a chaise lounge, and watched as two men, neither helmeted, emerged from the forest. The young soldier and, of course, the older bloke who'd bested him. He looked like he'd been alive five thousand years and fought at Troy, Marathon, Waterloo, and Ypres. Face the shade of lion leather on Swahili shields. His skin had the texture of the road up the hill to Thermopylae. Wrinkles twisted beyond mapping. What was it? Hemingway was always quoting it, hoping it would make him so, but it never did. The American, stoic, isolate, a killer. Something like that. No surprise flickered in this fine fellow's eyes, which calmly studied the scene.

He dismissed the young soldier, holstered his pistol, and approached.

Swagger holstered his .45, then approached the dying man.

"I say," Brix called in his Brit English, "got a cigarette?"

Swagger knelt to him, pulled a Camel from his pack, put it in the fellow's blood-flecked lips, and lit it with his G.I. Zippo.

The Swede inhaled, drawing broadly, enjoying the flavor and the slight vibration of dizziness against his other sensations. Then he exhaled and a tiny column of smoke spiraled upward from the hole in his chest, syncopated to a slight whistle of a wheeze.

"Not exactly encouraging, is it?" he said.

"Doesn't look too good," said Swagger.

"Superb shot, old man."

"H&H .240 Apex. I got it from your friend Wilson."

"Ah, Robert. He's had it in for me ever since he discovered I slept with his wife."

"He didn't mention it."

"The Brits, you know. All buttoned-up. They do build beautiful rifles."

"Don't they, though? This one's a beaut. I hate to give it back."

"I don't blame you. Say, old chap, sorry I'm taking so long on this bit. You really should be going. I'm sure Von Klumphumklopper or whatever his name was will be sending a crew of Bavarian pig farmers after you. A shame to see your celebration ruined."

"I got time," said Swagger.

"Professional courtesy. It's rare in our profession. Alone on the hunt, alone at hunt's end, that sort of thing. Appreciated."

"Anything to convey?"

"Tell Karen—well, no, tell her nothing. God knows where you'd find her anyhow. Tell Ernest—no, he'd make it about himself. Tell Robert he was the best. If he mentions the wife, tell him to forgive her and that it was just the great Brix being Brix. Caught up in my own bloody legend. I think I had some other wives but I can't remember their names. Tell four hundred Kikuyu maidens to remember me well as I remember them. Tell—oh, hell," he said.

He looked upward at nothing, coughed slightly.

"Oh, hell," he said again, and died.

Swagger made it in ten minutes after Archer. Much congratulation. Leets had come over to wait too and was exuberant. The Dog Company CO, Sergeant McKinney, Battalion G-2, with his rimless specs, all the patrollers, all the stay-behinds, they had a little party. No one knew how it happened, as Army regulations strictly prohibit such, but somehow a case of cold French beer was produced and all enjoyed. Even the Germans were polite enough to stay away.

"Shouldn't you call it in, sir?" Leets asked. "They're waiting."

"You call it in, Lieutenant," said Swagger, beer in one hand, cigarette in the other, Brix's M41 resting against the table.

Leets beckoned the radio guy over, took up the SCR-300 transceiver, clicked the transmit button twice.

"Blue Leader One, this is Red King Three, over."

Snap, crackle, crackle, snap. Then, through the grit of the radio universe: "Receiving Red King Three, over."

"Red King Three reporting mission accomplished, zero casualties, coming home, over."

The colonel came on, too excited for radio protocol.

"Swagger got him?"

"Put him aboard the express to Valhalla," said Leets.

Part Five

MR. RAVEN

CHAPTER 74

Maltby's

He was an old man in a dry season. He ached everywhere, most profoundly in his soul. He took his time showering, powdering, putting on new shirt and tie, making certain Teddy had polished his shoes brightly.

"Do watch your drinking, David, dear," called his wife from the bed to which her barbiturate habit—the Mellon millions were of no help—had condemned her.

"I shall, darling," said the colonel, though it was a lie, as he hungered for Scotch, lots of it.

The driver was late; it didn't matter. He got lost; again, it didn't matter. New chap.

"Sorry, sir. I'm nervous on the backwards driving rules."

"Not to worry. You'll get used to it soon enough," said the colonel, diplomatic even to tech 5s from Omaha. "Try not to get us hit by a buzz bomb, young man," he added, and the boy said, "Yes, sir," not getting the joke.

Maltby lived not quite in country but definitely not in town. It was

427

the sort of Victorian monstrosity lots of new money bought, clearly bespeaking no lineage and family but only money and power. Coal bought it, steel bought it, railroads bought it, but nobody who'd ever lived there had fought at Blenheim or even knew what Blenheim was.

The driver dropped the colonel at the big house's big door, which was encapsulated in some clown's idea of a drawbridge design, and, taking a breath of melancholy air, the colonel entered.

Phew! It smelled of smoke like Hamburg after a night's bashing by Lancaster. The noise of chatter had reached highest buzz. While a butler bowed and scraped, took his hat, then led him to the grand room overlooking the terrace and then the grounds, the colonel charted his strategy. It involved a direct assault on Maltby's bar for a fortifying drink, a quick confab with Sir Colin and HMS *Devastator*, a round of hellos and handshakes with those high muckers of Six and Five as he knew them, perhaps a meet with a new chap who might become useful sometime or other, a nod to diplomats, a chummy chat with any high American officers who happened to be present, a few minutes, Scotched up again, to gander at the beauties, a hello–good-bye to the fool Maltby and the child actress he had married (number three, was it?), and then out before the crowd.

Oh, so much easier if Millie were there!

Millie, I miss you so!

We all miss you so!

Why did that fool fighter pilot boy manage to get himself shot down today of all days. Why did this Zora choose to have her nervous breakdown now? Had the woman not heard of delayed grief? So inconvenient.

He went into the large room, took a blink at the high drama of the lighting, a dry swallow at the wall of smoke that belted him in his face, looked about for Sir Colin, found him, waited patiently for eye contact, achieved it finally and—

"He's here!"

"It's Bruce of OSS!"

"Hip hip hooray!" someone else said.

"Good show!"

"Well done, old chap!"

"Three cheers for the U.S. of A.!"

"Three more for Oh So Social!"

In seconds an audience had formed, pink-faced drunks in exotic uniforms or double-breasted bankers' monkey suits, drinks held high in salute. At each shoulder, a woman's face bloomed with admiration. He felt the love broadcast upon him as if he were having a heat wave, a tropical heat wave.

"Well, ah—"

Sir Colin was next to him suddenly, and the fool Maltby, and someone from MI6 known only as X (well, everybody who mattered knew his real name), and they all squeezed around him, shaking hands, patting back, clapping shoulder.

"Speech! Speech! Speech!" came a chant.

"You must address your worshippers, old man," whispered Sir Colin. "Really, one only gets a single night like this, and yours has arrived. Make it count."

He faced them.

Was he at a loss for words?

Are you kidding?

"Thank you, thank you," he said. "Ah, could someone get me a Scotch, please? Glenlivet, please."

Laughter, but indeed a glass of amber fluid rotating on diamond cubes of ice was thrust magically into his hands, and just as magically he took a calming sip.

"Ah, thank you very much. I can only say that what we accomplished was by dint, first, of teamwork of which I am merely the symbol, and, second, by closely following our British uncles, masters of the game, for inspiration, advice, and can-do, will-do attitude."

He raised his glass, took a rather stiff belt—ah, the blur, the wham, so much better!—and continued more or less in the same line, only repeating himself six or nine times, until he felt he'd used up enough oxygen in the room, big as it was, and needed more Scotch.

"And so, in conclusion, despite the joy we all now feel, we must understand that it is but one step, triumphant though it may be, on the trek to victory. As always, triumph will not always occur and tragedy might instead. But inevitably, by spirit, by courage, by will, under superb leadership, we shall prevail!"

The next stage of the ceremony, obviously, was The Mingle. He hated it, of course, but one had to do what was required. It was called "duty." He roamed, was petted and stroked and congratulated, with squashed-bubby hugs from a variety of mystery women, and pretty much passed around the room like a religious relic at a High Mass or a whore at a low one. He smiled, drank, enjoyed the bubby play, the handshakes not so much, and eventually felt he'd done his utmost.

Back to the bar for replenishment. Lord Glenlivet, at your service, sir! Then a straight shot to Sir Colin, some maneuvering for privacy, and finally, finally, *finally* he got to ask, "Colin, what in God's name is this about?"

"You don't know? Good God, man, what a brilliant performance. You really don't know?"

"No idea."

Colin reached into his uniform coat, pulled out a sheet of paper.

"One of our chaps at SHAEF got hold of this early and sent it over. Right now, it's being distributed to the whole theater."

The colonel unfolded the paper, saw it was a feeble mimeograph, letters slightly blurry and too small.

He got out his glasses, hung them on nose and ears, took another bolt of the Glenlivet, and read:

RESTRICTED

HEADQUARTERS FIRST UNITED STATES ARMY

GENERAL ORDER: APO#30

NUMBER 26: 23 July 1944

I–Headquarters announces a successful conclusion to OPERA-TION TOTO this morning.

II–Under a plan developed by a top secret G-2 entity and implemented by officers and men of two infantry divisions in a sector holding in the bocage region of Normandy, a specialized WAFFEN-SS sniper initiative was destroyed.

III–Ten enemy snipers were either killed or wounded and captured. The German unit, code-named SS-STURMGRUPPE TAUSEND, consisted of marksmen specially trained to operate in low light conditions. The unit had been responsible for KIA of many patrol leaders since the invasion.

IV–Destroying this unit should have great impact on enemy morale, especially their sniper program, in the coming weeks.

Gen Bradley, CO

CHAPTER 75

Sebastian

No, he didn't want to join battalion G-2. No, he didn't want to join division G-2. No, he didn't want to join corps G-2. No, he didn't want to join army G-2. No, he didn't want to join SHAEF G-2, and being asked by a General Smith, Eisenhower's hatchet man and butt-kicker, was an honor, since usually only bridge players got that nod.

"Thank you, sir. I hope I've been of service here. And I've enjoyed being a major. But the Corps is both my home and my future. It's my family. There's islands out there left to bust and someone's got to lead the young guys whose job it'll be to bust them. That's where I fit in. That's where I belong."

"Major," said the reedy, precise General Smith, "you won't take affront if I send General Vandegrift a letter pointing out to him that he ought to resign immediately and appoint you commandant?"

"Sir, I don't think the general has had a good laugh since Navy beat Army, whenever that was. I'm sure he'll appreciate it."

Then there was crap that all militaries swear they hate but are addicted to: reports, debriefings to a variety of staffs so that nobody would feel left out, as well as travel arrangements, folding and packing, checking weapons for safe transport, returning to London standards of appearance. Swagger's last official act for First Army was to write a Silver Star recommendation for Archer. Maybe he'd get it, maybe he wouldn't. Told the Army wanted him to accept some stuff as well, he asked them not to. Couldn't wear it on his Marine dress uniform.

Late evening a day after, the B-26 Marauder—the medium bomber was referred to in the colloquial as the Baltimore Whore, for the city in which it was built and for the fact that, with smallish wings mounted on a fattish fuselage, it was held to be fast, with no visible means of support—took them to an AAF airfield near Milton Hall, ninety miles or so north of London, the OSS training and supply location. All combat uniforms, boots, web gear, weapons, ammunition, and knives were turned in and checked off as accounted for. Back in summer Class As, they waited for Sebastian.

The car approached.

Hmm, right car, wrong driver.

This one, getting out and snapping to with a smart salute, was tall and willowy, spiffy in tailored enlisted As, but weirdly orange in the lamplight of Milton Hall.

"Major Swagger, Lieutenant Leets, my name is Spec 5 Roger Evans. I've been assigned by Colonel Bruce as your new driver and general assistant."

The two men exchanged glances.

"Colonel Bruce would have come himself," said the boy, maybe nineteen, obviously another Ivy League novice hand-delivered into a choice assignment by a line of connections as long as a monkey's arm. He had to be from an old family and college, by the look of him. The snappy wardrobe said old money too. "We just didn't have a car big enough," he continued. "But the colonel would like to see you as soon as you get in."

He opened the Ford's doors; they entered.

"Why are you so tan, Evans?" asked Swagger as they prowled across the dark landscape toward London. "The Pacific?"

"No, sir. I'm a tennis player, sir. Number two singles at Har—"

"What happened to Sebastian?" asked Leets, not giving a shit about tennis.

"Ah, he transferred out, sir."

"Jesus Christ," said Leets. "Was this job too rough on him?"

"He tried very hard to get it done, sir. You know how the Army works. He knew people; he—"

"Where is he now? Camp Beverly Hills? Fort Manhattan? Our embassy in Geneva?"

"No, sir."

"Well—"

"He transferred to the 1st Ranger Battalion in Italy, sir," said Evans. "Since he wasn't Ranger trained, he had to get special dispensation. It wasn't easy. He said you'd understand."

"I do," said Swagger.

CHAPTER 76

The Waiting

He was the man in the noose as it was tightened. Nothing, just the sense of something constricting his neck. He couldn't go out, he couldn't accept new jobs, he was hung up in nowhere land, waiting, waiting, waiting.

He lay, completely dressed, in the dark of his bedsitter. The ceiling offered nothing but more darkness. The window was open; random sounds, meaningless, of London washed in and out leaving not a trace.

The spies! Damn the spies! They were such tricky bitches, feline and cunning in their plotting, enmeshed in conspiracy within conspiracy, agenda within agenda. If you signed on with them, you signed on for a voyage into madness. If you—

At last, the knock came, proving there was a real world.

"Yes?"

"Oh, Mr. Raven, you're there, are you, dearie? Chap has just called. Wants a call back. Left a number. Shall I slip it under the—"

No need for under the door. He wrapped his shame in scarf as he rose, skipped two short steps to the door, opened, took the slip from the old lady, her overly smeared makeup especially repellent today, and walked on past.

"Have a good one, Mr. Raven, sweet."

He went not to the first nor the second but the third booth he found, checking for followers. None at all, the streets filling up as the night progressed, revelers, lovers, maids and machinists, the mad whirl. He entered the red box, folded the door shut for privacy, addressed the receiver, put in his tuppence, and waited for operator.

"Hullo, general telephone, exchange and number, please."

He gave it, new to him.

"Yes?" The voice was also new, male, possibly queer in its affectation. Were they all queer?

"Yes?"

"Raven here."

"That was quick."

"Get on with it, man! Enough time has passed."

"Not our fault, old chum. Beyond control."

"Fine."

"By the way, you rather roughed up the last lad we sent you, you naughty boy."

"Is he still on the floor of the loo, soaking in piss?"

"I believe he's rallied manfully."

"Little toff made an indecent proposal. Had to set him straight."

"Such high standards we have, eh?"

"Get on with it."

"Plenty of time. No need of a cab, even; the tube will get you there with an hour to spare. The hero lad is back from the war, now an even bigger hero. He will meet his young lady tomorrow night, or so we are assured. Lovers reunited amid the whispering leaves of Mayfair. Seen it in the flickers a dozen times."

"Not so happy an ending this night."

"You know what to do, then? By our latest instructions? It has to be done a certain way, not with mess or spill, not with melodrama or spectacle. We are paying you for banality. This is why we came to you and pay so much."

"I have never failed any of my clients yet."

"There's an extra fifty quid in it for you if you perform perfectly. Tidy counts."

"About time somebody recognized my worth."

"Indeed. And, Raven, this is our way of making sure you understand how quite important the outcome is to all sorts of people. You are being counted upon. There's a good lad."

CHAPTER 77

The Office

They sat on the leather couches. It was close to 0400 British summer war time. London outside was quiet, dark, secure. A doodle had landed earlier, but the fuel measure was way off and it hit east of the city, turning an empty field into an empty crater, probably doing everyone a bit of good. Fritz was perhaps tired too and gave it up for the day.

Three of them, one in his forties, one in his thirties, one in his twenties, pretending for now those decades apart in birthing years meant nothing. Bushmills fine Irish. One lamp, the building quiet. No dog pictures visible on the walls, no file cabinets against the wall. No wall. A fire would have made it more ceremonial, but since it was in the seventies, far too warm for fire; the lamp in a far corner had to stand in for illumination purposes. It tried hard but came up short, leaving the room rent by shadow and dark.

It had started with war stories, with Brix's rifle, which Swagger had given the colonel.

"By God," said the man, "that will be on the mantel of every house

438

I own, and my eldest grandson's as well." He wedged it on this mantel, where it sunk into darkness.

"Now, please. Do tell all."

Leets delivered a summary of how it was planned, how it was executed, how it succeeded. So impressive. If the colonel was upset at being out of the loop, he didn't mention it. He felt too good.

And, in fact, he moved next to a note of triumph. Colonel Bruce was almost in tears. He told them of the party.

"Gentlemen, I've never been so moved, so proud. I can't say enough. Harry and the President must hear of this. They'll be pleased too, I'm sure. Now, I've heard, Earl, if I may, that you're most eager to return to the Marine Corps. I do understand and will see that it happens ASAP. But I'd be remiss if—" and he launched into his own recruitment pitch, guaranteeing instant promotion to lieutenant colonel and command of the Special Operations division, Tyne's old bailiwick.

"I think when we've won," the older man continued, "they may close OSS down. It hasn't been without its controversies, as even General Donovan would admit. And perhaps I wasn't the best choice to take the London helm. But somehow, within a year or so, it'll be reborn under a different name, mark my words. And it'll be staffed—it has to be—with outstanding, experienced OSS personnel. You could play a part, Earl, especially with my recommendation. A big part."

Swagger did his routine turn-down, which Leets had heard before too often, but managed this time, despite fatigue and the lateness of the hour, to sell it solidly.

"Earl, I know recruiters will come to you again. I want you to be aware of that. It's never too late. You'll always have a home among the spies. It's your métier."

"Thank you, sir."

"Here, some more Bushmills," said the colonel.

Each took a shot. The stuff was good.

The talk was low but pleasant, meandering. Sebastian's transfer came up and how many big people got involved. It consumed a whole day of office time.

"Millie was run ragged!"

Then Leets's future. Still medical school? After all, his fine record in OSS could mean doors opening in all sorts of interesting areas. Mustn't be too hasty.

Yawns. It seemed to be over. No. Two of them didn't realize yet that it hadn't even begun. It was 0500 British summer war time, by the clock on the mantel, still visible in the shadow.

Swagger said, "By the way, sir, there's a loose end I'd like to tie up. Do you mind?"

"Ah—well, I suppose."

"Actually, it's Lieutenant Leets who'll help us tie it up. Leets, you know, there's a story you've never told me. I've never asked you. But I know that inside you something is and has been gnawing. You try to hide it, and maybe you could from the officers, but I'm a sergeant. I see stuff officers don't. So let's have it."

Leets looked most uncomfortable.

"Major, I don't—"

"We have lots of time. I want Colonel Bruce in on this too. Come on, Lieutenant."

"I really don't—"

"Casey," said Swagger. "It's time to tell me about Casey."

It took an hour. Swagger asked questions.

"The Brens were pulled during the firefight?"

"How did the SS Das Reich people get there so fast?"

"Any indication from St. Florian that Group Roger could have been infiltrated?"

"The fat guy, the butcher who fought in Spain—do you know who with? Wasn't POUM, was it?"

"And in all the checking, not a word on Captain St. Florian? Did anyone mount any kind of search? Are there reports of executions after the incident on file?"

"How about your debriefing here? Did it seem thorough? Did you confide in them as you've confided in us? No? Why? What was eating you?"

"I must say, Major," said the colonel, "I don't see where this is headed. I suspect history will judge Operation Jedburgh quite harshly for being ill-planned, hastily implemented, rather a botch, actually. I'm sure I'll have to answer for it in many history books. Too busy at parties, not enough supervision and target planning, inept coordination with the maquisards. But then, that's what happens in war, isn't it?"

"Sometimes," said the major.

Leets reached the end. It was 0607 British summer war time.

"Casey was betrayed," he said. "I know it."

They let it sit.

Then the colonel said, "Lieutenant, please file a report on these allegations with Millie tomorrow. I'll assign someone from outside the office to look at them—someone perhaps with investigative skills. I'm thinking—"

"Sir, he can't file it with Millie," said Swagger. "She's the spy."

CHAPTER 78

Somewhere in France

"All right," Archer said, "new guys on me."

Much drama aroused in the dark, as it was clear something big was happening. Ignorant armies preparing to clash by night. A sense of large vehicles moving on congested roads, formations of men easing through the trees, flashlight beams slashing everywhere, commands sharp and hard cutting the air, just the vibration of a big parade or convoy disassembling, rearranging, smoking, and hurrying up to wait.

The kids gathered before him, their tentativeness evident in the awkward stutter with which they moved. About seven beardless warriors, new to the bocage, new to Dog 2-2, new to the war, new to the closeness of death. He saw eyes wide open, apprehending everything, understanding nothing.

"At ease, smoke 'em if you got 'em, take a load off, relax."

They obeyed except for the relaxation part, which was impossible for them—for anyone, actually—in the 9th Infantry Division, or any of the other eleven divisions in First Army.

"I know you're scared," Archer said. His grease gun hung from a strap around his neck and he wore a waistcoat of fragmentation grenades over his M41 field jacket. "I'm scared; everybody's scared. There's going to be a lot of shit flying through the air in a few hours. Some guys, maybe some of you, will get hit, some guys killed. That's what happens up here and I am not going to sugarcoat it.

"Just remember two things: in combat, confusion is normal and no plan survives contact with the enemy. So no matter how many times the captain has explained it to you, it won't be like that. It'll be smoke, lots of noise and flash, and you'll quickly lose orientation to your map points. You probably won't see the steeple at Saint-Gilles that's our objective. But I'm here to tell you that's okay. The main point is not to lose contact with the company. You want our guys visible to you. If you lose that, you could get in big trouble. Just stay low, move when the line moves.

"No heroics, at least not on the first day. You may see Germans but you probably won't. They come and go like ghosts. I would keep my safety on while moving, but if we are stopped, then punch it off and look for targets. It's not killing, it's shooting, and you've been well trained."

"Sarge," a seemingly twelve-year-old asked, "what do we do about prisoners?"

"Let the more experienced men handle them. Give cover, keep your eyes open. You don't shoot the surrendered. That's not how we do things here, no matter what you've heard. Anything else?"

Either there wasn't, or nobody had the nerve to ask, "Will I die?"

"Okay," Archer said, consulting his watch. "A few hours until jump-off yet. Again, relax, grab some sleep if you can. Tomorrow, listen to Sergeants Blikowicz and Roselli. They're good men; they'll take care of you. You also take care of each other."

Maybe he'd helped them a bit, maybe he hadn't. Who knew? But it was all he could do. The boys rose to shuffle back to their squads. But one or two looked at him with something other than the usual indifference. They had a kind of worship in their eyes.

That's when he knew: he had become a war god.

CHAPTER 79

Berkeley Square

The talk was all the big attack. Operation Cobra, it was called, as the boys smashed through German lines smack in the face, through Saint-Gilles and Marigny. Leets realized that was why there'd been such a rush, such urgency. They wanted to get out news of success against the snipers before launching such an adventure as a last-second morale booster, telling the G.I.s that a night patrol wasn't a ball-buster, that the Germans were as blind after twilight as they were now that this special unit had been destroyed.

"You must be so proud," she said. "Really, it all came down to an OSS major and a first lieutenant, the whole thing, and you delivered against all the odds."

He laughed.

"The major delivered. I held his coat. That was about it."

"So modest. God, where do they make men like you?"

"Much to be modest about," he said.

They walked. It was just after 7. He'd left her a message that morning saying he'd gotten in late, was going on forty-eight sleepless hours, had to crash. He'd sleep the day away and pick her up at 70 Grosvenor at 7.

And there she had been. Standing in front of the prosaic building as the lights were just beginning to take effect, and no cinematographer could have done a better job casting the planes of her classical face, the luster of those mysterious eyes, the lithe grace of that long body in a veil of glow. She was a goddess in the uniform of a second lieutenant of the WACs and managed to make even that dowdy garment glamorous. She smiled; radiance blossomed in an otherwise radiance-free world.

God, he loved her. God, he hated her.

They had walked a bit.

"You're not hungry, darling?" she asked.

"No, they crammed me with Spam and pineapple upside down cake. I think it's turned into sludge in my stomach."

"Let's go to the park. Let's enjoy the twilight. Then cocktails and a slow walk back. We don't have to talk about anything. The future will take care of itself."

They held hands; their shoulders brushed, and the tingle of flesh on flesh went through his body. That was sex in 1944. It was enough.

They entered the park as the last hues of setting sun empurpled a few clouds in that sector of sky. Yes on the birds, yes on the breeze agitating the leaves of the London planes, yes on the fragrance of the flowers, yes on her fragrance. The vapors of a low fog began to infiltrate, giving the whole thing an over-art-directed aspect, almost unbelievable. But, yes again, things like this do happen.

They sat.

"The colonel," she said, "was out all day. I'm sure he was at Bushy Park, getting briefed on Cobra. God, I hope this is finally the beginning of the end."

"How's your friend Zora?" he asked. "Is she going to make it?"

"She's tough, you know. She will. I can't wait to introduce you. You'll love her."

"I can't wait," said Leets.

"Poor Tom. He went down before Cobra and never knew."

"Maybe he's in a POW camp."

"We hope and pray."

"By the way," he said after a pause, "a P-51 hasn't been shot down in fourteen days. And also, there's no one at OWI named Zora. It must be a code name for a spy."

Another pause. She got out a cigarette, lit it, exhaled a plume of thick smoke.

"We know," he said. "Millie, we know."

"I don't know what you're talking about."

"You're working for someone. Not OSS. You're reporting to them."

Another pause.

"You're talking crazy, darling. Did you take some drugs or something? Has somebody been filling your mind with fantasy? Why, for God's sake, would I work for the Nazis? I loathe and despise them. I hate what they're doing. I hate the murders, the slaughter, the arrests. I hate their hate. I—"

"Not the Nazis," he said. "The Russians."

Again the pause. What did it signify? Astonishment? Strategic recalculation? Both?

"That doesn't even make sense. Jim, they're our allies."

"In the current war. But they know they've already won it. They've known since Kursk in '43. They've already moved on to the next war. The one against us that we haven't even thought about. Hot or cold, they're fighting the war of 1984."

"I hardly—"

"They know France will be in play when Berlin is taken. They control hundreds of guerrilla groups there already who are stockpiling arms for that battle. And they want our efforts in France to be a mess. They want us blowing up churches, bombing bridges and railways, razing villages, killing civilians, burning forests. They want something they call 'the People' to hate us. It's the fastest route to 1984. It's Realpolitik."

"Jim, you haven't a shred of proof."

"We have all the proof we need. It was the major who—"

"That man hates me. Maybe he hates you too. He'll twist and distort and—"

"No, actually, he doesn't hate you. You just think that because he's the only one you know who isn't in love with you, unlike me or the colonel, or that poor idiot Frank Tyne. That's your greatest weapon; you use it brilliantly."

"Jim—"

"Please shut up and listen to me. When we went on our first patrol, the Germans had no idea we were there. That's because it was never reported in those summaries you do. That's how Swagger knew the Germans wouldn't have sentries out; they thought they had the night off. Then, a few days ago, to test the thesis, he arranged through First Army that you were given a SHAEF theater summary to distribute to the office. It was like all the other theater summaries you've been doing at 1600 every day since you got here. Except this one didn't go anywhere but to you. You typed it on mimeo, gave it to a tech to crank out and distribute. Sebastian got it from the tech. It never went anyplace. You were the only one who saw it. Yet all the snipers of Sturmgruppe Tausend were in place and waiting. They were using your information. You got your info to Zora, who got it to her NKVD contact, who got it directly to the Germans. In fact, the Germans have always known where and when we were sending out night patrols. NKVD told them. And NKVD ordered the butcher to pull the Brens at Tulle. The NKVD source got SS Das Reich to send trucks ahead; that's how they arrived so fast. The trucks were on the way before we even hit the bridge."

"I didn't know Basil. I didn't know you. It wasn't personal, it was political."

"Tell me, Millie. Tell me about it. Tell me how you killed Basil."

CHAPTER 80

Millie Again

Enter Millie Fenwick again. Millie, from Millicent, from the Fenwicks, you know, *the* Fenwicks of the North Shore. Millie was a lovely girl, clever as the devil. She graduated with high marks from Smith but never bragged or acted smart; got her first job working as a secretary at *Life* in Manhattan for the awful Luce and his hideous wife; spent some time on a Senate staff (her father arranged it); and then, when the war came, she gravitated toward the Office of Strategic Services just as surely as it gravitated toward her. People knew where they belonged, and organizations knew what kind of people belonged in them, so General Donovan's assistants fell in instant love with the willowy blonde who looked smashing at any party, smoked brilliantly, had languid, see-through-anything luminosity in her eyes. Everyone loved the way her hair fell down to her shoulders; everyone loved the diaphanous cling of a gown or blouse to her long torso; everyone loved her yards and yards of legs, her perfect ankles well displayed by the platforms of the heels all the girls wore.

By '43 she'd transferred to London Station at 70 Grosvenor in Mayfair, under Colonel Bruce, one of whose assistants she'd become, and wore the uniform of a second lieutenant in the WACs. She was in charge of the colonel's social calendar. She answered his phones or placed his calls, but it was more than that. She also knew the town and so was able to prioritize. The colonel was hopeless and said yes to every invitation in the days before she arrived on station.

She was indispensable, she was ruthless, she was efficient, she was beautiful and brilliant at once, and she was the ranking NKVD agent in OSS, the star of INO (Foreign Intelligence Section), who had been trained at Shkola Osobogo Naznacheniya, the Special Purposes School, in Balashikha, fifteen miles east of the Moscow Ring Road when everybody thought she was rusticating in Cap d'Antibes.

Millie sniffed something up at 3 p.m. that afternoon, when Colonel Bruce's mood immediately brightened. The issue of the day had been Operation Jedburgh, by which three-men teams of OSS/SOE/FFI agents had parachuted behind the lines to wreak havoc on German communications and transportation lines in the immediate wake of the Normandy show. So far, no good. No teams had hit a target; many had drifted apart in the descent and failed to link up with Maquis units whom they were supposed to lead; several had never acknowledged arrival by radio and were considered combat lost. It was looking like a washout, and Colonel Bruce knew he was meeting with Sir Colin Gubbins, head of SOE, and that Gubbins would blame the muck-up on the American third of the units. It was *so* important that the teams did well!

But around 1800, the SOE liaison informed the colonel that radio intercepts strongly suggested one team was in position and would strike that night at midnight against a bridge on Das Reich's route to the beachhead.

"Millie, do you see? This is what we needed."

The great issue with OSS was that it was considered immature—inferior and amateur in comparison to the far savvier British intel outfits—and it drove both General Donovan and his factotum Colonel Bruce mad.

"Yes, sir."

"Oh, the boys," said Colonel Bruce. "Those wonderful, wonderful boys, they make me so proud. Here's to Casey at the bat!"

Millie, of course, was not privy to code names and didn't know which groups were operating where; she just scooped up all available information and turned it over to her NKVD control, a fellow named Hedgepath who'd been big in WPA and then network radio PR before the war and was now big in the Office of War Information, reporting directly to Mr. Sherwood. She adored Hedgepath because of course he was one of the few men on earth who didn't yield to and couldn't be budged by her blandishments, charms, and beauty. She had no way of knowing he was a sexual deviate and therefore immune to such. From any gal.

She called him from a phone in the Accounting Section, feeling utterly secure because no one monitored internal calls between American entities such as 70 Grosvenor and the London OWI headquarters nearby. It was Kate Jesse's phone, and Kate thought Millie used it to speak to a secret lover, an RAF bomber pilot. Kate's problem: she read *Redbook* magazine too earnestly.

"Hullo," said Hedgepath.

"Millie here."

"Of course, my dear."

She reiterated what she had learned that day, the colonel's schedule, his incoming calls, reports, office tidbits, expenditures, the nuts and bolts of it. Finally she mentioned some kind of show that was set for the evening, and the colonel's curious explosion of glee: "Casey at the bat."

"Oh, baseball," said Mr. Hedgepath. "I loathe baseball. It's mostly standing around, isn't it? Awfully boring. Who's this Casey?"

"It's from a famous poem. 'Mighty Casey,' they call him, a sort of Babe Ruth figure. All hopes are on him. It's very dramatic."

"Who knew there was drama in baseball?"

"At any rate, 'Casey at the Bat' is about a hero's chance to win the big game. As I recall, he fails. It's regarded as a tragedy. I think Casey has to do with something they're calling Operation Jedburgh."

Jedburgh?

"Hmm," said Hedgepath. He knew from Moscow NKVD Center that the terrible Zyborny had sent a flash to GRU earlier, but the center wasn't completely able to penetrate the GRU code and only knew the subject of the message was a Brit-Yank-Frenchy thing called Operation Jedburgh, some silly blowing-up of structures that would have to be expensively rebuilt after the war. But NKVD did not want GRU operating with impunity anywhere and the two agencies cordially hated each other. NKVD Center was suddenly interested in Operation Jed not as part of the war against the Germans, which it knew was won, but in the war against GRU for postwar operational control of the intelligence mechanism.

"Urgent you penetrate Jed," NKVD Center had ordered.

"My dear Miss Fenwick," said Mr. Hedgepath. "Can you focus tonight on this 'Casey'? There's a lot of interest in it. Possibly flirt it up with one of the cowboys and get me some information soonest? I'd like to pop a line to Our Friends before bedtime if possible."

Millie sighed. She knew exactly what she had to do. Drinks with Frank Tyne, a horrible New York Irisher and former cop who was all swagger and bluster. He'd been in and out of France for two years now, or so it was said, and it was rumored had actually killed several Germans. More to the point, he adored her and had been asking her out for weeks.

That night his dreams came true.

"They must be so brave," said Millie to poor, hopelessly-in-love Frank Tyne. Frank's Irish heritage, or so he claimed, made him a special favorite of General Donovan, whom he routinely referred to as "the General." He was not above using such information to advance himself. He was crude, direct, horny, stupid, supposedly a hero but utterly full of himself and other noxious substances.

"Good guys. See, the deal is, it was time to show Jerry some action. The General knew that. So these teams, I put them together as an opportunity for the outfit to show its stuff."

She knew he hadn't put one and one together to get two.

"And tonight's the night?"

"Tonight's the night," Frank said, with a wicked gleam in his eyes that suggested that maybe he was assuming tonight was the night in more ways than one.

They sat in the bar of the Coach & Horses, amid smoke, other drinkers, and trysters.

"Frank, you should be so proud. It's your plan, after all. You're really doing something. I mean, so much of it is politics, society, canoodling, and it has nothing to do with the war. I just get depressed sometimes. Even Colonel Bruce, he tries so hard, he's such a darling, but he's ineffectual. You, Frank—*you* are stopping the Nazis. That is so important. Somebody has to do the fighting!"

She touched Frank's wrist, and smiled radiantly, and watched the poor mick melt. Then, fighting the sudden rush of phlegm to his throat, he said, "Look, let's get out of here."

"Frank, we shouldn't. I mean—"

"Miss Fenwick—Millie . . . May I call you Millie?"

"Of course."

"Millie, it's the night of the warrior. We should commemorate it. Look, let's go back to my office; I have a little stash of very fine Pikesville Rye. We can have some privacy. It'll be a great night and we can wait for news of Team Casey's strike to come in and celebrate."

Millie played up the I'm-considering look, going through several Yes-why-nots? and several No-no-it's-wrongs before seeming to settle on the Yes-why-not?

"Yes, why not?" she said, but he was already pulling on his raincoat over his uniform.

It was spread out before her on Frank Tyne's desk: Operation Jedburgh. It was a facsimile of the map in Operations two floors below, now staffed and busy. But it was close enough to actuality for government work.

She could see all the locations for the teams, and all their targets, laid out across the Cotentin Peninsula and southwestern France, all the boys who'd gone in with darkened faces and knives between their teeth. Teams Frederick and Hugh, Harry and Ian, Willis and Felix, Francis and David, with the mission to set Europe ablaze.

"Oh, Frank," she said. "And to think you thought it up. That's your plan. Those magnificent men fighting and killing, and all under your direction."

Frank swelled a bit, then turned modest.

"Sweetie, you have to understand it was a true team effort, and it involved logistics and liaison between three entities. I just conceived and organized it, that's all. It's my bit. Nothing dramatic. I don't want you thinking I'm a hero. The kids are the heroes."

Her eyes scanned the map with incredible intensity, and if dumbbell Frank had a whisper of sense in his brain, he would have noted how inappropriate her concentration was, but of course he was way gone. He was over the edge. His dick was as big as a wine bottle.

"Oooooh!" she squealed girlishly. "What's this one? Casey."

"You must have heard the name in the air. Casey's on for tonight. There's a bridge, right smack in a German panzer division's route. Casey's going to hit it, *ka-boom!* No tanks, not on my watch."

"Such heroes."

"If there's room for heroics. First, you have to get through the bullshit—oh, excuse me—the bull crap about politics. France is not only fighting the Germans but the French themselves are always trying to skew this way or that for political advantage after the war."

He wanted to show her what an insider he was. "Casey was hung up for some reason because a commie guerrilla outfit wouldn't give them support. But I was able to make certain phone calls—can't say to who, you understand—and the Commies were ordered to pitch in." He smiled smugly, loosened his tie, took another swig of rye.

"And it's happening tonight?"

He looked at his watch, worn commando-style upside down on his wrist.

"Real soon now. We should know by dawn."

"It's so exciting."

"Millie, why don't you come over here on the couch and we'll relax for a bit, have a few more drinks. Then I'll wander down to Operations and see if anything's come in on Casey."

"Oh, Frank," she said. She sunk down on the old sofa that constituted his office furniture, beside the desk and the battered filing cabinets and the safe, and snuggled close to him, and felt him groping to get his beefy arms around her.

"Oh, Millie, Millie, God, Millie, if you only knew, Jesus, Millie, I've had the same feeling for you that you have for me, I'm so glad the war has brought us together, oh, Millie . . ."

She smiled, and when he closed his eyes to kiss her, she brought a handkerchief full of knockout drops—chloral hydrate, mixed with alcohol—to his nostrils and felt him struggle, then go limp.

She got up quickly, went to the map, marked the coordinates for Casey's operational area, and then realized of course they would know all this. The big info was that a red group had agreed to assist the Jeds, which meant assisting the FFI. She knew Moscow would go through the roof on that one! It felt so wrong to her, so unjust. If you helped the FFI, then the war would have been for nothing; when it was over, it would just go back to what it was, with big money ruling everything and the little guy squashed to nothingness and all the bullies and all the rich scum and all the boys who'd pawed her at Smith, brutal, smelly, drunken Frank Tyne, all those men would be triumphant, and what, really, what would have been the point? The only hope was the Soviet Union, the greatness of Uncle Joe, the justice of a system that didn't depend on exploitation but that enabled man to be all that he could be, noble and giving, generous and loving. That was a world worth fighting for, and if she didn't have a gun, she had a telephone.

She picked it up and dialed, knowing that nowhere on earth would anyone see anything suspicious about Frank Tyne of OSS calling David Hedgepath of the Office of War Information at 2214 on the night of June 8, 1944.

CHAPTER 81

The Raven

The fog was most helpful. Across the street, he was secure in the bushes, standing in the darkness of one of the great residences surrounding the park and yet awarded a solid view. The vapors rose, not much at first, then to shoe level, then up, heavier to the waist, and finally a fine scrim on all of the park, all of London, really.

He could see them through the circle of plane trees that defined the center of the park, sitting on a bench, lost in conversation. He hoped they'd stay. A few other walkers roamed the park; so much easier if they departed. Then a bobby on foot patrol, lamp in hand, whistle in tunic, wandered by and seemed to utter something. Raven heard the hero lieutenant answering, "Same to you, Officer." The policeman completed his rounds and headed off, and Mr. Raven, who had a prodigious memory for police routes and times, knew he wouldn't be back until nearly 11. It was but 8:30 now.

He waited, he waited, he waited. The park's last visitor, a single gentleman with a Scottish terrier on a leash, left by the far exit and the two Americans were alone. It was time. He felt the pistol heavy in his hand in the folds of the coat. At this point, so close to action, he found himself tumescent. It was not unusual.

"I had no idea who 'Leets' was until the colonel took me to see you in hospital. I saw this large, handsome man trying so hard to deflect praise from himself. I also saw the pain on his face, but more: the weight of the loss he'd experienced. I knew I was responsible for it all. And I suppose you think the love I feel for you is a fraud, part of my red half. But it's not, Jim. No matter what happens, it's not."

A policeman wandered by. Decent fellow, friendly.

"Evening, sir and madam," he said, and Leets answered, watched then as he drifted away. He turned back to her.

"I could be cynical and say you used the charm and beauty on me as part of your cover. If I loved you, and dammit to hell, I do and always will, I'd never see you for what you were. I could never be realistic, I could never force myself to look at the evidence, I would keep my suspicions to myself."

"I swear, I never thought of that. Yes, I manipulated that idiot Frank Tyne and I suppose I did the same to the poor colonel. I knew I'd last until a realist came along. He came sooner than anybody anticipated. But none of that is about you. Everything I have said to you, I have meant."

"God, I wish there was some other way."

"There is, Jim."

"Don't."

"Just listen. You could come with me on my journey. You could have a big career ahead of you with your record in the war and find yourself in high places. There you could work for a new world. You could do so much good. The whole point is to find meaning and worth in all the slaughter and destruction. If we just go back to the way it was, it's all been for nothing."

"I doubt Private Goldberg would agree."

"Private Goldberg?"

"The late Private Goldberg. He thought he was dying for his country and was willing to do so. True also of Captain St. Florian: despite his cosmopolitan ironies and sophistication, a believer. And all the French kids shot down by Das Reich on the slope at Tulle. It's not America or the Allies. It's them. I owe them, much as even right now I'd like to take you in my arms."

"Poor Jim," she said.

"Here's my pitch. We go to the FBI tomorrow. I know who the guy is in the outfit. You confess. They'll get you on a plane out the next day. You go to Hoover, you spill everything. You tell who recruited you, who you met, how and where you were trained. You give up Zora. You give it all up. As you say, the Russians are our allies, at least formally. And the FBI knows a lot of good-hearted Americans have fallen for the line about a better tomorrow. Maybe that'll cut you some slack and keep you out of jail for life. Then . . . well, we'll let 'then' take care of itself."

"Jim, I can't. You don't understand. I *believe*. It's not about getting my father to pay attention to me or getting revenge on my drunken mother. It's not because I was seduced by a red professor at college or am striking out at a world that has ignored me while noticing my face. I *believe*."

A small man emerged from the fog. He wore a derby, an overcoat, and a scarf over his face. His eyes seemed odd.

"Evening, sir and madam," he said. "Hope I didn't startle you."

He had a pistol in his hand.

Now at last.

He was so close, he could hear them. It was a conversation of some urgency—earnest, he judged, on both their parts—driven by emotion that was nevertheless, as it is among people of their sort, held in.

And for the first time in his life, he felt sympathy.

Am I really to do this? Must I do this? Suddenly it seemed wrong.

They were so perfect, so in love, so beautiful. It was a scene from a romantic painting, something from before the Great War. Something from a myth, a medieval tale, an old book, a collective folk memory. Lancelot and Guinevere, Héloïse and Abelard, Tristan and Isolde, Romeo and Juliet. To interrupt seemed impolite; to destroy, blasphemous. He yearned to walk away. It would be his end, of course. His reputation shattered, what else could a man with his face do? He scared children; he made women turn away and men wince. There was only this life.

He stepped forward.

"Evening, sir and madam," he said. "Hope I didn't startle you."

He broke their intensity. Both stared intently at him.

He presented the pistol.

They did not panic or cry; they did not scream. They simply looked on, waiting, accepting what must happen. The woman uttered something to the man and took his hand.

He followed his orders.

He did what he must. He fired.

The report was loud in the quiet of the London park, shrouded in fog.

He turned. He walked away, cursing himself and his duty.

The man had an almost sheepish look in his eyes, for his eyes were all that was visible. He had come to kill, almost embarrassed by the nature of the mission.

"Jim, I do love you," she said, taking his hand. "But I also know the Revolution is sometimes cruel to the few in order, someplace else in time, to be kind to the many."

The little man fired.

The bullet was kind to her beauty. It punctured her above the right eye, destroying nothing, ruining everything. She toppled to the right, to the bench.

CHAPTER 82

RAF Horham

Evans drove Leets and Swagger to RAF Horham, in Suffolk, home to the Eighth Air Force's 92nd Bomb Group. After being ID'd at the gate, they pulled in next to the administrative office in the control tower.

"Evans, go in and see if the major needs to sign in or something."

"Yes, sir," said Evans, departing.

They watched him go, young asshole who knew nothing, so beautiful in his tailored Class As.

"So what does the colonel have for you?" Swagger asked. "Has he told you?"

"It's not really for me. It's for Evans, so he'll have his afternoons free to give tennis lessons to various London big shots. Meanwhile, back at 70, I'm heading up something called SWET: Small Weapons Evaluation Team. It's a huge unit consisting of me and, when available, Evans. The idea is to evaluate new-generation German small arms as they come into our possession and to write technical reports. The more technical the better, because it'll eat up time and keep anybody from ever reading them."

"Sounds like you'd get some range time."

"If Corporal Evans's schedule permits."

"Are you okay about the girl?"

"Ah, well . . . ," he said. "I suppose a few more sleepless nights or weeks ahead. Regrets, yeah, sorrow, of course. Pain, but there's always pain in a war. Not as much as Basil, not as much as Goldberg. She believed in what she was doing, and that means, whether she knew it or not, she had to accept the outcome. Her choice, no one else's."

"She was the girl who knew too much. They couldn't let her be taken."

"Had she figured that out, or was it just as much a surprise to her as to me? We'll never know. Suicide or murder? I'll wonder for the rest of my life."

Evans knocked on the window. Leets rolled it down.

"Straight to the flight line. It's the number two ship, *Duffy's Circus*. They're ready to go."

Leets nodded. The kid got in, only checking his watch once to see if he'd have to cancel on General Lehman at 1600, and drove them. The car passed along a row of huge warbirds canted upward on their landing gear, four-engine behemoths with proud tails reaching skyward, plexiglass and silver gleaming, guns jutting, bullet holes patched, folks around them busy loading the bombs that looked like gigantic rusted sausages for the day's run to Berlin or Munich or wherever. B-17s *in excelsior!* Aviators in A2s and crushed forty-mission caps, soon to be targets at twenty-four thousand feet for the entire Luftwaffe, stood around the giant tires and ladders into the fuselage hatches, joshing, laughing, smoking, all of them.

They arrived at *Duffy's Circus*.

"Earl, dammit, are you sure you don't want to take that commission? It's not too late. It kills me to think of you shot to pieces in some jungle shithole in a place I can't even pronounce. It's such a waste."

"I think it'll be pronounced PELL-I-LOO, if it matters. Worst-kept secret in Washington. A waste? Maybe. I don't know. I'm not cleared for discussions on waste. That's for generals and politicians. To me, we're

461

fighting so we can stop fighting. If it has to be done, it better be done by someone who knows what he's doing. Less dying that way."

"Then take a Marine commission. You could have one in thirty seconds."

"Believe it or not, when it comes to fighting Japs, sergeants are more useful than majors. It's sergeant's work."

They shook hands.

"Take it easy, Lieutenant. You're the best."

The older man turned and went to meet his aircrew.

From the observation deck of the control tower, Leets watched the Flying Fort taxi to the runway, orient itself, pause a second, rev, tremble, and then launch. It sped across the English tarmac, gathered enough speed, and left the earth behind. It banked, its landing gear folding into the inboard cowlings, and headed out.

He watched all the way. It seemed to be headed toward Valhalla, or Olympus, someplace more majestic than, ultimately, a scrap of coral, which would come very high, called PELL-I-LOO. It climbed amid towering castles of cumulus, a big bird serenaded by the sun. It became a profile, a blur, a silver speck. Then it disappeared into the blue.

He was thinking: Where do we get such men? And what do we do if we run out of them?

ACKNOWLEDGMENTS

I can track this book to an exact moment. Sometime in 2018, Barrett Tillman and I were exchanging bits of sniper lore via email. Barrett, by trade an aviation/The War historian, told me that Omar Bradley was so enraged at German sniper predation in the Normandy campaign in July 1944, he ordered captured *Feldgrau* marksmen executed on the spot. Cooler heads talked him out of it.

In that nanosecond I saw a book. In another nanosecond I calculated that, by my own accounting, Earl Swagger was "available," having survived Tarawa and not yet arrived to Peleliu. I had long wanted to get back to Earl and The War, as anyone who lived in the forties and fifties would call it. That he was a Marine sergeant and not an Army officer I saw as a challenge, not an obstacle. In a third nanosecond I saw how I could knock off some unfinished business from a story I had written in 2010 for Otto Penzler called "Casey at the Bat." Not bad for three nanoseconds.

What happened next? Damned if I know. Possibly I drifted off, possibly some mandate from Big Publishing changed my course, possibly it was rejected by somebody. But it was gone with the vapors. Then, in 2020, I'm sitting in my friend Gary Goldberg's backyard with cigars and bourbon and two friends from Pennsylvania, Dave Dunn and Tony Clements. What would be my next book? They all wanted to know—and so did I.

Out poured *The Bullet Garden*. It arrived from Annex B-19, Cavern 11, Tunnel R-4, of the Hunter subconscious, where it had been frozen solid in pristine condition, shrink-wrapped and dense as a boulder. Thawing it on the fly, I was amazed how well my friends responded and how well I responded. We all agreed, especially me, that I had to do it.

Publishing action was called for and my agent, Esther Newberg, adroitly got me out of one deal and into another, this time with Emily Bestler, whose label goes forth under the auspices of old friends at Simon & Schuster. Superb work all around. I only hope I have equaled it.

I should say that I am fully aware that if the book is a sequel to "Casey at the Bat," then it is also a prequel to my very first novel, *The Master Sniper*, published forty-three years ago. I am also aware, if anyone cares to remember a relic from so long ago, that the joinery between this book and that is far from perfect. Leets's wound, as an example, was far more serious in that one. And I think he had a new girlfriend already. My hope is that if this book succeeds, someone might be interested in publishing something entitled *The Master Sniper: Fixed Up Real Good*, meant to get Steve's War in accord. That would be so cool!

You may notice a few more-vivid-than-usual turns of phrase. These are almost certainly pinched from the great correspondent Martha Gellhorn's *The Face of War*. (The Germans looking like "some kind of dead vegetable" in the field after the night attack on Dog 2-2 is my favorite.) I asked my great friend Lenne Miller to read *The Face of War* and highlight especially vivid images. He had no problem finding them. I also pinched Rick Atkinson's close-in description of the hedgerow from *The Guns at Last Light*. As well, Rick, an old *Post* colleague, answered questions on the bocage campaign for me.

As well, I got a lot of uniform and equipment questions answered by consulting the busy online colony of World War II reenactment fabricators, who definitely know the difference between 1943 and 1944 SS camouflage patterns (as do their customers). Believe me, they are folks who live and breathe this stuff. I even bought an M41 field jacket, cool enough for jeans and a sweater in a bar. AttheFront.com is the one I recommend.

Otherwise, the usual suspects pitched in. Gary was great on lots of computer issues and arranged for the manuscript to be formatted and assembled by Brooke Hart. Jeff Weber, the great Jim Grady, Dave Dunn, Bill Smart, and Mark Keefe of NRA performed as usual to my great benefit. Barrett became my go-to man for dozens of arcane issues (the personalities of Francis Gabreski and Robert Johnson, for one). Mike Hill, who actually knows something about cricket, kept me from appearing too ignorant on the sport. And Ed DeCarlo, of On Target Range, provided excellent early intel on the Swedish M-41.

I also must thank Professor Rob Fitzpatrick, of Australia's University of Adelaide, a leading authority on forensic soil analysis, for help not with this book but with *Basil's War*. Production requirements prevented acknowledgments in that one, and Professor Fitzpatrick is owed even belated recognition.

Professionally, Esther, Emily, and Emily's associate, Lara Jones, got it all turned into an actual book. And Otto, of course, set everything in motion by commissioning "Casey at the Bat" for *Agents of Treachery* in 2010. And my wife's coffee, as usual, got me awake and kept me awake. It was prepared even as she flourished in her own career as the great Jean Marbella of the *Baltimore Sun*.

As usual, these fine people are free of blame for errors, foolish decisions, follies, and misunderstandings, which are the sole responsibility of the proprietor.